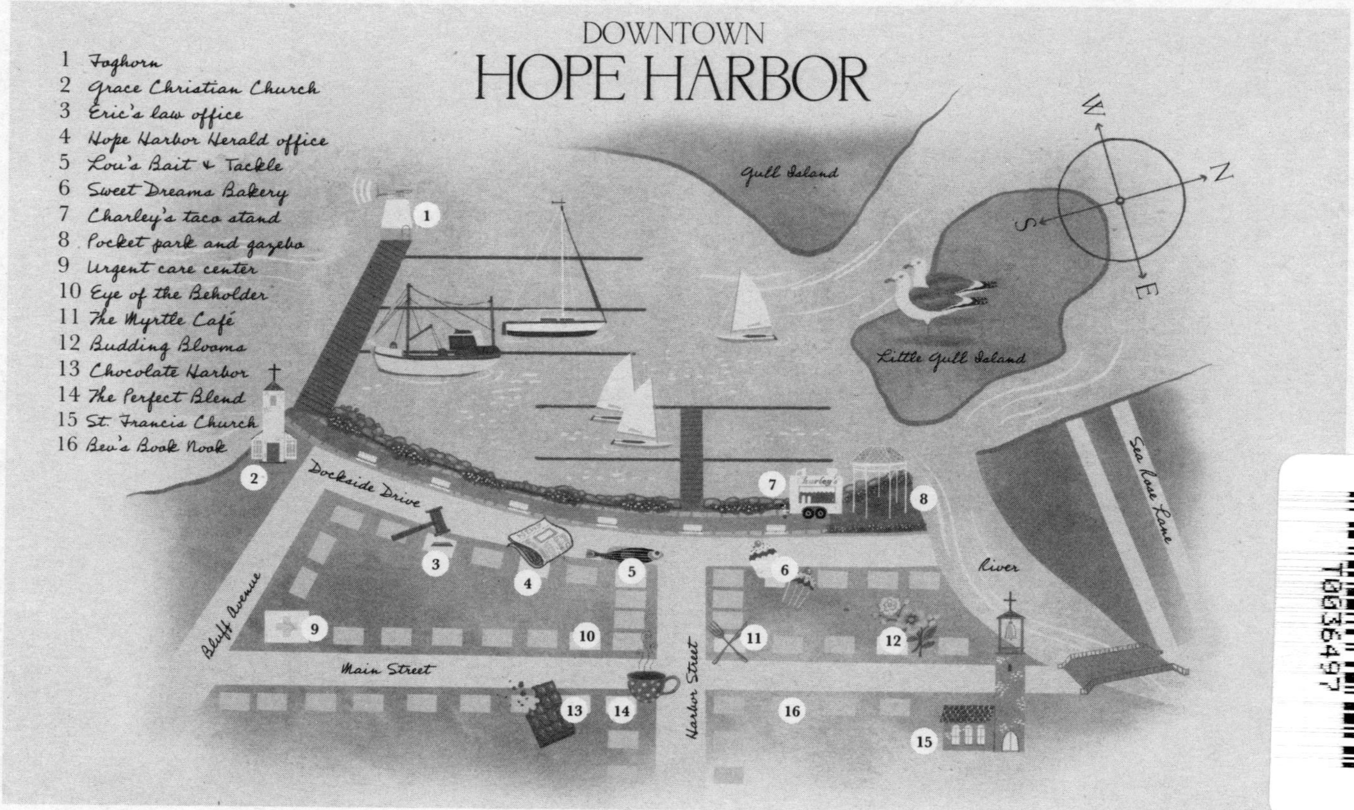

DOWNTOWN HOPE HARBOR

1 Foghorn
2 Grace Christian Church
3 Eric's law office
4 Hope Harbor Herald office
5 Lou's Bait & Tackle
6 Sweet Dreams Bakery
7 Charley's taco stand
8 Pocket park and gazebo
9 Urgent care center
10 Eye of the Beholder
11 The Myrtle Café
12 Budding Blooms
13 Chocolate Harbor
14 The Perfect Blend
15 St. Francis Church
16 Bev's Book Nook

Gull Island
Little Gull Island
W
N
S
E
Dockside Drive
Bluff Avenue
Main Street
Harbor Street
River
Sea Rose Lane

Sandcastle Inn

Books by Irene Hannon

Heroes of Quantico

Against All Odds
An Eye for an Eye
In Harm's Way

Guardians of Justice

Fatal Judgment
Deadly Pursuit
Lethal Legacy

Private Justice

Vanished
Trapped
Deceived

Men of Valor

Buried Secrets
Thin Ice
Tangled Webs

Code of Honor

Dangerous Illusions
Hidden Peril
Dark Ambitions

Triple Threat

Point of Danger
Labyrinth of Lies
Body of Evidence

Undaunted Courage

Into the Fire

Hope Harbor

Hope Harbor
Sea Rose Lane
Sandpiper Cove
Pelican Point
Driftwood Bay
Starfish Pier
Blackberry Beach
Sea Glass Cottage
Windswept Way
Sandcastle Inn

Standalone Novels

That Certain Summer
One Perfect Spring

Sandcastle Inn

A Hope Harbor Novel

IRENE HANNON

a division of Baker Publishing Group
Grand Rapids, Michigan

Published by Revell
a division of Baker Publishing Group
Grand Rapids, Michigan
RevellBooks.com

Printed in the United States of America

Library of Congress Cataloging-in-Publication Data
Names: Hannon, Irene, author.
Title: Sandcastle Inn : / Irene Hannon.
Description: Grand Rapids, Michigan : Revell, a division of Baker Publishing Group, 2024. | Series: A Hope Harbor novel
Identifiers: LCCN 2023031287 | ISBN 9780800741921 (paper) | ISBN 9780800745677 (casebound) | ISBN 9781493444809 (ebook)
Subjects: LCGFT: Christian fiction. | Romance fiction. | Novels.
Classification: LCC PS3558.A4793 S25 2024 | DDC 813/.54—dc23/eng/20230714
LC record available at https://lccn.loc.gov/2023031287)

This book is a work of fiction. Names, characters, places, and incidents are the product of the author's imagination or are used fictitiously. Any resemblance to actual events, locales, or persons, living or dead, is coincidental.

Baker Publishing Group publications use paper produced from sustainable forestry practices and postconsumer waste whenever possible.

24 25 26 27 28 29 30 7 6 5 4 3 2 1

To my brother and sister-in-law,
Jim and Teresa Hannon,
as you celebrate your 25th anniversary.

May all your tomorrows be as happy as your yesterdays.

And may you always be blessed
with the three things that abide—
faith, hope, and love.

I love you both. Now and forever.

1

Good grief.

What on earth had Kay gotten herself into?

Matt Quinn braked, gravel crunching beneath the tires as his Mazda came to a stop in front of his sister's new business.

No. Scratch new.

Beachview B&B might be new to Kay, but that adjective didn't come anywhere close to describing this cedar-shake-covered structure with the whimsical turret on one end.

Exhaling long and slow, he wiped a hand down his face as his hopes for the much-needed R&R that had fueled his long drive north from San Francisco evaporated.

His sister may not have summoned him for help with her business, but how could he ignore the elephant in the room?

An elephant that likely wouldn't be here if he'd done what he should have done and asked way more questions nine months ago when she'd announced that she was going to buy a B&B on the Oregon coast. Or even come up here to look the place over. He could have accomplished that in a weekend trip if necessary.

One more regret to feed the gnawing guilt that had been his constant companion for two long years.

Knuckling the road grit from his eyes, he tried to coax the ever-present knot in his stomach to untwist. After all, it was possible the few rotted pieces of shake siding above the foundation, the missing roof shingles, the potholes on the inn's access drive, and the listing shutter on the second floor weren't an omen of what was to come inside.

Nevertheless, the empty parking lot suggested he wasn't the only one who'd been put off by a negative first impression.

Did his sister have *any* customers?

The knot cinched tight again, like a hangman's noose.

But this whole scenario did have one bright side.

There would be plenty to distract him from his own problems while he was here.

The front door opened, and Kay stepped out, shadowed under the large A-frame roof above the entryway at this twilight hour.

Since it was too late to drive away even if that had been an option, he pulled into a parking space, set the brake, and pushed the engine stop button.

She jogged over, waiting to speak until he opened the door and slid from behind the wheel. "I've been watching for you." Her lips tipped up, fine lines feathering at the corners of her eyes as she held out her arms. "Welcome to Oregon on this beautiful June day."

"Thank you." He gave her a hug.

After returning the squeeze, she eased back to scrutinize him. "You look tired. Tell me you took a couple of breaks during the drive."

"I did." But only long enough to fill up with gas.

"This wasn't an emergency, you know. You didn't have to make it a marathon."

"A nine-hour drive isn't exactly a marathon."

She rolled her eyes, just as she'd been doing for the past twenty-six years whenever he exasperated her—which had been often in the early days. Few eighteen-year-olds thrust into a dual parenting role were equipped to deal with a grieving nine-year-old who tended to get into a lot of messes.

If Kay had ever resented being saddled with such a heavy responsibility at that young age, though, she'd never let on.

One of the many reasons he loved her.

"Hey." He put one hand on her shoulder and used the pad of his other thumb to smooth out the furrows on her brow. "No frowns allowed. I'm here, safe and sound."

Her features relaxed a hair. "That's one worry off my plate, anyway."

Meaning there were others. Plural.

And one of them had to include the condition of the inn.

But that discussion could wait until he'd clocked some z's and his brain was fully functional again. Better to focus on the situation that had summoned him here.

"Is Cora still trying to convince you not to go back to Boise for her surgery?"

"Yes. But it's a major operation, and she doesn't have any family. I don't want her to go through that alone."

"I don't either. She may not be related to us by blood, but I'll always think of her as a grandmother."

"Me too. I don't know what I would have done if she hadn't unofficially adopted us after we moved into the other half of her duplex. She was always there to lend a hand or offer advice when I was at my wit's end."

He propped a hip against the car and folded his arms, mouth bowing. "Not to mention the chocolate chip cookies she plied us with."

"That too." The twin creases reappeared on Kay's forehead. "I know bypass surgery is a common procedure these days, and her heart is healthy other than the blockage, but she's getting up in years."

"She'll be fine, Kay. She's a strong woman, physically and mentally."

"Do you talk to her often?"

"Yes." Though that was more Cora's doing than his over the past two, dark years. How often, when he'd most needed to hear an encouraging voice, had he answered the phone and found her on the other end? Too often to count. It was as if, across the miles, she'd sensed his plunges into despair. "She told me the doctors gave her a very optimistic prognosis."

"I heard the same story." Kay sighed and brushed back a few strands of wind-ruffled hair. "I've missed her these past five months. I mean, I love the ocean, and this inn is a wonderful opportunity to start a new chapter in my life, but . . ." Taking a deep breath, she put on a bright face. "Let me help you with your bags." She circled around to the trunk and waited.

Rather than probe for more information about her regret-infused *but*, he took her lead and followed her to the trunk. There should be ample opportunity to get the lay of the land with the inn and with her before she left for Boise in three days.

After giving her the smaller of his two bags to tote, he picked up the heavier one, closed the trunk, and followed her inside to the spacious foyer.

A quick perusal revealed a small room to the left that appeared to be an office. A wide doorway on the wall that faced the front door offered a glimpse of the sea through windows at the rear of the structure. A staircase led to a balcony above the foyer, and two doorways on the second level were visible before a hallway disappeared to the right.

At first glance, there were less obvious signs of wear and tear inside than out.

That was encouraging.

"Do you want to drop your bags here and have something to eat, or would you like to freshen up first?" Kay stopped in the center of the foyer. "I made the spaghetti sauce you always liked."

His stomach rumbled, and he gave her a sheepish grin. "Sorry. My last meal was hours ago." And the drive-through burger he'd wolfed down hadn't put much of a dent in his hunger. "Give me five minutes to dump my bags in my room and wash my hands."

"That'll work. I'll get the noodles going. Your room is up the stairs and down the hall, last door on the left."

"Got it." He took the smaller bag from her. "See you in five."

He had no trouble finding the spacious room that was cluttered with too much furniture—nor spotting a few signs of wear as soon as he entered. While the space appeared to be spotlessly clean, scrubbing couldn't erase the faint vestiges of two sizeable stains on the carpet. Nicks in the doorframe and baseboards were past due to be touched up. A few marks above the luggage rack suggested the entire room could use a fresh coat of paint.

But the view from the sliding door that led to the balcony?

World class.

Matt left his bags at the foot of the bed and crossed to the far side of the room.

Through the expanse of glass, the azure ocean stretched to the horizon past several dramatic sea stacks. Billowing clouds tinged with gold and pink massed where sky met sea as the sun began its grand exit for the day. To the left, on a tree-covered headland, the top of a lighthouse soared over the distant point. And straight in front, visible through the branches of the spruce and pine trees that nestled the inn? A gorgeous, secluded beach that extended as far as he could see to the right behind a long stretch of low dunes.

Wow.

The location alone would sell this place to potential customers—if they could look past the obvious deficiencies in the inn itself.

So why hadn't Kay corrected them? Had she spent every dime of her husband's insurance money on the purchase price alone? Was she living on fumes and regretting her hasty purchase?

Those were among the questions he'd ask before she left for Boise.

But that discussion would have to be handled with kid gloves, and after almost a full day on the road, it would be wiser to keep their conversation on the lighter side tonight.

Except Kay had other ideas.

After giving him five minutes to down a significant portion of the large serving of pasta she set in front of him, she wrapped her fingers around her glass of iced tea and angled toward him on the stool at the counter where he'd elected to eat. "So tell me how you're doing—and how you managed to take a month off from your vet practice. You didn't give me a straight answer on the phone."

The last bite he'd taken stuck in his windpipe, and he fumbled for his glass of Sprite. Took several gulps while he tried to formulate a response that was short on details but sufficient to satisfy his sister.

"I'm fine. I got a glowing report at my physical six weeks ago. And my backlog of unused vacation days was getting unwieldy."

She narrowed her eyes. "You know I'm not talking about your physical health, and unused vacation days never compelled you to take time off in the past. Especially four weeks in a row. It's not like you to leave your partner in the lurch for that long."

If he told her Steve was the one who'd suggested he not only take a break but extend it even longer than he'd finally agreed to, he'd have to tell her why.

Another discussion he didn't want to have tonight.

Or ever.

He put on his dancing shoes.

"Steve was fine with the idea. We have a recent vet graduate on temporary staff who wanted to get a feel for working in a private practice setting, and she's more than capable of filling my shoes while I'm gone."

"Sorry. Not buying. Someone fresh out of vet school wouldn't have all your experience."

"Steve was comfortable with the arrangement." And that was all he was going to say on that subject. "You should be glad I was able to get away."

"I am, trust me." She motioned to his plate. "You want another helping?"

"Yes. But heavy food and sleeping don't mix, and sleep is next on my agenda." He gathered up the remaining noodles on his plate. "What's on the schedule tomorrow, other than a crash course on how to run an inn?"

She flashed him a smile that seemed a bit strained. "Why don't you sleep in after your long drive? Maybe take a walk on the beach. The tide pools about half a mile to the north are worth visiting. You could do that while I run a few errands in the morning."

"What if a guest shows up or needs help while we're both gone?"

Faint creases marred her brow as she focused on the melting ice cubes in her glass. "Don't worry about that."

Suspicion confirmed.

There were no paying guests at Beachview B&B.

The pasta he'd ingested hardened in his stomach.

It appeared the light duties he'd agreed to handle last month in exchange for some R&R while she was gone would be far lighter than he'd anticipated.

Tempted as he was to ask questions about her new business, however, he was too tired to tackle what could be a hard discussion tonight.

After swigging the last of his soda, he rose. "This may be the earliest I've called it a night since you made me go to bed at nine when I was a kid."

"A battle we fought every night." She shook her head, lips twitching as she stood and gave him another hug. "Sleep well."

"Thanks."

But as he returned to his room, taking in the drywall cracks where the walls met the ceiling and the worn tread on the stairs, his chances of having a restful slumber plummeted with each step he climbed.

Because Kay had a mess on her hands—and now he was in the middle of it.

Slinking home to Oregon with her tail between her legs was the last thing Vienna Price had ever expected to do.

But when all the rules in your carefully planned, by-the-book life got thrown out the window, the familiar tended to beckon.

Braking at the top of Bluff Ave, she cranked down her window, inhaled a lungful of the briny air, and scanned Hope Harbor spread out below.

The soothing ambiance seeped into her pores, dissipating the tension in her shoulders as she drank in the view.

This was exactly how she remembered the charming town from the occasional weekend trips she and Mom had taken here during her growing-up years.

The planters that served as a buffer between the sloping pile of boulders above the waterline and the sidewalk still brimmed with lush flowers. As on previous trips, boats rested safe and secure in the placid harbor that was protected by a long jetty on the left and a pair of rocky islands on the right.

Vienna shifted her gaze to the other side of Dockside Drive, where storefronts with colorful awnings and window boxes faced the sea, matching the image in her memory to a T. Farther down the two-block-long, crescent-shaped road that dead-ended at the river, the same charming white gazebo graced the tiny pocket park.

Best of all, the taco stand with Charley's name emblazoned in colorful letters over the serving window remained ensconced beside the park.

Her lips curved up as memories flitted through her mind of her last trip here with Mom ten years ago during one of her brief visits to the state of her birth, to celebrate her new MBA and plum job offer. In those days, the renowned artist had still been dispensing philosophy and gentle wisdom along with his famous fish tacos.

Of course, it was possible he'd sold the business and moved on. Things changed—sometimes overnight.

Mouth flattening, she heaved a sigh, put the car in gear, and continued down the hill, turning right onto Main Street.

If fate was kind, change hadn't beset Charley. Having an empathetic sounding board would be a godsend when she and Mom clashed, as they inevitably would. Much as they loved each other, a free-spirit mother paired with a by-the-book daughter generated a subtle but ever-present tension that often led to conflict.

"Your destination is on the right."

As the voice on her phone spoke, Vienna slowed and glanced inland.

There it was, the second building past the intersection of Main and Harbor.

Bev's Book Nook.

Once she pulled into a parking space and set the brake, Vienna read the banner that hung over a display of books in the front window.

Start a New Chapter!

An appropriate tagline for Mom, from both a business and personal standpoint. How many retirees would launch a new business after wrapping up a thirty-year career? Weren't most people at that stage of life happy to have fewer responsibilities and more free time?

Then again, Bev Price wasn't most people. Never had been, never would be.

Vienna picked up her purse, slid from behind the wheel, and locked the doors. Probably not necessary in Hope Harbor, but the habit was hard to break after living in a city the size of Denver for the past ten years.

"Vienna! Welcome to Hope Harbor!"

At the enthusiastic greeting, she swiveled toward the shop as the door was flung open and a woman emerged.

Vintage Mom, from the bright, patterned muumuu more appropriate for a luau than an Oregon seaside town to the purple swath in her long, flowing locks. While the silver streaks in her hair were far more prominent than they'd been during their last in-person visit at the retirement party in Eugene two years ago, her expression radiated exuberance and joy.

Her new life agreed with her.

Despite Vienna's diligent effort to contain it, resentment bubbled up inside her at the irony.

The woman who'd never cared about climbing the corporate ladder, who did her job with passion during the work day but cherished her free hours, who lived a paycheck-to-paycheck and go-with-the-flow philosophy, had retired from a stable job after three decades and pursued her dream business while the fast-track daughter who'd toed the line and devoted herself to work 24/7 was out on her ear.

Another example of how life wasn't always fair.

Shoring up her flagging spirits, Vienna circled the car.

Her mother met her in the middle of the sidewalk, arms extended, and pulled her into a tight embrace.

The familiar scent of jasmine swirled around her, stirring up memories of the bedtime kisses Mom had bestowed every night as she tucked in the covers and whispered, "Happy dreams, sweet girl. Never forget how much Mama loves you."

Vienna's throat tightened.

How sad that their diametrically opposed personalities had always created a barrier between them despite their mutual love.

"Hi, Mom." She tried for a light tone as she returned the hug, shifting slightly away from the purple hair tickling her nose. "Your prodigal daughter has returned."

"Prodigal." With a snort, Mom released her and waved the comment aside. "That implies extravagance, recklessness, and imprudence. You don't have an ounce of any of those in your body."

True. Her DNA came from her maternal grandparents, not Mom. And maybe from her father, based on the little Mom had told her about him.

"It's been a while since my last visit, though."

"I'll agree with that. It's been way too long. But I know that job of yours keeps you hopping. I want to hear all about your latest adventures as soon as you get settled in."

Somehow Vienna hung onto her smile.

In hindsight, it might have been easier to tell Mom about her career disaster on the phone. Except once she'd said she was thinking about coming out for a visit, it had been hard to get a word in edgewise or put a damper on her mom's enthusiasm.

Nor was there an urgent need to spring it on her this moment. Why not catch her breath after the early morning flight and the drive down from North Bend?

"I promise to fill you in on everything, but first I want to see your shop."

Mom gave the façade of Bev's Book Nook a satisfied sweep. "You mean my pride and joy." Beaming, she pushed open the front door, setting off a musical tinkle of wind chimes, and ushered her in.

Given her mother's propensity to cram every available space with color, crafts, items she'd collected on her international travels, flea market finds, and natural art like feathers, shells, shiny rocks, and displaced birds' nests, Vienna braced for a sensory onslaught.

Three steps inside the door, she jolted to a stop.

The shop's website only featured the front of the building, and the photos Mom had emailed as she prepared for the opening six months ago had been close-ups of bookshelves and décor rather than overall views.

They hadn't hinted at the oasis within.

Yes, there were eclectic elements that gave a subtle Bohemian vibe to the space. A wicker swing chair in one corner, padded with comfortable-looking cushions. An intricate macramé wall hanging. Pottery lamps. A few pieces of wave-sculpted driftwood on the bookshelves. A patterned jute rug on the polished hardwood floor. Two woven baskets filled with glass floats. A flat-topped inlaid wood trunk with a Moroccan motif, two cushioned rattan wicker swivel chairs beside it.

Many of the items had been in their apartment while she was growing up, lost in the general clutter of the small space crammed with Mom's treasures.

But here, used as accent pieces, they stood out and enhanced the quiet, restful, welcoming mood.

"You're speechless." Mom took her arm and drew her deeper into the shop, amusement sparking in her irises.

"Um . . . it's not quite what I expected."

"Which goes to show you should never judge a book by its cover." With a wink, Mom swept a hand down her attire.

While true in general, that adage hadn't applied to Mom in the past. What you saw was what you got with Bev Price.

Apparently the adage applied now.

The orchid-and-fern-bedecked fabric of her muumuu was a major disconnect with the peaceful, soothing, book-filled haven she'd created in her shop.

"It's just that I thought you'd have more . . . that the shop would be . . ." Vienna's voice trailed off.

"Jammed to the gills like our apartment back in Eugene?" Mom gave her arm an understanding pat. "Not anymore. The sign in the window says it all. I started a new chapter when I moved here. I took inventory of my life, literally and figuratively, and let go of a bunch of stuff I'd been hanging on to for too long."

Major disconnect.

Not to mention a bit unsettling.

What other unexpected changes were in store?

The disconcerting question added yet another ripple to the already turbulent waters of her world only minutes into a visit she'd assumed would be comforting due to its predictability.

Once again the wind chimes pealed, followed by the appearance of a middle-aged couple.

"Welcome to Bev's Book Nook." Her mother leaned around her and lifted a hand in greeting. "I'll be with you in a sec."

"No rush. Vacations are meant for unhurried browsing with your favorite girl." The man slipped his arm around the woman beside him. "Especially on an anniversary trip."

"Well, congratulations to you both. You may want to take a look at the jewelry near the checkout. I make all of it myself. You might find a memento to help you remember your trip."

"We'll do that. Thanks."

While the couple ambled toward the display case, Mom took her arm and tugged her toward the back room.

Vienna let herself be led as she digested the news about her mother's handiwork. "I saw the jewelry display in one of the photos you sent me. I didn't know you made it."

"I took a class about six years ago, remember?"

Vaguely, now that Mom had reminded her. But her mother took all kinds of classes. In general, they were one-offs.

"Yes. I didn't realize you'd stuck with it, though."

"I didn't expect to, but I fell in love with the creative process. It started out as a hobby, but after people began asking to buy pieces, I decided to launch an online business."

"Why didn't you ever mention that?"

Mom shrugged. "It was just small potatoes for a long while. But several jewelry stores in Eugene did carry my work. Who knew a labor of love could end up being profitable?"

One more surprise.

Mom pushed through a swinging door into a stock room/office and stopped at a desk to rummage through her purse. "I'll give you a key to the apartment so you can unpack. Help yourself to the lunch fixings in the fridge. I plan to close early today and take you out to dinner. The Myrtle has an amazing spinach quiche."

"Why don't I take you to dinner instead?" Unless her mom's financial philosophy had changed too, her bank account would be lean. Excess cash had always been in short supply in the Price household. And once her offspring had flown the nest, Mom had begun spending her hard-earned money on theater tickets, travel, yoga classes, and who knew what else. Perish the practicality of saving for a down payment on a house.

"No. First dinner is on me. But I'll let you treat me to Charley's tacos while you're here."

Vienna's spirits took an uptick. "So he still owns the stand?"

"Of course. The man is a town fixture. Hope Harbor wouldn't be the same without him. He's on a visit to Mexico right now, though." Mom withdrew a key and handed it over. "My place is easy to find. Just head north on 101 and hang a left on Starfish Pier Road. Sea Haven Apartments are on the right. There isn't much else down that way."

"What time will you be home?" Vienna slid the key into her pocket.

"As soon as the delivery I'm expecting arrives. I have several customers waiting for those books."

"You don't have to close early because of me."

"Yes, I do. I want to take full advantage of this rare treat." The comment was matter-of-fact, with no hint of recrimination, but guilt pricked at Vienna's conscience anyway.

"Won't your customers be disappointed if they stop by and find the shop closed?"

"No. Hope Harbor is laid-back. People here go with the flow. Is it any wonder I love this place?" She reached over and once again pulled her close. "It's so good to see you, sweet girl. I love our phone chats and Zoom sessions, but nothing beats a hug."

Vienna inhaled the jasmine-infused air as she squeezed her mom back, letting the love envelop her and seep into her soul.

Leaving Denver behind temporarily had been a smart move. While she and Mom didn't agree on much, at least her mother's love was predictable.

Unlike the future she'd planned with such meticulous care.

As she left the shop behind, Vienna paused at her rental car to read the sign in the window again.

Start a New Chapter!

A worthy mantra during her stay.

For perhaps here, in this quiet seaside community, she'd discover a new path for her life after the unexpected detour that had thrown her so off course.

2

No way.

Poised at the door of the bedroom in Mom's apartment, her mother's note in hand, Vienna reread the sheet that had been waiting for her on the kitchen counter.

> *Welcome again! The bedroom is down the hall, on the right. I've cleared space in the closet for you. Bath is at the end of the hall, fresh towels on the vanity. Make yourself at home.*
>
> *Love, Mom*

Vienna exhaled.

She wasn't about to take the sole bed in the small, one-bedroom, one-bath apartment.

Why hadn't Mom told her the place only had one bedroom?

She'd have to find other accommodations fast.

She retraced her steps, moving past the galley kitchen with its pass-through counter to the living room/dining room combo.

Truth be told, had she and Mom been more simpatico, sleeping on the couch in this uncluttered space wouldn't be too bad. The earth-tone palette, punctuated by bright spots of color from a few items her mother had brought with her from Eugene, was as restful as the shop. Also night and day from the messy apartment of her youth.

But in such confined quarters, disruptive flare-ups would likely rear their ugly heads in short order. So to preserve family harmony, it would be wise to find other living quarters sooner rather than later.

Vienna pulled out her cell and googled hotels in Hope Harbor.

First up was the Gull Motel, where she and Mom had stayed on their occasional visits to the town. Small, family run, and clean, with basic rooms. Fine for travelers on a budget, but she could afford to splurge on more upscale digs.

The second possibility that popped up sounded promising. According to its website, Seabird Inn offered two spacious suites and a gourmet breakfast each morning.

Vienna tapped in the number and proceeded to ask the friendly man who answered about availability.

No go. Only random nights were open for the next month.

Which left choice number three, Beachview B&B.

She squinted at the name.

Was this the place she and Mom had considered staying for their first weekend excursion to Hope Harbor two decades ago? The newly opened B&B that had ended up being too expensive for their lean budget?

She clicked on the website and scrolled through the inviting photos. Read the history of the twenty-four-year-old inn.

Yes. This must be it. The timing fit. And this go-round, the price wasn't a deal breaker. It was higher than the Gull Motel, but cheaper than Seabird Inn. It was also located off the very road where Mom lived, close to the beach.

Assuming they had a room available, this would be perfect. Far preferable to the Gull or commuting from Bandon or Coos Bay.

Vienna entered the number, wandered over to the fridge, and took a quick inventory.

Containers of chicken salad, potato salad, and coleslaw were front and center, while whole wheat rolls, chips, and a plate of brownies sat on the adjacent counter.

Either Mom's latest vegan phase had ended or she'd stocked up just for her visitor.

As the phone continued to ring, Vienna opened a cabinet, pulled out a glass, and filled it with water from the fridge dispenser.

"Hello. This is Beachview B&B. I'm sorry, but we are not currently taking reservations. Please try us again on your next visit. Have a great day."

Well, shoot.

It appeared the Gull Motel won by default.

With a resigned sigh, Vienna fixed a plate of food, tapped in the motel's number, and reserved a room through the weekend. After that, she'd play it by ear. Who knew how long it would take to regroup after the setback that had sent her reeling? It was possible she'd regain her balance and come up with a plan for her future faster than she'd expected.

She could hope, anyway.

Settling onto a stool at the counter between the kitchen and living/dining room, she checked her sparse emails while she ate. A couple of brief procedural questions from a former colleague. A notification from her gym about a change in hours. Junk mail.

Strange not to have dozens of messages to respond to or meetings to attend or financial reports to prepare or marketing campaigns to plan.

Also strange not to have a jam-packed work schedule that kept her on the go from early morning until she fell into bed at night.

This new normal was going to take some getting used to for an ambitious, disciplined high achiever who'd set her sights on a secure career that would let her amass a comfortable financial cushion with nary a worry about paying next month's rent or whether the budget would allow for steak or dictate macaroni and cheese.

Yet what had all her work and sacrifice and planning gotten her?

A big fat zero.

Instead of climbing the corporate ladder, she was—

The doorknob rattled, and Mom swept in, bringing a swirl of high-octane energy with her.

"The delivery arrived early, praise the Lord! I'm not usually anxious to leave the shop, but today was an exception." She stopped as she spotted the suitcases sitting by the door. "I thought you'd be unpacked already."

"I was hungry." Vienna dabbed at her lips with a paper napkin and indicated the plate on the counter in front of her. "Thank you for all the goodies."

"It was my pleasure, sweet girl. Have you tried the brownies? They're from Sweet Dreams bakery. I remember how much you liked them on our visits."

"No. I haven't gotten to dessert yet."

"Shall I join you, or would you like to unpack first?"

Vienna took a steadying breath and wadded her napkin into her fist.

This wasn't going to be easy.

"There's only one bedroom here, Mom."

"And it's yours for as long as you can stay."

"I can't take your bedroom. Where would you sleep?"

Her mother motioned toward the couch. "That will suit me fine for a few nights—or longer, if your busy job can spare you for more than that."

Another sticky subject she'd have to broach soon. After she dropped the bomb about the Gull Motel.

"I'd feel guilty if you slept on the couch."

Her mother dismissed that concern with a flip of her hand. "Don't be silly. In my wild and crazy pre-Vienna vagabond days, I slept in places that would make a sofa bed in an apartment even as modest as this one feel like the Taj Mahal. Of course you'll stay here."

"I can't, Mom." She swallowed. "The sleeping issue aside, I think we both need our space."

Mom studied her, a fusion of hurt and hope in her expression. "We don't have to clash, Vienna. We're both adults. You've made your choices and I've made mine. Maybe we can learn to accept each other as we are and not let our differences lead to dissension."

A reasonable plan in theory, but if their history was any indication, the likelihood of it happening was slim to none.

"We can try. But I still think it's better if we have our own space while I'm here. These quarters are a bit small."

Her mom's features tightened a hair. "The apartment's clean, in case you're worried about that. Almost up to your standards. I may have missed a speck of dust here or there, but there's no toothpaste in the sink or hair balls on the carpet. Not that those would kill anyone."

And so it began.

The cleanliness of their apartment in Eugene had always been an issue between them. While she liked everything spic and span and in its place, Mom only dusted if a rare cleaning mood struck, and she was always trying to find her car keys amid the clutter. The key holder Vienna had given her one Christmas and installed the next day had ended up holding necklaces and rubber bands and stray shoelaces. Anything but keys.

In light of her mother's piqued response, the decision to hole up elsewhere was wise.

"I called the Gull Motel and booked a room before I ate lunch, Mom. But we can meet for coffee or breakfast every morning and have dinner together every night. And I'd love to go sightseeing with you."

After a few beats, her mom nodded. "Okay. Whatever works for you is fine with me. Why don't we have a brownie and you can tell me what's new at your job?"

Vienna stifled a groan.

From the frying pan into the fire.

"Sure." If she could somehow choke down the treat while she shared her news with Mom.

"What can I get you to drink with dessert?"

"Whatever you're having is fine."

Her mother's mouth twitched as she rounded the counter into the hall and reappeared in the kitchen. "You may want to rethink that. I'm having vanilla-flavored oat milk. A favorite from my vegan days."

Vienna tried not to grimace. "Um . . . could I have a cup of tea? Decaf, if possible."

"Will herbal tea do? I have mango pear, hibiscus, chamomile, and sage."

Naturally Bev Price wouldn't have an ordinary tea like English Breakfast or Earl Grey.

"Any chance you have decaf coffee?"

"Yep. My old standby, Folgers. Never broke that habit from my youth."

"Sold."

"I'll have it ready in a jiffy." She opened a cabinet and selected two mugs.

"Why don't I plate the brownies?"

"Thanks for the offer, but this kitchen is too tight for two butts."

"It *is* on the small side." Vienna broached the subject that had been on her mind since she walked in the door. "Did you think about buying a house here? That would have given you more space." And equity.

"There's plenty of space for me in this apartment. And I'd rather spend my money on travel and theater and experiences than a pile of bricks. Besides, who wants to worry about maintenance issues when there are books to read and jewelry to create and places to go?"

The same kind of response she'd always offered whenever Vienna brought up the logic of investing in property rather than paying someone else's mortgage.

Some things never changed.

Curbing her exasperation, Vienna slid her lunch plate aside as her mother set a brownie and fork in front of her. "Thanks. This brings back memories."

"For me too. Happy ones. They were a big factor in my decision to open my shop here, and I'm glad I did. This town suits me." She flicked the switch on the coffeemaker and circled back to claim the other stool. "Enough about me. Tell me how your career is going. Your experiences at that high-end boutique hotel chain remind me of that old TV show. You know, *Lifestyles of the Rich and Famous*."

Vienna broke off a bite of brownie and braced. "Those were the exceptions. Most days I was hunkered down at my desk until all hours crunching numbers or stuck in conference rooms trying to sell management on a marketing program or struggling to get a consensus on a new campaign."

Mom's forehead puckered. "Did I hear a past tense in there?"

Bev Price might march to the beat of her own sometimes frustrating drummer, but she'd always been a master at picking up nuances in the spoken word.

"Yes. The career that was supposed to be my ticket to long-term security is history." A hint of bitterness crept into her inflection despite her attempt to contain it.

"Oh my goodness." Mom set her fork down and reached over to grasp her hand. "I don't know what to say. You busted your buns for that company. What happened? Did they get bought out? File for bankruptcy? Get a new CEO who wanted to shake things up?"

If only. Any of those explanations would be far less embarrassing.

"No. They reorganized my division. The promotion I was supposed to get went to a lower-level colleague, and my job was eliminated."

"But . . . I don't understand. How could they do that to you?

You've been there since you got your MBA, and you worked so hard for them. Too hard, in my opinion. Did they say why you didn't get the promotion?"

"No."

Yet in hindsight, their rationale had been clear. The woman they'd chosen had been a hard worker too. No denying that. But all the nights she went out socializing with the team while Vienna toiled extra hours at her desk had paid dividends. Schmoozing, it seemed, trumped experience and zealous diligence.

Her colleague's outgoing personality hadn't hurt either.

"I'm sorry, Vienna. I know that had to be a huge blow. You gave up so much for that company."

Too much.

Mom didn't say *too* this time, but the message was clear. She'd never been shy about sharing her views or nudging her workaholic daughter to create a life apart from the job.

But single-minded focus and dedication were how you achieved success.

At least, that's how the rules were supposed to work.

"It wasn't fair, Mom." Her throat clogged, and she forced herself to swallow past the lump. "I poured my heart and soul into my job. I gave them everything they asked for, and more. This isn't how it was supposed to play out."

Several seconds of silence ticked by as her mother's demeanor grew pensive. "I don't know, sweet girl. Hard as it may be to believe at the moment, this might be exactly how it was supposed to play out."

What?

"How can you say that? This is a disaster. I'm out of a job and I have no idea what to do next. I don't even have an up-to-date resume. I never thought I'd need one again."

"Are you financially secure?"

"For the immediate future. I have a fair amount of savings, and I got a generous severance package."

"So you don't have to rush into anything, make rash decisions. That's a blessing."

Leave it to Mom to find a bright side to this dark cloud.

"I don't think our definition of blessing matches." So what else was new?

"Blessings can be hard to identify in the moment. But with a financial cushion, you have time to explore options, think through priorities, find a new road to travel."

"I liked the road I was on."

A melancholy smile whispered at Mom's lips. "Sometimes the road we think will take us where we want to go ends up being a dead end. It's better to recognize that and find a new path rather than lament over a journey that's over."

Her mother was now a philosopher?

Vienna throttled her annoyance and poked at her brownie. "Be that as it may, you're not supposed to get thrown out of the game if you play by the rules."

"That's why I never put much stock in rules. Why I always encouraged you to spread your wings and push the boundaries."

"Yeah." She gave a soft snort. "Like the time you told me I didn't have to color inside the lines for the kindergarten assignment I brought home."

Mom cocked her head. "I don't remember that."

"I do." The painful lesson was etched in her mind, as was the humiliation. "The next day, in front of the whole class, the teacher told me I'd done it wrong and made me sit in the corner while I colored it again."

"Why am I only hearing about this now?" Mom bristled with indignation. "If you'd told me back then, I would have given that teacher a piece of my mind."

The very reason she'd kept it to herself.

"I survived. But I learned that in general, life is a lot easier and more predictable if you follow the rules and color inside the lines."

"Also more boring." Her mom rose and circled back to the

coffeemaker. "I'm not saying the world could function without rules. Some serve a legitimate purpose. But I'm not certain the rules of the rat race are among them." She poured the coffee into the two mugs. "As comedian Lily Tomlin once said, the trouble with the rat race is that even if you win, you're still a rat. Present company excluded."

Vienna let that comment pass. She was in no mood for humor.

"At least I have a healthy 401(k), money in the bank, and a hefty amount put aside for a down payment on a house." Her reply came out sharper and more critical than intended, but it was hard not to be defensive—and hurt—when the person you loved most in the world disapproved of your choices.

In all fairness, though, Mom no doubt felt the same about her.

So much for accepting each other's priorities without judging.

"I'm sure you do. And that's wonderful, because those are important to you." Mom came back around the counter.

"But you don't think they should be."

"I never said that."

"Maybe not in those exact words. But what's wrong with caring about financial security? Don't you ever worry about what would happen if an emergency cropped up and you didn't have any reserves to get you through?"

"I'm not wired that way, sweet girl. I have more money in the bank than I've ever had, but I'm not any happier or more content. My joy comes from the people I meet and my bookshop and jewelry making and long walks on the beach. You're much more like my parents than I ever was."

Not exactly a compliment, given that her nonconformist mom had always clashed with her super-strict, hypercritical engineer and actuary parents, who'd done everything by the book.

Was it any wonder Mom had left home at eighteen and led an unconventional life until an unexpected pregnancy forced her to tame her wild ways so she could give her daughter a more stable home?

"I am who I am, Mom."

Her mother patted her hand. "I know. Me too—although I think I'm mellowing with age." She motioned toward the brownies. "Why don't we put aside heavy discussion for today and enjoy our treat? Your first day back should be a celebration." She hoisted her mug. "To turning the page and starting a new chapter right here in Hope Harbor."

Vienna lifted her mug and clinked it with Mom's.

But as she took a sip and sampled the brownie, she doubted the toast would come true. The odds of finding anything more in this small, seaside town than peace and quiet to regroup had to be minuscule. Hope Harbor was a waystation on her road of life, not a destination.

After all, what could a tiny place like this offer to entice someone with her skills and ambition to stay?

It was worse than he'd thought.

Matt slid onto a stool at the counter in Beachview B&B's kitchen and stared at the list of issues he'd compiled after two hours of inspecting the property and googling various review sites for guest comments.

It filled an entire legal-sized sheet of notepaper.

And this was just what he'd discovered after a cursory look.

He blew out a breath and forked his fingers through his hair.

Why on earth had Kay bought this aging white elephant? Had she done any due diligence at all?

A low rumble from the garage door vibrated in the house, and Matt's pulse picked up.

His sister was back from her morning errands—and it was time for answers.

Psyching himself up for the exchange to come, Matt took a sip of the coffee he'd brewed after a walk on the beach that he'd hoped would calm him down and help him come up with a plan to rescue Kay.

It had done neither.

Kay pushed through the door from the garage into the mudroom, pausing when she caught sight of him at the counter. "Good morning."

"It's almost noon, but good morning to you too." He kept his tone mild, despite the churning in his stomach.

"Did you sleep well?" She continued into the kitchen and deposited a bakery box on the counter.

Under other circumstances, the enticing cinnamon aroma wafting toward him would have activated his salivary glands. But stress could ruin a person's appetite.

"Not especially."

"I'm sorry." Parallel creases marred her brow as she flicked a glance at the sheet of paper in front of him. "Were you overtired?"

"No. Over worried. And I'm more worried than ever after a walk-through of the inn and an hour of online research."

Biting her lip, she leaned a hip against the counter and folded her arms. "I know the place needs a little work."

"More than a little, based on this list." He lifted the corner of the sheet in front of him. "The gardens are pristine—thanks to your magic touch with all things horticultural, I assume—but everything else is in desperate need of TLC."

"I'll concede the place has some issues. I guess the previous owners let maintenance slip as they approached retirement."

"No guessing about it." He tried hard to keep his tone level and non-accusatory. "Kay, did you even get an inspection?"

Her chin tipped up. "Of course I did. The inn is structurally sound. All of the issues the inspector identified were cosmetic."

"That may be true, but there are a ton of them. Didn't you realize the scope of the repairs when you visited the property to look it over?"

She dropped her gaze. Scrubbed a finger over a spot of tomato sauce on the counter, a souvenir from last night's dinner.

His stomach bottomed out as shock ricocheted through him. "You did visit the site in person before you signed on the dotted line, right?" But he already knew the answer.

"The agent sent hundreds of photos and a video. I had the inspector's report. The guest reviews on the inn's website were glowing. I saw the books. Everything seemed fine on paper. I was afraid if I didn't snatch it up, someone else would beat me to it. And I had money in reserve for repairs and cosmetic updating."

"Enough to cover everything?"

"Almost. I got a bid from a local contractor. They're booked too far out to use, but based on their estimate, a few of the minor updates may have to wait."

Otherwise, she'd run out of funds.

The silent caveat hung between them.

Unfortunately, no new money would be coming in until she had a steady infusion of guests—a long shot, thanks to the online reviews he'd found that counteracted the glowing recommendations on the inn's website.

"Have you had *any* bookings, Kay?"

"Yes. I inherited some from the previous owners and took a few reservations myself after I got here."

"I googled reviews. The ones in the past couple of years aren't pretty."

"I saw some of those too, but the reviews on the B&B website were stellar. I figured some guests had just been too picky. But after I got here, I realized how much work needed to be done." The corners of her mouth drooped. "That's why I decided about three weeks ago to cancel the few upcoming reservations and shut down while I figure out what I'm going to do. I haven't pulled the trigger on the repairs because I didn't want to throw good money after bad." Her voice caught, and her eyes began to glisten. "Dealing with this alone has been kind of . . . overwhelming."

A word he never used flashed through his mind.

If he'd been a decent brother, he'd have jumped into the situation the day Kay mentioned her idea nine months ago. Finance wasn't her forte, as they both knew. And she had zero innkeeping experience. After all she'd done for him, after all she'd sacrificed, he owed her a debt he could never repay.

Instead, he'd been so mired in his own problems he'd left her to fend for herself.

Now she was neck deep in trouble and sinking fast.

Meaning that instead of attending to a few light inn duties and taking long walks on the beach for the next month, as planned, he'd have to dive in and try to help prop up her failing business.

Since he could put everything he knew about innkeeping in the palm of his hand with room left over, that looming task was more than intimidating.

It was downright terrifying.

But admitting that to Kay wouldn't ease her mind on the cusp of her departure for a mission of mercy.

Quashing his panic, Matt stood and pulled her into a hug. "You don't have to deal with it alone anymore."

"Y-yes I do. This is my mess, not yours. Besides, you already have a full plate."

"I'm here for the next month. Much as I'm looking forward to walks on the beach and trying those fish tacos in town you told me about that are made by a famous artist, I'm not used to downtime. A project like this will keep me occupied." To put it mildly.

"I don't want to burden you with this while you're here. You need a vacation." She backed off a few inches, hope warring with indecision in her eyes.

"Vacations are overrated. Why don't we sit down together and dig into the financials? I want to get a feel for the situation. Then we can plan out next steps. If you want to proceed with repairs,

I'll line up a contractor while you're helping Cora and get the work rolling. If you decide to go a different route, I can coordinate that too." Like passing the inn on to someone more equipped to manage this type of business.

A tear formed on her lower eyelid. "It's too much to ask, Matt."

"You're not asking. I'm offering."

"Big brother to the rescue." She offered him a watery smile. "Funny how the passage of years has reversed our roles. I remember nursing many a scraped knee and defending you from bullies in grade school."

"I remember that too—and much more." He squeezed her arm. "It's just you and me now, kid. We have to stick together." Though he tried for humor, his voice rasped as the stark truth of that statement ripped at his soul.

"You'll always have me, Matt." She wrapped her arms around his waist and laid her cheek on his chest as she offered that gentle but firm assurance. "I love you."

He held her tight. "I love you back. And we'll get through this, like we've gotten through everything else. Okay?"

"Yeah." After a few seconds, she pulled away and pushed the box on the counter closer to him. "I brought you a cinnamon roll from Sweet Dreams bakery. They're famous in these parts. Why don't you top off your coffee while I freshen up and then we'll dive into the numbers?"

"Works for me."

"Give me a couple of minutes." She pivoted toward the innkeeper's quarters off the kitchen.

After the door closed behind her, Matt opened the bakery box and swiped a finger through the icing on the huge roll. Licked it off while he crossed to the coffeemaker.

Sweet as it was, however, the sugary confection couldn't offset the sharp taste of anxiety on his tongue.

Kay was leaving in forty-eight hours, and her ability to help with the inn from Boise was limited. Plus, her focus there would be on Cora.

So while they were in this together in theory, he'd be carrying the bulk of the load here.

And for a guy who spent his life keeping beloved pets healthy, he was way out of his element trying to cure the ills of an ailing inn.

3

"I feel bad about leaving you on your own here to deal with the inn, Matt."

"Don't." He hefted Kay's two sizeable suitcases into her trunk. "All I have to do is follow the plan we agreed on over the past two days."

She pulled out her sunglasses as the early morning sun crested the hemlock, pine, and spruce-covered hills to the east. "Do you honestly think I should go ahead with the repairs? I don't want to throw good money after bad."

"I know it's a big expenditure, but if you end up selling the inn, you'll get a higher price for a structure that's in tip-top shape. If you decide to follow through with your original plan to operate it, you won't be able to attract guests to a place with such obvious signs of wear. As far as I can see, it's the only logical choice."

"I suppose so." She sighed. "I just never expected to have to deal with this much stuff right out of the gate."

The "as is" clause in the purchase contract he'd reviewed should have tipped her off to potential problems, but that was water under the bridge at this point.

He called up an encouraging smile. "It will work out, Kay. You'll have almost a month in Boise to think about what you want to do. Don't feel rushed. I'll keep you informed about the progress here, and we can continue to discuss pros and cons by phone."

"You're a lifesaver, you know that?"

His lips flatlined. "Hardly."

"Oh, Matt." Distress tightened her features. "I'm sorry. I didn't mean—"

"Hey. It's okay." He forced air into his lungs. Rested a hand on her shoulder. "You better get rolling. I'm not thrilled about you making the long drive alone, and I don't want to have to worry about you on the road after dark."

"I drove out here by myself. I'll be fine." She gave him a hug. "I wish we'd had more of a chance to visit. All we've talked about since you arrived is the inn and *my* troubles."

Fine by him. Rehashing his issues would have stirred up feelings he'd rather leave undisturbed.

"We can catch up during our phone calls. Remember to text me every few hours with a progress report on your trip."

"I will. And stop worrying. I'm used to being on my own." She slipped on her sunglasses. "I have been for quite a while."

At her soft admission, he frowned.

That was the closest she'd ever come to acknowledging her marriage hadn't provided the kind of love and companionship she'd hoped for when she'd said "I do" to the over-the-road truck driver fourteen years her senior who'd proposed after a whirlwind courtship. How could it, with her husband gone most days of the week and taking on freelance jobs in between his regular hauls?

Hal hadn't seemed like a bad guy, but Kay had deserved a full-time husband.

"I'm sorry, Sis."

She offered a resigned shrug. "Life's not a fairy tale, as we both know." She glanced toward the inn. "Which means I should have realized an opportunity that appeared too good to be true probably was."

"Don't write this place off yet. I think it has great potential, if you decide to stick it out."

"Really?" She refocused on him.

The truth?

He had no idea.

But why add to her stress by sharing his doubts just as she was heading off to play Florence Nightingale? For now, it would be kinder to punt.

"We're both smart people. Getting this place in shape isn't rocket science. It should be a piece of cake for a decent contractor. Your location is world class. You have the contact information for the housekeeping service the previous owners used. The only cooking you have to do is breakfast. Scrambling a few eggs shouldn't be difficult."

"You make it sound simple."

Those parts might be.

The biggest challenge was going to be lining up guests, thanks to all the negative reviews floating around in cyberspace.

A formidable hurdle to overcome if ever there was one.

"Not necessarily simple, but doable."

"I wish I had your confidence."

He forced up the corners of his mouth as he closed the trunk and stretched the truth. "I have enough for both of us."

"Hold that thought." She gave the inn another sweep. "It doesn't look half bad in the morning light, does it?"

"Not bad at all." Thanks to the warm, golden hue that tempered a multitude of sins. "You sure you don't want a cup of coffee to go?"

"Yes. I'm wide awake." She circled around to the door, tossed her purse onto the passenger seat, and turned back to him. "You're the best."

"Not even close." The words rasped past his throat.

"Matt." She touched his arm, her voice gentle. "What happened wasn't your fault."

The same reassurance everyone had offered. Dana's family. Cora. Steve. His pastor.

But they were wrong. All of them. Everything that had happened had been his fault.

"Thanks for saying that." Untrue as it was.

"You need to believe it."

"Maybe someday." Like light years from now, in a galaxy far, far away.

Kay studied him, brow crinkling. "Are you going to be okay here by yourself?"

As her meaning registered, he struggled to maintain a neutral expression.

It appeared she was as worried about his mental health as his vet partner was.

But he was holding his own. While guilt continued to plague him, his grief was beginning to lose its power to steal the breath from his lungs and suck him into crushing darkness. Day by day, the pain of loss was transitioning from sharp to dull.

As far as he was concerned, that was progress.

"I'll be fine, Kay. Trust me on that."

She chewed on her lower lip as she assessed him. "Only if you promise to touch base with me every single day. Deal?"

A small concession to ensure her peace of mind.

"Deal."

After one more hug, she slid behind the wheel, started the engine, and drove down the drive with a toot of the horn and a wave out the window.

Leaving him alone with an inn and a heart that were both in need of a heaping dose of TLC.

Why was the Gull Motel calling her?

From the bench she'd claimed at Pelican Point lighthouse,

Vienna squinted at caller ID, shading her phone from the bright afternoon light as it vibrated in her hand.

Maybe they wanted to know if she planned to extend her stay beyond the five days she'd booked. The motel had been busy this morning when she'd set out early to take a drive along the coast.

She tapped talk, put the phone to her ear, and greeted the caller.

"Ms. Price, this is Madeline King, the manager at the Gull Motel. I'm afraid I have bad news. The housekeeper discovered a major water leak in the bathroom in your room that's caused extensive damage. We think a pipe broke. All of your personal items appear to be fine, but we're going to have to take the room out of service while we do repairs."

Vienna closed her eyes.

First a firing, now a flood.

What other disasters were lurking in the shadows, waiting to pounce?

"I appreciate the heads-up. Would you like me to come back and move my belongings to another room?"

"That's the problem. We're fully booked for the next three days. There's a family reunion in town, plus a small tour group."

Vienna watched two seagulls ride the wind currents as she absorbed that news, along with the ramifications.

She was being thrown out.

This was becoming a disturbing pattern.

"I guess I'll have to find other accommodations." She tried not to let her frustration show. No point blaming her bad luck on the messenger. "Do you have any recommendations?"

"There are several places in Bandon, which isn't too far, and Coos Bay has multiple lodging choices. Would you like me to give you a few names and numbers, or call them for you myself?"

"Isn't there anything closer to Hope Harbor?" It was possible the manager knew about a spot that hadn't surfaced in her Google search.

"The Seabird Inn is lovely, but I expect it's booked."

"What's the story on the Beachview B&B?"

"I don't believe they're currently taking reservations."

"They aren't—but do you know why?" Depending on the reason, they might be amenable to taking in one guest if she promised not to be demanding.

"No, but the previous owners retired not long ago and sold the B&B. Rumor has it the place could use sprucing up. The new innkeeper may have closed while that work is being done."

"So the owner is on-site?"

"As far as I know. I saw her in Sweet Dreams last week when I passed by the shop."

Vienna's brain began clicking.

If the B&B had even one room that wasn't torn apart for renovation, would the owner let her stay there? The breakfast part of the B&B was irrelevant. All she required was the bed component. And noise shouldn't be an issue. Work crews would be gone at night, taking their sleep-disrupting racket with them, and she wouldn't be on-site much during the day.

Staying there would be far preferable to driving back and forth from Bandon or Coos Bay.

"Thanks for the information." Vienna stood and picked up her purse from the bench. "I'll make other arrangements myself. And I'll come by to get my things within the hour."

"I'm really sorry about this. I'll be glad to give you a 10 percent discount on your stay for the inconvenience."

"That's not necessary. The pipe break wasn't anyone's fault." And small businesses were struggling enough these days. Why penalize this one for an accident?

Besides, it wasn't as if she'd planned to stay much longer anyway. Now that the initial shock from her unexpected career detour was receding, she needed to get herself in gear and figure out next steps.

"I wish you'd take the discount. We don't want dissatisfied

customers. Our reviews are always favorable, and we'd like to keep it that way."

A top priority for anyone in the hospitality industry, as Vienna knew firsthand.

"Don't worry about that. My stay was fine. You offer excellent value for the price. That's what my review will say, with no mention of the water break."

"Thank you so much." The woman's relief was obvious. "I'll have the housecleaner move all of your things out of harm's way. Stop in at the office when you get back and I'll help you collect everything. And I'll contact you as soon as we have a vacancy."

"Thanks." Vienna ended the call and started down the path from the lighthouse toward the parking lot, weighing the phone in her hand.

Why not call Mom and see if she had any inside information about Beachview B&B? A town the size of Hope Harbor likely had an active grapevine, and Bev Price had never met a stranger. She might even know the innkeeper.

It was worth a try. Approaching the owner with more rather than less information would be as smart in this situation as it had been in her job.

Picking up her pace down the gravel path, she tapped in the number for the shop.

Mom answered on the second ring. "Hello, sweet girl. What are you up to this morning?"

"I took a drive and stopped in at the lighthouse. Are you busy?"

"Never too busy to talk with my favorite daughter. What's up?"

Vienna filled her in on the Gull Motel saga. "Bottom line, I have to find a new place to stay, and I'd rather not traipse back and forth from Bandon or Coos Bay."

"There's a bedroom with your name on it at Sea Breeze Apartments."

"I appreciate that, but I had another idea. Do you know anything about Beachview B&B? It's not far from your apartment complex, down a drive that branches off Starfish Pier Road near the beach."

"Yes, I've seen the sign. The owner is a woman by the name of Kay Marshall. I believe she bought the B&B not long after I moved to town."

"Do you know her?"

"That would be stretching it. We exchange a few words whenever our paths cross in town, but she always seems a tad distracted and worried. I got the impression she's on her own at the B&B."

Vienna relayed what the manager at the motel had told her about the state of the property. "It's possible the place needs more work than she expected."

"That could explain the stress I picked up from her, especially if she bit off more than she can chew. Are you thinking of staying there?"

"I called the day I got here, but the message said they aren't taking reservations." Vienna stopped beside her car as two seagulls landed a few feet away. "Unless the whole place is torn apart and uninhabitable, I'm thinking about trying to convince her to let me stay. Since I won't be there much during the day, construction noise won't be an issue."

"I can't see any harm in asking. Worst case, she'll say no and you'll end up commuting or staying at Chez Bev."

The gull on the left flapped its wings and emitted a raucous squawk that sounded almost like *absolutely not*.

Her exact sentiments.

Angling away from her avian audience, she tried for a diplomatic response. "Those are always options."

"More like last resorts." Her mom's wry tone suggested she'd seen through her daughter's attempt at diplomacy.

"I wouldn't go that far." But close. "Besides, wherever I end up will be short term. Long gaps in resumes raise questions."

"There's nothing wrong with taking time off between jobs to chill and explore and play."

With that attitude, it was fortunate her mother had never set her sights on climbing the corporate ladder.

"That's not how it works, Mom."

"You may be surprised. From what I've read, the Covid crisis wrought dramatic changes in the workplace. Employees have much more power and flexibility than they had before. I don't think anyone would fault job candidates who want time for themselves. Priorities shifted, thank the Lord."

To a certain degree that was true. And it would be nice if she could take this downtime in stride. Enjoy the moment and ignore the money leaching from her savings, with no replenishment on the horizon.

But she wasn't wired that way. Security had always been a top priority.

Debating her mother on that topic, however, would serve no purpose.

"You may be right, Mom, but I'm not certain I want to test that theory. I have decades of work ahead of me, and I don't want to sabotage my shot at a plum position by slacking off for too long. Are we still on for dinner at that pizza place you told me about, up 101?"

"It's written in ink on my calendar. Frank makes the best pizza this side of Italy."

"My treat."

A sigh came over the line. "Are we going to argue over the dinner tab every night?"

"Only if you want to."

"Let's compromise on Dutch treat."

"Agreed. I'll meet you at your apartment at six."

As they said their goodbyes and Vienna slid the phone back into her purse, the two gulls continued to give her their rapt attention.

"Sorry, guys. If you're waiting for a handout, you're out of luck."

The gull on the right looked at its companion and gave a laugh-like cackle.

A second later, the two of them departed in a flutter of wings, soaring north against the blue sky in the direction of Beachview B&B.

Her next stop.

And as she took her place behind the wheel, Vienna sent a silent plea heavenward that Kay Marshall would be receptive to an unexpected and undemanding guest who wanted nothing more than an uncomplicated stay in peaceful Hope Harbor.

4

How could so much go so wrong so fast?

Expelling a breath, Matt swiped the mop at the noxious-smelling waste that had spilled onto the bathroom floor and trickled into the hall from the toilet in the first-floor guest bathroom.

If this was an omen of what was to come, he was in serious trouble. Kay had only left five hours ago, for crying out loud.

Teeth gritted, he scrubbed at a stubborn glop of muck.

Taking his coffee out to the patio after using the facilities had been a big mistake. If he'd stayed inside, he'd have realized much sooner that the commode had morphed into overflow mode.

Instead, the modicum of calm he'd managed to achieve during the half hour he'd spent watching the ocean while he sipped his java was evaporating as fast as the capricious fog that had briefly descended after Kay drove away.

A splatter of gunk from the mop arced toward his light beige chinos, and he grimaced.

A shower and change of clothes would be in order as soon as he cleaned up this mess.

Averting his nose from the stench, he leaned down and wedged the mop behind the commode to scrub the floor back there.

As soon as he was done here, he'd have to plunge or snake-out the toilet. Assuming Kay had the appropriate tools on hand, of course. If she didn't, he'd have to scrap his plans for the day and round up a plumber who could—

The doorbell chimed.

He straightened up.

Seriously? Someone wanted him to answer the door *now*?

Not happening.

No guests were booked, and he didn't know a soul in town. If this was a delivery, the driver could leave the package at the front door.

He went back to mopping.

Thirty seconds later, the bell rang again.

He ignored it.

Another half minute passed.

Ding-dong.

Blast.

Whoever had come calling wasn't going away.

Jamming his fingers through his hair, he tossed the mop aside, marched to the door, and flung it open. "Yes?"

At his abrupt greeting, the slender, thirtysomething woman on the other side gave him a fast once-over and took a step back. "Um . . . is Kay Marshall here?"

"No."

"Do you know when she'll be back?"

"Not for a month."

"Oh. Um . . . who's in charge of the B&B?"

"You're looking at him."

Her nose twitched, and she retreated another step.

The stink must be wafting her way.

"I was, uh, hoping to . . ." She gave him another perusal as her voice trailed off.

The woman was clearly discombobulated.

Apparently being greeted by a disheveled man reeking of sewage had freaked her out.

While she inspected him, he took his own inventory.

Five-fourish, using his six-foot frame as a reference. Wavy, long brown hair secured by barrettes on either side of a center part. Jeans that hugged her curves and had designer written all over them. A soft-looking sweater the same deep blue hue as her eyes. Slightly asymmetrical features that kept her from being a classic beauty but gave her face an arresting quality more than sufficient to prompt a second glance from men in the market for female companionship.

Which excluded him.

But what was she doing here, and why did she want to talk to Kay?

"You were saying?" He folded his arms.

"Um . . . that's okay." She groped through her purse and withdrew her keys. "It wasn't that important. Have a nice day."

She swiveled away and took off at a trot for her car. Even from a distance, he could hear the locks click into place after she slid behind the wheel and closed the door. Then she backed out, leaving the B&B behind in a spurt of gravel. Fleeing as if the hounds of hell were after her.

Weird.

And she'd never said what her business was with Kay.

As the dust cloud behind her car dissipated and she vanished from view, he shrugged and closed the door.

Back to his revolting task.

But he jolted to a stop when he caught sight of himself in the large mirror above the credenza in the foyer.

Whoa.

His hair looked like he'd stuck his finger into an electrical outlet, there was a smear on the front of his shirt, and the sewage splash marks on his pants had migrated upward.

Add in the smell, and it was no wonder the woman had turned tail and run.

Plus, he hadn't exactly been welcoming. A smile might have spooked her less than a scowl.

Oh well.

He continued back to his discarded mop and resumed cleanup duties. It wasn't as if he'd ever see her again. Unless he'd misread her, the lady had no intention of darkening the Beachview B&B doorway again anytime in the foreseeable future.

Fine by him.

He had work to do here, starting with this misbehaving toilet, and he didn't need any distractions.

Especially the kind an attractive woman could cause even for a man with zero interest in romance.

Well, *that* strange visit had dashed any hopes of finding a temporary home at Beachview B&B.

Halfway down Starfish Pier Road, Vienna finally slowed her car after escaping from the house of horrors.

From its rutted road to its wobbly shutters to its missing shakes, the place was in desperate need of sprucing up. As was the foul-smelling, glowering man who'd answered the door.

Who was he, anyway?

And where was the owner?

He hadn't offered either of those pieces of information—but it was doubtful he would have answered her questions if she'd broached them. He hadn't come across as the warm, welcoming, talkative type.

Not that it mattered.

If the owner was gone, she was out of luck.

It appeared a daily commute was in her future.

She hung a right on 101 and accelerated back toward town. A Sweet Dreams brownie would help mitigate her disappointment over the B&B while she lined up other accommodations.

If nothing else, the drive back and forth between wherever she landed and Hope Harbor might spur her to get on the stick and begin giving serious thought to her future instead of spending her days taking walks on the beach, sightseeing, and putzing around with her resume.

She turned off the highway and drove through town, passing the street that was home to Mom's bookshop. On Dockside Drive, she hung a right, scanning the street for a parking place near—

Wait.

Charley's window was up.

The resident sage and taco-making artist must be back from Mexico.

Great news.

Switching plans, Vienna grabbed the closest parking spot she could find and picked up her purse. In her present state of mind, an order of tacos served with a side of philosophy would offer much more comfort than a brownie.

No one was in line as she approached the stand, a rarity based on past experience. She and Mom had always had to join a queue during their visits.

Charley swiveled toward her from behind the serving window as she approached, his long gray hair pulled back into a ponytail beneath his usual Ducks baseball cap.

As she drew close, a gleam of recognition sparked in his dark irises, and he gave her one of his dazzling smiles. The kind that had always made her feel like he was delighted to see her and that she'd have his undivided attention for as long as she needed it. "Well, if it isn't Vienna Price. Long time no see."

"You remember me." A rush of warmth filled her heart.

"Of course."

"But Mom and I only visited a few times, and our last trip was ten years ago. You must have a remarkable memory."

"Not for everything. But the people who cross my path? Absolutely. Can I make you an order of tacos while we chat?"

"Please." Her lips flexed at the "cash only" sign taped to the window. "I see you still haven't entered the electronic age."

"Never. I prefer greenbacks in my hand to digital wallets, and face-to-face conversations over texts. Both are much more real." He opened a cooler and pulled out a couple of fish fillets. "What brings you to our charming little town, aside from visiting your mom?"

She narrowed her eyes as he began chopping a red onion.

Why would he think she had another reason for coming—unless her mother had mentioned her visit to him since he'd returned from Mexico?

"What did Mom tell you about my trip?"

"Not a thing." He tossed the red onion on a sizzling griddle, set three corn tortillas on the grill beside the fish, and angled toward her. "I left ten days ago and only returned last night. You're my first customer of the day. I assume your trip was spur of the moment or Bev would have mentioned it before I left."

She gave the wharf a sweep.

No one must yet have noticed Charley was back in business or there would be a steady stream of customers descending on the stand.

An ideal, private opportunity to share her story.

"As usual, your reasoning is astute. I lost my job." She gave him a quick recap of her career crisis.

Concern softened his features. "I'm sorry to hear that. From everything Bev's told me, it sounded as if you'd found your niche. But I'm glad you came here to regroup. Hope Harbor is a wonderful refuge for those seeking healing and peace."

"I'm searching more for direction than anything else."

"You may find that here too. Stranger things have happened." He flipped the fish. "Are you staying with Bev?"

Another sticky subject.

"No. We have very different personalities that sometimes clash. Sharing her small apartment could be problematic. I was staying at the Gull, but that fell through this morning." She filled him in.

"Have you tried Beachview B&B? It's not far from Bev's apartment. I know it was shut down for a while, but it may be open again." He began assembling the tacos, sprinkling them with seasoning from a shaker can and adding a dollop of his special sauce with a squeeze bottle.

"I just came from there. It's still not open, but I was hoping to convince the owner to let me have a room, minus the breakfast. The man who answered the door told me she was gone for a month."

"Kay was gone, and a man answered the door?" Charley began wrapping the tacos in white paper. "I'll have to catch up on everything I missed during my trip. So what are you going to do?"

"Find a spot in Bandon or Coos Bay, I guess. The commute will be manageable for a short-term stay." If inconvenient.

"Maybe other accommodations will turn up closer to home."

Not much chance of that with the Gull unavailable, Seabird Inn booked, and Beachview B&B out of service.

But Charley had always been the optimistic sort.

"I suppose that could happen." She dug her wallet out of her purse, counted out several bills, and slid them across the serving window.

"Anything is possible." His confident tone suggested that a better solution to her housing dilemma was already a done deal. "I added a bottle of water to your bag. Why don't you mosey over there and enjoy the view?" He motioned to an empty bench down the wharf, past one occupied by a young couple.

"I'll do that. I can't wait to sink my teeth into these." She lifted the bag from the counter. "My mouth always waters whenever I think about them from past trips."

"Music to a taco maker's ears." He flicked a glance past her shoulder as several people converged on the taco stand.

"News of your return must have spread. I'm glad I got here first."

"I am too. Enjoy your lunch. And welcome home."

Before she could respond, he greeted the approaching customers.

Leaving the stand behind, she mulled over his parting words.

Welcome home, not welcome back.

Sweet, if off base.

Hope Harbor was a lovely place to visit, but it would never be home. There were no jobs in her field here. At least none with the potential to give her the perks and benefits and salary that came with the executive-level position she'd always set her sights on.

As she approached the man and woman who were deep in conversation on the first bench, snippets of their exchange filtered toward her.

"—never expected to have to start over." The woman's comment was tear-laced.

"I'm sorry, Paige. If I could change what happened, I would."

Dejection hovered over the duo like a dark rain cloud.

Vienna gave them a surreptitious peek as she passed.

Twentysomethings, dressed in casual attire, shoulders slumped, heads bowed, seemingly oblivious to their surroundings.

She kept moving, but their voices followed her.

"I still can't believe Jack betrayed us." The woman's words were choked.

"I know. And why would he take a chance that could ruin his life? *Did* ruin his life."

"It also ruined our reputation. Oh, Andrew." Her voice caught on a sob. "Now we've lost everything we worked so hard for. And the leaky tent is—"

Their voices faded as Vienna continued down the wharf and claimed the empty bench.

Apparently she wasn't the only one in town with problems. Others, it seemed, had even bigger issues than she did. She may have lost her job, but she hadn't lost everything—including her reputation. She'd rebound. Yes, getting sacked had been a terrible blow, but the resume she'd been revamping was impressive. She'd find another position long before she had to dip too deep into her financial reserves.

It didn't sound like that couple's prospects were anywhere near as hopeful as hers.

Vienna pulled out her bottle of water, giving them another quick assessment while she unwrapped the first taco.

Their huddled posture was defeat and misery personified.

It was a shame she couldn't help them in some way.

But they were strangers. All she could do was offer a prayer on their behalf and hope they found a resolution to whatever calamity had befallen them.

5

Mission accomplished.

Plunger in hand, Matt leaned down and flushed the toilet again.

The water swirled, drained, refilled.

Whew.

At least one crisis had been resolved.

Now he just had to round up a rehab outfit that could start on the B&B sooner than the firm Kay had contacted.

His number one priority come Monday morning.

For today, though, it was on to a hot shower and a trip to town.

Less than forty-five minutes later, he was in line and inching toward the taco stand on the wharf that Kay had raved about.

When it was his turn, he stepped up to the window and scanned the interior of the white trailer for a menu.

"I only make one kind of taco a day." Eyes twinkling, the taco chef smiled at him. "Today I'm featuring rockfish. That work for you?"

"Sure."

"New in town or passing through?" He selected an avocado from a bowl, examined it from all angles, and began chopping it.

"Both. But my pass-through is on the long side. I'll be here for about a month."

"You're a rarity. Most visitors spend a day or two in our fair town, tops. Unless you have family here?"

"My sister owns Beachview B&B."

"Ah. That would explain what I heard earlier."

Matt squinted at him. "What did you hear?"

"That there was a man on the premises. I'm Charley Lopez, by the way. A pleasure to meet you."

Matt introduced himself and returned the sentiment as he did the math.

Since he'd only run into one person during his stay, Charley's source had to be the woman he'd scared off this morning.

"News must travel fast around here."

"That it does." He put three corn tortillas on the grill and tossed a handful of red onions on the griddle. "I also heard Kay will be out of town for an extended period."

Further evidence the man's intel came from the visitor he'd spooked.

"Yes. She went back to Boise to help a friend who's having major surgery."

"Kudos to her. The world could use more compassion and kindness. It's generous of you to watch over the place while she's gone."

"There are benefits for me too. I was due for some R&R." Which was dwindling with every passing hour.

"Leisure is excellent for the soul." The taco chef flipped the fish. "I was sorry to hear Kay had stopped taking reservations, but I understand her rationale. First impressions are critical in any business, and the inn could use a bit of TLC."

"More than a bit."

"Are you planning to tackle the repairs?"

Matt snorted. "No way. I managed to unclog a stopped-up toilet this morning, but that stretched my handyman skills to the limit. A dog or a cat, I can fix. Buildings are beyond me."

"Are you a vet?"

"Yes."

The man gave an approving nod as he stirred the onions. "Caring for God's creatures is a worthy occupation. Right, Floyd?"

Matt angled away from the window. No one was in sight, nor was anyone waiting in line behind him.

A cackle sounded at his feet, and he lowered his gaze.

Two yards away, two seagulls sat side by side on the pavement, their attention fixed on him.

He turned back to Charley, who grinned.

"Meet Floyd and Gladys. I expect you'll see them around while you're in town. They seem to have taken a fancy to you."

He gave the birds an amused once-over. "You name the seagulls?"

"These two are special."

This guy was a character.

Charley withdrew a bottle of water from a cooler. "I can toss this in the bag, but if you're a coffee lover, I recommend a visit to The Perfect Blend. One of their Americanos would be an excellent accompaniment to your tacos, and the atmosphere can't be beat. It's laid-back, relaxing, and contemplative."

Exactly the kind of environment he craved after his stressful morning.

"Sold."

"It's one street up, on the corner of Main and Harbor. You can't miss it." He set the water aside, then wrapped the three tacos in white paper and slid them into a brown bag. As Matt reached for his wallet, Charley shook his head. "No charge for the first visit."

The man was offering him free tacos?

"Do you do that for everyone?"

"Not the day trippers. But you'll be here for a while, and I want to encourage you to come back."

"Count on it."

"See? My generosity is good for business." Mouth quirking,

he adjusted the brim of his Ducks cap. "Enjoy the tacos and The Perfect Blend. I think you'll like the ambiance there."

"I'll do that." He hefted the bag. Hesitated.

Charley appeared to be connected in town. Might he have any suggestions about contractors?

"Change your mind about the water?" Charley reached for the bottle again.

"No. I was just wondering if you happen to know any handymen or carpenters in the area. The one Kay asked to bid isn't available for weeks."

"That would be BJ, I assume."

Matt tried to call up the name on the bid. "I think the paperwork said Stevens Design & Construction."

"That's BJ. She's the only game in town. First-rate operation, which is why she's booked solid."

That nixed the idea of finding another option in Hope Harbor.

He stifled a sigh.

"I guess I'll have to expand my search to Bandon, or even Coos Bay."

"You never know. Someone closer to home may turn up."

"I can hope, anyway." But he wasn't going to count on it. If the Stevens operation was Hope Harbor's main construction offering, it wasn't likely he'd stumble across any other viable options in such a small town. "Thanks again for the tacos." Crimping the bag in his fingers, he set off in search of The Perfect Blend.

As Charley had predicted, it was easy to spot. And the ambiance was as calming as the taco maker had promised. The clean, simple design featured close-up, poster-sized nature photos on the walls, with tables tucked between them and around a free-standing fireplace in the center.

Just what he needed.

Five minutes later, an Americano in hand and seated at a table by the picture window that offered a view of the street, he bit into his first taco.

Flavor exploded on his tongue.

Wow.

The combination of tender fish, avocado, red onion, and the other ingredients Charley had tossed in along with his special sauce and seasonings was magic.

Kay hadn't exaggerated.

Taking his time to savor every morsel, Matt ate all three tacos, washing them down with the best Americano he'd ever had.

Hope Harbor might be a mere speck on the map and an unknown in the culinary world, but its tacos and coffee were second to none.

Another selling point to generate traffic for the B&B if Kay decided to keep the place.

Whether she did or not, though, it was up to him to find someone willing and able to start repairs next week. And lingering over his coffee wasn't going to help him accomplish that task.

Matt drained the dregs, wiped his mouth with a napkin, and mentally bullet-pointed a plan as he stood.

Google handymen and construction types. Skim through the ads in the recent copy of the *Hope Harbor Herald* Kay had left in the kitchen. Ask a few more people in town who seemed approachable if they had any recommendations. It was possible there was someone Charley hadn't thought of.

Armed with that strategy, he disposed of his trash and wandered toward the door, glancing at the amiable barista behind the counter who'd prepared his coffee.

Might he have any suggestions to offer?

No harm in asking.

He veered toward him. "Your Americano was exceptional."

"Thanks." The guy wiped his hands on a towel and flung it over his shoulder. "We aim to please. Passing through?"

"I'll be here for a month. My sister owns the B&B off Starfish Pier Road."

"Kay. Nice woman."

No surprise his sister was known in town. Unlike her brother, who often found it easier these days to communicate with animals than humans, she was a people person through and through.

"Yes, she is." He held out his hand and introduced himself.

"Zach Garrett. I own this place." The man returned his firm shake.

"You wouldn't by any chance have a recommendation for a carpenter or handyman in town, would you?"

"Have you talked to BJ? She's top-notch."

"So I've heard. My sister got a bid from her, but she's not available for at least a month."

"Doesn't surprise me. I don't know anyone else offhand. Have you checked the community bulletin board at Bev's Book Nook?"

"No."

"You may want to give that a try. She put it up when she opened the shop about six months ago, and it's become a huge draw. Everyone in town stops in at least once a week to see the new postings—and buy a book or a greeting card or sample a cookie from her jar. Great marketing idea. I wish I'd thought of it first." He offered an affable grin.

"I'll swing by there."

"It's straight down Main toward the river, second shop past the intersection. Good luck."

"Thanks. I'll take all of that I can get."

"Well, you know what they say." The man motioned out the window, toward the portable A-frame signboard on the sidewalk in front. "A thought for the day, courtesy of The Perfect Blend."

Matt peered at the saying that had been handwritten on the board.

If your ship doesn't come in, swim out to it.

In other words, don't wait for luck to come to you. Make your own.

"I'll keep that in mind." Though its application to his present situation was dubious. If everyone he found was too busy to help with the B&B, it wouldn't matter how hard he swam—or persisted. The answer would still be no.

And every day the B&B was closed, Kay was losing money. All because he'd been too preoccupied to ask any pertinent questions or offer assistance when she'd told him her plans.

Quashing a surge of guilt, he struck off down the sidewalk. Rather than fixate on things he couldn't correct, better to focus on the problem at hand.

Once he crossed Harbor Street, Bev's Book Nook came into view.

At the door to the shop, he paused to read the sign in the window.

Start a New Chapter!

Was everyone in Hope Harbor into pithy pieces of advice? Even Charley had offered a few philosophical thoughts.

Shaking his head, he pushed through the door.

A woman who appeared to be in her mid- to late-fifties looked up from a worktable off to the side as he entered and gave him a genial smile. "Welcome to Bev's Book Nook. I'm the shop's namesake. Can I help you, or would you like to browse?"

"I was told there's a community bulletin board here."

"Yes, there is. You're the second person today who's come in search of it. Most of the locals make a beeline that direction when they enter the door, so I assume you're a visitor?"

This woman was as chatty as Charley.

"Yes. My sister owns Beachview B&B."

"Ah. Kay!" Her face lit up and she rose.

As she crossed to him, he tried not to stare at the long purple swatch in her hair or the psychedelic tunic top or the wide-legged silky pants that seemed larger-than-life on her tall, big-boned frame.

"It's lovely to meet you." She extended her hand and gave his a hearty shake. "I bet Kay is delighted you came to visit. I haven't seen her out and about much lately, and it's not healthy to spend too much time alone. It will be wonderful for her to have company."

"Actually, she won't have. Not here, anyway. She's back in Boise, helping a friend through a health crisis."

"That's very kind of her." Bev tipped her head. "So you're in charge of the B&B?"

"There isn't much to be in charge of. It's closed for the indefinite future."

"No guests at all?"

"No. And none for the foreseeable future."

"Shoot. Vienna will be disappointed to hear that."

He arched his eyebrows. "Vienna?"

"My daughter. She's also in town for a visit. Her room at the Gull Motel got flooded, and she was hoping to convince Kay to find her a spot at the B&B."

Matt frowned.

Was it possible this Vienna could be the woman who'd come to his door earlier? The same one Charley had gotten all his intel from, who'd exuded class and understated elegance?

"Someone did stop by this morning. A woman in her thirties, long dark hair parted in the middle, blue eyes, driving a Focus?"

"Sounds like her. So you two have met."

That was stretching it.

"Not exactly. I was in the middle of a plumbing disaster, and I think I scared her away. We only exchanged a few words."

"She didn't ask about booking a room?"

"No."

"Strange." Bev's forehead wrinkled. "I can't imagine why else she would have stopped by."

He shifted his weight. "Maybe she changed her mind after I told her Kay would be gone a month and I was alone on the premises." No need to mention the stench or his unkempt appearance.

"That could be. Vienna's the cautious type, unlike her mother." She winked at him, then grew more serious. "But she was willing to live on a construction site, if the rumors in town are true that a rehab is in the works. Unless all the rooms are torn up, of course."

"None of them are torn up. But they should be. That's why the B&B is closed."

"What a shame." Bev tut-tutted. "I hope your sister isn't overwhelmed or discouraged."

Yes, she was.

They both were.

Until Kay decided what she wanted to do with the place, though, dwelling on negatives would be counterproductive.

"At the moment, we're more frustrated by the long wait to get any work done. I'm hoping a local carpenter or handyman may have posted an ad on your bulletin board."

"You know . . . there was a woman in here a couple of hours ago who tacked up an ad for her husband. I didn't recognize her, and she didn't stay to chat, but I read the ad afterward. It could be the answer to your prayer."

She led him over to the board and pointed out the small sheet of paper that had been neatly hand lettered.

Skilled carpenter seeks work, large jobs or small. Available immediately. Call for a bid.

A name and phone number were included.

Matt's spirits took an uptick.

This was like manna from heaven.

He pulled out his cell and snapped a photo of the ad. "This could have potential. Are you certain the name doesn't ring a bell?"

"Yes, but I'm new here too, like Kay. It's possible there are people in town I haven't met."

Not according to Zach at the coffee shop.

This carpenter must either be new to Hope Harbor or an itinerant workman.

Hiring someone without a local track record might be dicey,

but desperation could compel a man to take risks. However, there was zero risk in talking to the man.

"I may give him a call." Matt slipped the phone back in his pocket.

"Couldn't hurt. I got the feeling from his wife that they were down on their luck." She pursed her lips as she regarded him. "You know, if there are any problems at the B&B beyond cosmetic, Vienna may be able to offer you a few pieces of advice. She worked at a boutique hotel chain for years."

Boutique as in high-end, impeccable, and plush?

No wonder she'd turned tail and run after getting a load of the Beachview B&B and the temporary manager. In light of that first impression, she probably wouldn't set foot inside even for the offer of a free stay.

But it could be helpful to pick her brain about the B&B. Heck, it was possible Kay would be willing to pay her a consulting fee, assuming his sister decided to move forward with her plan to operate the place.

He folded his arms. "How long will she be here?"

"Unknown. She's between jobs. Would you like me to ask her to give you a call?"

In light of her hasty retreat, it was doubtful she'd want anything to do with the B&B. But maybe this was the ship he was supposed to swim out to.

"If you wouldn't mind, I'd appreciate it."

"Happy to help. What's your number?" Bev whipped out her cell and tapped it in as he recited it. "I'm having dinner with her tonight. I'll pass this on. Who knows? She may be willing to barter with you. Advice for a room."

"If she ends up being here for an extended period, wouldn't she rather stay with you?"

"No. I only have a one-bedroom apartment, and she refuses to impose. As if that were possible. But she's also concerned we might clash. Not that we don't love each other, you understand.

It's just that our personalities are as different as Oscar and Felix from that old TV show, *The Odd Couple*, despite the genes we share. Go figure." She chuckled. "That's why a barter arrangement might work."

The bookstore owner's candor was refreshing, even if her daughter might not appreciate the comparison Bev had just offered.

"I doubt she'd be interested in that, given the condition of the place. But thanks for offering to ask her to get in touch."

"My pleasure."

The tinkle of wind chimes signaled a new arrival, and Matt pulled out his keys. "I'll let you get back to work."

"Hang on a sec." Bev hurried over to the checkout counter, lifted the lid on a clear glass jar, and extracted a cookie with a square of bakery tissue. "Gooey butter. I made this batch last night." She held it out as she rejoined him. "Good luck with the carpenter. I hope he works out for you."

"Thanks."

She moved on to the customer, who was perusing a table with a selection of books.

He let himself out and wandered back toward his car on the wharf, taking a bite of the rich, tender cookie as he strolled.

Bev had been the second person today to wish him luck, and he'd take every crumb of it that fate was willing to hand out.

Because he either had to get the B&B in shape to sell or leave it in excellent condition so Kay could begin attracting customers again and start to refill her dwindling coffers.

No matter how pristine the place was, though, getting past the bad reviews would be a challenge.

He took another bite of the melt-in-the-mouth cookie.

It was possible Bev's daughter could offer a few suggestions on that score, if he could convince her that he wasn't a spin-off Hitchcock character from *Psycho*. Assuming she even called him.

But first he'd get in touch with Andrew Thompson and hope

the carpenter whose wife had posted an ad at the bookshop really was the answer to a prayer. Otherwise, he'd be back to square one.

So until he had a contractor lined up, he'd forget about Bev's daughter.

Why waste brainpower trying to figure out how to correct the bad impression he'd made on her if the B&B continued to make a bad impression on everyone who ventured down the narrow road that led to his sister's impulsive folly?

6

"This pizza is amazing." Vienna popped a mushroom into her mouth and wound a strand of mozzarella across the top of her slice. "I would never have expected such culinary artistry from the looks of this place." In truth, if she hadn't spotted Mom's car already parked in front of the rustic building with the garish neon sign, she'd have waited for her to arrive rather than venture inside alone.

"Another example of why it's a mistake to judge a book by its cover. And speaking of books, you'll never guess who stopped in at the shop today."

"I'm sure I won't. I don't know a soul in town other than you and Charley. He's back, by the way."

"Wonderful news. We'll have to pay him a visit next week. But you've met one other person."

Vienna took a sip of water as she searched her memory. "Nope. During my walks on the beach, I've become acquainted with an acrobatic dolphin and a belching seal, but my contact with humans has been limited."

"You met Kay's brother today."

She blinked. "The guy at Beachview B&B?"

"That would be him. Matt Quinn. You didn't tell me you'd followed through on your idea to talk to Kay."

"There was nothing to tell. It was a dead end. Her brother didn't come across as very approachable."

"Really?" Mom helped herself to another piece of pizza. "I thought he was most pleasant. Handsome too."

Vienna stared at her. "Are you certain we're talking about the same man? When I saw him, his hair was sticking out in all directions, his clothes were dirty, and a noxious odor was wafting from his direction."

"The smell must have been from the plumbing problem he mentioned. But it had to be him. There's no one else on the premises. Besides, his description of you was spot on. Including your eye color."

Vienna stopped chewing. "He noticed my eyes?"

"Of course he did. Any man would notice your eyes. They're the same vivid blue as your father's. Anyway, Matt's about six foot, dark hair and eyes, very buff. Sound familiar?"

"To be honest, I was too busy trying not to gag at the stink to pay much attention to his physical attributes." Though the image of him she called up in her mind did fit Mom's description.

"Your loss. If I were twenty-five years younger . . ." The corners of her mouth flexed.

Vienna sent her a skeptical look as she took another bite of pizza. "You told me you'd written men off long ago."

"I did and I have. After you came along, I decided it would be you and me against the world. Men require too much energy, and I wanted to give you all of mine. By the time you were grown, I'd decided I liked the flexibility and independence of being single. But if I were a couple of decades younger, this guy might tempt me to change my mind."

Vienna stopped chewing again. "You never told me I was the reason you didn't have a boyfriend or go on dates while I was growing up."

"You weren't the only reason. Just the main one."

"But I wouldn't have minded. You didn't have to sacrifice your personal life for me."

Her mother laid down her pizza, wiped her fingers on a paper napkin, and reached across the table to touch her cheek. "Loving you was never a sacrifice, sweet girl. Don't ever think that. I lived my life the way I wanted to, and I have no regrets—except for the mistakes I made raising you."

What?

A piece of pepperoni slid off the slice of pizza in Vienna's hand and plopped onto her plate as she gaped at her mother.

Since when had Bev Price harbored any misgivings about her child-rearing strategies? Or the appropriateness of her relentless and unsuccessful attempts to raise a spunky daughter who was willing to color outside the lines?

Mom's lips curved into a wry twist. "Wisdom does come with age, it seems. Like realizing that part of loving is giving the other person what *they* need, not what you think they need. I wish I'd learned that lesson years ago."

Apparently bombshells were on the menu tonight along with pizza.

"I don't know what to say." Vienna set her pizza down.

"You don't have to say a thing. I should have waited to bring this up at a more appropriate time and place. But you know me. I tend to blurt out whatever pops into my head."

"What prompted you to start thinking about all this, anyway?"

"I'm not certain." Her expression grew pensive. "I expect all the changes in my life played a role. Retiring, moving here, opening the shop. Who knows? But it's been on my mind for the past few months. I do know that some of my conversations with Charley played a role. Not that I ever mentioned anything specific about us, but his comments are often thought-provoking."

"I remember that from past trips."

"Well, as long as the subject has come up, I want you to know

I'm sorry for trying to force you to become more like me instead of accepting that my personal philosophy of life wasn't one-size-fits-all."

Vienna's throat tightened. "Your intentions were good, though."

"That's true. But the road that's paved with those tends to lead you know where."

Mom must not have been kidding a few days ago when she said she'd mellowed.

And since they were in apology mode, she ought to reciprocate. "The fault wasn't all yours. I'm sorry for all the aggravation I caused you—and for disappointing you."

"Disappointing me?" Shock flattened her features. "Never! But I will admit you confused me. I assumed if I exposed you to new experiences, encouraged you to broaden your horizons and spread your wings, you'd soar. Instead, my strategy backfired. You became *less* willing to take risks." She shook her head and raised her face toward the heavens. "Lord, I made a boatload of blunders."

"But I turned out okay." Vienna touched her hand. "And while we may differ in our approach to life, I never doubted your love. Why do you think I ran here when my world went into a free fall? Because I knew you'd catch me and encourage me and set me on my feet again." Her voice caught.

"Thank you for that. It's worth more to me than all the stock options and bonuses and perks those high-powered executive jobs offer." She sniffed, dabbed at her nose with her paper napkin, and motioned to their pizza. "We better get ourselves under control and eat this or we'll have a soggy mess on our hands, and that would be an insult to Frank's masterpiece."

Vienna picked up her pizza, took another bite, and steered the conversation back on track after their unexpected detour. "So why did the innkeeper's brother come to your bookshop?"

"To check my bulletin board. He's in the market for a contractor to do updates at the B&B."

"It could use a few. From what I saw of the outside, the rumors about the condition of the place are true. Why is he handling the repairs?"

"Kay's out of town."

Vienna continued to eat while Mom filled her in on the details, waiting until she finished to comment. "So basically his sister ran out and dumped the mess on him." No wonder he'd seemed frazzled.

"I don't know if that's the appropriate term under the circumstances, but he *is* planning to get repairs underway while she's gone." As Mom leaned forward and lowered her volume, a drop of grease dripped from the pizza in her hand to the table. "To be honest, I think he's in over his head. Kay gave me the same impression. So I told him about your background, said you might be willing to lend him your expertise. I also threw out the idea of a barter—a room for advice."

Share a roof with that foul-smelling, unfriendly man?

No thank you.

A conversation, however, might be okay.

"I guess I could talk to him." Vienna pulled a napkin from the metal dispenser and scrubbed at the spot of grease on the table. "But I'm not keen about staying there. It would only be the two of us, and my first impression of him wasn't pleasant." An understatement if ever there was one. The man had been downright unsociable.

"He was very cordial to me. But I imagine dealing with sewage could sour a person's disposition."

True. And at least a plumbing crisis would explain the stench.

"I suppose I could give him the benefit of the doubt."

"Always a wise strategy. I think he'd appreciate your advice. And I assume there are locks on the guestroom doors, if you want to pursue the barter idea. You could also ask for references if you're worried about his character. Staying there would be more convenient than driving back and forth from Bandon every day.

Of course, there's always a room for you at my place, if you want to reconsider. We may be more compatible than you think."

That was possible. They hadn't clashed much yet on this trip. But living in close quarters could rock the boat on what so far had been a smooth voyage. Why take the chance?

"Let me think through the options. Do you want to text me this guy's contact information?"

Mom pulled out her phone and tapped a few keys. "Done."

"I'll call him tomorrow."

For the rest of their meal, Mom entertained her with stories of customers who'd stopped in at the shop, shared tidbits about various Hope Harbor residents, and offered suggestions for sightseeing outings.

As they finished, Mom wadded up her napkin and smiled. "This was fun. Much more pleasant than ordering pizza to go and eating alone at home. Maybe you can visit more often after you settle into whatever new job you take."

"Count on it." Since giving up weekends and working through vacations didn't appear to be a prerequisite for success—or even a guarantee of job security—she wasn't going to make that sacrifice again.

"Are we still on for church in the morning?"

"Yes. Shall I swing by and pick you up?"

"Why don't I meet you there? I have to go early to help set up for the doughnut-and-coffee social afterward. I could wait for you in the vestibule a few minutes before the service."

"That'll work." Vienna slid from the booth, and Mom fell in behind her as they wove through the small, packed restaurant toward the exit.

In the parking lot, Mom leaned over and gave her a hearty hug. "Drive safe."

"You too. See you tomorrow." With a wave, she continued to her car, settled in behind the wheel, and accelerated north on 101.

What a pleasant evening this had been. In fact, other than a few subtle clashes her first day in town after she'd insisted on staying elsewhere, Mom had been totally chill. No advice, no criticism.

And perhaps there was a lesson in Mom's new mellower demeanor for her too.

After all, Mom didn't bear all of the blame for their often prickly relationship. How many times had she been critical and judgmental in the past too? Dug in her heels and refused to even consider Mom's suggestions? Shut her bedroom door—and shut Mom out? That had no doubt been as hurtful to Mom as Mom's perceived disappointment and frustration had been to her.

She flipped on her blinker and passed a slow-moving car, peering at the bumper sticker on the small travel trailer it was pulling.

The tortoise wins the race.

She snorted.

The driver was certainly living that philosophy.

But slow and steady did have a certain allure after the harried life she'd led, even if that meant paring back her executive aspirations a tad. Like Zach Garrett, the owner of The Perfect Blend, had done. From what Mom had said over dinner, he'd left behind a high-powered job in Chicago and was happy and content with his new, lower-key lifestyle.

Or was there something about the laid-back vibe in Hope Harbor that insidiously undermined valid and reasonable ambitions? And if it did, would she fall under its spell if she stayed too long?

She frowned as she pondered, then dismissed, that concern. There was nothing here to compel her to stay. The town didn't offer a single job in her field.

But this place did suit Mom.

Vienna flicked on her headlights as dusk deepened around her.

And if nothing else worthwhile came from her career disaster, maybe during her short tenure in Hope Harbor she and Mom could start a new chapter in their relationship, just as her mother had started a new chapter in her life by opening a bookshop after retiring from a decades-long career.

She could also use this opportunity to do a good deed and help Beachview B&B start a new chapter too.

Assuming Kay Marshall's taciturn brother was more willing to communicate next go-round than he'd been during their brief, uncomfortable exchange this morning.

"Andrew? Why didn't you answer that?" Paige ducked into the tent, letting the flap close behind her as his vibrating cell went still on the nylon floor.

No response.

She finger combed her damp hair, pressure building in her throat as she looked down at him.

In the fifteen minutes she'd been gone, he hadn't moved a muscle. He was still lying on the sleeping bag, face to the wall, back to the door of the tent. Only the slight, steady rise and fall of his midsection indicated he was breathing.

A wave of despair washed over her, and her shoulders sagged.

She couldn't go on like this. Couldn't keep living in a borrowed tent, showering in state park bathrooms, cooking over a camp stove, depleting their meager reserves day by day . . . and watching her husband of six years give up.

Yet after three weeks of vagabond living, of wandering aimlessly, they were no closer to coming up with a plan for their future than they'd been when they'd set out from Portland, disgraced and disheartened.

And if they didn't settle somewhere soon and find jobs, how were they ever going to dig themselves out of this mess?

Wrestling a surge of panic into submission, she crossed the tent, knelt beside the phone, and scanned the screen. "You have two voicemails, Andrew."

No response.

"Andrew!"

"They're probably spam calls." His defeated tone did nothing to lift her flagging spirits.

"You want me to listen to them?"

"I don't care."

His response to everything these days.

Fighting back tears, she sat cross-legged on the floor, opened his voicemail, and put the phone to her ear as the first message from early afternoon played back.

"Mr. Thompson, this is Matt Quinn at Beachview B&B in Hope Harbor. I saw your ad at Bev's Book Nook and would like to talk to you about a potential job. Please call at your earliest convenience."

"Andrew." She prodded him, a spark of hope flickering to life in her heart. "A guy called about a job."

"I bet it's a scam."

"I don't think so. He sounds legit."

"Even if he is, nothing will come of it."

"You don't know that." The frustration and anger she usually managed to contain escaped, sharpening her tone. "At least I'm trying. You wouldn't even take the ad into the bookstore."

Clenching the cell in her fingers, she put it on speaker and played back the message that had come in minutes ago.

"Mr. Thompson, it's Matt Quinn again. If you're not interested in my project, would you let me know so I can look elsewhere for a contractor? Thanks."

He'd called twice?

That had to be an encouraging sign.

"Andrew, I think this is for real. It's the same guy who left the earlier message. He must really want to talk to you."

Several seconds ticked by, but at last he rolled toward her. "With our luck it's probably just someone who wants a piece of siding replaced. That won't pay enough to live on."

"You have no idea what the job is."

"Don't get your hopes up."

"Why not? We're due for a break. This could be it." She held out the phone, trying hard to control the quiver in her voice—and in her fingers.

His gaze dropped to her hand, and his eyebrows dipped into a V. "You're shaking."

"I've been shaking since the day this started. Take the phone, Andrew. Return the call. We need to pick a spot to land soon. I can't get a job until we do, and our checking account is running on fumes. I'm tired of living in this tent, but we can't afford an apartment until one of us is working. Please. Just see what he has to say."

After a moment, he sat up, took the cell, and called the number.

Paige twisted her fingers together into a tight knot as she listened to his side of the conversation.

"Mr. Quinn, Andrew Thompson. I'm sorry I missed your calls. How can I help you?"

Thank goodness he'd managed to summon up the professional tone he reserved for customers instead of the dispirited one he'd used with her since the catastrophe had knocked their world off its foundation.

A long stretch of silence followed before Andrew spoke again.

"Yes, all of that work is within my capability. What's your timetable on the job? . . . That could be problematic. I'm a one-person show . . . Yes, I'd be happy to. When would be convenient? . . . Yes, that will work. Let me jot down the address." He made a writing motion, and Paige scrambled to pull a scrap of paper and a pen from her purse, scribbling down the information as he repeated it. "Got it. I'll see you tomorrow at noon." He pressed end and set the phone down.

"That sounded promising." She handed him the slip of paper.

"It would be if I had my old crew. He wants a whole B&B rehabbed ASAP."

She bit her lip. "Maybe his timetable is more flexible than you think."

"I didn't get that impression."

"But you're an excellent carpenter, and you also have a lot of other construction skills. Plus, you work hard and fast."

"I'm not the one you need to convince."

"If he agreed to meet with you, he must be open to adjusting his schedule."

Andrew scrubbed a hand down his face. "Even if he is, he may not want to hire me once he hears my story."

A drop of water dripped off her hair, leaving a dark splotch on the floor of the tent. "Are you going to tell him everything?"

"He'll ask about my background and credentials, Paige. I'm not going to lie."

"But nothing that happened was your fault."

"I hired Jack as our business manager. I didn't have business theft insurance. I didn't keep a close enough eye on the books."

"We never thought that kind of insurance was necessary. We were a small operation. Like a family. Jack's credentials were solid. And when would you have carved out the hours to review financials? You already worked sunup to sundown."

"I took care of the books until I hired Jack."

"The operation was smaller then. It's harder to run an office *and* do field work when you have a dozen employees and a mushrooming workload. I stand by my comment. What happened wasn't your fault."

He shrugged. "It's a moot point now. The business is ruined, and any company that has illegal activities under its roof is tainted forever—as is the owner. At the very least, it suggests I wasn't as conscientious as I should have been."

"But we did everything we could to make it right. We sold our house and emptied our bank accounts to pay all the outstanding bills and meet payroll."

"Matt Quinn may not care about that. His primary concern will be competence and reliability, and he'll ask for references to verify those. I can give him the names of satisfied clients, but one of them could mention what happened. I'd rather he hear it from me than them."

He was right. Deep inside, Paige knew that. Honesty was always the wisest route, even if it didn't necessarily lead to the desired destination.

"Let's hope he has an open mind."

"I think it will depend on how desperate he is to get someone lined up fast." He twined his fingers with hers, lines of strain bracketing his mouth and aging him far beyond his twenty-eight years. "I'm sorry, Paige. This"—he swept a hand over the tent—"isn't the life I promised you."

"It's not forever." She infused her voice with all the positivity she could dredge up. "We'll get through this as long as we stick together."

His chin dipped, and he ran his work-roughened thumb over the simple gold band he'd slipped on her finger the day they'd said "I do." "I wouldn't blame you if you dumped me."

At his muted, ragged words, her pulse stuttered. "You can't be serious."

No response.

"Andrew." She squeezed his fingers. "I promised to stick with you for better, for worse."

"I bet you never expected the worse to be this bad."

"No. I didn't." Why lie? "But we can start over. And Hope Harbor may be the place to do that. The fact that you got a call the very day I put up the ad seems providential."

"Or a fluke." He sighed. "But you've always been a lemonade-out-of-lemons kind of woman."

Once upon a time, that had been true. Not so much lately. If he could see into the darkest corners of her heart where she tried to shove all her fears and worries, he'd know her usual sunny outlook was on shaky ground.

One of them had to remain upbeat, though, and despite her meltdown on the wharf today, she'd managed to do that during waking hours over these past weeks. Only at night did the demons of doubt infiltrate her mind and chase sleep away.

More so on nights when Andrew was distant in heart and spirit if not in body. When he turned away and left her feeling alone and abandoned despite his physical presence.

She angled toward him and touched his hand. "Let's make lemonade together."

"You're better at that than I am." He eased his hand out from under hers, stood, and moved toward the door. "I'm gonna take a walk."

Without waiting for her to respond, he lifted the flap and disappeared outside into the fading light.

Silence wrapped around her like a shroud.

So did loneliness.

Squeezing her eyes shut, she choked back a sob.

Maybe her optimism was misplaced. Maybe tomorrow's meeting would be a bust, and Matt Quinn wouldn't hire Andrew. Maybe the timeframe necessitated by a one-man show would end up being a deal breaker.

But if they couldn't get a break in a town with the name of Hope Harbor, where would they go from here?

7

As his cell vibrated, Matt swung into a space in the Grace Christian Church parking lot and pulled out his phone.

Kay.

"Hey there." He set the brake. "I thought you'd sleep late after your long drive yesterday."

"I did too. But an overdose of coffee and high-carb snacks during the trip nixed that plan. I figured you'd be up and wanted to give you a call before the day got rolling here. I was too distracted catching up with Cora and settling in last night to focus on our phone conversation, but you have my full attention today. How on earth did you find a new contractor mere hours after I left?"

"Correction. *Potential* contractor. TBD whether he ends up being a fit for the job. I'm meeting with him at noon. I'll fill you in after we talk."

Another car swung into a parking spot farther down the row, and he flicked a glance at it. Did a double take as Bev's daughter opened the door and swung her legs out.

He homed in on them.

Nice.

Very nice.

And very wrong.

Scowling, he yanked his gaze away.

Dana had only been gone for two years, and he loved her as much as he ever had. Why was he suddenly noticing women's legs?

"Matt?"

He tuned back in to the conversation with his sister. "Sorry. I'm in the parking lot at church, and the activity is distracting."

"Huh. The early service isn't usually that busy."

"The tourist season may be picking up." He shifted away from Bev's daughter. "What did I miss?"

"I said if your take on this outfit is positive, hire them. The B&B has been out of commission too long."

And the lack of cash flow was worrying her.

Message received.

"I don't want to burst your bubble, but it's not an outfit. It's a him. One guy. The project may be too big for a one-man show, or it could take too long."

"Maybe he can bring in a few people to help if we sweeten the pot."

"The budget we agreed on won't accommodate much sweetening."

She sighed. "I know, I know. I'll let you decide how to handle this. I trust your judgment. But if he doesn't work out, what then?"

"We go with plan B. Expand the search to Bandon or Coos Bay."

"Let's hope it doesn't come to that. Hang on a sec." A door closed in the background. "I think Cora's stirring. I should go. You should too. The service starts in two minutes. Call me later with an update."

"You got it. Give Cora my love. I'll talk to her later when I call so I can wish her well on the surgery tomorrow."

"She'll appreciate that. Enjoy the service."

Matt ended the call and scanned the walkway leading to the front door of the church.

Bev's daughter was hurrying toward the entrance, as he should be. But it would be awkward to run into her if she'd decided not to follow up on the contact information Bev had no doubt passed on by now. Better to wait until she was inside to avoid an uncomfortable encounter.

Stowing his phone, he remained behind the wheel as she approached the door, the silky blouse she'd tucked into her slim skirt shimmering in the morning sun.

Quite a change from yesterday's jeans and sweater.

The high heels that accentuated the curve of her calves were also a step up from the casual flats she'd sported at the B&B.

A tingle rippled through him, and he frowned.

Was that . . . attraction?

No. Impossible. Dana had been his one and only.

Besides, after all that happened over the past two years, he didn't deserve another chance at love.

Spirits tanking, he checked his watch as Vienna slipped through the door. The service was either on the brink of getting underway or had already begun. Should he write off this trip to town and come back later for the second service to avoid any possibility of running into her, or control the situation by choosing a seat near the back and leaving the instant the first notes of the closing hymn sounded?

The latter was more logical. Who would detain him, anyway? He'd met only a couple of people in town, and they likely wouldn't spot him in the back even if they were in the congregation. Why make two trips?

Controlling his reaction to Vienna, however, was a different matter altogether.

But he couldn't afford to let unruly hormones undermine his commitment to help Kay, and Bev's daughter was his preeminent resource for that.

So if she called him, he'd have to rein in his misbehaving testosterone and concentrate on correcting the bad first impression he'd made. Because he needed her professional savvy.

Nothing more.

Even if he couldn't quite erase the image of her killer legs and vivid blue eyes that was imprinted on his mind.

Was that Kay's brother?

As Vienna paged through her hymnal in search of the next song, she gave the tall, shadowed man in Grace Christian's very last pew a surreptitious survey.

"Well, look who's here."

At the quiet comment in her ear, she angled sideways to find her mom fixated on the same man. "Don't stare." Vienna nudged her.

"Why not? He isn't paying any attention to us."

The organ began the intro for the hymn, and she leaned closer to her mother. "That's Matt Quinn, isn't it?"

"None other."

The congregation launched into the song, cutting off their conversation, but as Vienna joined the chorus, she risked a few more peeks at the dark-haired man clad in a tailored sport jacket that emphasized his broad shoulders.

Night and day from the disheveled guy who'd answered the door at the B&B yesterday.

No wonder Mom had been enamored with him. This well-groomed version of Matt Quinn reeked of respectability and, near as she could tell in the dimmer light at the back of the church, he was silver-screen handsome.

Too bad she hadn't called him last night. It would have been easier to break the ice by phone rather than in person after their awkward encounter yesterday. On her cell, she could have mentioned the plumbing issue and made light of her spooked-deer escape without worrying about him seeing the hot spots of color that would probably bloom on her cheeks.

If she was lucky, though, he'd be long gone by the time she

collected her purse, straightened the hymnals in the rack, draped her sweater around her shoulders, and employed whatever other delay tactics she could come up with after the service.

For the next thirty minutes, she tried hard to direct her attention to the sanctuary and the minister's excellent sermon. Only when the organ launched into the final hymn did she venture another peek toward the back of church.

Kay's brother was already slipping his hymnal into the slot on the pew in front of him, preparing to leave.

Yes!

Awkward in-person encounter averted.

"Vienna." Mom leaned closer. "I have to leave or the coffee won't be ready when the crowd descends. Why don't you come with me? We can always use another pair of hands."

"Um . . ." She checked on Matt out of the corner of her eye. He was still in his pew. "I'd, uh, like to stay until the end, if you don't mind. Especially since the fog during my drive down from Bandon delayed me and I missed the opening."

"Okay. Hang a left in the vestibule and follow the hungry horde to the fellowship hall when the service is over." Mom slipped out of the pew and hustled up the side aisle.

Vienna continued singing as the minister exited via the center aisle, toward the vestibule, waiting until the last notes died away and the congregants began to follow in his wake to scope out the back of church.

Kay's brother was gone.

She exhaled.

The coast was clear.

Nevertheless, she didn't rush gathering up her belongings. Nor did she hurry toward the rear of the church. Hopefully he wouldn't detour for coffee and doughnuts, but unless she'd read his body language wrong, he'd been anxious to leave.

Vienna fell in behind the crowd surging toward the exit, scanning the vestibule for Matt as she left the sanctuary behind.

He was nowhere in sight.

All she had to do was find a spot in the fellowship hall and hang out until Mom was ready to leave for their breakfast date at the Myrtle. Which could be a while, given her mother's propensity to chat up everyone she—

"Vienna! I've been watching for you."

At Mom's voice, she swung around.

Her mother was wedged beside one of the open doors that led to the sanctuary, Kay's brother beside her.

Well, crud.

Short of being rude, she couldn't ignore Mom's summons.

Taking a deep breath, she wove through the crowd and joined them. "I thought you were making coffee."

"One of the other volunteers offered to get it started while I welcomed Matt to our church. Let me introduce you two."

As her mother did so, Matt extended his hand. "I think I owe you an apology for my less-than-gracious greeting at the B&B yesterday. Not to mention the foul smell." He hiked up the corners of his mouth, and an endearing dimple dented his cheek.

Her gaze got stuck there for a moment before she pried it free and returned his firm clasp. "I'll admit it wasn't an auspicious meeting—on either of our parts. I don't usually bolt."

"And I don't usually bite."

Mom's head oscillated between the two of them, an enigmatic glint sparking in her eyes. "Now that you two have met, I'll leave you to talk. I don't want to shirk my hostess duties. Feel free to come to the hall if you'd rather converse over doughnuts."

With that, she trotted off at a brisk clip.

"I take it you were waylaid." Vienna nodded toward her mother.

"We happened to emerge into the vestibule at the same time. Sorry to put you on the spot. I know Bev filled you in on my predicament, but don't feel pressured to give me an answer now."

"I was going to call you later this morning anyway and see if you wanted to get together to discuss the situation. I'm having breakfast with Mom after the social hour, but other than that, I'm available anytime."

"Thank you. Any and all assistance and advice would be appreciated. Kay and I are both in over our heads, and an empty B&B isn't tenable for long. The sooner we can get a meeting scheduled, the better."

"In that case, do you want me to swing by today, after Mom and I have breakfast?"

He hesitated. "I don't expect you to work on Sundays."

She offered him a wry smile. "Trust me, that's not a problem. Sunday work was par for the course in my previous job."

"Then I accept. With gratitude. I'm meeting with a potential contractor at noon. Otherwise my day is wide open."

"I expect my breakfast with Mom will wind down about eleven thirty, since she opens the shop at twelve on Sundays. Rather than go back to my room in Bandon, I'll kill an hour or two in town. How long do you expect your meeting to last?"

Again, he hesitated. "I don't want to monopolize your day, but you're welcome to sit in on the meeting if you like. I'm going to give him a tour of the place, and you may find that useful for our discussion."

"Yes, I would. In fact, unless you have other plans, why don't I come as soon as Mom and I finish breakfast and you can fill me in on the non-cosmetic issues at the B&B? The more background I have, the easier it will be to come up with recommendations."

"Makes sense. I'll expect you around—"

"Good morning. Welcome to Grace Christian."

Vienna turned.

"Reverend Paul Baker." The minister moved toward them, his hand extended toward her. "I'm always delighted to welcome a new couple to our congregation—or are you just visiting our lovely town?"

Vienna sent Matt a sidelong glance as she took the man's hand.

His sudden ruddiness suggested he was as taken off guard by the reference as she was.

"Um . . . we're not actually together. I'm Vienna Price, Bev's daughter."

"And I'm Matt Quinn, Kay Marshall's brother." He shook the minister's hand too.

"Sorry. I shouldn't have jumped to conclusions."

"Putting your foot in it as usual, I see." A jovial-looking man carrying a few extra pounds and wearing a Roman collar bustled toward them, his comment booming across the vestibule that had mostly cleared out as congregants departed or moved on to doughnuts. "Morning, folks. Father Kevin Murphy. Happy to meet you." He pumped both their hands.

The minister sent him a disgruntled look. "Father Murphy is the pastor at St. Francis church on the other side of town—where he should be on a Sunday morning. What are you doing here, anyway?"

"I came between Masses to collect the box of golf balls you owe me." The padre directed his next comment to her and Matt. "The two of us have a standing golf date on Thursdays, and my clerical friend here has a terrible left hook nothing short of a miracle could cure. He's always in the hock to me for the balls he borrows—and loses."

"I could have given them to you Thursday. You just came over to eat our doughnuts."

"Perish the thought." The priest dismissed the accusation with a flick of his hand. "Our homemade ones are far superior to your store-bought offering."

The minister offered him a smug smile. "But we have Danish too."

Father Murphy blinked. "Since when?"

"Since this week."

"Why didn't you tell me you were expanding your menu?"

"You eat too much high-cholesterol food as it is."

"Not always. I gave up sweets for Lent. Healthy for the soul *and* the heart. I'll have to sample your Danish before I leave."

Based on the twitch in Matt's lips, he was enjoying the good-natured banter between the two men of the cloth as much as she was.

"I'll go with you." The minister folded his arms.

"Don't bother. I know the way." The priest leaned closer to them and lowered his voice. "A word of advice. If you want real doughnuts, come visit us at St. Francis. Kay stops in on a regular basis."

"What? Are you stealing my congregation now, along with my doughnuts?" The minister arched an eyebrow.

"Would I do that?" The padre's expression was the picture of innocence.

"Is the pope Catholic?"

"Let's leave the Holy Father out of this, shall we?" Father Murphy turned back to Matt. "Kay enjoys our meditation garden. She's quite knowledgeable about flowers. We've had many a pleasant discussion amidst the flora."

"I have to admit he does a wonderful job with that garden." The minister patted him on the back. "You two should visit while you're in town. It's a little taste of heaven right here in Hope Harbor."

"Thank you for that." The priest gave a jaunty salute. "And I'll second the invitation. Stop by anytime. All are welcome. Now, would you two like to walk over to the fellowship hall with me?"

"Thank you, but I have to get back to the B&B." Matt pulled out his keys.

"I heard Kay was on a mission of mercy in Boise, God bless her." The priest made the sign of the cross.

"Where did you hear that?" Reverend Baker stepped back into the conversation.

"I keep my ear to the ground."

"Hmm. Better to live quietly and mind to your own affairs."

The priest squinted at him. "Are you quoting Thessalonians to me?"

"Wonder of wonders." The pastor steepled his fingers and raised his face heavenward. "He knows the source."

"I am not debating Bible fluency with you again." Father Murphy turned his back on him. "Vienna, can I interest you in a doughnut?"

"Or a Danish." Reverend Baker leaned around his Catholic counterpart.

"Mom's helping serve today, and I promised to join her. So yes. Either one would hit the spot. I'll see you later, Matt."

"No rush. Reverend Baker, Father Murphy, a pleasure to meet you both." Kay's brother strode toward the door across the empty vestibule.

"Pleasant young man." The priest watched him push through the door, then swept a hand toward the hallway on the right. "Shall we?"

Vienna took the cue, and the clerics fell in on either side of her, launching into a spirited discussion of the most worthy sights for her to see during her visit.

But her mind wasn't on the gardens at Shore Acres State Park or tea at the lavender farm, though both sounded appealing.

Instead, her thoughts were on the intimidating man who'd scared her off at the B&B yesterday but who she was suddenly eager to see again ASAP.

8

She was here.

Matt stepped back from the front door sidelight as Vienna pulled into a parking space in front of the B&B. Scanned the foyer for any dust balls or missed evidence of yesterday's plumbing disaster. Sniffed the air for any lingering stench. Angled toward the mirror to verify his hair was behaving and his shirt was tucked in.

Everything was copacetic.

He was as ready as he could be to continue the effort he'd launched at church this morning to correct yesterday's bad impression.

Taking a deep breath, he returned to the door and pulled it open as she approached the entrance.

Her step faltered. "Were you watching for me?"

"Guilty as charged." He called up the teasing smile he hadn't used in a very long while. "I'm a desperate man, and after our last encounter here, I wouldn't have blamed you if you'd bailed."

"I said I'd come, and I always honor my promises. But the fog slowed me down. Again. Sorry to keep you waiting." Shaking her head, she picked up her pace. "Fighting the fog coming down from Bandon for church was the pits, but twice in one day is too much."

"I hear you. I'm no fan of fog myself, even though I should be used to it after living in San Francisco."

"Have you lived there long?"

"A number of years." To avert a follow-up question, he opened the door wide and motioned her in. "Would you like to sit on the terrace while we talk, now that the sun's back out?"

"Sure."

He led the way toward the rear of the house, but she halted as the wall of windows in the great room came into view.

"Wow." She gave the scene a slow sweep. "What a stunning vista."

"Yes, it is. It's a huge asset for the B&B. The interior? Not so much, as you'll see on the tour." He continued across the room, opened a sliding glass door, and ushered her onto the terrace. "Can I offer you a beverage?"

"No, thanks. I ODed on OJ at breakfast." She chose a seat at the patio table that offered a panoramic view of the beach beyond a low dune draped in ground cover.

As she gave the unobstructed stretch of sand a slow perusal, she also gave him an unobstructed view of her flawless profile—delicate jaw, full lips, classic cheekbones, thick fringe of lashes, oh-so-soft-looking hair. The kind a man's fingers could—

"I don't know the extent of your infrastructure problems, but you couldn't improve on the setting. And the seclusion would be a huge selling point for couples."

Her comment jerked him back to the moment, and he cleared his throat. "Yes, it would." He pulled out the chair beside hers, moving it a few inches farther away as a disconcerting buzz in his nerve endings and a hovering sense of danger activated every defensive reflex in his body. "It reminds me of a place my wife and I visited on our honeymoon."

As that personal tidbit slipped out, he furrowed his brow.

Why had he mentioned Dana to this woman, who was almost a stranger?

Whatever the reason, his comment appeared to have surprised her as much as it did him.

In addition, for the briefest moment before she called up a smile that came across as a bit forced, an emotion that looked like disappointment flickered in her eyes. As if she was sad to hear he was taken.

But he had to be mistaken. They were barely acquainted. Why would she care about his marital status—especially after the impression he'd made on her yesterday?

"You should stress that in your marketing."

Hard as he tried, he couldn't remember what they'd been talking about.

As if sensing his dilemma, she spoke again. "This place is secluded. It would be a fabulous honeymoon destination. You could suggest that in your marketing copy."

He fumbled for the sunglasses in his pocket. They were missing. Naturally. "I would, if we had any marketing copy."

"What about the website?"

"It's outdated and misleading. Have you had a chance to read it?"

"I gave it a fast skim the day I was trying to find accommodations closer to town."

"Did you notice the reviews?"

"I didn't read them, but I saw lots of stars, and the pullout quotes are impressive."

"They're also old. After I arrived, I dug into other review sites. All the recent comments are thumbs-down."

Her forehead crinkled. "That's a major concern. No matter the product, online reviews are a go-to source for potential customers."

"I know."

She folded her hands on the table. "If this is none of my business, feel free to tell me, but may I ask why your sister bought the place, knowing how difficult it would be to overcome bad reviews?"

He leaned back, crossed an ankle over a knee, and watched

two seagulls cavort offshore as he carefully composed a reply that didn't paint Kay in too bad of a light. "My sister is a wonderful person who thinks the best of people and tends to be too trusting. After her husband died a year ago, she decided to start over in a new place. Beachview B&B was it. Suffice it to say, she sometimes sees the world through rose-colored glasses and leaps before she looks. In this case, she didn't do enough due diligence."

"I can only imagine how disappointed she must be if she walked in expecting a guest-ready inn. I'm sorry."

"I think she's beginning to feel the same way. I know she's overwhelmed by the challenges."

"How did you enter the picture?"

"I came up here expecting R&R for a month while she went to help a friend in Boise who's having surgery. When I arrived and realized she had a mess on her hands, I offered to help her try to straighten it out."

A flicker of admiration . . . approval . . . warmth . . . sparked in Vienna's eyes. "I'm impressed. I doubt most brothers would be that magnanimous."

The two seagulls dipped low overhead and settled down in a flutter of wings on the dune beyond the paved terrace as he pondered how much more to tell her. His uncharacteristic earlier lapse aside, he wasn't the type to run off at the mouth about personal issues to friends, let alone new acquaintances.

But if Vienna was willing to offer them her expertise, didn't he owe her a few insights into who she was helping?

Yeah, he did.

He linked his fingers over his stomach. "I can't speak for most brothers, but our history has made us extra close. By the time I was nine, we'd lost both of our parents. Kay was only eighteen, but she took on the job of raising me. She gave up college, worked two waitressing jobs, played the role of both mom and dad. Tag-teaming it with the B&B was a no-brainer. I could never in a million years repay her for all the sacrifices she made for me."

"She sounds like a remarkable, selfless woman. I can see why you'd come to her rescue."

"I'm not certain how much rescuing I can do. I should be able to find a contractor to handle physical repairs, but the well of funds is only so deep. And I don't have a clue how to fix a negative image."

Vienna tapped a finger on the arm of her chair. "Changing an image is a huge challenge in this digital age. Most stuff never disappears from the internet. You can delete content, but often pieces of it have been cloned or copied and lurk in places you don't control. Any reference to Beachview B&B will always surface in a search, including bad reviews."

Not the news he wanted to hear.

"In other words, we're hosed." May as well be blunt. Why dance around what appeared to be a looming disaster?

"Not necessarily." She tipped her head. "Did Mom tell you I worked for a boutique hotel chain?"

"Yes. But nothing more."

"I was on the team that evaluated prospective acquisitions. My job was primarily numbers related, but since my MBA had a double concentration—finance and marketing—I also got involved in promotion and advertising. Many of the properties we identified had problems that had hurt their business, bad reviews being a major one. But if we thought we could fix the issues and turn the place around, we'd make an offer. Also, it wasn't a chain in the usual sense. We searched for small inns that met our criteria for size, location, and growth potential, and then created a distinctive identity for each."

Matt stared at her.

How in the world had he and Kay lucked out and had a woman like this drop out of the sky into their backyard? With an MBA, no less.

Wait until he gave his sister *this* news tonight.

Still digesting Vienna's credentials and obvious savvy, he began formulating questions. "How do you turn an inn around if the bad reviews stay out there forever?"

"At my company, we took it out of service, fixed the problems, created a new image for the property, and changed the name."

A name change.

Of course!

"I have to admit it never occurred to us to change the name. Which is a sad commentary on our expertise in this industry."

"When you're dealing with a major dilemma, it can be easy to overlook the simplest and most obvious answer. We tend to assume that complicated problems require complicated solutions." Her mouth flexed, drawing his attention.

Not appropriate.

Yet fixing his attention on her blue irises, with their glints of gold, wasn't any less distracting.

But where else could he look without suggesting to her that he was bored or uninterested?

"I suppose that's true." He scooted his chair back a few more inches on the pretext of eluding a persistent bee. "In hindsight, a new name seems like an obvious remedy."

"I'm not suggesting you go that route yet, though. I'm just tossing it out as a possibility to consider. I want to do more online research, take the tour with your contractor to get a feel for the inside, talk to you or your sister about your vision for this place and the type of guest you want to attract."

"I have a feeling she'll like your idea about making this a couples destination."

"How do you think she feels about the current name?"

"As far as I know, she's not married to it. She hadn't intended to change it, because the plan was to build on the customer base and favorable image that was out there. But now that she has neither, I'm sure she'd be open to other names. What do *you* think of the name?"

"The alliteration is clever, and it's descriptive of this"—she waved a hand over the scene in front of them—"but it doesn't have any magic. Nor does it suggest a couples destination, which is what I'd aim for with this property. If I was branding this location with that in mind, Beachview B&B wouldn't cut it. You'd need a name with whimsy and romance. Something that suggests fantasy and dreams and fairy tales and happily-ever-afters."

He gaped at her.

Ask him to diagnose a colicky cat? Done. Create an ambiance imbued with whimsy and romance? Not happening.

"That's a tall order for someone like me. I'm not skilled at wordsmithing. And I doubt Kay would factor all the appropriate nuances into that sort of decision either. Do you have any ideas in mind?"

"Not off the top of my head. When we renamed properties, it was a weeks-long process involving tons of research, focus groups, surveys, and brainstorming meetings with the team."

Wow.

This was light years out of his league.

"We don't have unlimited weeks. Or a team. And I wouldn't know where to start with focus groups and surveys."

"For a standalone property, I don't think all of those are essential. I just wanted you to know that a great deal of thought went into a rebranding program with my former employer. I'm confident the three of us can settle on an appropriate name, assuming we go that route."

"I'm glad *you* are."

"Hey." She leaned forward, erasing the distance between them to rest her hands on the table, one on top of the other. "Don't panic. We'll figure out a plan."

Maybe about the B&B.

But panic nevertheless bubbled up inside him as he studied her graceful fingers. Panic that had nothing to do with Kay's predicament and everything to do with the woman sharing this secluded terrace with him.

Because it would be easy to pull in his chair and link his fingers on the table, close enough to hers for the heat radiating from her skin to seep into his pores like the warmth of her encouraging smile was infiltrating his defenses. To let the light of her presence brighten the dark corners of his heart.

So easy.

But physical proximity couldn't bridge the chasm between them. A solitary life was his lot. He deserved nothing more. Romance wasn't in the cards for him.

Not now.

Not ever.

"I appreciate the pep talk." He left his chair where it was while he filled his lungs and forced himself to make eye contact.

As their gazes tangled—and locked—Vienna's breath hitched and her lips parted ever so slightly. With fingers that didn't appear any too steady, she tucked a breeze-tossed lock of hair behind her ear.

His pulse began to thunder.

What was going on here?

How was he supposed to—

Ding-dong.

It took a second for the ring of the doorbell to register, but the instant it did, he vaulted to his feet. "That must be the contractor." His voice rasped.

She gave a slow blink. "Yes. I guess so."

"I'll be back in a minute."

He pivoted and escaped as fast as he could, questions tumbling through his mind as he put as much distance between him and his visitor as possible.

Was she as blindsided by the electrical storm that had just swept across the terrace as he was?

Was she also as much off balance?

Or had she even felt the potent wattage arcing between them?

Potent on his end, anyway.

The answers to his questions eluded him. Maybe he'd misread

her reaction. Maybe she'd simply been thrown off guard by his intense scrutiny. Perhaps been uncomfortable with it.

But it wasn't hard to make an educated guess about what had sparked the sizzle on his end.

Loneliness, pure and simple.

After all the desolate months filled with nightmares and insomnia and guilt and recriminations and grief, his empty heart craved love like a parched, drooping plant longs for water.

But Vienna Price was here to help him fix the B&B, not mend his heart. Period. He couldn't let himself forget that.

Nor could he let personal feelings deter him in his mission to help Kay get out of the corner she'd painted herself into.

So he'd work with Vienna on a professional level with the B&B, but he wouldn't venture into personal territory with her.

No matter how tempted he might be to cross that line.

9

Oh. My. Word.

As Matt disappeared through the sliding door at the back of the B&B, Vienna tried to jump-start her balking lungs.

What had just happened here?

One minute she and Matt were talking about business, the next her heart was sputtering as she watched the very tantalizing lips of a man who was asking for her professional help.

A very married man.

How in the world could she be attracted to someone who was already taken? That wasn't her style.

And in light of his almost panicked escape when the doorbell rang, he'd noticed her inappropriate reaction. Who knew what sort of look she'd had on her face in those few, charged moments?

Warmth spread across her cheeks, and she picked up her notebook. Fanned her face.

She had to get a handle on her wayward emotions before he returned. Behave in a businesslike manner.

Heck, maybe she even owed him an apology for her indiscretion.

But how could she bring up the subject without further embarrassing them both?

Could she pretend it had never happened? Compose herself and behave with proper decorum for the rest of this visit?

It was worth a try.

The door slid back open, and Matt reappeared, followed by a familiar man who was two or three inches shorter than Kay's brother.

She did a double take.

The guy from the wharf was Matt's potential contractor? The one who'd been deep in conversation with a woman at an adjacent bench? The one who'd sounded like he was in trouble of some sort?

As Matt introduced them, she stood and shook the man's hand. He gave no indication he recognized her, but that wasn't surprising. He and the woman had seemed insulated in misery that day. Oblivious to their surroundings.

"Vienna is assisting with marketing for a relaunch of the B&B." However flummoxed Matt may have been by those few incendiary seconds before the doorbell rang, his even tone suggested he'd recovered his equilibrium. Lucky him. "I asked her to sit in on our meeting and join us on our walk-through. Shall we start with the tour to give you a feel for the scope of work?"

Andrew hesitated, shoulders stiffening as he clenched his fingers. "If you don't mind, I'd like to fill you in on my background first. There's a reason I'm looking for work with an ad on a community bulletin board, and if you're not comfortable with my situation, it would be best for both of us to know that up front."

Vienna sent Matt a quick glance.

Other than a slight elevation of his eyebrows, he gave no indication he was surprised by the man's unexpected request.

"No problem. Please, have a seat." He motioned to the patio table.

Once they all claimed chairs, Andrew folded his hands on top of his clipboard. "Based on what you told me about the job, I believe I'm capable of handling everything that has to be done. I can confirm that after the walk-through. The biggest issue, aside from what I'm about to tell you, may be the timetable."

"It's possible we can make it work, depending on your assessment of the length of the job after you review the scope of work."

He nodded. "You didn't ask about my experience on the phone, but I've worked in construction for more than a decade. I was with a large outfit in Portland for four years, then started my own business, which was very successful."

Vienna studied him.

So far his story wasn't matching the scene she'd witnessed on the wharf.

"I take it that changed?" Matt voiced the very question running through her mind.

"Yes." A bead of sweat popped out on Andrew's forehead. "As we won more and more bids, I expanded our crew. In the beginning, I not only worked in the field but handled all of the office duties. Eventually that got to be too much, so my wife took over the paperwork and bids. Three years ago, we also hired a business manager to handle finances—invoicing customers, paying bills, payroll. I was acquainted with him from high school, and he had a solid resume. That's when our trouble began, though we didn't know it at the time."

As the man swallowed and fell silent, parallel grooves dented Matt's brow. "If you'd rather not continue, please don't feel—"

"No. I believe in being honest. If you hire me, I want it to be with full knowledge of my background." His knuckles whitened, and a muscle in his cheek ticced. "To cut to the chase, a few months ago we discovered he'd embezzled almost a million dollars."

Vienna sucked in a breath.

No wonder he and the woman who must be his wife had been dejected on the wharf.

And his story provided a heaping dose of perspective. She may have lost her job, but her life hadn't been ruined.

"I'm sorry to hear that." Compassion softened Matt's features. "Has he been prosecuted?"

"Yes, but the money is gone and we weren't insured against that type of loss. So my wife and I liquidated all of our business assets and most of our personal property, including our house, to pay our suppliers and keep part of our crew on long enough to finish the jobs that were underway. We believe in honoring our commitments."

"How did you end up here?" Matt rested his elbows on the arms of his chair and steepled his fingers, giving the man his full attention.

"After the dust settled, we put our few remaining belongings into storage in Portland, borrowed a friend's camping equipment, and drove south for some breathing space. We've been wandering for the past three weeks while we try to figure out what to do next, but we're getting low on cash. It was my wife's idea to post the ad in the bookstore. To be honest, I never thought anything would come of it."

"Your timing was impeccable for me. Almost providential."

"That's what my wife said." The corners of Andrew's mouth lifted for a microsecond before flattening out again as he motioned toward his clipboard. "I put together a list of references for jobs we did in Portland, but if my company history is a deal-breaker, I won't waste any more of your time."

A few seconds ticked by as Matt regarded him.

"I'll tell you what. Keep the references handy. If you're interested in the job after the walk-through and we can agree on a timeframe, I'll check references before you work up a bid. Sound fair?"

A tiny bit of the tension in the man's features eased. "More than."

"Let's move on to the tour, then. Vienna, feel free to jump in and ask any questions you have as we make a circuit."

"I will." She picked up her notebook and followed along as the men talked paint and drywall cracks and hardware and missing shingles and a host of other problems. All of which would have to be addressed to realize the full potential of the property.

But she also focused on the softer items that were no less important to guests. While Matt and Andrew examined a warped window frame in one of the bedrooms, she zeroed in on worn spots in the upholstery, toiletries in the bathroom, towels, bedding, and decorating, scribbling copious notes.

Forty-five minutes later, after a full circuit inside and out, she'd filled several pages.

This was not a small job.

But tackling it could be an interesting challenge. More satisfying in many ways than being on the acquisitions team in her prior position, where every decision had to be consensus based and often took forever. Here, only Matt or Kay would have to sign off on ideas, meaning they could be implemented much faster.

It would be fun to get the project rolling before she left town to go wherever her next job took her. And that had to be soon. Taking two or three weeks to regroup was fine. A longer gap might be off-putting to potential employers, no matter what Mom thought.

They finished their tour in the foyer, where Matt asked Andrew for a topline assessment.

"I can handle all the repairs we discussed." He tucked his clipboard under his arm. "Best case, I'd estimate it will take me five to six weeks to complete the work, depending on availability of materials. I can call suppliers as I prepare a bid and give you a firmer completion date in a few days. If you want me to take that step."

An almost palpable tension radiated from the man as he waited for Matt's verdict, and Vienna's heart contracted in sympathy.

What must it be like to be in such dire need of work?

Hopefully she'd never find out firsthand.

But you had to admire a man who refused to sugarcoat or cover up his past to win a desperately needed job. Who'd offered absolute honesty and candor. That should count for something.

Did count with her. If she was making the decision, she'd proceed in a heartbeat.

Matt's next comment confirmed their conclusions were in sync.

"I'd like to go ahead and contact a couple of your references. If I get positive reports, we'll proceed. Bear in mind that anything you can do to shorten the job without sacrificing quality would be helpful."

Andrew exhaled, pulled out the list of customers he'd compiled, and handed it over. "Thank you for this opportunity. If it's okay, I'll go through again and take measurements while I'm here."

"That's fine. I'll be on the terrace when you finish. Vienna, would you like to join me?"

Yes, she would.

But no way could she sit alone again out there with him, where a lingering bolt of electricity might zap her. At least not until she processed the earlier unsettling interlude and figured out how to deal with it going forward.

"Actually, I should be leaving." To emphasize that, she pulled out her keys. "I want to dig into my research and sort through the notes I took during the tour."

He didn't try to deter her. On the contrary. An emotion that resembled relief washed across his face.

"I'll walk you out." He crossed to the front door and pulled it open.

It would be better if they said goodbye in the foyer. But left with no choice, she sidled past him and stepped out, trying to ignore the musky scent of aftershave that tickled her nose. A vast improvement over the pungent smells permeating this spot during her previous visit.

He closed the door behind him and joined her under the covered entranceway. "What do you think?"

"About the condition of the B&B or Andrew?"

"Both."

"I'd be inclined to give Andrew a chance, if his references pan out and you can agree on a schedule." She relayed her encounter with him and his wife on the wharf. "I think they're in a tough spot. It's one thing to lose your job, like I did, in a corporate reorg. It's another to have your business wiped out by treachery from someone you trusted. But he went above and beyond to make it right. Most people would have filed bankruptcy and let clients with in-progress jobs fend for themselves."

Matt's forehead pleated. "I agree with you about Andrew. And I'm sorry about your job. I didn't realize you'd been let go."

Vision misting at his caring tone, she gave a stiff shrug. "It happens. I'll admit I never expected to be a corporate casualty after all the hours I worked and everything I sacrificed for the company. But I was, and that was a wake-up call. One I probably needed, as I'm sure my mom would agree. She always thought I worked too hard."

"You did mention earlier that Sunday work wasn't unusual for you. No day of rest in your schedule?"

"On occasion. But I expect everyone works a Sunday now and then." If not every Sunday, like she had. "Don't you?"

"Only in emergencies."

Vienna gave him a wry smile. "People have different definitions of what constitutes an emergency."

"In my case, it was a life at stake."

She digested that piece of news. "Are you a doctor?"

"Veterinarian." His mouth flexed. "And in many cases, my animal patients are beloved, faithful companions that often provide their owners with more comfort than human friends or relatives do. So . . ." He swept a hand over the B&B and guided the conversation back to business. "What do you think about this place?"

She forced herself to shift gears. "All the cosmetic work you and Andrew discussed is essential. From there, it depends on your sister's vision for the place. There's a big difference between a mid-range, casual B&B and a high-end luxury property that generates top dollar. This has the potential to be the latter, if she wants to go that direction and feels confident she can pull it off. Everything from amenities to service to food would have to be first-class."

"Define top dollar."

"For a location like this, more than you may think." She threw out a number that would probably send a shockwave through him. But she also added a caveat. "That's assuming a major redo. The décor is dated, and much of it should be upgraded. I would recommend investing in premium-quality linens too, like plusher towels and higher-thread-count sheets. Indulgent toiletries would also be a selling point. Names like Oscar de la Renta, Ferragamo, Hermès."

He gave her a blank look. "You lost me back on thread count."

"Sorry." She flashed him a smile. "I didn't mean to overwhelm you. Why don't you worry about getting the structural repairs going and let me focus on the branding side? But first your sister should weigh in on what sort of image she wants for the place. There's more money in a high-end operation, but not everyone has the skill set to deal with a demanding clientele. Once she gives us direction, I'll work up some ideas."

Faint creases scored his brow, and he shoved his hands into his pockets. "I'm not expecting you to invest hours on this project for free, Vienna. If this is going to turn into a true consulting gig, I want to talk to Kay about compensating you."

She waved that aside. "Putting together a few preliminary recommendations is no big deal. If my role expands beyond that, we can regroup. For now, I'm happy to help out. Let me know what Kay says on the image question, and then I'll dive in. I can give you a call Tuesday or Wednesday and let you know where I am."

"That works. And thank you for coming out today."

"It was my pleasure. I hope you and Andrew can reach an agreement on timing." With a wave, she pivoted and strode to her car.

He waited until she was pulling out to lift a hand in farewell, then retreated inside.

As she drove down the gravel drive, she lowered her window and drew in a lungful of the crisp sea air.

What an intriguing challenge.

And what an intriguing man.

Matt Quinn seemed like one of the good guys. After all, how many people would invest such a significant amount of time and effort to help a sibling?

No wonder some woman had nabbed him.

Except . . . where was his wife?

Vienna hung a right on Starfish Pier Road and tooled back toward 101.

Perhaps she had a demanding career back in San Francisco that didn't allow her to get away for the extended stay Matt had planned.

But whatever the explanation, the question was irrelevant. Matt Quinn was off limits. The surge of electricity on the terrace had been a one-sided aberration, and it would *not* happen again.

Period.

Besides, even if he was available, they were both temporary residents of Hope Harbor. Ships passing in the night—or, in this case, the fog. Getting involved with anyone here could mess up her plans for the future, restrict her options and opportunities. The executive-level career she wanted was far away from the quiet seaside town Mom now called home.

At the intersection, she paused, checked both directions to verify the road was clear, and pulled onto the highway. While she accelerated north, she put her cell on hands-free and rang her mom. If she didn't report in, as she'd promised to do when they parted after breakfast, Mom would call her. She'd seemed inordinately captivated by the Beachview B&B project.

"Hello, sweet girl. How was your meeting?"

"Interesting. Do you have a minute to talk, or are you busy with customers?"

"It's quiet here at the moment. I'm working on a necklace in my jewelry corner. Are you going to be able to help Matt and Kay with the B&B?"

"I offered to put a few ideas and recommendations together, but the place needs a massive makeover."

"You could always stay longer, spearhead the effort for them. With all your experience, I bet turning that place around would be a piece of cake for you."

"I have to find a real job, Mom."

"That would be a real job."

"Not on a resume."

"Why not? A consulting gig is a consulting gig. And saving a floundering B&B would be a feather in your cap. Plus, you could use the project to buy yourself more time here. Turn an extended visit into a career asset instead of a liability."

Huh.

She pursed her lips as a diaphanous tendril of fog descended and executed a sinuous dance around her car.

Her mom's idea wasn't half bad. A success story with the B&B would indicate she was a self-starter with excellent organizational and marketing skills.

That could be an impressive credential for her resume.

"You're thinking about it, aren't you?"

As Mom spoke, she peered at the pavement, which was playing hide-and-seek as more wisps of fog joined in the dance. "Yes. Matt actually mentioned paying me to consult, but I got the impression finances are tight."

"Do it for free."

"I guess I could offer that." It wasn't like she had to tell anyone she'd provided her services gratis. "But I'm not certain he'd go for it."

"You could always suggest the barter idea again that I threw out to him in the shop."

No, she couldn't.

Staying alone on the same premises as a married man would be pushing the bounds of propriety, however innocent the arrangement might be.

"I don't think that would work, Mom."

"Why not? You're not still worried about your safety, are you?"

"No." Not her physical safety, anyway. The pleasant, conscientious, churchgoing man who'd greeted her at the door had come across as eminently trustworthy.

It was her heart she couldn't trust, after the incident on the terrace.

But she couldn't admit that to Mom.

"Then what's the problem?"

She'd have to go with propriety, despite the fact that that excuse wouldn't cut it with Bev Price, who'd always been a march-to-the-beat-of-her-own-drummer kind of woman. While she'd mellowed in some ways, her refusal to let decorum dictate her decisions hadn't likely changed.

"I'm not certain it would be appropriate to stay on the property alone with a married man. He may feel the same way. That could explain why he didn't latch onto your idea."

A beat of silence ticked by.

"Did he tell you he was married?"

"He mentioned a wife."

"That's strange. While Kay and I were waiting for our orders at The Perfect Blend a few weeks ago, she told me he was a widower. I'm sure if he'd been planning to remarry in the immediate future she'd have said so, as long as we were on the subject."

Vienna squinted at the center lane marking as it appeared and disappeared in the mist, throwing off her sense of direction.

That put a different spin on a whole lot of things.

"His marital status aside, it may not be wise to stay there." For a ton of reasons.

"But consider the convenience factor."

Not to mention safety. It was getting harder and harder to see the road.

"I'll think about it."

"Well, if I were you, I'd . . . Whoops. Zipping the lips right now.

I'm done pushing and prodding. It's your life and your decision. Are we still on for cinnamon rolls at Sweet Dreams tomorrow morning?"

"I wouldn't miss it."

"What's on your agenda for the rest of the afternoon?"

"I'm going to noodle on ideas for the B&B."

"Could be fun. Let me know how it goes."

They rang off, and Vienna made a course correction as the car drifted a tad too close to the shoulder.

Enough with the fog.

Maybe she'd follow up with the Gull Motel tomorrow, get a best-guess estimate on when a room might be available. Or suck it up and give Mom's place a try.

Or broach the barter idea with Matt.

A tingle rippled through her at the thought of sharing the same roof with him.

But of course she had no intention of exploring the sizzle of attraction that had blindsided her on the terrace. This was all about practicalities. Commuting in pea soup wasn't fun, and adding to her woes with a rental car accident would be the pits. It would also be much easier to work on ideas for the inn if she was living on-site.

The fact that the temporary innkeeper was hot, charming, and available had nothing to do with her sudden willingness to consider that option.

Nothing at all.

And she'd keep repeating that mantra until she convinced herself it was true.

10

Andrew turned into the state park campground and trundled toward the primitive tent site he and Paige would have to vacate in a week, when they hit their fourteen-day maximum and were forced to find a new park. Camping on public land like national forests would be cheaper, but at the very least he owed his wife access to running water and a hot shower.

In truth, he owed her much more than that.

Stomach clenching, he tightened his grip on the wheel as he took the fork in the road that led to their campsite.

Maybe he should urge her to go back to her parents' home. Her decision to quit college after one year and marry a carpenter in defiance of their wishes might still be stuck in their craw, but they'd welcome her in a heartbeat if she ditched the high school dropout with a GED who worked with his hands and wasn't anywhere close to the white-collar professional they'd set their sights on for their only child. Not even his business success had been sufficient to soften their hearts.

The truth was, no matter what he did, he'd never be good enough for them.

And maybe he wasn't good enough for Paige.

As he dodged a rut in the road with a sharp yank of the wheel, his shoulder slammed against the door.

He probably should be noble about this and cut her free.

But what he *should* do and what he had the strength to do were two different things.

How could he encourage her to go when she was the only bright spot in his world? The only reason he got up in the morning and kept on keeping on? The only thing that breathed life into his bruised, hurting heart?

Without her, he'd be finished.

But that was doubtless what he deserved after his epic fail.

Convincing her to leave would be a hard sell, though. She'd believed in him and his dream heart and soul, walking with him every step of the way as they built the business from the ground up, working menial but reliable jobs that offered them a steady paycheck and benefits until he had a financial foothold and she could join him at the company.

Paige wasn't a quitter, that was for sure.

As their campsite came into view, he slowed.

Despite her reassurance that the disaster with the company wasn't his fault, he should have paid more attention to the books instead of trusting a man whose amiable demeanor had hidden a growing heroin problem and serious gambling addiction.

It was too late to change the past, though. All he could do was try to minimize his mistakes in the future

Including his mistakes with his wife.

He had to do what was best for her.

But God help him, he wasn't certain what that was anymore.

The flap of the tent opened, and Paige emerged. Froze when she caught sight of him.

He picked up speed, pulled into their parking spot, and stepped down from the cab. At least today he had more upbeat news to share.

She crossed to him, hands gripped together in front of her, a tentative hope blooming in her eyes. "How did it go?"

"I told him my story, and he didn't throw me out. He also took my references. But the job is big. It could take me as long as six weeks, working alone. I know he'd like it done faster than that."

"Did he ask you to bid?"

"Not yet. He said he'd contact my references and let me know."

"That must mean he's willing to work with you on the schedule."

"Don't count on it, Paige." Much as he hated to dampen her spirits, it would be foolish to get their hopes up. Breaks hadn't been their lot lately.

She chewed on her lower lip. "If timing is a deal breaker, I could help you speed the job up."

"How? You're not a carpenter."

"No, but I can paint and pick up supplies and hand you tools and clean up the construction mess and place orders with suppliers and manage the books for a job of this scale. It's not like running a whole company and doing payroll and filing taxes."

"You didn't sign on for all of that."

She mashed her lips together, a definite sign she was digging in her heels. "I signed on the day I said 'I do.' Whatever it takes to make this job work, I'm willing to do it. We're in this together, Andrew. I can also stop at that café we saw in town and see if they're hiring. I haven't waitressed in a while, but I've had experience. I could try to get early morning or late shifts so I can help on the job site."

His throat constricted.

What had he done to deserve this woman?

"I don't want you to have to wait tables again. Or work sixteen hours a day."

"It won't be forever. Once we're back on our feet, I can quit the restaurant gig. But a steady income will allow us to get a decent place to live, with running water and electricity and heat on chilly nights."

All the comforts she deserved.

Gritting his teeth, he dug deep for the courage to say what had to be said. "You could always go home. Your parents would be glad to have you back."

His suggestion went over about as well as he'd expected.

"Home is where you are. And I won't go back to my parents' house until you're welcome there too."

"That's never going to happen. If they didn't relent when the business was booming, it's not likely they ever will."

"Then you're stuck with me."

He shoved his hands in his pockets. "I think you've got that backwards."

She moved closer, stopping inches away. Close enough for him to catch a subtle whiff of the bewitching floral scent from the shampoo she favored. To see the faint, endearing sprinkle of freckles across her nose. To hear the slight catch in her words as she spoke.

"I will never in my life feel stuck with you, Andrew. I wish I could convince you of that."

"You could have done a lot better than me." His voice hoarsened, and he cleared his throat.

"Better how? Could I have found a man with more integrity? A more admirable work ethic? A kinder heart? More humility?"

"You could have found one with a higher-class background. Your parents didn't like mine." And who could blame them? A guy with an abusive father and a mother who drank too much wasn't a promising marriage prospect for a woman like Paige, with her genteel upbringing.

"They never got to know you like I did. Their loss."

"Yours too. I never meant to drive a wedge between you and them."

"You didn't. They did. I'm sorry they couldn't accept you. I'm sorry they couldn't accept that I was old enough to make my own decisions, even if those decisions didn't meet their approval. But as long as I have you, I'll be fine." She touched his arm. "I need you, Andrew. Please don't shut me out."

At her pleading tone, his vision misted. "I only want what's best for you."

"Then don't do what my parents did and try to override my feelings. Trust me to make my own choices."

"I just don't want you to feel like you have to stick with me. I know we took vows, but I would never hold it against you if you decided staying together is too hard. This isn't the life I promised you."

"The life you promised me is less important than the love you promised me. And it will only be too hard if you keep shutting me out. Pushing me away. Please don't do that, Andrew." A sheen appeared in her eyes, and she reached up. Laid her palm against his cheek.

He ought to move back, break the connection.

But he didn't.

"Let's not wait to work on the bid." She smoothed her thumb over his cheek, sending ripples of warmth through him. "Let's go ahead and get it rolling. Together. I bet we can figure out ways for me to help that will shorten the timeframe. And if you get this job, the news will spread about your work ethic and your skills. We might be able to make a new start here."

How was he supposed to resist her entreaties while she was standing inches away, her gentle touch wreaking havoc with every resolution he'd made to keep his distance until he was certain he could dig them out of the mess he'd created?

How was he supposed to resist *her*?

It would take a man with far more self-discipline than he possessed not to cave.

Mistake or not, he slowly covered her hand with his, slipped his arms around her, and tugged her against his chest.

A simple hug, that was all he needed. A moment of comfort to help get him through the challenges ahead. To lighten the loneliness.

She came willingly, nestling close as she melted into his embrace, the familiar curve of her body against his bringing sweet memories of happier times as he absorbed the tiny quivers running through her and inhaled the scent of her hair while the slight frizz of her curls caressed his temple.

The temptation to move beyond a simple caress was strong. Almost too strong to resist. But somehow he summoned up the willpower to ease back. For now, a hug had to suffice.

He maintained his hold on her hands, however, as he looked down at her. "Are you certain you want to help me on the site?"

"Yes."

"And you don't think it's jumping the gun to start working on the bid?"

"No. How could any of the references you offered be anything but complimentary about your work? I guarantee the guy at the B&B will hire you as long as we give him a schedule he can live with. And we will. Whatever it takes."

At the conviction in her tone, a glimmer of hope flickered to life deep inside him. "I guess it wouldn't hurt to research local suppliers and work on a timetable. Why don't we find a coffee shop with Wi-Fi and boot up the laptop?" Their old cells would have come in handy today, but a pay-by-the-minute flip phone had been more budget-friendly during their weeks of wandering.

"I'm in. There's a coffee shop in Hope Harbor, but the woman at the bookstore mentioned it was a Wi-Fi-free environment."

"There has to be one in Bandon or Coos Bay. A library could work too."

"Let me get my purse." She squeezed his hand. "And try not to worry. I have positive vibes about this job."

He watched her jog back to the tent, this woman who'd caught his eye the day they met at the café where she was studying for finals and he was measuring the counter for a remodel job.

Who could have known their flirty, teasing conversation would lead to romance and love and marriage?

But it had been an ideal match for almost six years, despite her parents' misgivings and disapproval.

Until the bottom fell out of their world.

Paige could be right, though. Maybe here in Hope Harbor they'd find the new start they so badly needed.

If Matt Quinn was willing to give him a chance.

"So tell me how the meeting with the contractor went. I've been waiting with bated breath."

As Kay cut straight to the chase after greeting him, Matt watched the two seagulls that had taken up residence at the edge of the terrace cuddle up beside one another.

Cell pressed against his ear, he gave them an envious look.

Nice for them that they had each other for companionship.

Angling away from the cozy duo, he focused on a solo silver-white harbor seal perched on a craggy rock offshore, its doleful expression a more apt reflection of his own mood. "The meeting went well for the most part."

She listened while he recapped the story Andrew Thompson had relayed, speaking only after he finished. "He sounds like an honest man. Not everyone would be up front about that sort of experience."

"I agree. Vienna Price did too."

A beat ticked by.

"I know a Bev Price. She owns the bookstore in town."

"Vienna's her daughter. She's here on a visit. You won't believe her background." Once again, Kay listened without interrupting as he filled her in. "I don't know how we lucked out, but she's willing to help us while she's here."

"For real?"

"Yes. She toured the inn today with the contractor, and she's already thrown out more ideas than you or I would probably come up with in a month." Or a year.

"I'm all ears."

He gave her the rundown, ending with the notion of changing the name of the B&B. "What do you think about her suggestion to make this a couples destination?"

"I like it. The location is secluded, and the scenery is world-class. But I don't have a clue how to go about . . . what did you call it? Rebranding?"

"I expect she has a ton of ideas on that score too."

"Okay." A note of caution crept into her inflection. "How much is this going to cost?"

"The initial pass is free, but if she gets more involved, we should offer to pay her."

"I don't think we have the budget for that."

The two seagulls rose in a flutter of wings and settled on the railing of the balcony of one of the guest rooms.

Guest rooms.

Bev's comment about bartering advice for a room replayed through his mind. As did Vienna's comment about her aversion to driving in the fog.

Would a free place to stay, despite the fact that it didn't hold a candle to the inns she was accustomed to dealing with, be sufficient compensation for her counsel?

More importantly, would it be safe to even offer that, given his reaction to her today?

"Do we?"

At Kay's prompt, he redirected his attention to finances. "Depends on the bid from the contractor, assuming his references check out. Vienna also asked me about your vision for the place. Are you looking to make it mid-range casual or a high-end destination that brings in top dollar?"

"What's top dollar?"

He repeated the number Vienna had tossed out. "That's assuming we do serious updating."

"Wow." Her response came out hushed. "I say we aim for high-end. I can't do the math in my head, but multiply that by five rooms, times three hundred and sixty-five—wow again. For that kind of income, it may be worth taking out a loan to do the updates."

"Except I doubt you can count on 100 percent occupancy year round."

"Oh. Yeah, that's true. Did she say anything about what occupancy rate we *could* expect?"

"Not yet, but I assume that will be part of her research." As it should have been part of Kay's. But he left that unsaid.

"Even at 50 percent, that would be a decent income."

"You'll also have expenses. Like housekeeping staff."

A huff came over the line. "Are you trying to be Mr. Negative?"

"No. I'm trying to be realistic. Assuming she thinks you can expect a reasonable occupancy rate, however, it may be worth taking out a loan if there aren't sufficient funds in reserve to cover all the expenses. And if you decide down the road to move on, a rebranded, high-end inn would be easier to sell than the Beachview B&B you bought. However . . . Vienna did say clients at those kind of places can be demanding, and they'll have elevated expectations for everything from amenities to service to food. Are you up for that?"

"For a higher return, yes. Hang on a sec." Muffled voices came over the line. "I'm passing the phone over to Cora. She's champing at the bit to talk to you. Will you keep me in the loop?"

"Of course."

After a pause, Cora spoke. "How's my favorite vet doing?"

At her familiar gravelly, no-nonsense voice, the cloud hovering over him lifted a hair. "He's holding his own. I'm more interested in how *you're* doing."

"I'll be right as rain after they roto-rooter my ticker. Don't you worry about me. You take care of yourself and that B&B your sister saddled herself with. I've been hearing quite a few stories about the sad state of affairs out there."

"We'll get it all sorted out."

"I expect *you* will—if you get my drift."

Yeah, he did. Cora knew Kay as well as he did, both her many wonderful qualities and her foibles. "I'm not the savviest businessman, but I'll do my best."

"From what I overheard of your conversation, sounds like you have someone out there who may be able to lend a hand."

"I think so. Her background is tailor-made."

"I'm sure I'll get the scoop from your sister, but how on earth did you happen to cross paths with her?"

He filled her in. "She came out to the B&B today, and she seemed willing to help us."

"You're about due for a break. She vacationing there with her family?"

One of the gulls above him squawked, and he glanced up. They were both watching him with rapt attention.

Weird.

"She's here to see her mother. No family in tow."

"Is she married?"

Uh-oh.

Apparently her health issues weren't deterring Cora from the less-than-subtle campaign she'd been waging for the past couple of months to remedy his solo status.

"I don't think so. She didn't mention a husband, and neither did her mother."

"How about that. An eligible woman literally on your doorstep."

"I'm not in the market, Cora."

"You should be. The Bible verse says it all, right there at the beginning, in Genesis. It isn't good for man to be alone."

"You never got married."

"But I wasn't alone. I have a ton of friends, and I have you and your sister. Who do you have, other than me and Kay and those animals you take care of?"

"At least they don't try to give me advice."

"Ha-ha. But you know what? That's the first snappy comeback I've heard from you in a while, and there's a hint of the old lilt in your voice. Something—or someone—out there is perking you up."

An image of Vienna popped into his mind.

He erased it at once.

"Could be the sea breeze."

"Nope. You have that in San Francisco. My money's on a someone. Call me again in two or three days, after the effects of the anesthesia wear off. I want a clear head to keep tabs on this new development."

"You should be worrying about yourself, not me."

"I don't need worrying about. You do. So does your sister. And let me tell you, that's been a full-time job these past two years. Just say a prayer for me tomorrow and put everything in God's hands."

"I will. I'm also coming to see you soon."

"I'd like that, but Kay needs you more than I do right now. You take care of business for her while she takes care of me, and maybe I'll come out and see that B&B you're working on after it's all snazzed up and the doctor gives me the green light."

"You could come back with Kay for a visit after she's finished playing nurse."

"I'll consider that. Love you, Matt."

Pressure built in his throat at her typical matter-of-fact expression of affection that hid quiet depths of emotion.

How blessed he and Kay had been the day they'd moved in next to this caring, generous, slightly rough-around-the-edges woman who'd taken one look at them, realized they were hanging on by their fingernails, and tucked them into her heart. If she hadn't thrown them a lifeline, who knew where they'd have ended up?

"Love you back, Cora."

They said their goodbyes, and as he set his cell on the patio table, he gave the vast expanse of ocean a slow sweep.

Truth be told, he'd been thrown a lifeline on this trip too, thanks to the unexpected arrival of a carpenter and a consultant just as he was beginning to get desperate.

Whether Kay's B&B ended up being the center of the new life she'd planned remained to be seen. His main goal was to get it to a point where she could walk away whole if she chose.

And even though he hadn't contacted Andrew's references yet or seen detailed ideas from Vienna, every instinct in his body said that with them on his side, he could not only bail out his sister but perhaps add a bit of light to the darkest corners of his soul.

11

Mom had arrived. Right on schedule too.

Vienna waved as the older-model red Mini Cooper edged onto the shoulder at the end of Starfish Pier Road with a toot of the horn.

Had her mother ever been on time in the past, other than for work?

Not that she could recall.

Vienna pushed off from the fender as she waited for her mother to set the brake and kill the engine, memories of her childhood flitting through her mind. The harried, late departures for school and church. The tardy arrival for doctor appointments and social events. The last-minute hurricane-like flurry of activity as her mother raced to get ready for work each morning.

Yet during this visit, Mom hadn't been late for a single get-together. In fact, she'd arrived early at Frank's.

This new punctuality, plus her restrained decorating and curbed opinionating, was requiring a seismic adjustment.

But one thing hadn't changed.

Her mother's eclectic taste in fashion.

As Mom emerged from the car, Vienna surveyed her pirate-style blouse, cinched with a belt at the waist while its full sleeves flapped in the breeze, as well as the handkerchief hem of the bohemian skirt billowing over her sport shoes.

Her lips quirked.

Typical mom.

And reminiscent of the eclectic muumuus and caftans and tunics she'd worn to school events while festooned with enough baubles to sink a ship. A stark contrast to the tailored slacks and sweaters favored by her classmates' moms—and a never-ending source of embarrassment for an introverted, blend-into-the-background daughter.

"Am I late?" Mom hurried over.

"No. I got here early. I built in a few extra minutes in case of a fog slowdown, but the sky was clear."

"Isn't it glorious?" Lifting her face toward the expanse of blue, she swept a hand over the heavens. "This is an ideal day to see the tide pools. Let's do this." Without further delay, she scaled a small dune while Vienna fell in behind her, setting a brisk pace up the sand toward the far end of the beach. "You're going to love this spot. It's one of my favorite places to visit. I come every week."

"By yourself?" Vienna eyed the long expanse of deserted coastline. Other than Beachview B&B in the opposite direction, there was no other development at the end of the road.

"Of course."

"Is it safe?"

Her mother sent her a get-real look. "This is Hope Harbor, not Eugene or Denver."

"I know, but . . ." She motioned ahead to the rough rocks that housed the tide pools. "I mean, those have to be slippery. What if you fell and got hurt?"

"I have my cell." She patted her pocket.

"But what if you dropped it? What if . . . what if you couldn't move and the tide came in?"

"I suppose that could happen." Mom shrugged. "Trouble is, if you live your life what-iffing and worrying, you're going to spend half of it on the sidelines."

Hard to argue with that.

"Couldn't you bring someone with you, though?"

"Sweet girl, if I waited around until other people showed up to do anything, I'd rarely leave my apartment. And much as I like my little nest, I have places to go and marvels to see. Like this." She extended a hand toward the dark rocks up ahead. "I've lived alone for a very long time—before you came along, and after you left for college. I'm used to doing things on my own."

That was true. Mom had lived solo for a hearty chunk of her life. By choice.

But had she ever second-guessed her decision to go it alone?

"I know you like to be self-reliant." Vienna lengthened her stride to keep up with her mother's energetic pace, giving voice to a question she'd never asked. "But don't you ever get lonely?"

Her mother's smile faltered for a nanosecond. Stabilized. "Every lifestyle comes with pros and cons. I wanted independence, and I wanted to live life my way. That can cause friction in relationships, as ours demonstrates. It can also cause conflict in a marriage. Staying single was less disruptive, and it suited me. Now let me introduce you to this wondrous world." She stepped up onto a large, craggy rock. "Follow me."

Vienna did as instructed for their tour of the tide pools, but following in Mom's footsteps into a solo life had never been her intention.

Yet thanks to her all-consuming job, the family she'd always hoped to have still tantalized on the distant horizon. Had it not been for her unexpected career detour, it could have languished at the margins of her ten-year plan until it evaporated like a Hope Harbor mist.

Perhaps a realignment of professional *and* personal priorities was in order as she charted her new course.

Letting such weighty matters distract her while she climbed over dangerous rocks, however, could be disastrous.

So for the next hour, Vienna focused on her footing as she and Mom peered into pools at vivid purple sea urchins, fragile and delicate-hued anemones that closed in on themselves at the first hint of danger, and huge, vibrant orange, purple, and burgundy starfish.

It was amazing.

Even more amazing?

She was enjoying this outing, just as she'd enjoyed everything she and Mom had done together on this trip. Kind of like during their Hope Harbor mini vacations in the old days. Here, there had been fewer clashes. Probably, in hindsight, because the opinion of strangers hadn't mattered as much. If Mom had embarrassed her here, no one would have been able to use it against her.

Frowning, Vienna bent low for a clearer view of a hermit crab, which scuttled out of reach when she got too close.

Why had she cared so much what other people thought about Mom or her, anyway? Life would have been far less stressful if she'd let criticism and snide comments and hurtful teasing bounce off her instead of closing into a protective tuck, like the anemones did.

But that wasn't easy to do, especially for a hypersensitive kid. And youthful peers could be hateful.

"Vienna! Come see this." Mom motioned her over, her attention on the tide pool at her feet.

She crossed to the next rock and leaned over beside Mom.

"There." Mom pointed to a shimmery, bluish-white creature with orange fringe.

"What is that?"

"An opalescent nudibranchs. A variety of sea slug. They come in all different shapes and colors. I saw one a few weeks ago that was fairy-like. It had dozens of wing-like projections, all rimmed in white. Two weeks ago, I spied the bright yellow sea lemon version. I don't always spot one. This is your lucky day."

Vienna stared at her mother, who'd been a veritable encyclopedia as they'd explored the craggy rocks. "How do you know all this stuff?"

"I enjoy learning about subjects that interest me." Her lips curved up, and she reached over to squeeze her hand. "But I must admit, it's a pleasure to have someone to share this with."

A rare occurrence, based on her earlier comments.

Not that outgoing Bev Price would ever lack for friends in a town like Hope Harbor, where everyone seemed welcome.

Still, it wasn't like having family close by.

Another consideration to ponder as she launched her job search. If she found a new position somewhere that was a quick flight away, she could visit more often.

"I think we'd better wrap up." Her mother shaded her eyes against the dipping sun and motioned toward the westernmost edge of the tide pools, where the sea was already encroaching. "Besides, I'm getting hungry. I put a pot roast in the slow cooker this morning. I thought we'd eat in tonight."

Vienna's mouth began to water. "I love your pot roast."

"I know. I should have made it more often while you were growing up. But I believed it was important to expose you to all kinds of food."

"I remember." The tofu stew, eggplant lasagna, chickpea pancakes, and a host of ethnic dishes that had rotated through their kitchen were etched in her memory. Even eating had been an adventure in their household.

Her mother offered her a rueful smile. "Instead of making you a more daring eater, though, I drove you to French fries and chicken nuggets."

Which had only added to her childhood woes.

But that was history now.

"You'll be happy to know I've broadened my culinary horizons. I even eat sushi. But pot roast sounds wonderful tonight."

"Then let's head back before we're washed away in the tide."

As they hiked back down the beach, Mom chatting away, Vienna kept tabs on the rising tide that was making serious inroads on the sand. Maybe they ought to pick up their pace and—

"I do believe that's Kay's brother."

As her mom spoke, Vienna yanked her gaze back to the beach ahead.

In the distance, a lone figure sat on a piece of driftwood, angled slightly away from them, his focus on the horizon. Though he was a football field away, and it was impossible to see any detail in his features, his bearing was familiar.

"I think you're right."

"He must have gone for a walk. I expect he's lonely at the B&B all by himself."

"Kay lived there alone too."

"And I suspect she was also lonely. Strange how they both lost their spouses within twelve months of each other. Kay mentioned once that her husband was quite a bit older than she was, so I suppose age could have been a factor in his heart attack. But I wonder what could have happened to Matt's wife. I assume she was quite young."

"Whatever it was, it had to be tragic." And it would account for the sorrow and desolation visible deep in his eyes, if one looked close enough.

Without ever glancing their direction, he pushed himself to his feet and began trudging back down the beach, his hunched shoulders telegraphing discouragement and worry and perhaps lingering grief over whatever heartbreaking circumstances had robbed him of the woman he loved.

"And now he has to deal with his sister's B&B." Mom shook her head. "At least he has you to get him started on the road to improvement."

The perfect opening to share the decision she'd reached a couple of hours ago.

"Actually, I'm going to take your advice and offer my services for the duration of the redo. Matt texted me that Kay wants to go high-end, and I'm certain I can turn the place around if they have the budget to do what needs to be done."

"You mean you're going to stay in town for a while?" Her mother stopped and swung toward her, delight sparking in her eyes.

"Yes. If they want me to help."

"That's wonderful! But . . ." Mom's brow puckered. "Have you talked about your fee yet with Matt? I have a feeling Kay isn't rolling in cash."

"I got the same impression. I'm only going to charge if he insists, and nothing more than a nominal amount. Having a successful turnaround property on my resume is more than sufficient payment."

"You could always suggest the barter arrangement if he's uncomfortable with free." Mom continued down the beach, skirting a broken sand dollar.

"I'm debating that." Or at least the notion of proposing the idea.

"Even when the Gull has an opening, you can't live in a hotel long term. It would be too expensive. If you don't want to pursue the barter idea, stay with me."

"I can't take your bedroom, Mom. And I don't know if my back would appreciate being subjected to the couch for an extended stay. I'm not eliminating that option, but it's not ideal."

Her mother huffed out a breath. "I should have rented a two-bedroom unit."

"Just so I could stay there on occasion? Don't be silly. I'll work this out."

"If you're reluctant to bring up the barter idea, do you want me to broach it? I could stop in at the B&B with a plate of sweet potato brownies. They're gluten free, vegan, and sugar free. Very healthy—unlike the cookies I bake for the shop, though everyone in Hope Harbor loves them."

Somehow, Vienna had a feeling Matt would prefer the cookies.

But having her mother run interference for her wasn't on the menu, anyway.

"Let me see how it goes at our next meeting. I plan to call him tomorrow and schedule a time to get together. After two and a half days of research, I have enough information to lay out preliminary ideas and costs."

"I'll be happy to step in if you want me to. I'm the one who brought up the barter concept in the first place."

"I'll keep that in mind."

As they arrived at the spot where they'd crossed the dune, Vienna paused to give Matt one more perusal.

He was far up the beach now, near where the B&B was snuggled among the coniferous trees.

It would be interesting to see if he brought up the idea about her staying on-site after she offered her services for free.

If he didn't, she might yet end up on Mom's couch. While the Gull's rates were reasonable, and she could no doubt negotiate a weekly price, it would still be expensive for an extended stay. She'd have to find an alternative. But she wasn't going to push herself on Matt.

All she could do was hope he had a healthy guilt complex that would nudge him to offer her a room.

Especially if she dropped a few judicious hints.

"That should hold us for another couple of days." Andrew finished dumping the bag of ice from Lou's Bait and Tackle shop on top of the perishables in their cooler.

Paige's stomach rumbled as he secured the lid, and she sent him a sheepish look. "Sorry. The scent of cinnamon is getting to me." One hand pressed to her midsection, she motioned down Dockside Drive with the other. "It must be coming from the bakery on the next block. I passed it the day I brought the ad into town."

"You want to check it out?" Andrew closed the tailgate.

"No. Cinnamon rolls are pricey at bakeries." At the flash of remorse in his eyes, she called up a smile. No need to make him feel any worse than he already did about the Spartan life they were leading. "Besides, they're loaded with calories and carbs."

He gave her a quick sweep, forehead wrinkling. "Like you have to worry about either. You need to eat more, Paige."

Yes, she did. But the stress of waiting to hear back from Matt Quinn had killed her appetite. Even the enticing aroma of cinnamon couldn't tempt her while their future hung in the balance.

"So do you. You've lost weight over the past few months. Too much." That was no exaggeration. His jeans hung slack on his lean hips, and she'd felt every rib as he'd pressed her close on Sunday.

"I'll put it back on once everything gets—" He froze. Pulled out his cell. Lost a few shades of color as he skimmed the screen. "This is it."

Heart lurching, Vienna groped for the edge of the truck and held on tight. As Andrew pressed talk and put the phone to his ear, she grasped his hand and twined her fingers with his.

"Good morning, Mr. Quinn . . . No, not at all. We're early risers . . . I understand. I'm sure returning a phone call was low on their priority list." He listened for another few moments, then released a shaky breath and nodded.

Paige closed her eyes.

Thank you, God.

"I'm glad to hear that." A subtle tremor ran through his voice. "As a matter of fact, knowing you wanted to get the job underway ASAP, I went ahead and prepared a bid. I'd be happy to drop it off for you. I'm in town and could swing by in less than fifteen minutes . . . No trouble at all. See you soon. And thank you." He ended the call, slid the phone back in his pocket, and squeezed her fingers. "We're in. As far as the bid, anyway."

"I told you the references would come through for you." She continued to hold tight to his hand as a surge of buoyancy thrummed through her. "And the bid is bare bones. He won't find anyone who will do the work for a lower price."

"But he may be able to find someone who can do it faster, despite the days we shaved off."

She stepped in front of him and wrapped her arms around his waist. Few people were about at this early hour, but she lowered her volume nonetheless. "He's going to hire you, Andrew. I know it."

One side of his mouth flexed. "Women's intuition?"

"Logic. No one will beat your price, and if necessary, we'll find a way to trim a few more days off the schedule."

"We're already stretching ourselves to the limit."

She inched closer, until his warm breath feathered her face. "We can do this. Together." She wasn't letting him get cold feet now. Not after all the hours they'd labored over this bid. Not when this could be their opportunity for a fresh start.

"If he accepts the bid."

"He will. You want me to wait in town until you're finished meeting with him? You could come back and pick me up after you're done."

"I've been thinking about that. Maybe you should come along, since the timeframe on the work is contingent on his willingness to let you help me. He may want to meet you once he realizes you're part of the deal."

"Now?" She eased back and scanned her worn jeans and faded sweatshirt in dismay. "I'm not dressed for a job interview."

"You are for a construction job." He took her hand. "Come with me, Paige." His voice rasped, and he gave her a shaky smile. "Strength in numbers and all that."

She hesitated—but only for a second. If her presence gave him moral support and helped them get this job, she'd deal with her own case of nerves.

Because if this fell through, they'd be back where they were four days ago.

Nowhere. With no light at the end of the tunnel.

"Okay." She propped up the corners of her mouth, praying her show of enthusiasm and optimism would bolster his confidence. "Let's give this our best shot." After squeezing his hand, she circled around to climb back into the truck.

But as Andrew pointed it north, the knot in her stomach coiled tighter.

For despite the assurances she'd offered him, until this job was in the bag, she wasn't going to count on dropping anchor in Hope Harbor.

12

Pulse picking up, Matt crossed the foyer in response to the summons from the doorbell.

Andrew Thompson had arrived with his bid. Hopefully one that was affordable and offered a workable timetable. Because after hearing nothing but praise from three of his former clients yesterday, he had no qualms about hiring the man.

If the bid didn't meet his parameters?

He'd have to expand his search for a contractor to Coos Bay and Bandon, losing precious time with every day that passed. Time Kay couldn't afford. She'd sunk too much of her nest egg into this up front, and if she didn't begin generating income soon, her assets would continue to dwindle.

Matt opened the door to find not only Andrew on the other side but also an unfamiliar young woman.

"Good morning." He extended his hand to Andrew. "Thanks for coming so fast after my call."

"Like I said, the bid was ready." Andrew motioned toward the woman. "This is my wife, Paige."

Matt shook hands with her too as he introduced himself, her icy fingers suggesting she had a major case of nerves.

"I brought Paige along because without her help I couldn't meet the timetable outlined in the bid. I want to be sure you're comfortable with our two-for-the-price-of-one proposal." Andrew flashed him a stiff smile.

His wife intended to help him on the job?

That was unexpected.

But if it expedited the work, why not?

"I'm open to that."

"If you have a few minutes, I can review the bid with you rather than just drop it off, in case there are any initial questions. I can also explain Paige's role."

"Sure. Come on in." He stepped back to admit them, waving toward the back of the house. "Let's talk in the kitchen. It's too cool this morning for the terrace."

They followed him to the rear of the B&B, tension radiating from both of them.

As Vienna had intuited that day at the wharf, they must be uber-stressed about their situation.

"Have a seat." He indicated the dining table off to one side. "Would you like coffee or tea?"

When both declined, he picked up his mug from the counter and took a seat. "I apologize again for the delay in getting back to you. It took a couple of calls to reach one of your references. But I heard only glowing reports from everyone. I'm more than ready to see the bid."

"The numbers and timeframe are all in here." Andrew removed several stapled pages from the manila folder he'd set on the table in front of him and handed them over. "I've itemized the items so you can adjust the scope of work if necessary to accommodate the budget."

Matt moved his mug aside and set the papers in front of him. "Let me take a quick pass and see if any immediate questions pop up. I'll give it a more thorough review later and call you if anything else comes to mind."

The room fell silent as he skimmed through the detailed, professional, and comprehensive document.

Andrew had done a stellar job.

While there was much to digest, he homed in on the two most pertinent pieces of information—timeframe and the bottom-line cost.

Timeframe popped up first.

Four weeks.

Shorter than Andrew had originally estimated, no doubt due to the assistance of his wife. Longer than was ideal, though. Kay would have to oversee the last part of the project alone, since his break from the vet practice would be up in three weeks. But if the price was right . . .

He zipped through the detailed spec sheets and flipped to the last page. Did a double take at the total-cost number near the bottom.

That couldn't be correct.

Had he misread something?

He went back to the beginning, gave the document another pass—and found his answer.

The estimates for materials were reasonable. It was the labor charge that was way out of line.

He looked over at the Thompsons, who were perched on the edges of their seats. "The labor cost is much too low for four weeks of work. Could there be a mistake here?"

"No. The number is correct." Andrew exchanged a glance with his wife. Covered the hand she'd fisted on the table with his. "I need the work, Mr. Quinn."

Paige leaned forward, posture taut. "We consider the labor for this job an investment in our future. If you're happy with the work, we hope word will spread and more jobs will come our way. We'd like to make a new start here."

If ever a couple deserved a second chance, it was these two.

Matt zeroed in on the number again.

The temptation to accept the bid as written was strong. The total was far below the budget Kay and he had put together, and it would leave a significant amount in reserve for the softer changes Vienna had recommended.

But taking advantage of other people's adversity wasn't ethical.

Neither was keeping them in limbo about the job.

He set the sheets aside and wrapped his fingers around his mug. "From what I can tell after a quick read, your bid is well within our budget. And I can live with a four-week turnaround. Where I'm running into a roadblock is the labor. While I appreciate your willingness to work for such low wages, that's not fair to you."

"Opportunity has value, and that will more than make up the difference between what I'm charging and my normal wage." Andrew kneaded the edge of the folder between his thumb and index finger. "And we put in enough to live on."

"I'm also hoping to get a job at the café in town or another restaurant nearby to supplement our income," Paige said.

She was going to work two jobs?

Given their dire straits and their commitment to building a new life, he'd have to figure out how to structure an arrangement that was fair to all of them.

"I'll tell you what. Let me give this a more careful read and talk with my sister. It's really her call. Sound fair?"

"Yes." Andrew drew in a lungful of air. "Would you like us to explain how Paige would be involved in the project?"

He picked up his coffee and leaned back. "Yes."

As the two of them clarified her role, and Andrew made it clear they would have to be on-site far beyond normal working hours in order to accomplish the four-week turnaround, the wage they were charging became less and less adequate.

Maybe he ought to offer to help with the painting part of the project. He wouldn't know where to begin with a drywall patch, but he could wield a brush. And what else did he have to do around here except walk on the beach, anyway? Besides, if he helped paint, it might speed up the job.

Definitely worth thinking about.

Matt drained the last of his coffee as the man finished. "I appreciate all the information. As far as I'm concerned, you have the job. But let me talk with my sister about the labor piece. May I call you later today?"

"Yes. That would be fine." Andrew scooted his chair back, and Paige followed suit.

Matt stood and led them to the door, following them out as they exited.

"The gardens are pretty." Paige paused to examine the beds on either side of the covered entry.

"My sister loves flowers, and they love her back." He inspected the ground, where weeds had already begun to encroach in the week since his arrival. Stifled a sigh.

One more chore to add to his to-do list. There was no money in the budget for a gardener.

"I could take care of them for you while we're on-site." Paige leaned down to examine a hydrangea flower. "I had a garden at home."

At the wistful note in her voice, Andrew slipped an arm around her waist.

Okay.

These two were getting the job, even if he had to supplement Kay's budget from his own savings to pay them what they deserved. He could always position it as a loan if she balked at an outright contribution.

"I'll mention that to Kay too. Expect to hear from me by early afternoon, unless I have trouble connecting with her."

"Thank you again for the opportunity." Andrew shook his hand.

Paige repeated the sentiment.

He remained by the front door until the truck disappeared

down the drive through the trees, then turned back toward the house.

As he entered the foyer, his cell began to vibrate. After closing the door behind him, he pulled it out and checked the screen.

This must be the day for his support crew to check in.

He put the phone to his ear. "Good morning, Vienna."

"Morning. I hope this isn't too early to call."

"Not at all. I just finished a meeting with Andrew."

"You decided to let him bid?"

"Yes. All his references were stellar. He dropped off his numbers a few minutes ago, which are much lower than I expected. I can fill you in at our next meeting."

"Speaking of that . . . are you at the B&B?"

"Yes."

"If you have a few minutes, I could swing by now. I have a ton of research to share, along with recommendations and costs."

"That would be fine. My whole day is open, and I'd like to get everything rolling here as soon as possible."

"Watch for me in twenty or thirty minutes." The line went dead.

Matt continued toward the kitchen to brew a second cup of coffee, lips curving up in anticipation of another one-on-one with Vienna.

"Something—or someone—out there is perking you up."

As Cora's observation replayed in his mind, his mouth flattened.

Despite the tingle that had zipped through his nerve endings during their meeting Sunday on the patio, he wasn't interested in anything but Vienna's business acumen.

That didn't mean he was immune to her charms, however. But awareness and attraction weren't the same thing. And he wasn't attracted. Lonely, yes. In the market for romance, no—as he'd told Cora. He'd had his chance to fill his life with love, and he'd blown it.

Twice.

Gut clenching, he gritted his teeth.

His interactions with Vienna had one purpose, and one purpose only. To help Kay. Period.

And he'd keep that priority front and center, no matter how much he might be tempted to let his guard down and crack open the door of his heart.

By the time she arrived twenty-five minutes later, he had his game plan ready. Light and easy, that's how he'd play this. Grateful but not beguiled.

He swung open the door, paying zero attention to the black leggings that showcased her spectacular legs or the soft, touchable sweater that hinted at her curves. "Welcome back to Beachview soon-to-be-something-else B&B."

"I have ideas on that score." She lifted the satchel she was toting.

"Come in." He ushered her into the foyer. "I thought we'd sit in the kitchen in case the fog descends."

Not likely, with clear blue sky stretching to the horizon, but the utilitarian, commercial-grade space was far less atmospheric than the terrace—and far less apt to engender another electrical storm.

He hoped.

Motioning to the table as they entered the room, he detoured toward the coffeepot. "Would you like a cup? Freshly brewed."

"Do you have tea, by chance?"

"We do." He retrieved the well-stocked tea caddy Kay had prepared for the guests that had been in short supply. Set it on the table. "Let me nuke you a mug of water."

While he did that, she began unpacking her satchel, and when he joined her three minutes later, there was a fat file folder to her right and her laptop was booting up.

"I don't want to overwhelm you, but I know you're on a tight timetable, so I'm going to throw a bunch of stuff at you today. First, though, I have good news. I've decided to extend my stay in town and help with the redo and rebranding. Assuming you'd like me to."

He set her mug of hot water beside the laptop and took a seat, his spirits ticking up. Maybe he was going to be able to pull off this project for Kay after all.

"A safe assumption—if we can afford you."

She waved that aside as she selected a tea bag. English Breakfast, not one of the more exotic varieties Kay stocked. "No charge. As Mom pointed out to me, this gives me an excuse to prolong my vacation and add a plum item to my resume."

He shook his head. "We can't ask you to do all this work for free."

"You're not asking. I'm offering. A successful image makeover will give me bargaining power for my next career move. That's worth its weight in gold. And I'm determined to snag a primo job." She smiled as she swirled her teabag through the water.

His gaze got stuck on the endearing dimple that dented her cheek.

Somehow he managed to shift his attention back to her animated blue eyes. "I'm sure you will." His voice roughened, and he grabbed his coffee. Took a gulp. Tried not to wince as the scalding liquid sluiced down his throat.

A beat passed as she squinted at him, but then she continued. "The real question is whether you can afford to tackle the ideas I'm going to offer. If we're too constrained budget-wise, it will be tough to do a full-scale high-end rebrand."

"We may have more capital to work with than anticipated." He filled her in on Andrew's bid and the man's plan to meet the timeframe he'd outlined.

Her forehead wrinkled. "So they're both willing to work here for a wage that isn't adequate for one person, let alone two?"

"That's the offer on the table. But I'm not comfortable taking advantage of their hard luck. I doubt the amount in the bid for labor would even cover rent."

"That may not be an issue. From the conversation I overheard that day on the wharf, I have a feeling they're living in a tent."

He blinked. "Seriously?"

"I could be wrong, but that's the impression I got from the snippet I heard."

"Do you think they've been living in a tent all the weeks they've been wandering around?"

She lifted one shoulder. "It's cheap housing if you're low on funds."

He took a more careful sip of his coffee, an idea beginning to percolate in his mind. "I wonder if they'd accept a room here for the duration of the job as a supplement to their wages."

"I like that idea. It would definitely beat living in a tent—or a hotel room, for that matter."

Only someone who was very dense would miss her broad hint. She wanted him to extend the same offer to her. And he did owe her for the work she was planning to do gratis.

He tapped a finger on the table.

Maybe he should consider it. After all, having her under his roof 24/7 with chaperones present was far less dangerous than inviting her to stay with just the two of them on-site.

Until he got buy-in from the Thompsons on his idea, though, it was safer to act oblivious.

"Living in a tent for a weekend is fine." He kept his tone conversational. "Living in a tent for weeks would get old. If Kay endorses the idea, I'll broach it to them later today."

Unless he was mistaken, a shadow of disappointment swept across her eyes as she lifted her mug and took a sip of her tea.

Understandable.

Staying here would not only be more economical for her, it would also be safer. As she'd already admitted, commuting from Bandon in the frequent fog was stressing her out. Even driving around in Hope Harbor could get dicey when the town was blanketed in mist.

Nevertheless, he had to play this smart.

She set the mug back on the table and opened the folder without making eye contact. "Did your sister have any suggestions for names?"

"No. I think she's open to recommendations. Do you have any?"

"I do. Over the past two and a half days, I solo brainstormed, researched beachy themes and local customs, did a word association exercise, and put together an online survey question to test the top three names I came up with."

"Who are you planning to survey?"

"It's already done. I know a number of influential travel bloggers from my previous job, and I tapped two of them with a large following to post the link to the question. Here are the results. I circled the winning name."

His guilt ratcheted up.

He and Kay were going to owe Vienna a huge debt.

The least he could do was offer her a free room in exchange for all her work. He ought to put his personal feelings aside and do the right thing.

But it wouldn't hurt to wait until the Thompsons weighed in on his offer, assuming Kay approved. Once he issued an invitation, he'd be on the hook to honor it.

He took the sheet she held out. "Have you been spending every waking hour on this project?"

"A fair number. But to tell you the truth, it's been fun. Much more rewarding in many ways than working on a team like I did in my prior job. I get to run the show here. With customer input, naturally." She motioned to the paper. "See what you think."

He gave the page his full attention.

The survey question was at the top of the sheet.

"If you wanted to book a secluded, romantic getaway at a small, intimate inn, which of these names would most entice you to investigate the property?"

Matt read the list of six names, homing in on the circled one that had won a far higher percentage of the vote than any of the others.

Sandcastle Inn.

How perfect was that?

"As far as I'm concerned, that's a winner."

"I think so too. Let's hope your sister concurs."

"I can almost guarantee she will. It has all the qualities you described in our last meeting. Whimsy and fairy tales and romance."

"Those are the feels it gives me too. Once we clear the name with her, we can move full speed ahead on the rebranding, beginning with a teaser campaign. I asked Mom about local resources, and she referred me to Marci Weber Garrison, the editor of the *Hope Harbor Herald*, who also has a PR business that does websites. I've already talked to her and have preliminary costs." She pulled out another piece of paper and passed it over too. "I have contacts for these sorts of services from my previous job, but I like to keep business local whenever possible."

He gave the price sheet a quick perusal. "I don't know much about website creation, but these amounts don't seem out of line. And as I said, thanks to the low rehab bid, we have more money in the budget than expected. I'll get Kay's sign-off on this today."

"Once we have that, we'll take down the current site while Marci dives into creating the new one. We'll populate it with scenic images and close-up shots at first, until the inn is rehabbed and we can get interiors. I can take the initial photos. If Andrew could give façade repairs priority, that would allow us to post exterior shots faster. We'll continue to add photos to the site as work progresses. That will build excitement and anticipation."

At her rapid-fire download, he reached behind him for the pen and notepad he kept on the counter for to-do list items. With all the information Vienna was throwing out, he'd need a script to work from when he talked to Kay. "Won't it be hard to attract guests without any reviews?"

"It could be. That's why it would be smart to offer an incentive to early guests. One suggestion is half-price rooms for the opening week. It also offers the inn a window to work out kinks before full-price guests arrive."

"I can see the logic in that."

"But there are tactics we could use to jump-start business too. I have one in particular in mind. It's more involved and will cost some bucks, but it could pay huge dividends."

"How many bucks are we talking about?"

"That depends on a number of factors. I can price it out if you're interested in the idea, see if it fits in the budget."

"Kay mentioned taking out a loan if necessary—assuming projected occupancy rates would justify that step. Do you have any data on that?"

Vienna nodded and riffled through her file. Pulled out another sheet. "I ran occupancy stats for inns on the Oregon coast in the same category as this one will be."

Of course she had.

While Bev Price came across as a bit flighty, her daughter appeared to be totally buttoned up.

She passed him the sheet. "I calculated projected profit numbers based on the occupancy rates I found. This should be a very lucrative operation."

A quick scan was all it took for him to concur. "You've convinced me. Now tell me your idea for jump-starting the business."

"Remember those travel bloggers I mentioned? They have huge followings. If they go on a trip and write a glowing blog post about their experience, bookings for the places mentioned tend to skyrocket." As she talked, energy pinged off her, and animation lit up her face.

He tried hard to focus on the business they were discussing instead of the vibrant woman across from him. Really hard. "So how do we get these bloggers to visit?"

"After the inn is ready, we invite them for a two-night stay, all expenses paid. After the soft opening would be ideal, to give us a chance to work out any glitches. We also keep them entertained while they're here."

"Entertained how?"

She smiled. "This place is loaded with activities, according to Mom. We can cram their days full if we want to. Take them to the lighthouse and Shore Acres State Park. Give them a tour of the town, with a stop in the meditation garden at St. Francis Church. Treat them to tea at the lavender farm. Set up a tour at Bayview Cranberry Farm, complete with a sample of their famous cranberry nut cake."

Mind whirling, Matt jotted furiously. "I had no idea there were that many things to do around here."

"And let's not forget the food. Travel bloggers love to write about local specialties. We should take them to Charley's for tacos and Sweet Dreams bakery for cinnamon rolls and brownies. Gourmet breakfasts, plus delicious treats and beverages in the afternoon here at the inn, are a must. Then we send them home to spread the word."

"Wow." He continued writing as fast as he could, trying to capture everything she'd said. "This is a lot to take in."

Her dimple reappeared. "Sorry if I overwhelmed you. I've been living and breathing this, so it's all front-and-center in my mind. Why don't we pause here, and I'll answer any questions you have?"

He went with the first one that popped into his head. "Tell me about the gourmet breakfasts and afternoon treats. What do you have in mind?"

"For breakfast, smoothies or a fruit plate, followed by eggs Benedict, Belgian waffles with fresh fruit, locally sourced sausages. Those sorts of entrées. And there should be home-baked muffins and pastries. Afternoon treats could be anything from a charcuterie board to tea and scones."

Matt frowned.

While Kay was a decent cook, their budget growing up had

only allowed for simple fare. But it was possible she'd upped her game in preparation for her new life here.

At least he hoped she had.

He jotted a note to ask her about that during their call later.

"I like all your ideas. I know Kay will too. I don't see any problem with the half-price soft opening from a budget standpoint, but I'm concerned about the all-expenses-paid trips. What kind of dollars are we talking about?"

"Airfare would be the biggest cost, but we could invite bloggers who live within a reasonable distance. There's one in Portland who could drive down. Once they're here, it's just food and organized sightseeing."

"Organized like with a tour guide?"

"Yes, but it doesn't have to be an official guide. As a matter of fact, it may be more charming to use locals. When I mentioned this to my mom, she rattled off several candidates, including a man who ran a successful tour business in town as a teen and is now a respected expert on area history. And she offered to lead the tour of the tide pools herself. We were down there the other night, and she blew me away with her knowledge."

"We'd still have to pay the guides, though."

"Maybe not. Mom thinks people would do it for free. Apparently if someone in Hope Harbor is in need, everyone rallies. Many of the residents have met your sister, and Mom said they'd all like to see her succeed here."

Was this place for real? No one did anything for free anymore.

Except, it seemed, in this unique little seaside town, where seagulls spooned, dolphins frolicked, and famous artists served up tacos on the wharf.

Vienna's lips curved. "I know what you're thinking. I had the same reaction. Hope Harbor reminds me of the line from *The Wizard of Oz*. We're definitely not in Kansas anymore. Or, in my case, Denver."

"All I can say is that if Kay had to buy a white elephant somewhere, I'm glad it was here." For multiple reasons. Including the skilled carpenter whose timing had been impeccable and the vivacious hotel expert across from him who'd dropped from the sky.

It was almost like a miracle, even if divine intervention had been sorely lacking in his life these past two years.

"I think she's lucky the B&B is in Hope Harbor too. Now that I've laid out my marketing ideas, shall we move on to décor?"

"That's not my forte, but I can listen and pass on information to Kay."

"You may want to pull your chair closer. This is where the laptop will come in handy. It's easier to show you what I have in mind online."

Getting close wasn't smart.

But what excuse could he offer to keep his distance?

He edged his chair over, steeling himself against the familiar, slightly floral scent emanating from her skin as she showed him countless photos related to decorating, furnishings, color schemes, and amenities.

When she wrapped up an hour or so later, he had a dozen pages of notes.

And a raging case of hormones.

"I think that's it for today, except for costs." Vienna pulled yet another sheet from her folder. "I did a rough budget for everything I'm suggesting. Bear in mind that most of these are one-time expenditures. At least until the next major redecoration, which should be far down the road. And with this investment, you'll have a world-class inn." She handed over the page.

He gave it a fast once-over, dropping down to the number at the bottom of the page.

Whoa.

That put a damper on his hormones.

Any construction savings, plus a big chunk of Kay's contingency fund, would be gone after this project.

But he couldn't disagree with any of Vienna's suggestions. If his sister wanted to create a successful high-end inn, she'd have to bite the bullet.

"I'll share this with Kay." He tried to school his features to hide his shock.

"Let me know what she says. If you'd like to give me her email, I can send her the links to the decorating references I showed you."

"That would be helpful. Photos will be far superior to my descriptions." He recited Kay's email address as Vienna entered it into her phone. "I can also set up a conference call if you like."

"Let's see what she says about the ideas and the cost first." Vienna shut down her laptop and slid it and the file folder back into her satchel. "If everything's a go, I'll take measurements and start placing orders ASAP. We should also set a firm opening date. I'd build in a few days after Andrew's finished to get all the furnishings in place." She glanced at her watch and stood. "I have a lunch date with Mom, so I should get going."

He rose and followed her to the door. "I don't know how to begin to thank you for everything you've done."

"Like I said, it's been fun. And I'll benefit from this too. Let me know what your sister says." With a farewell wave, she strode to her car, stowed her bag, and rolled down her window as the engine revved up. "Don't forget the drive will need to be repaired too. Potholes don't make a great first impression." She grinned, waggled her fingers, and drove off.

One more item to add to the repair list.

As the dust settled behind her car, he ambled back to the kitchen and picked up their empty mugs from the table, mouth flexing at the hint of peachy color on the rim of Vienna's.

Hesitated.

He ought to call Kay instead of staring at a lip-printed mug. Update her on his meetings with Andrew and Vienna and check on Cora. Then he should call Andrew and lock him in for the job.

And he would. In a minute.

But first, he sat back in his chair, set the two mugs side by side on Kay's table, and for just a moment let himself pretend that someday there could again be two mugs on *his* kitchen table.

Even if that notion was as unsubstantial as the fairy tales and dreams and fantasies Vienna had used for inspiration as she conjured up a new name for his sister's floundering inn.

13

He hadn't bitten at her not-so-subtle hint.

As she reached the end of the drive from the inn, Vienna hung a right and sighed.

Short of asking Matt outright to offer her a room, she couldn't have been any more obvious in her effort to wrangle an invitation.

But if he didn't want her living there, that was his prerogative. And with all the work that would be going on, it might end up being too disruptive anyway. The Gull would be quieter, once a room was available, as would Mom's. Plus, either of those would be sizzle free, providing a far more relaxing environment.

And she needed relaxing.

Sheesh, even today, with zero encouragement from Matt, her fingertips had been tingling during their encounter. Especially after he'd scooted his chair closer and his subtle but oh-so-masculine aftershave had invaded her senses.

She fumbled for the button on her door and lowered her window, filling her lungs with the mind-clearing salt air.

Better.

It was possible, of course, the pitiful dearth of romance in her life was the cause of said tingle. That Matt per se wasn't the source. That he'd simply been the first eligible male to enter her orbit in too long to remember.

Yes. That was a logical explanation.

And letting herself get all hot and bothered about a man who was mourning his late wife was foolish.

Resting her arm on the window well, she guided the car with one hand as she tooled toward town.

From here on out, she should stick to the task at hand and view her involvement with the inn from nothing more than a professional perspective. As a resume-enhancing project that would impress potential employers.

Besides, even if Matt had invited her to stay, the Thompsons would likely be in residence too. If their living conditions were as primitive as she suspected, they'd jump at his offer to move into the inn. Too many people bustling about could distract her from her task.

It would be much more prudent to find other accommodations.

In addition, it might be wise to suggest to Matt that Kay be her contact for the day-to-day decorating decisions. His sister was the owner, after all, and thanks to Covid, video conferencing had become a standard business practice. That would be far safer than hanging around Matt. The last thing she needed was to get carried away with crazy ideas that would send her on yet another career detour.

Not the outcome she'd intended when she'd come to Hope Harbor.

Shoring up her resolve, she finished the drive into town, zipped into a parking spot, and scanned the wharf.

No sign of Mom, but she was a tad early. And a few minutes of quiet bench-sitting while she waited would be welcome after the past couple of intense hours.

She left the car behind and strolled toward the waterline, pausing as her cell pinged with a text from Mom.

Customers showed up as I was flipping over the "Be back soon" sign. Didn't want to shut the door in their faces. Can we defer lunch for a few minutes?

She typed in an affirmative response and continued along the sidewalk that passed Charley's stand.

He lifted a hand in greeting as she approached. "Someone must be in the mood for tacos."

"Mom and I are meeting here for lunch, but she got delayed at the shop. I'll wait to order until she arrives." Vienna stopped by the serving window.

"I heard you're staying on for a while."

She stared at him.

Only Mom and Matt knew about her decision, and when would either have had the opportunity to pass on the news?

"Where did you hear that?"

He smiled. "The grapevine is alive and well in Hope Harbor. Let's just say a little bird told me."

That didn't make sense. Her news wouldn't have had time to travel through the grapevine. Unless . . . had Mom mentioned it to a customer at the shop this morning, who'd passed it on?

Before she could query him further about his source, Charley asked a question of his own.

"Bev told me you've visited the B&B and were thinking about lending a hand. Is that what prompted your extended stay?"

"Yes."

"I imagine your assistance will relieve Kay's mind. I could tell she was worried about the condition of the place whenever we talked."

"It would definitely benefit from sprucing up."

"I wonder if she's having second thoughts about buying it." The taco chef rested his forearms on the serving counter and leaned down, bringing him closer to eye level.

"Could be. Buyer's remorse isn't uncommon." Especially if you got stuck with a lemon.

"That's true. Sometimes we see something that looks appealing and put all our efforts and resources into getting it, only to have the reality turn out to be less than we expected."

Kind of like her career.

Not that she'd ever admit that to anyone.

But the truth was, now that she'd been away from it for going on three weeks, the job seemed less and less worth the slavish dedication that had come at the expense of a personal life.

"I suppose we all have to learn that the hard way."

"Experience does tend to be an exceptional teacher. And that's not necessarily bad, as long as we take the lesson to heart and try not to repeat our mistakes."

Vienna shifted her purse on her shoulder.

Was he still talking about Kay? And if so, why did it feel as if his comments were meant for her?

"How goes it with your mom?" Charley continued to give her his undivided attention.

"Fine."

"Glad to hear it. I think she's been a little worried there might be a few rough patches."

"Mom told you that?" No surprise if she had. Bev Price was nothing if not outspoken.

"Not in so many words. How did she phrase it to me?" He squinted and looked toward the sky. "Ah yes. I remember. She said that when God pairs an incorrigible nonconformist with a staunch conventionalist, sparks can fly."

That sounded like Mom.

"I'm sure it wasn't hard to figure out who fell into which camp."

He smiled. "Not hard at all. I hope there haven't been many electrical storms since you arrived."

"No." Not with Mom, anyway. The vet at the inn? Different story. "She's changed since she retired from her library job and moved here."

"Is that right? How so?"

"For one thing, I think she finally accepted that I'm never going to be a daring free spirit like her."

"And what about you?"

Vienna cocked her head. "What do you mean?"

"Have you accepted that she's never going to be a staunch conventionalist?" His tone remained conversational, and his expression was open and pleasant, but the question seemed to be more than casual chitchat.

"I accepted that long ago. And over the years I've learned to tolerate Mom's idiosyncrasies."

"Mmm." A few beats passed as he regarded her. Then he straightened up, the corners of his mouth flexing northward. "There's a fine line between acceptance and tolerance, isn't there? One of the many small nuances of life that can have huge consequences."

"Yoo-hoo! I'm here!"

As her mom called out, Vienna swiveled toward Dockside Drive, processing Charley's comment.

Or had it been a criticism?

No, that wasn't Charley's style. He was more the give-people-food-for-thought type.

But *had* she accepted Mom? Had she embraced the idiosyncrasies she'd mentioned to Charley, or did she merely tolerate and endure them? Did she give Mom the impression she'd prefer to do a makeover on her, as she was doing with Sandcastle Inn, instead of celebrating who she was?

Questions worth considering—but a taco stand on the wharf wasn't the place for heavy contemplation.

Charley lifted a hand in greeting as her mother drew close. "My favorite bookseller has arrived."

"I bet you say that to all the booksellers. Oh, wait. I'm the only one in town." Mom grinned at him as she handed a flat bag across the serving counter. "Your order arrived. As long as I was coming here for lunch, I decided to save you a trip to the shop."

"Thank you. I've been waiting for this one."

"I paged through it this morning. You'd never guess a skinny volume like that would contain such heavy subject matter. I didn't know C. S. Lewis wrote a book about grief."

Charley tucked the bag under the counter. "Most people associate him with The Chronicles of Narnia. But he was prolific on a number of topics. I assume you two ladies want tacos?"

"Is there anything else on the menu?" Mom arched an eyebrow at him.

"No." His smile broadened. "And the fish of the day is halibut. Yes or no to the jalapeno?"

"Yes."

"No."

As she and her mom spoke simultaneously, Vienna shrugged. "Too hot for me."

"What happened to your more adventurous eating?" Mom gave her a wink and an elbow nudge.

"Hot and adventurous are different concepts."

"That's a fact." Charley pulled several fillets out of the cooler and went to work.

"How did it go this morning with Matt?" Mom angled toward her.

"He was receptive to all the ideas." While Charley prepared their tacos, she launched into a thorough recap of their meeting, punctuated with questions from her mother. "I think the cost shocked him, though."

Mom lowered her voice as several people converged on the taco stand and joined the queue. "Did he agree to let you work for free?"

"I gave him a convincing argument, but I'm not certain I persuaded him. I expect he'll discuss it with his sister."

"No mention of the barter idea?"

"No."

"I can bring it up again, if you like. I have all the ingredients for those brownies at home, and a neighborly visit wouldn't be out of line."

"It may be more peaceful if I stay elsewhere, Mom. I think he's going to offer his contractor a room too, and from what I gathered, work will be going on at all hours. It could be noisy there."

"You know the door's always open at my place."

"I appreciate that."

"Here you go, ladies." Charley set a large bag on the counter. "Did I overhear you say Matt has found a contractor?"

"I think he has." Vienna counted out bills and handed them over. "Did you happen to notice the young couple sitting on the bench next to mine last week, while I ate my tacos?"

"I did. Is he the man Matt is going to hire?"

"Yes. His wife will be helping him."

Charley gave a slow nod. "That should work out fine. You ladies enjoy your lunch. There's a spot over there with your name on it." He motioned to an empty bench.

"Let's grab it quick." Mom took her arm and hustled her toward it.

Vienna kept a tight grip on their lunch until they'd staked their claim. "This was lucky."

"I know. The wharf benches are prime property. An ideal place to enjoy Charley's divine tacos."

Keeping tabs on two seagulls that fluttered down to the pavement a few feet away, Vienna doled out the parcels wrapped in white paper. "Anything interesting happen at the shop today?"

"As a matter of fact, I did have a bit of excitement. I got a call this morning from a regional bookselling trade organization I joined when I opened the shop. Bev's Book Nook has been named best independent bookstore of the year."

Vienna stopped unwrapping her taco. "That's fantastic. Congratulations. Did this come out of the blue?"

"No. I knew I was in the running. But I didn't think I had a chance of winning."

"Why not?"

Mom dipped her chin and worked a stray piece of red onion back into her taco, giving the task more attention than it deserved. "My store is eclectic, as you've seen. Typical for a woman who's always marched to the beat of her own drummer." Her lips curved into a wry twist. "And aside from the gift of a wonderful daughter, I've never been rewarded for following my heart or taking the road less traveled."

Never.

By anyone.

Not her parents. Not her wonderful daughter.

As Charley's comment about the fine line between acceptance and tolerance replayed through Vienna's mind, regret bubbled up inside her.

When had she ever told Mom she was proud of her? Embraced her unique attributes instead of merely put up with them? Celebrated or praised her mother among her acquaintances? How often had she let other people's opinions undermine her gratitude for the unconditional love Mom had always offered her?

She took a slow, deep breath.

It was too late to undo all those mistakes. The past couldn't be changed. But neither did it have to be repeated.

"I think this is wonderful, Mom—and well deserved. You worked hard to create a shop that's unique and popular and welcoming. It's more than a bookstore. From everything I've seen and heard, it's become a community gathering spot. It deserves to be recognized. *You* deserve to be recognized."

The soft flush that stole over her mom's cheeks was yet another first. And another indication of the short supply of praise in her life.

"I appreciate that, sweet girl." She reached over and gave her hand a squeeze. "It means more than I can say."

Vienna squeezed back. "Tell me about the award."

Her mom complied as they ate their tacos and threw occasional tidbits to the patient gull duo cuddled nearby.

"So I asked them to ship it to me after the awards ceremony two weeks from Saturday." Her mom finished off her second taco.

"Wait." Vienna stopped eating. "You're not going to get it in person?"

"No. There's a conference in Seattle the prior week, and the awards dinner is the finale. I didn't expect to win, and closing the shop during tourist season to make a trip up there would put a dent in my revenue. So I didn't sign up."

"But I'm here now. I could take care of the shop while you're gone."

Mom hesitated . . . then shook her head. "You didn't come out here to work in my shop. Besides, it's too late. The deadline to register for the conference was weeks ago."

"Couldn't you at least go for the dinner? I bet they wouldn't say no to a winner if she was able to attend the awards program at the last minute. This is a big deal."

Mom patted her mouth with a paper napkin. "You really think I should go?"

"Absolutely."

"And you wouldn't mind watching the shop?"

"Absolutely not."

"Well, maybe I will."

"No maybe about it. You should go. I wish I could be there too."

"I believe I read somewhere that they're going to livestream the program, if you want to watch."

"You bet I do." She wiped her fingers on her napkin and took her mom's hand again. "I'm proud of you and what you created here, and I'm glad you got your dream with the bookshop."

Her mom sniffed, and a shimmer appeared in her eyes. "You know what I'm most glad about? That we're sitting here together on a bench and enjoying each other's company. This"—she lifted their linked hands—"was always my biggest dream." With one more squeeze, she released her grip. "Now let's enjoy these tacos before they get cold."

For the rest of their meal, Vienna filled her in on more details about her meeting with Matt, and by the time they parted at her car and Mom continued on to the shop, she was already thinking ahead to next steps with Sandcastle Inn.

Working on-site would be easier in many ways while she pulled all the pieces together, but it wouldn't be difficult to run back and forth as necessary once she relocated to either the Gull Motel or Mom's. And she wouldn't have to deal with the distraction or discomfort of noise and dust and construction chaos . . . and Matt. Which was good.

Because what if Kay's brother had offered her a room, she'd accepted, and he began to feel the sparks as much as she did? What if those sparks combusted?

That could wreak havoc with her career plans.

The key to finding a stellar position that met all of her criteria—including personal time—was to keep her geographic options open, not limit them to a single market.

Like San Francisco.

So as she worked on the inn project, she'd consult with Matt by phone and email as much as possible to keep in-person contact to a minimum. She'd also confine her on-site visits to working hours when Andrew and his wife would be roaming around the inn rather than sequestered in their room.

That was her plan—and as long as she stuck to it, she ought to be safe.

14

Matt yanked a weed from one of the gardens that flanked the front door of the inn and added it to the growing pile in the bucket beside him.

Tempted as he was to let Paige take on this job too, she'd have her hands full helping Andrew at the inn and waiting tables. And it didn't take any special skill to pull weeds. Only elbow grease and sturdy knees.

As he reached for another interloper hiding among the hydrangeas, his cell began to vibrate.

He wiped his palms on his jeans and pulled it out.

Kay.

Finally.

He stood, pressed talk, and put the phone to his ear. "Is Cora okay? All of my calls this afternoon rolled to voicemail."

"She's doing fantastic. I just noticed the three missed calls. It can be hard to get a signal in the hospital, and I—"

A loud crash drowned out her words.

Matt frowned, tracking the progress of a pelican cruising by overhead. "I missed the last part. What was that noise?"

"I came down to the cafeteria for lunch, and someone dropped a full tray of plates. Let me try to find a quieter place." As he waited, the background buzz of conversation gradually faded away. "Are you still with me?"

"Yes."

"I ducked into a small waiting room near the cafeteria. It's vacant at the moment, but I don't know how long that will last."

"First, tell me about Cora."

"She's up and walking. She was already halfway down the hall with an aide when I left to get lunch. The doctors think she may go home Friday, which will be better for both of us. I slept in a chair here Monday night, but Cora insisted I go back to the duplex last night."

"Smart. You won't be much help to her after she goes home if you're exhausted."

"That's what she said. I know you and I need to talk, but I may have to call you back in an hour or so. I'm meeting someone for lunch in the cafeteria. Do you remember Liz Norman?"

He ran the name through his memory. Came up blank. "No."

"I knew her in high school, but after Mom died and Liz went to college, we lost touch. Long story short, her mom is here recovering from heart surgery. I ran into her in the hall yesterday. She owns a nursery, so we talked flowers and plants. It was a welcome break from the hospital stress—not to mention all the stress back in Oregon. Anyway, we decided to have lunch together today."

"I may be able to relieve some of your Oregon-based stress. Why don't I give you the highlights now and fill in the details when you call me back after your lunch date?"

"That works."

He launched into a rapid-fire overview of both meetings.

Kay didn't say a word until he finished. "My head is spinning."

"I hear you. And that was the short version. I do need your input ASAP on several questions. Are you okay with me hiring Andrew, and do you agree we should offer him and his wife a place to stay for the duration to help make up for his low labor charge?"

"Yes. The rooms are empty anyway."

"What do you think about the name Vienna suggested?"

"I love it—and all the other ideas you rattled off. I know my bank balance will be on fumes, but if her occupancy rate information is correct, I should be able to begin replenishing the coffers fast. Do you feel confident about her research and expertise?"

"One hundred percent. She's an experienced pro."

"Then let's pull the trigger. But we should compensate her for her work. It's not fair for her to do this for free, despite the rationale she gave."

"We're on the same wavelength. Let me think about how to address that." And see if Andrew took him up on the offer to move into the inn. If Kay hadn't had an issue with the Thompsons staying there, it was doubtful she'd balk about adding another guest who was providing gratis services.

"I'll noodle on it too and call you after lunch."

"In the meantime, I'll email you the decorating links Vienna left with me. That's more your bailiwick than mine. If you have a few minutes while you're at the hospital, you can browse through them."

"Your timing is impeccable. Cora tends to doze off, and the book I'm reading isn't very compelling."

"One more question. This one about food." He told her what Vienna had said and relayed a few of the menu examples she'd offered. "How close is that to what you were planning to serve?"

For the first time in their conversation, there was a pause before she responded.

"It's fancier. I did prepare menus and test dishes at home, and the previous owners left a few favorite recipes, but nothing along the lines of eggs Benedict. And I wouldn't know where to start with a charcuterie board."

This could be a problem.

"We may have to find someone to help out in the kitchen."

"That will eat into profits—pardon the pun."

"According to Vienna, food matters to guests at upscale inns. Big time."

"Well, I can work on developing and testing higher-end menus once Cora goes home to recuperate."

But she didn't sound all that enthusiastic about the task.

Wonderful.

Another potential glitch to worry about.

"Call me later and we'll talk more." He swatted at a persistent bee. "I'll go ahead and give Andrew and Vienna a thumbs-up."

As they ended the call and he slid the cell back into his pocket, Matt propped his hands on his hips and surveyed the gardens that had quickly succumbed to weeds in Kay's absence.

Without TLC, nothing flourished. Gardens. Inns. Pets.

Hearts.

The garden and inn, he should be able to fix. And every beloved pet he treated got an abundance of TLC.

His heart was a different story.

Cora might be right about someone in Hope Harbor lifting his spirits, but it wasn't a long-term fix.

Because barring an unexpected change in plans, in three short weeks he'd be driving south to San Francisco, leaving behind the source of sunshine that had briefly brightened his shadowed heart.

While Paige stocked up on provisions in the small market at the edge of town, Andrew examined the front tire of the truck. Could be a pound or two low. He'd have to check it after it cooled down. They didn't need to add a deflated tire to their list of woes.

As he straightened up, he scanned the mint-condition 1957 Silver Thunderbird parked two spots down.

Now that was a classic. You didn't see many of those on the road anymore.

He strolled over, cataloging the distinctive features. Whitewalls on the tires, porthole windows on the sides of the white fiberglass convertible top where it dipped down in the back, tailfins, metal eyebrows over the headlights, oversized grill.

This was a car.

He leaned down and peered in the window. The T-Bird's interior was also pristine, from the seats to the steering wheel to—

"She's a beauty, isn't she?"

As a voice spoke behind him, Andrew jerked upright and pivoted.

A man of indeterminate age with a Ducks cap over a long gray ponytail strolled toward him, toting a brown sack.

Wasn't this the guy from the taco stand on the wharf?

"Charley Lopez." He extended his hand as he approached.

Yeah. It was him. That was the first name on the stand.

He returned the man's firm shake. "Andrew Thompson. Is this yours?" He motioned to the car.

"Yes." He gave the car an affectionate once-over. "Bessie and I have a long history."

As the man moved beside the car, the delicious aroma wafting from the bag activated Andrew's salivary glands. It was the same enticing smell he'd sniffed on occasion at the wharf. The one that always tempted him and Paige to splurge on an order of tacos whenever they caught a whiff of them.

But their limited food dollars went further on pasta, beans, tuna, and eggs.

He angled away from the bag, back toward the car. "She's definitely a beauty."

"She wasn't when I found her, though. She'd taken some hard knocks and was pretty battered and beat up. Most people would have written her off, but I looked inside, saw that the inner workings were sound, and decided to stick with her."

Kind of like Paige had done with him, despite all the mistakes he'd made and the mess he'd created in their lives.

"She was lucky you came along." He shoved his hands in his pockets.

"It worked both ways. I gave her a chance to shine, and she's never disappointed me. She's provided shelter in storms and taken me places I would never have gone on my own. The two of us have traveled many a memorable road together through the years." He rested a hand on the tailfin. "It makes a big difference to have a car you can count on. Removes a lot of the stress from life."

Andrew gave the T-Bird another sweep.

That was true about cars—and people.

What would he have done these past few months without Paige's constant encouragement and support, despite his efforts to shut her out? Through it all, she'd stuck by his side. Loving him. Letting him know he could count on her. Trying hard to repair his aching heart and broken spirit, as Charley had repaired Bessie.

He studied the car again.

Could there be a lesson here for him? Unlike Bessie, he'd disappointed the person who'd stood by him. Repaid her care with well-intentioned aloofness as he tried to protect her from the loser she'd married.

But maybe it was time to believe in himself again. In them. To be grateful she hadn't written him off despite the hard knocks he'd taken. To let her know he wanted to travel the road ahead with her. For always.

Another tantalizing whiff wafted his way, and his stomach rumbled.

"Sorry." Warmth crept up his neck, and he backed off a few feet.

"Don't be." Charley gave him a wide smile. "I'll take that as a compliment to my cooking. And speaking of food . . . if you haven't eaten dinner yet, would you like these?" He lifted the bag. "One of the guys in the market asked me to drop an order off on my way home, but he left early. The baby he and his wife are expecting decided to arrive ahead of schedule." He swung the bag back and forth. "If you don't take them, they'll go to waste."

Andrew hesitated. In all the weeks he and Paige had pinched

pennies, he'd never once considered taking any sort of charity or handout.

But if Charley was going to throw the tacos out anyway . . .

"Are you certain you don't want them?"

"I've eaten my fill." He held out the bag.

"Thank you." Andrew took it. "I know my wife and I will enjoy these."

"I hope so. Stop by the stand sometime when you're on the wharf. I like to stay in touch with all the townsfolk." He pulled out his keys, lifted a hand in farewell, and climbed into Bessie.

As the man pulled out of the parking lot, Paige came through the door of the market and crossed to the truck, juggling two bags of groceries.

Andrew joined her at the back and opened the tailgate, setting Charley's gift on top.

"What's that?" She deposited her bags, pulling out items that had to be iced as he reached in for the cooler.

"Tacos." He told her about his encounter with Charley.

"You mean he gave them to us?" She stared at the brown bag.

"Yeah."

"People don't do that kind of thing."

"I know, but he did. Should I have turned him down?"

"No way! I've been dying to try those since the first day we smelled them. Let's eat in the truck."

They finished stowing the food at warp speed and retook their seats in the cab, but before he could open the bag, his cell began to vibrate.

One glance at the screen, and his appetite stalled. "It's Matt Quinn. I guess he talked to his sister."

The phone buzzed again.

Paige took the bag from him. Crimped her fingers around the top. "Let's hope this is a celebration meal."

Steeling himself for whatever news the man was about to share, he punched the talk button and greeted him.

"Hi, Andrew. It took me all afternoon to connect with my sister, but she agreed that it's a go on the job."

He swallowed. Gave Paige a thumbs-up. "That's great news. When would you like us to start?"

"ASAP."

"Would tomorrow be too soon?"

"Today wouldn't be too soon—but tomorrow is fine. I do have one issue to discuss with you. Both Kay and I are uncomfortable with the low labor cost."

"Please don't be. Paige and I are fine with the number. Our needs are simple, and that amount will pay our bills until we get established."

"Nevertheless, we want to be fair. I realize you'd prefer not to increase your bid, so I have a proposal that will help salve our conscience. I know you're new to town. If you don't already have more permanent lodging, we'd like to offer you a room at the inn while the job is in progress. Of course you'd have full access to the kitchen and laundry facilities too. I'm also prepared to give you an advance on the labor if that would be helpful."

It took a moment for Andrew to digest the man's offer. "That's very generous, Mr. Quinn."

"Make it Matt."

"Let me talk to Paige. May I call you back in an hour or two?"

"No hurry on my end, but I hope you'll take us up on this. Kay and I will both feel guilty if you don't."

"I'll pass that on to Paige. Thank you again."

As they said their goodbyes and he ended the call, Paige leaned forward, brow pinched. "You didn't take any more money, did you?"

"No, but he made a counteroffer."

When he relayed it, her eyes widened.

"You mean he offered us a free place to stay in that fabulous inn?"

"It will be a construction zone while we're there, but yeah. We wouldn't have to worry about rent for a month. Or trek to public bathrooms. Or take showers in state parks. It would give us breathing space to save up money for an apartment."

She sank back against the cushions. "Is this town for real? First free food, now a free place to stay. It seems too good to be true."

"I know. But the smell from that bag is real, and the inn isn't a figment of our imagination. We've been there. I think the stars are finally beginning to align for us."

"No complaints from me about that. We're due for a break. I think we should stay there, don't you?"

"As long as you're comfortable with the arrangement."

"Anything would be an improvement over a tent, and with the long hours we'll be working, it will be more convenient for us to be on-site."

"I'll call him back after we eat our tacos. It would be a crime to let them get cold."

She dug into the bag and passed him a packet wrapped in white paper. Took one for herself. "After we settle into the inn tomorrow, I'll drive into town and check with the Myrtle Café. If our luck holds, they'll have a part-time opening for a server." She smiled. "Things are looking up, Andrew."

"Yes, they are. No thanks to me."

"What do you mean? You got the job."

"*We* got the job—and we wouldn't have known about it if you hadn't insisted on putting that ad in the bookstore." He touched her cheek. "In case I haven't told you lately, I think you're an amazing woman. I'm sorry I've been so down . . . and distant. It's just that I always wanted what was best for you, and I was beginning to think that wasn't me."

Her features softened. "It's always been you, Andrew. Please believe me about that."

"I'm beginning to. And I promise not to shut you out anymore. To be here for you, heart and soul. I appreciate how you stuck with me these past few months, and I promise you can count on me from here on out." His mouth curved up. "Like Charley counts on Bessie."

Her face went blank. "Who's Bessie?"

"Long story. I'll tell it to you sometime, but right now we have tacos to eat and a camp to pack up . . . and maybe a private celebration to have in our tent. If you're in the mood."

Her irises began to glisten. "I've been in the mood since the day we left Portland and set out on this journey."

"The journey isn't over yet."

"Doesn't matter, as long as we're together. But you know what? I think the literal journey may be over. That this is destined to be our new home." She squeezed his hand, her eyes alight with hope. "Now let's have dinner so we can move on to that celebration you mentioned."

He followed her example and dived into the best tacos he'd ever eaten.

And though the cab of a truck in the gravel parking lot of a small grocery store at the edge of a tiny town didn't have the ambiance of the famous French Laundry restaurant down the coast in California, he wouldn't trade it for a million bucks.

Because sharing it with Paige was as close to paradise as he'd ever get this side of heaven.

So going forward, he'd give this job his all, let news spread about the quality of his work, and hope nothing went awry that would sabotage the fresh start they hoped to make in this seaside town filled with goodness, generosity, and kindness.

15

Practical justifications aside, this was probably a huge mistake.

Vienna eased back on the gas pedal as she passed her mom's apartment complex, laptop on the seat beside her, her two suitcases in the trunk.

If Matt hadn't caught her in a frazzled state last night after she'd battled yet another round of fog on her drive back to Bandon, she might have mustered the resolve to decline his invitation to stay on-site as token compensation for all her work on the project.

But it wasn't too late to back out. He wouldn't care if she changed her mind. She could give Mom's couch a shot instead, see how that worked out.

Except what excuse could she use after subtly wrangling for an invitation before common sense prevailed? A sudden case of cold feet? Worries about another electrical storm? Fear?

Accurate as those were, admitting such qualms would raise all kinds of questions. Ones she couldn't answer without adding a whole new layer of awkwardness to the situation.

Flipping on her blinker as she approached the drive to the inn, she faced the truth.

She was stuck.

If staying here proved too uncomfortable, though, she could always find an excuse to leave. Too much noise. Too much dust. Lack of privacy. A change of heart about staying with Mom. Something. Anything.

But there was safety in numbers, and if she focused on the task at hand, stayed hunkered down in her room at the inn, or took her laptop to The Perfect Blend or Mom's apartment and worked there during the day should both Andrew and Paige be off-site, she ought to be able to avoid too many one-on-one encounters with Matt. Especially now that she and Kay had touched base via email to discuss decorating ideas.

She maneuvered around a pothole.

Everything should work out fine. And if it didn't, she'd vacate the premises on a trumped-up excuse.

She finished the drive and parked beside a pickup truck as the woman from the bench on the wharf appeared in the doorway of the inn, followed by Andrew. He spoke to his wife, and they approached as she set the brake.

"Nice to see you again, Andrew." She greeted him as she slid from behind the wheel.

"Likewise. Since we're all going to be roommates for a few weeks, let me introduce my wife."

Vienna shook her hand as he did so. "It's a pleasure to meet you."

The too-thin brunette returned the sentiment. "We just finished putting our stuff in our room. Can we give you a hand with your luggage?"

"Thanks, but all I have is a laptop and two suitcases. I can manage."

"Why don't you let me take one of the suitcases?"

"I can do that, Andrew." Matt appeared from around the side of the house, wiping his palms on his dirt-smudged jeans. "I heard the car pull up, and I have to show Vienna her room anyway."

"Okay. I'll see Paige off, then get back to work."

The two of them walked hand in hand to the truck.

Vienna gave Matt a sweep. "Whatever job I interrupted must be messy."

He grimaced. "Gardening. Kay has a master touch with flowers, and she kept a lid on the weeds while she was here. But they've gone rogue in her absence. I don't have any expertise at decorating or installing drywall, but I can wield a paintbrush and pluck weeds. I decided that for the remainder of my stay, my main job will be slapping on paint and keeping the jungle at bay. Standing around watching other people work doesn't sit well."

The grin he gave her turned her insides to mush.

Oh, brother.

This wasn't a promising start.

Maybe playing their encounters pert and perky would help disguise the more unruly emotions he stirred up in her.

"Far be it from me to divert you from such a worthwhile task on this bright, sunny Thursday morning. We don't want our fairy tale inn to turn into Sleeping Beauty's bramble-barricaded castle. If you'll give me directions, I'm sure I can find my assigned room."

"Nope. I'll take you up. Pop the trunk and I'll get your suitcases."

Since his offer of assistance didn't appear open to discussion, she did as he asked.

While he pulled them out, she reached back into the car for her laptop.

"The lady travels light." He circled back to her with her two carry-on-sized bags.

"I didn't plan to stay more than a couple of weeks. Funny how plans can change, right? Who knew I'd get pulled into a This Old Inn redo?"

"Having second thoughts?"

"Nope." Not about that, anyway. "I'm excited to tackle this challenge. Did Kay tell you we've been emailing?"

"I got a short text from her last night. Late. She said the two of you had touched base and that she was devouring all the links you sent."

"I figured it made sense to begin communicating with her directly, unless you want to be involved in everything."

An emotion that read as relief washed across his face. "No. I'm more equipped to discuss construction than interior decorating."

So he was fine with them keeping their distance.

That was good.

It really was.

She called up her brightest, perkiest smile. "In that case, lead me to my room, oh grungy guide."

His lips quirked. "Follow me. And watch your step."

Oh, she'd be doing a ton of that in the weeks ahead.

He guided her up the stairs and down the hall. "Your room should be the quietest spot, not that anywhere will be super quiet while the Thompsons are working. But Andrew says the walls are well-insulated, which should help. He and Paige are in the first room on the other side of the stairs. I moved into the innkeeper's quarters off the kitchen. That means we should all have plenty of space to ourselves. As I told you on the phone, though, the kitchen and laundry room are community property. Feel free to use both."

"I appreciate that, but I tend to eat bagels for breakfast and yogurt and fruit for lunch. No cooking necessary. All I need is a small spot in the fridge."

"What about dinner? I'm planning to provide the evening meal for everyone."

That was news.

"You cook?"

He hiked up one corner of his mouth. "No, but I'm excellent at picking up takeout. As I've discovered over the past few days, the food at the Myrtle is almost as tasty as homemade. Charley's tacos will also be on the menu. I understand there's a world-class pizza place up 101 too."

"There is. Mom and I ate there last Saturday. But I've been having dinner with her every night and will probably continue that for the rest of my stay. We haven't spent much time together for years, and I want to take advantage of my stay here to see her as often as possible."

"Understood. But you have a standing invitation to join us."

"Thanks."

He stopped at the last door and pushed it open with his shoulder. "Everything should be spotless. No one's been in here since the cleaning crew's last visit, other than our walk-through with Andrew. This room and the one the Thompsons are using will be the last to be rehabbed. Neither of you will have to play musical rooms until the very end, and then only one switch."

She followed him in. Near as she could recall from her whirlwind tour, this was the most spacious room in the inn, with a sliding door on one side that led to a balcony and a large window on the adjacent wall that also offered a spectacular view.

Far, far nicer accommodations than her cramped quarters at the small motel in Bandon, and a huge step up from the Gull, homey as the latter was. In fact, once the redo was complete, this would be the premier room in the inn.

"I love this space. And it has huge potential." She set her laptop on a soon-to-be-gone easy chair upholstered in a dark-green flocked fabric. The nicked headboard was also slated for banishment. At least all the mattresses were of excellent quality, based on the inspection she'd given them during her first visit. "I can visualize this once it's done in a natural palette with more contemporary furnishings."

"I'm glad one of us can." He set her suitcases at the foot of the bed. "The Thompsons moved in earlier and I've already seen Andrew roaming around with a hammer and T square. Expect the noise and dust to descend soon."

"Not a problem. I can work around him for any measurements I have to take. I can also hang out at the coffee shop in town or Mom's apartment during the day if it gets too distracting here. My aim is to stay out of everyone's way as much as possible. Kay and I should be able to handle most decisions by phone or email, so I'm not expecting to have to corner you with fabric swatches or paint chips."

"For that, you've earned my eternal gratitude. Well . . ." He wiped his palms on his jeans again. "Back to the jungle. If you need anything, don't hesitate to let me know."

"Thanks. I will."

She edged aside as he walked toward the door, a faint whiff of his aftershave tickling her nostrils and setting off a flutter in her stomach.

Closing the door behind him, she took a deep breath.

It was going to be tricky to mask her interest in the innkeeper's brother, but she'd dealt with harder challenges.

Maybe.

As long as she kept her distance as much as possible, though, this should be manageable. After all, he hadn't given any indication the attraction was mutual.

So unless that changed, she should be fine.

Andrew was never going to believe this.

Mouth bowing, Paige swung into the inn's drive and wove around the potholes, the construction supplies she'd picked up in Coos Bay rattling around in the back of the truck.

Vienna's car rounded the copse of trees ahead that hid most of the inn from view, and she edged over on the narrow drive, returning the other woman's wave as they passed.

Interesting that she was staying on the premises too. Why would she do that if she was from around here? And if she wasn't, how had she ended up getting pulled into the inn redo? Was it because she and Matt were involved? That wasn't out of the question, with all the sparks pinging between them.

Yet there was no outward indication they were a couple.

Curious—but the news she had to share took precedence over musings about the connection between their housemates.

After parking the truck, she went in search of Andrew.

She found him at the back of the inn, prying off rotted shakes.

"Hey." She crossed to him and leaned over for a kiss.

He returned it with an enthusiasm that suggested his promise to her last night to make up for lost time had been sincere.

"Mmm." She wrapped her arms around his neck and erased the distance between them. "Is Matt around?" The words were muffled against his lips.

"He's in the shower. I heard it running while I was inside getting a refill on water." He deepened the kiss for an instant before backing off. "How did it go at the Myrtle?"

"They hired me."

"For real? I didn't think a small place like that would have much turnover."

"They don't. The timing was once again providential. One of their morning shift servers was supposed to go on maternity leave in five weeks, but she had the baby early last night. They need someone to take her slot for the next three months."

"Huh. I wonder if that's the wife of the guy Charley mentioned last night. The one whose tacos we inherited."

"Could be. The important thing is I'm in. Long enough for the income to supplement our pay here and for the word to spread about your work."

"What are your hours?"

"Tuesday through Saturday, six to eleven. That will give me every afternoon to help out here on my work days."

His brow rumpled. "That's an early start. You're going to be exhausted."

"What time do you plan to clock in?"

"Matt and I agreed on eight."

She shrugged. "I can always crash for an hour in the afternoon if I get tired. Let's not look a gift horse in the mouth. This is an incredible stroke of luck." She gave him another quick kiss. No way did she want him worrying about her when they had so much to be grateful for. "Now tell me what I can do to help."

"My next chore is unloading the material you picked up from the building supply store."

"Why don't I give you a hand with the heavy supplies, then you can go back to what you were doing while I get the smaller items?"

"Did you buy a pair of work gloves, like I asked?"

"Yep. They're in the truck."

"Put them on and we'll get to work."

As they walked through the house, Paige glanced toward the innkeeper's quarters, where the faint sound of running water indicated their boss was still in the shower. And Vienna was gone. Nevertheless, she lowered her voice as she spoke. "Did Matt tell you how Vienna got involved in this project?"

"Not directly. He did say she used to have a big job with a hotel chain, and she's in town visiting her mom. That's the woman who owns the bookstore where you posted the ad."

"So why is she staying here?"

"No idea."

"Hmm." She pushed through the front door.

"What does that mean?" Andrew fell in beside her as they walked to the truck.

"Did you pick up the sizzle between them?"

"Sizzle, like in attraction?"

"Yeah."

"No. I don't think they even knew each other until she came to town to visit her mom."

"It doesn't take long for romance to happen." She smiled and shoulder-bumped him. "Look at us."

He shook his head. "I'm not seeing it." He opened the tailgate and hoisted himself up. "You just have stars in your eyes because you married the handsomest guy around."

At his eyebrow waggle, she giggled. Like she had in the pre-scandal days, when good-natured banter had been the rule between them rather than the exception. "Don't forget modest."

"That too." He winked and began working a sheet of drywall loose while she retrieved her gloves from the front seat. "But I think your imagination is working overtime about Matt. For all we know, he has a girlfriend back wherever he's from."

She waited until she had the gloves in hand to respond. "Nope. He looks too sad and lonely. You can see it in his eyes."

He squinted at her. "Not me. But you were always better at picking up nuances." He slid out the drywall. "Let's tackle this first. It's not heavy, but it's bulky."

She pulled on the gloves and caught the edge, balancing it until he jumped down and took the other end of the sheet.

As they reentered the foyer, Matt appeared in the doorway that led to the kitchen, his hair still damp. "You two aren't wasting any time."

"There's none to waste if we're going to meet the schedule we agreed on." Andrew veered toward the stairs.

"That's what Vienna said. Have you seen her?"

"She was driving out as I drove in." Paige shifted the drywall to get a clearer view of his face.

"Oh. Well, if you need a hand with anything, let me know."

They continued up the stairs juggling the drywall, Andrew in the lead as she watched Matt retreat.

Her husband might be oblivious to subtle nuances of attraction, but the expression that had flitted across Matt's face when he'd realized Vienna had left was easy to identify.

It was disappointment. No question about it.

Whether their temporary boss realized it or not, he was definitely interested in the woman who'd come to help spruce up the inn.

So perhaps, in light of all he'd done for them, they could return the favor by helping him spruce up his heart with a little romance.

As soon as she got Andrew on board with the plan.

16

Two walls down, two to go. In this room.

But there were at least a dozen more waiting.

Matt rotated his shoulders and dipped the roller back into the tray of paint recommended by Vienna and endorsed by Kay. Seashell Magic, per the label on the cans. A fancy name for off-white, as far as he was concerned. But if Vienna said it was a sound choice, who was he to argue?

Not that she'd communicated much with him in the fifteen days since she'd moved in. Heck, he hardly saw her. She was either flitting about rooms taking measurements, heading out with her laptop, or hunkered down in her room after having dinner with her mother.

But she had her finger on the pulse of everything that was happening, and the inn redo was progressing at a remarkable pace. The website would launch this weekend, and Kay was gearing up to field inquiries that came in through the form embedded in the site.

Everything was good.

He ran the roller up and down, following the stroking rhythm he'd developed after Andrew began greenlighting certain walls as ready to paint. It had taken some fast talking on his part to convince the Thompsons to let him add sweat equity to the job, but with the two of them working dawn to dusk and him at loose ends, they'd accepted his logic in the end.

Vienna appeared to be working long hours too, albeit mostly off-site. And bypassing him to deal directly with Kay did make sense. His sister was the owner, after all. He was just the stand-in.

He dipped the roller into the paint again and continued stroking Seashell Magic over the walls, adding a new luminescence to the dull surface.

Truth be told, though, he missed talking with her—despite the fact that most of the information she shared about furniture styles and color palettes and fabrics was like a foreign language.

But keeping their distance was smarter. Less risky. Because even though he wasn't in the market for romance, and even though it was too soon to get involved with another woman if he *had* been open to the idea of a new relationship, Vienna would be one huge temptation.

Far better to inhale paint fumes instead of the beguiling scent that lingered in the air around her.

He took another swipe at the wall, reworking a spot that was reluctant to accept the paint, despite all the prep Andrew had done. Or maybe his roller was running dry. He bent down to—

Ding-dong.

He paused.

Huh.

Must be the driveway guy, come early to give him a bid on the pothole repairs. Like two hours early. And with Vienna off-site as usual, and Andrew and Paige in town restocking the meager food supply they kept on hand, he was the doorman.

He set the roller back in the pan, wiped his hands on a damp rag, and jogged down the hall toward the stairs.

When the bell rang again, he picked up his pace. Someone must be anxious to see him.

He clattered down the steps and pulled the door open.

Charley stood on the other side, a 1957 T-Bird parked behind him, his face creased with concern. "I'm glad you're home, Matt. Can I persuade you to put your vet hat on for a few minutes?"

Frowning, he recalibrated from maintenance mode to medical mindset. "I'm not equipped to handle much here at the inn. What's up?"

"Have you met Eleanor Cooper?"

"No. I haven't gotten into town much. This place has been a hard taskmaster." He swept a hand over the inn.

"Eleanor is one of our longest residents. I stopped by her house with an order of tacos and found her trying to deal with an injury to her cat's paw. Her housemate is an EMT, but he's on a twenty-four-hour shift, and her usual vet in Coos Bay is on vacation. Would you mind taking a quick look at Methuselah? I could have run him to an emergency clinic or pet hospital up the coast, but you were closer."

"Sure. If you want to bring him into the kitchen, I'll grab my bag."

"Much appreciated."

While Charley returned to his car to get the patient, Matt strode toward his room, dug out the vet travel kit he always took with him on trips, and washed his hands. After pulling two clean towels from a shelf in the hall closet, he returned to the kitchen.

A slow parade was filing into the room when he reappeared, led by a woman who appeared to be in her late eighties or nineties, white hair pulled back in a soft bun, features taut as she pushed a walker. Charley took up the rear, a small satchel hooked over his shoulder, a black-and-white striped cat in his arms, one of its front paws wrapped in what appeared to be a dishtowel.

"Matt, meet Eleanor Cooper. Eleanor, this is Dr. Quinn. Kay's brother."

The older woman dipped her head in acknowledgment. "Pleased to meet you, Dr. Quinn."

"Make it Matt. I'm not in town in an official capacity. But I'll be happy to take a look at your friend here."

"Where would you like the patient?" Charley edged around Eleanor.

Matt spread a towel on the island. "This will work as a makeshift examining table."

"A word of warning." Charley carefully set the cat down. "He can be somewhat temperamental."

"Crotchety and cranky are more like it, but he's been a faithful companion for many years." Eleanor trundled up next to the island and stroked the cat.

"Tell me what happened." Matt snapped on a pair of latex gloves.

"It was all my fault." Eleanor continued to caress the tabby, lines of distress etching the corners of her mouth. "I dropped a glass in the kitchen, and before I could clean up the pieces, Methuselah decided to investigate. The next thing I knew, there was blood all over the floor. That's when Charley arrived. He managed to corral Methuselah, which wasn't hard. This poor cat has more arthritis than I do. He put pressure on the wound, but we thought it might need stitches."

"Let's take a look. Charley, would you mind assisting me?"

"Happy to lend a hand."

Matt set out his supplies, then opened the other towel and wrapped the cat in it, leaving his head and injured paw exposed. "Since Methuselah and I aren't acquainted, and he may not appreciate me poking at his sore paw, this will help keep him contained. Charley, I'd like you to hold him at the back of the neck and keep his leg in position. Like this." Matt demonstrated.

"Got it." Charley took his place.

"Eleanor, if you want to rest your hand on his hind quarters, he'll know you're close by. That would be comforting." Not so much for Methuselah, but giving the older woman a role might help calm her.

After she did as directed, he examined the pad on the foot Charley had immobilized.

"Is it bad?" Eleanor leaned in, her voice wobbly. "It bled quite a bit."

"We'll find out in a minute, but let's not worry too much yet. The pads have a lot of blood vessels, meaning minor injuries can bleed a fair amount." He cleaned the cut with gauze and examined it gently as Methuselah mewed, checking for any shards of glass that may have gotten stuck in the wound. "I don't see any debris in the cut, and it's not too deep. No call for stitches. All I have to do is treat it with antibiotic cream and bandage it."

"Thank goodness." Eleanor heaved a sigh.

Matt took care of the task with practiced efficiency. After applying a nonstick bandage, he secured it with self-adhesive vet wrap and tape. "You'll want to change the bandage every couple of days and keep the cut clean and dry."

"Luis will help me with that."

"He's her housemate." Charley scratched behind Methuselah's ear.

"Wonderful man. I'm blessed that he left Cuba behind and came into my life at a most opportune time."

"It sounds like there's a story there." Matt stripped off his gloves.

"Indeed there is. I'll tell it to you one day when we don't have an injured cat to deal with. Can we unwrap him now?" Eleanor plucked at the towel.

"Yes. Do you happen to have an E-collar at home?"

"I do. With a cat his age in the house—not to mention a human of advanced years—I have plenty of medical supplies on hand."

"Use it for about ten days. To ward off infection, he should also have an antibiotic."

"We have those too. Charley?" Eleanor motioned to the small satchel her chauffeur had carried in. "I brought everything I had at home for him in case you asked, including any medications that hadn't expired."

Charley carried the satchel over to the table and began unpacking it.

"He's a handsome fellow." Matt unwrapped the towel from around the cat.

"Yes, he is." Eleanor patted him. "We have a long history together. He can be ornery, but we understand each other."

Juggling a handful of pill bottles, Charley joined them. "Will any of these work?"

Matt scanned the labels and selected a bottle. "These will do the trick. Seven days should be sufficient, and there are more than enough in here to cover that."

"I'm very grateful, Matt." Eleanor opened her purse. "I don't know what the usual bill would be for this sort of emergency service, but—"

He stopped her with a touch to the hand. "No charge. This one's on the house."

"No." She shook her head. "I expect to pay for services rendered."

"I understand how you feel. But someone did me a favor recently, and I'd like to pay it forward. Besides, I was happy to help." He jotted his cell number on a slip of paper and handed it over. "If anything concerns you about the cut, call me."

"That's very kind of you." She took the paper, the corners of her lips flexing. "And I have a little thank-you in mind."

"Ah." Charley's eyes began to twinkle. "I believe you're in for a treat. Eleanor's fudge cake is legendary in these parts."

"You do like chocolate, don't you?" Eleanor tucked the slip in her purse.

"Doesn't everyone?"

"A man after my own heart." Her smile got bigger. "You'll accept that, won't you?"

"With pleasure." Just as the Thompsons had accepted his offer of a room. That gesture didn't compensate for their reduced-rate bid, but it had soothed his conscience. No doubt the cake would do the same for Eleanor's.

"Watch for it soon. And thank you again, young man. I'll sleep easier tonight knowing Methuselah has been treated by your skilled hands."

Charley repacked the satchel, scooped up a docile Methuselah, and turned toward Eleanor. "Ready to go?"

"Yes. We've disrupted Matt's day too much already. I expect he wants to get back to whatever he was doing before we arrived." She positioned her walker and trucked toward the foyer.

"To tell you the truth, I was happy for the interruption." He fell in behind the duo while Methuselah serenaded them with meows. "I volunteered for painting duty, and I'm discovering muscles I forgot I had."

"On the bright side, physical labor can be healthy for both body and soul." Charley grinned over his shoulder.

"The paint fumes aren't all that wonderful for the sinuses, though."

The taco artist chuckled. "I won't argue with you on that."

Matt accompanied them to the car and helped Eleanor in while Charley held Methuselah. Once the older woman was settled, Charley carefully placed the tabby in her lap and closed the door.

"Thank you again for your kindness." Charley shook his hand. "I know Eleanor is grateful. She'd be lost without that cat."

"I'm glad it wasn't anything more serious." Matt gave the car an admiring perusal. "You have a classic here. Have you had it long?"

"A number of years. Bessie's fun to drive, and she's a wonderful conversation starter. I've crossed paths with any number of special people thanks to her." He pulled out his keys. "I should get Eleanor home. Methuselah too. They've had more than their share of excitement for one day."

"I'll stop by your stand for another round of tacos for the three of us in a day or two."

"Bev told me Vienna's staying here too. I'm surprised she's turning down my tacos."

"I don't think she would be if she and Bev weren't eating dinner together every night."

"Ah. That makes sense. They have a great deal of catching up to do. Why not feed the crew at lunchtime one day so she can join in?"

"I don't think switching to lunch would help. She tends to keep herself scarce during the day."

Charley studied him. "I wonder why she would do that?"

Excellent question. Because it was getting to the point where it almost felt like she was making a concerted effort to avoid him.

"Beats me. But it's probably better anyway."

Blast.

He shouldn't have let that comment slip out. It begged too many questions.

Of course Charley asked the most pertinent one. "Why is that?"

Shifting his weight from one foot to the other, he shoved his fingers into the back pockets of his jeans and fumbled for a response that wouldn't lead to more questions. "There's constant activity at the house. If too many people are around, we could get in each other's way."

Charley offered him a gentle smile. "I've talked to many a person living alone who would be more than happy to have someone get in their way and liven up their quiet house. Ask Eleanor about that sometime. But her story had a happy ending, thanks to Luis. All because she was willing to open the door of her house and her heart to let someone new in." Charley touched the brim of his Ducks cap. "Enjoy the rest of your day. And don't let the paint fumes get to you."

He circled the car, slid behind the wheel, and drove away with a wave.

As the dust billowing behind the classic car dissipated, Matt wandered back inside to clean up his makeshift examining room.

Charley was right about the oppressiveness of a quiet, empty house that had once been filled with love and laughter.

And whatever Eleanor's story, it was wonderful that she'd found someone as a companion.

But it was doubtful she carried the baggage or grief he did. Or that she was as undeserving as he was of joy and contentment and affection. A woman who cared for a geriatric cat and made fudge cakes wasn't likely to have any skeletons in her closet that would prevent her from opening her house and her heart to someone new.

Like he did.

Quashing the familiar surge of despair that always hollowed out his stomach, he returned to the kitchen and focused on cleanup, putting away all his supplies and wiping down the surfaces with disinfectant.

When the counter was spic and span, he crossed to the table where Charley had unpacked the satchel Eleanor had brought. Halted as his gaze fell on a flat bag resting on one end.

That wasn't his.

And it hadn't been there before his unexpected visitors came.

He set his cleaning supplies down and picked it up.

The only one who'd been in this area was Charley. Could this be an item he'd taken out of the satchel and forgotten to put back in?

Matt peeked into the bag. A slim volume was tucked inside.

He withdrew it and read the title.

A Grief Observed, by C. S. Lewis.

That didn't fit with Charley's upbeat nature. He didn't seem like the type who would dwell on grief.

But who else could it belong to?

Matt opened the book. Read the first line.

"No one ever told me that grief felt so like fear."

He sucked in a breath.

That was exactly how he felt. In one pithy sentence, Lewis had captured an emotion that could only be understood by someone who'd been through the same kind of hell.

Matt flipped the book over and read the back blurb.

No wonder his grasp was spot on. Lewis had written this after the tragic death of his wife.

Book in hand, Matt pushed the cleaning supplies aside, pulled out a chair, and sat. What harm would there be in skimming through the book? Charley would soon realize he'd left it here and call, but until he did, why not see what other thoughts it had to offer?

Matt began to read, turning page after page, until the lock on the front door clicked.

Pulling himself out of the book, he twisted his wrist. Gaped at his watch.

He'd been reading for forty-five minutes?

As the voices of Andrew and Paige carried down the hall, he stood and slid the book back into the bag. Ducked into the innkeeper's quarters to stow the volume. Waited until their conversation faded away, then quietly returned to the room he'd been painting to avoid any conversation.

He picked up the roller, now stiff with drying paint.

But that was okay.

For in the slim volume Charley had left behind, he'd found refreshment for his parched soul.

And maybe, if he continued to read and absorb it, C. S. Lewis's words would provide some useful insights as he searched for a way out of the emotional wasteland he'd been living in for the past two long, lonely, agonizing years.

17

As the lyrical tinkle of wind chimes announced the arrival of the first Saturday customer at Bev's Book Nook, Vienna lowered the lid of her laptop and took a deep breath.

Hopefully the basic procedural instructions Mom had given her yesterday would be sufficient for a day and a half of work. Not that Mom had seemed in the least worried about leaving her shop in the hands of a rookie salesclerk. After the cursory briefing, she'd been more interested in enthusing about her road trip to Seattle.

But why fret? Her mom was a text away if anything went awry.

"Good morning." Vienna smiled as the twentysomething woman with triple-pierced ears and spiky, multicolor hair who was often behind the counter at The Perfect Blend entered. Bren, if her recollection of the woman's nametag was correct. "May I help you?"

"Is Bev here?"

"No. She's out of town."

"Oh." The barista didn't attempt to hide her disappointment. "She ordered a book for me, and while I was in town, I thought I'd stop by and see if it had come in."

"She didn't mention anything about it to me, but let me poke around in back. It's Bren, right?" She slid off the stool.

"Yeah. You're Bev's daughter, aren't you?"

"Yes."

"You've been at The Blend a lot the past couple of weeks."

"I know. I love the ambiance. I'm not much of a coffee drinker, but what I've sampled has been delicious. And your pastries are to die for."

"Zach's a stickler about quality."

"It shows. Give me a sec."

Vienna pushed through the swinging door into the back room, but a fast circuit of the stock on the shelving and her mother's desk didn't produce any results.

"Sorry." She returned to the shop. "I don't see anything."

"No worries. Bev usually texts me when a book arrives, so I had a feeling it wasn't here."

In that case, why had she stopped in?

The woman answered the unspoken question with her next comment.

"It must be great to have a mother like Bev."

Ah. She was here because she liked being around Mom.

No surprise there. Judging by Bren's appearance, she and Mom were kindred spirits. And if Bren's fashion idiosyncrasies weren't tolerated well by her own family, she'd found a sympathetic ear in Mom.

"She's an amazing person." Vienna slid back onto her stool.

"Also an awesome listener." Bren fiddled with the zipper pull on her jacket. "When will she be back?"

"Monday."

"I'll stop in after work."

She must really want to talk to Mom.

"If it's important, I could text her and ask her to call you."

"No. Thanks anyway." Her lips quirked up. "I just need a Bev fix. Seriously, your mom should hang out a shingle. Half the town parades through here looking for advice."

Huh.

Mom had always been gregarious and empathetic, but who

knew she'd become Dr. Phil? And why hadn't those skills helped her with her daughter and parents?

Then again, it was harder to connect with unreceptive subjects than with people who sought out your advice and counsel.

"Mom can always be counted on to offer an honest opinion." At the very least.

"That's true." Bren flicked a glance toward the cookie jar Vienna had filled earlier.

"Help yourself." She lifted the lid. "Mom baked a fresh batch last night. They've been calling to me, but I'm trying to resist. I won't be able to stop at one, and I don't want the calories."

"Thanks." Bren took a cookie with a bakery tissue and meandered down the counter to examine the jewelry in the glass display case. "Your mom is super talented. Katherine Parker is a regular customer. She wore a pair of Bev's earrings for her photo shoot for *People* and gave your mom credit."

Vienna's jaw dropped. "Katherine Parker, the actress?"

"Yep." Bren continued to examine the jewelry. "She married Zach, and now she runs Chocolate Harbor next door to the coffee shop. But she still acts too. Bev said orders skyrocketed after that article." Bren straightened. "If you talk to your mom, will you tell her I'll be by Monday?"

"Sure."

Bren disappeared out the door as Vienna digested this new piece of intel about her mother. Before she finished processing it, however, another customer entered.

Vienna switched mental gears and put her salesclerk hat back on. "May I help you?"

"I hope so." The woman joined her at the counter. "I live up in Coos Bay, but I was in here last month and put a deposit on a piece of jewelry. I wanted to pay the balance and pick up the piece, but I've misplaced my receipt. Could you check your records and see if you can find my transaction? I can give you the date and the amount I was billed."

Uh-oh.

This could be beyond her limited skill set.

"I'll be happy to try, but the owner is out of town this weekend and I'm filling in for her. Why don't you give me the information and I'll see what I can dig up?"

The woman recited it. "Don't hurry. I like browsing in this shop."

As the customer wandered off, Vienna tapped a finger on the register.

While the sales data was probably stored in Mom's point-of-sale system, instructions on how to access that hadn't been part of last night's crash course. But it was possible Mom also kept other transaction records.

Vienna retreated to the back room and booted up the PC on the desk. While she waited, she checked the shelves in back and found a box with the woman's name on it. No balance-due information attached, though.

She returned to the desk and dug out the passwords Mom had left with her in case there was an emergency. Riffled through the file drawers. All were neatly organized, but there was nothing that resembled a physical ledger.

No surprise there. Most records were kept online these days.

Once she was into the computer, she didn't have to look far to find a promising Excel document. It was on the left of the desktop, labelled "sales."

Vienna opened the spreadsheet and gave it a quick scan to get the lay of the land.

Mom kept her records by month, recording every online and in-person transaction in meticulous detail. This must be why her instructions had included not only checking customers out but keeping a list of what was sold and the amounts.

Yet the Excel document contained more data than that. Mom had typed in notes after many of the transactions. Like, "surgery coming up," "son deployed overseas," "issues with parents," "new job in offing."

No wonder her customers loved her. She cared about them as both patrons and people.

Vienna switched to the previous month, scrolled down to the date the customer had indicated, and inspected each transaction until she found a jewelry sale with a deposit that matched the amount the woman had provided. She jotted down the total and balance due.

As she prepared to stand, she skimmed the month-end totals at the bottom.

Did a double take.

Whoa.

Mom was *not* hurting for money.

Yes, there were expenses to running the shop, and book sales weren't staggering. But the amount from those sales ought to cover operating costs. It was the income from the jewelry that was mind boggling.

Bren must not have been kidding about Mom's sales skyrocketing.

Or perhaps they'd always been strong. After all, Mom had said several stores in Eugene had stocked her jewelry and that she'd had online orders even before she'd opened the shop.

Apparently the woman who'd once lived paycheck to paycheck and never cared about commercial success had developed a lucrative business and was a profitable entrepreneur in spite of herself. Based on her meticulous records, she'd also traded chaos for structure—at least in terms of finance.

Vienna shook her head.

One more Mom surprise to add to her growing list.

She picked up the slip of paper, retrieved the box, and returned to the front of the store. "I found the information. Here's the total and balance due, along with your purchase." She handed the woman the slip of paper and set the box on the counter.

"Thank you so much for your help." She withdrew her credit card as Vienna rang up the balance.

Once the woman finished the transaction and left, quiet descended. For all of five minutes.

Then a steady flow of traffic kept Vienna hopping through midafternoon.

Sheesh.

How did her mom ever carve out a few minutes to eat lunch?

By three thirty, as the wind chimes on the door signaled the departure of the last customer in the current crop, Vienna escaped to the back room to grab another bottle of water and scarf down the yogurt she'd brought for lunch. The fruit would have to wait until later.

Thank goodness she could lock the door in ninety minutes. And tomorrow would be a short afternoon shift.

Retail sales were definitely not for her, even if Mom appeared to thrive in this environment. Par for the course, though. Their interests had always been at opposite ends of the spectrum.

As she twisted the cap off the bottle and prepared to take a swig, the chimes sounded again.

Good grief.

It appeared her yogurt would remain uneaten too.

She set the water on the desk and returned to the front of the shop. Halted as the identity of the latest customer registered.

What was Matt doing here?

He seemed as surprised to see her as she was to see him, and his greeting confirmed that impression. "I didn't expect to find you here."

Pert and perky. That was her game plan.

She called up a smile. "I'm filling in for Mom." She gave him a topline about her mother's trip to Seattle. "Can I help you find a book?"

"No. I just thought I'd drop in while I was in town to pilfer a cookie. I was in the market for a sweet treat and some of the upbeat aura your mom radiated on my first visit."

So Matt had succumbed to her mother's charms too, like everyone else in town.

But why did he need to be around her upbeat aura?

Not a question she could ask.

"Sorry you got me instead."

"I'm not complaining." The corners of his mouth flexed a hair.

She squinted at him.

Was that a compliment? A come-on? A simple comment?

More likely a comeback he already regretted, given the flush creeping up his neck.

Wisest course was to let the remark pass and move on.

"I can offer you a cookie, though. Mom made them last night." She lifted the lid on the jar by the register.

After a tiny hesitation, he crossed to her.

She pulled one out with a piece of baker's tissue and held it out to him.

His fingers brushed hers as he took it, and her breath lodged in her throat.

Dang, this man could play havoc with her respiration.

Not to mention her heart.

He eased back, cookie in hand, faint furrows denting his brow. As if he was thinking about a very serious subject. Perhaps the one that had sent him in search of Mom's upbeat aura. Like his late wife? The problems with the inn, and the state of his sister's finances? The short-staffed vet practice he'd left behind in San—

"If your mom's gone, that must mean you're on your own for dinner tonight."

She blinked.

That wasn't remotely close to what she'd assumed was on his mind.

"Um . . ." She tried to get her stuck brain in gear.

Matt broke the lengthening silence. "I'm getting pizza from Frank's. Andrew and Paige love it. Why don't you join us?"

Her mouth began to water. If she'd eaten lunch, it would be much easier to resist his invitation.

But why not accept? Four people eating pizza together was

about as innocuous as you could get. And as soon as they were finished, she could escape to her room to watch Mom's awards program.

"I do like Frank's pizza."

"Then eat with us."

"Okay. I will. Thanks."

"What kind of pizza do you like?"

"I'm not picky. The one ingredient I avoid is olives. Everything else is fair game."

"No olives. Got it. What time works for you?"

"I close here at five. Why don't I bring Mom's leftover cookies for dessert—unless you already have that covered?"

"No. I keep ice cream on hand, but that's it. You don't have to bring dessert, though."

"I insist. In fact, since I'll be out anyway, would you like me to pick up the pizza too?"

"I appreciate the offer, but I'll take care of that. Why don't we plan to eat at six?"

"That'll be fine."

"See you then." He lifted his cookie, took a bite, and strolled toward the door.

As the musical chimes filled the shop, Vienna sank onto the stool behind the counter, a delicious tingle racing up her spine.

Dinner with Matt.

And Andrew and Paige too, of course.

Much more pleasant than a solitary meal at the Myrtle, or the leftover tofu-based stir fry in Mom's fridge from their dinner two nights ago that had been surprisingly tasty. Mom had suggested she eat it tonight for dinner, but it would keep another day or two.

Vienna rested her elbow on the counter and propped her chin in her palm.

When had she last shared dinner with a man? Six months ago, maybe? Yes. With the guy she'd met during the social hour after the multi-church Christmas concert. An engineer.

A date so unremarkable his name had evaporated from her memory.

That wasn't going to happen with Matt. No matter where she ended up after landing a new job, she wasn't going to forget him.

So why not enjoy tonight? Once Mom returned, the two of them would resume their nightly get-togethers for the duration of her stay. This would be her one chance to enjoy a meal with Matt, in the company of two chaperones.

It was an ideal setup.

Because what could possibly go wrong with a simple, casual, lighthearted pizza dinner?

18

Nothing could possibly go wrong with a simple pizza dinner. The niggle of apprehension in his nerve endings was unwarranted.

Nevertheless, as Matt drove back to Sandcastle Inn with the book he'd intended to return to Charley still on the seat beside him since the man hadn't been dishing up tacos today, he cracked his window to let air into his suddenly claustrophobic car.

Maybe he shouldn't have tempted fate while he was at the bookshop by asking Vienna to join them for dinner, but the invitation had popped out faster than he could stop it. And what was the harm? Andrew and Paige would be there, and sharing a pizza wasn't like lingering over a multicourse meal. If Vienna followed her pattern of keeping herself scarce, she'd chow down fast and disappear to her room.

"I wonder why she would do that?"

As Charley's musing from yesterday played back in his mind, he took a deep breath.

He could think of one reason.

The same one that made him keep *his* distance.

Namely, that the electricity between them was hard to resist and he was afraid if they interacted too much one-on-one, it might become more disruptive than it already was.

Not that Vienna would have any grounds to walk a wide circle around a buzz of attraction, as he did. She wasn't grieving a devastating loss that had left a boatload of guilt in its wake. Her reluctance would be related more to the folly of getting involved with a man who would be returning to his vet practice in the not-too-distant future while she went off to who-knew-where for the next step up on her career ladder.

Considering their circumstances, it would be foolish for either of them to allow hormones to divert them from the plans they'd laid out for their lives.

He swung into the driveway of the inn, dodging the potholes the contractor who'd come by yesterday afternoon had promised would be repaired next week. A job that would put another large dent in Kay's dwindling cash on hand.

Which had also been a motivation behind the volunteer painting gig he'd taken on that Andrew had initially resisted. The sooner they could get the inn up and running, the faster Kay could begin to replenish her resources.

As for the more immediate problem of dinner with Vienna—the invitation may have been a mistake, but despite his qualms, a meal shared by four people ought to be safe.

His illogical apprehension was much ado about nothing.

Quashing his misgivings, he parked in front of the house, next to Andrew's truck. No point pulling into the garage. He'd be leaving again to pick up pizzas in an hour and a half.

As he entered, the Thompsons were coming down the stairs.

He stopped inside the front door. "How does pizza sound tonight?"

"From Frank's?" Andrew's face lit up.

"Yes. Vienna will be joining us for dinner. Do you two want your usual supreme, or are you in the mood to mix it up?"

"The supreme is—"

"Andrew." Paige took her husband's arm and locked onto his gaze. "I thought we were going to have a beach picnic tonight. You know. We said the next warm evening, we'd take dinner down there and watch the sunset while we ate."

From the blank look he gave her, the beach picnic was news to him.

"Um . . ." Andrew scrutinized her, and some silent signal passed between them. The kind married couples sent, the message clear only to the parties involved. "Yeah. We should do the picnic." Andrew turned back to him. "Would you mind if we bail on dinner?"

They wanted to leave him in the lurch tonight of all nights?

Yeah, he minded.

But how could he tell them that without explaining why?

Besides, after all the hours they'd put in here, how could he object if they wanted a romantic dinner alone?

"No. That's fine. You two enjoy yourselves."

"We will." Paige smiled at him as she wove her fingers through Andrew's. "I hope you do too. Come on, Andrew. Let's finish up in the great room so we can run into town and get our picnic fixings." She tugged him through the foyer, toward the back of the house.

As they disappeared, Matt expelled a breath and forked his fingers through his hair.

This was a fine kettle of fish.

Short of canceling on Vienna, he was stuck. And reneging on a dinner invitation would be rude.

He'd have to suck it up, order their pizza, and do everything he could to make their dinner pleasant, polite—and impersonal.

Armed with that plan, he set out plates on the table in the utilitarian kitchen rather than on the terrace, despite the balmy weather and blue skies. Picked up the pizza. Paced in the kitchen while he waited for his solo dinner guest.

When the crunch of tires on gravel announced her arrival, he froze. Wiped his damp palms down the scuzzy jeans he'd donned in an attempt to position this as just another end-of-workday meal, even if it was Saturday.

A couple of minutes later, the knob rattled and Vienna entered.

Instead of making a beeline for her room as usual, however, she appeared in the kitchen doorway juggling a ziplock bag of cookies and her laptop. "I could smell Frank's pizza the second I opened the front door. It has a siren song."

"Try driving all the way home with it on the seat beside you."

She flashed her dimple at him. "No thanks. That would be too much temptation for me." She glanced at the single flat box on the counter as she set her offering beside it. Frowned. "Did Paige and Andrew eat theirs already?"

"No. When I got back from town they informed me they intended to have a picnic on the beach tonight. Meaning it's just you and me for pizza. What would you like to drink?"

"Um . . ." She caught her lower lip between her teeth, obviously as uncomfortable with this turn of events as he was. Unless his instincts were failing him, she'd bolt if she had half a chance.

But with their dinner sitting on the counter between them, she had to feel as stuck as he did.

Propping up the corners of his mouth, he motioned toward the fridge. "I can offer you a choice of soft drink, coffee, tea, water, or orange juice—but I doubt the latter would be compatible with pizza."

After a beat, she exhaled. "Any white soda is fine. Diet if you have it." She set her laptop case on the counter.

"Coming right up. Grab the pizza and have a seat." He waved toward the table and pivoted to get their drinks.

She chose a chair at one end of the table and began opening the box. As if she wanted to dive in, eat fast, and vamoose.

As expected.

He set her soda at her place and chose a seat at right angles to her, scooting his chair slightly farther down the table as he pulled it out.

"May I?" She indicated the pizza.

"Help yourself."

He waited until she'd taken a piece, then followed suit. "What time is the awards program you plan to watch?"

"Eight."

Two hours away.

Not an excuse she could use to cut out fast.

Without giving him an opportunity to respond, she found another reason to exit ASAP.

"I promised to call Kay, though. Text and email have sufficed until now, but a real conversation would be more efficient to deal with several questions and make a few pending decisions. We were scheduled to talk this afternoon, but it got crazy at the shop, so I texted her and switched it to tonight."

Before or after his impromptu invitation?

She didn't offer that piece of information.

"From what she's told me, the interior plans are moving along at warp speed."

"I wouldn't go quite that far." Vienna plucked a wayward mushroom off her plate. "But most of the soft goods have been ordered, along with the furniture. The website launched this morning too. Have you seen it?"

"Not yet."

"Let me show you." She wiped her fingers on a paper napkin and started to stand. As if she was glad to have an impersonal topic to talk about.

"You may want to wait until we finish the pizza. I'm not certain your keypad will appreciate tomato sauce and grease."

After a brief hesitation, she settled back into her chair. "I see your point. I monitored the site in the few spare minutes I had this afternoon, and it's already generating traffic. A few questions and comments have come in through the contact form too. Kay's fielding those."

"Where are you with the half-price soft opening and blogger promo you and I talked about?"

"Full speed ahead. Andrew says they're on track to finish a few days early, thanks to a third set of hands added to the painting staff." She took a second piece of pizza.

"I don't put in the hours they do, though. Five or six a day, tops."

"Mmm." She finished chewing a bite. "If no glitches arise, Andrew thinks he'll wrap up in less than ten days. Once he does, I'll put the interior décor in place, with Kay's assistance. We'll do the soft, half-price opening for a few days, followed by the blogger weekend at the end of July. It's too bad you won't be around to see us hit the finish line. Kay says you're scheduled to leave next Sunday, the day after she comes back."

"That's the plan. Duty calls."

"I hear you. I'll be moving on too. Once the bookings begin coming in, I'll polish up my resume to include a successful relaunch and send it out into the world. That will give me an edge on the opportunities out there."

"Your mom will miss you."

"I'll miss her too. More than I expected, in light of our history."

"Because you two had a tendency to clash?"

Her pizza slice stopped halfway to her mouth. "She told you that?"

"Uh-huh. The day I stopped in at the shop in search of the community bulletin board, after she suggested I offer you a room here in exchange for your work on the inn. She said you have very different personalities. I guess she felt like she had to explain why you weren't staying with her." It might not be wise to mention the Oscar and Felix reference.

Vienna's lips twisted. "Leave it to Mom to share our issues with the world. She's nothing if not outspoken."

"She also said you two love each other very much."

"Also true. But love doesn't always eliminate clashes. It's been more congenial on this trip, though. She's mellowed, and I've grown up."

"Sounds like a win-win."

"So far, so good. Which is nice, since it's always been just the two of us." She took a sip of soda.

Always.

That begged a follow-up question.

And given her matter-of-fact tone as she relayed that bit of information, maybe she wouldn't mind if he asked it.

Keeping his inflection casual, he took another slice of pizza, prepared to back off if she balked. "May I ask what happened to your father?"

"Never in the picture, but I know who he was. Mom was up front about that, like she is about everything. She says I have quite a few of his traits. Long story short, when she was twenty-four, she hooked up with a soldier who was stationed at a nearby military base. A few weeks later, he was deployed to the Middle East. Within a month, he was killed in action. Mom found out she was pregnant after he died."

"That had to be tough."

"Yeah. In a number of ways. I think she cared about him more than she ever admitted. Might even have married him, though she says it probably wouldn't have lasted, thanks to her independent streak. But in any case, my arrival changed everything. Another mouth to feed meant she had to make dramatic changes in her lifestyle to accommodate an unexpected daughter. She gave up being a vagabond, got a decent job, and raised me as best she could."

"You have to admire her for doing the right thing."

"I do. More and more as I get older."

"So tell me about your name. I've never met anyone called Vienna."

A distant echo of pain flared in her eyes, and Matt stopped chewing.

So much for what he'd assumed was an innocent question. Apparently she was more comfortable talking about her sometimes rocky relationship with her mom and her absent father than about her name.

Why?

Despite his curiosity, if the subject was one that caused her distress, he wasn't going to probe.

"Sorry. I seem to have touched a nerve. Can I get you another soda?"

"No thanks." She set the rest of her pizza slice down. Swiped a trailing bead of condensation off her soda can. "And no need to apologize. Few people know that my name is a sore subject."

"For what it's worth, I like it. It's unusual. And it suits you."

She gave a soft, mirthless laugh. "That's what the kids at school thought too."

"I have a feeling they didn't think that in a positive sense."

"Not even close." She wadded her napkin into her fist. "Growing up with Bev as a mother came with certain stresses. She was always different than the other kids' moms. Like, when it was her turn to provide a treat for the class, she brought a tray of international desserts instead of the usual cupcakes or cookies. She went to a global food market and got kataifi from Greece, cannoli from Italy, alfajores from South America, mini crème brûlées from France, kashata from Africa, sesame balls from China. I can remember the selection like it happened yesterday."

"Wow. That took a lot of effort."

"Tell that to a bunch of fifth graders."

"I take it they didn't appreciate her attempt to broaden their culinary horizons."

"No, and I got the brunt of their derision."

He stopped eating. "Explain that."

"Kids can be mean. Bullying wasn't as much on the radar back then, but that's what it amounted to. And that led to other problems. To compensate for being ostracized and for my lack of friends, I ate. More and more."

It was hard to believe the slender woman sharing his table had ever been overweight, but the motivation for turning to food for solace was understandable. Food could be comforting. It was also one aspect of your life you could control.

"I take it weight became an issue, and that turned into another source of ridicule."

"Bingo—and my name didn't help. Are you familiar with Vienna sausages?"

It wasn't hard to deduce where this was heading.

"Yes."

"So were my classmates. I became known as Sausage. If no one in authority was within hearing range, that's what they called me."

Living with that kind of harassment could dent the strongest ego.

"Did you tell your mother?"

She snorted. "Are you kidding? She'd have marched up to the school and had it out with the teacher and the principal. That would only have made it worse."

Yeah. It could have.

"I'm sorry, Vienna."

She lifted one stiff shoulder. "I survived. But bolstering my self-image was a long battle. By the time I got to college, I'd become anorexic. Thankfully, I had a counselor who realized what was going on and helped me work through it."

Yet scars remained.

No wonder she and Bev had a complicated relationship.

"I can see why you and your mom have clashed."

"There was blame on both sides. I was too sensitive, and she had difficulty accepting I would never be the free spirit she was." Vienna pressed her fingers against the little pile of crust crumbs she'd gathered up and deposited them on her plate. "Ironically, Mom always told me she felt like a square peg in a round hole growing up. Her parents were staid and straitlaced and discouraged her eccentric, daring streak. Yet she ended up with a daughter who felt the exact same way, despite Mom's attempts to be everything her parents hadn't been. On a happier note, though, we're finally finding our groove."

"I'm glad to hear that."

"Yeah." She summoned up a smile. "In any case, to answer the question that led to this long story, Mom named me after the city at the top of her bucket list of places to visit."

"Did she ever get there?"

"Yes. Five years ago." Vienna's brow pinched. "She asked me to go with her, but I told her I was too busy. So she went alone. I regret that in hindsight. In fact, I regret all the sacrifices I made for my job."

"The two of you could always plan a different trip together."

"True. And that may be smarter anyway. Thanks to my classmates, I have such negative feelings about Vienna that I almost did a legal name change while I was in college."

"I'm glad you didn't." When she lifted her gaze to meet his, he locked onto it. "I think it's a beautiful name. I associate it with grace and elegance and culture and charm."

The room went silent as they looked at each other. Only the faint boom of the surf pounding against the sea stacks offshore intruded, in rhythm with the sudden pounding of his heart as an emotion that was clear to read softened her features.

Yearning.

His fingers twitched as he fought the impulse to lift his hand and touch the delicate line of her cheek. Trace the soft curve of her lips. Stroke her lustrous hair.

As her sweet scent invaded his senses, crumbling the foundations of his rigid self-control, he swayed toward her and—

"I-I should go." The longing in Vienna's eyes changed to panic, and she scooted her chair back and leaped to her feet so fast it almost tipped backward. "I have to call Kay. Thanks for the pizza. It was great."

With that, she darted toward the foyer, snatching up her laptop en route.

Seconds later, her feet pounded up the stairs, followed by a quiet click that indicated she'd closed her bedroom door.

It took Matt a full five minutes to muster the strength to push himself to his feet and begin gathering up the remains of their meal.

This dinner hadn't ended anything like he'd expected.

But it had proved one thing.

Being around Vienna alone was dangerous. Their cozy twosome had given him all sorts of inappropriate ideas.

Based on her expression, she'd had a few of her own as well.

Thankfully, she'd had the sense to flee before mistakes were made that couldn't be retracted.

Of course, there was a logical explanation for what had almost happened. Loneliness, plain and simple. What else could be prompting his disconcerting thoughts and impulses?

He carried their plates to the sink, pausing as he passed the bag of cookies containing their uneaten dessert.

But he didn't need a sugar fix.

Because for one fleeting instant with Vienna tonight, he'd tasted a sweetness no high-fructose confection could come close to replicating.

And hard as he tried to deny it, he wanted more.

19

That had been a close call.

Unless she'd misread the situation.

Had she?

In the safety of her room, Vienna sank into the green flocked chair destined for a charity-based resale shop in Coos Bay.

Was it possible she'd misinterpreted Matt's intent? That he hadn't planned to kiss her?

But if a kiss *had* been on his mind, what kinds of signals had she been sending to encourage him?

Groaning, she slammed her eyelids closed and dropped her face into her hands.

Why, oh why, hadn't she declined his invitation for dinner?

And why, oh why, had she scurried away like a scared rabbit?

It was downright embarrassing.

All she'd have had to do to break the charged mood was grab a piece of pizza, stuff a bite in her mouth, and launch into a discussion about furniture deliveries or carpet samples or even the weather.

She was thirty-three, for pity's sake, not a sixteen-year-old in the throes of a crush.

How could she ever face—

The muffled, musical notes of her ringtone echoed inside her purse, and she straightened up. Pushed herself to her feet. Crossed to the bed and pulled out her phone.

It was Kay. Half an hour early.

But not early enough.

If she'd called ten minutes ago, the whole fiasco with Matt could have been averted.

She pressed the talk button and put the phone to her ear. "Hi, Kay."

"I'm sorry to call ahead of schedule, but I've been busy with Cora and may be busy again later. I thought I'd try you while I had a quick break. Is this convenient?"

"Yes. It's fine. I'm in my room. Once I boot up my laptop, we'll be good to go." She pulled it out of the case and set it on the bed.

"Are you certain you don't want me to call back later? You sound a little out of breath."

Imagine that.

"I'm fine." Or she would be, as soon as her pulse descended from the stratosphere and her lungs regained their rhythm.

"I'm glad we finally connected by phone. Email and texts have been efficient, but it's not the same as talking to someone."

"I hear you. How's your friend doing?" Not that she knew much about the woman whose surgery had prompted both Kay's trip to Boise and Matt's presence here, but it would be polite to inquire.

"Improving day by day, but recovery is a longer and slower process than either of us expected. On a more upbeat topic, I've been watching the hits on the website and fielding inquiries all day. Creating a touch of mystery about the inn appears to have been a smart strategy."

"I've popped in and out too. Now that the outside repairs are finished, I think it would be safe to give the exact location and begin promoting the half-price opening deal. We should populate the breakfast page too. Have you had a chance to put together a few sample menus or prepare any of the dishes we discussed so you could snap a few photos? You can have professional shots done after you're up and running, but the previews don't have to be at that level since the site still has an under-construction theme."

"I was hoping to do that tomorrow. I found a recipe for a sausage casserole that sounds tasty."

Casserole.

Vienna wandered over to the window that overlooked the expanse of ocean, watching the aerial display of two seagulls as she tried to formulate a diplomatic response. "I'm a casserole fan myself for quick and simple meals. But guests at the sort of high-end place we're hoping to create will want to indulge in fancier, more elaborate food at breakfast. Did you have a chance to look at the menus I sent from several popular inns?"

"Yes. To tell you the truth, they're kind of intimidating."

Hmm.

Was food going to be the weak link in their relaunch?

"I'm not much of a chef, but between the two of us we ought to be able to put together three or four menus that aren't too difficult to pull off. And since most guests will only stay a short time, we can just keep repeating the menu cycle."

Kay exhaled. "I wish I could cook like Dana."

That name rang no bells. "Who?"

"Matt's wife. She could whip up a gourmet feast without breaking a sweat. I had some Instagram-worthy dishes at their house." Kay sighed again. "Matt tried to make home-cooked meals for Grace's sake after Dana was killed, but his heart wasn't in it. He finally gave up and resorted to takeout dinners most nights."

Food dropped off her radar as Vienna processed the new information Kay had relayed.

Matt's wife had been killed? She hadn't died of an illness?

And who was Grace?

Brain buzzing, Vienna returned to the bed and sat beside her laptop. "Um . . . I think you lost me, Kay. Matt's never mentioned anyone named Grace."

A few beats ticked by.

"That's strange. I assumed, with you staying at the inn, he'd probably told you about his daughter."

A jolt ricocheted through Vienna.

Matt had a daughter?

She tightened her grip on the cell and tried for a conversational tone. "No. We don't actually see each other that much."

"Oh." More silence. "Maybe I spoke out of turn. He doesn't really talk about Grace, but I figured it would have come up somewhere along the way, with you two living under the same roof. Not that it's exactly dinner conversation."

"In general we don't eat dinner together."

"I thought he was providing the evening meal for everyone."

"Most nights I eat with my mom."

"That's a shame. I think he could use someone to talk to. I try to have meaningful conversations on the phone, but it's too easy for him to dance around hard stuff from a distance. So, back to the food. I'll work on the menus tomorrow. And I did review the choices you suggested for bedding. Can we start with the Italian company?"

That would be Frette.

Moving on autopilot, Vienna clicked on her saved link for the company.

But as they went through the final list of soft goods to order and made their selections over the forty-five-minute call, her mind was only half on that task as a parade of questions strobed through her mind.

How had Dana been killed?

Had it been an accident?

If so, had Matt been injured too?

When had it happened?

Why didn't he talk about it?

And most of all . . . where was Grace?

Uh-oh.

As Andrew paused beside the bed and read the text that had come in while he and Paige were having their picnic on the beach, his pulse picked up.

The brief message was after the one she'd sent to her father when they'd replaced their smartphones with a single burner cell months ago. A quick note to let her parents know how to reach them, if ever they wanted to connect.

They hadn't.

Until now.

And the curt "call me" directive her father had left wasn't comforting.

The shower in the attached bath shut off, and Andrew's stomach began to churn.

With all Paige had endured over the past months, she didn't need more stress.

But whatever had prompted her father's text was going to bring a boatload of it.

Guaranteed.

He sat on the edge of the bed and waited.

Five minutes later, the door clicked open and Paige appeared, smiling as she finger combed her wet hair. "The sand has been vanquished. I'm glad the wind didn't pick up until . . ." She stopped, her lips flatlining. "What's wrong?"

He rose and lifted the phone. "We got a text from your father."

The flush on her cheeks from the warm shower vanished, displaced by a sudden pallor. "What happened?"

"I don't know. He just said to call." Andrew held out the phone.

For a long moment, she remained where she was, eyeing the cell. Then she walked across the room, her gait stiff, and took it.

Her fingers were ice cold as they brushed his.

"Let's sit." He caught her hand and tugged her onto the side of the bed beside him.

"It has to be about Mom." Worry vibrated through her words. "Dad would never have texted on his own. Whatever it is must be bad."

"You don't know that until you talk to him." But she was probably right, based on the radio silence from his end after Paige defied him to marry the man she loved.

Paige lifted the phone and placed the call.

Two rings in, he answered.

"Dad? It's Paige. What's wrong?"

Andrew leaned closer to hear both sides of the conversation.

"Your mom appears to have had a stroke."

The unsugarcoated response hung in the air, stark and ominous.

Paige sucked in a breath. "How bad is it?"

"Unknown. The doctors are evaluating her. Her speech is garbled, but she kept repeating a word while we waited for the ambulance. I finally realized she was saying your name. I assume she wanted me to reach out to you."

But without his wife's prod, he wouldn't have called.

No surprise.

From what Andrew had picked up about the couple, Warren Reynolds was the one who'd decided they should cease communicating with the daughter who hadn't lived up to his expectations in terms of academic career or choice of husband, and Paige's mother had fallen in line. Perhaps more to preserve peace in her marriage than out of a desire to cut off her only child.

Distress carved grooves onto Paige's forehead. "Where is she?"

The name of the hospital Warren relayed was one of the largest in Portland.

Andrew leaned closer and spoke in her ear. "I'll drive you up. Tonight."

"Hold on a second, Dad." She muted the phone and looked over at him, her eyes conflicted. "How can we do that? We have commitments here. Matt's counting on us, and I'm too new at my job to ask for time off."

"Portland is less than five hours away. We're both off tomorrow, and you don't have to be back at the Myrtle until Tuesday morning. Worst case, you let the job go and stay up there while I come back here to finish the job."

"We need the money." Her voice had grown shakier.

"We'll make it work, Paige."

She chewed on her lower lip. "Are you really up for a middle-of-the-night road trip?"

No, he wasn't. After the long hours he'd been putting in at the inn, he fell into bed every night as if he'd been drugged.

But if Paige wanted to go to Portland, he'd get her there. Whatever it took.

"I can sleep when I get there."

"Are you sure?"

"Yes. Tell your dad we're heading out. ETA between three and four." He leaned close again to listen in.

After a brief hesitation, she relayed the information.

"It's dangerous to drive all night." Was that a thread of worry winding through her dad's words? "Where are you coming from?"

"A little town called Hope Harbor, down the Oregon coast."

"The coast roads are foggy. If you insist on coming, why don't you wait until morning? I can text you with news."

"But what if something . . . if something happens to Mom before then?" Paige's voice broke.

"Nothing's going to happen. She'll be fine. She has to be fine." His words rasped, a rare crack in the stoic front he always presented to the world.

Andrew took the phone. "We're on our way, Mr. Reynolds. I'll get Paige there safely. Please call us if there are any updates during our drive. We'll see you in a few hours." He pressed the end button. "Why don't you pack a bag for both of us while I let Matt know what's going on?" He stood and tried to pull his hand free.

She held on tight and rose, stepping close to wrap her arms around his neck. "You're the best, you know that?"

At the soft light of love in her eyes, his throat swelled. "You stole my line." He gave her a quick kiss and backed off. "I'll find Matt and make a cup of coffee to go. You want one?"

"No thanks. I'm already wired."

Too bad he couldn't tap into a smidgen of her adrenaline.

"I'll be back in five minutes."

He left her in the room, put a pod into the coffeemaker in the kitchen, and went in search of Matt.

The man was nowhere to be found.

Strange.

He checked the parking lot.

His boss's car was there, meaning he had to be close by. But where?

Rather than waste time on a further search, he pulled out his cell and punched in Matt's number.

The call rolled to voicemail.

He blew out a breath and disconnected. This wasn't the kind of news he wanted to leave in a voice message.

Maybe he could knock on Vienna's door, tell her the story, and ask her to pass it on to Matt.

Yeah. That would work.

He picked up his coffee, added a lid to the disposable cup, and went back upstairs.

Faint music came through Vienna's door, so at least she was on the premises.

He knocked, and the music ceased.

A few seconds later, she pulled the door open.

"I'm sorry to bother you, but Matt's not here and I'd rather talk to someone in person than leave a note or voicemail."

"No worries. The video presentation I was watching is over. What's up?"

He briefed her in a few succinct sentences. "Would you pass all that on to Matt tomorrow? And please let him know I'll be back on the job Tuesday at the latest and that I'll make up any time I lose on Monday."

"Don't worry about that. Family comes first. Will you tell Paige I'm sorry to hear about her mom?"

"Yes. Let Matt know he can call me if he wants to talk, and that I'll give him an update tomorrow."

"I'll take care of it. Just drive safe."

"That's my plan."

When he returned to the room, Paige was zipping her small overnight bag closed. His was also packed and ready to go. "I hope I didn't forget anything."

"If you did, we'll buy what we need in Portland. Ready to roll?"

"Yes."

He picked up their bags, and she followed him out the door, down the stairs, and into the night.

Once their bags were stowed, he slid behind the wheel of the truck and buckled up mentally as well as physically.

Because the road ahead could be rough—and unless Paige's father had had a change of heart, there wasn't going to be a warm welcome waiting for them at the end of their long, dark journey.

20

He ought to go back to the inn. It was getting late.

But he wasn't ready to turn in yet.

As the full moon disappeared behind a stray cloud and a shadow fell over the sea, Matt paused in his solitary trek down the deserted beach. A large log that had been battered by the elements and worn smooth by wind and waves beckoned, and he trudged over, sat on top, and fished out his wallet.

Hesitated.

The moon peeked out of its hiding place, casting a silver light on the scene, and he swallowed. After wiping his palm on his jeans, he worked his finger into the spot behind his driver's license and withdrew the laminated photo buried there.

Bracing, he angled the shot toward the lunar glow and examined the faces smiling back at him. Dana, vibrant and happy. Grace, eyes alight behind the candles of her birthday cake. Him, a hand resting on each of their shoulders and bending into the photo, sporting a carefree grin that had been absent for two long years.

It was a photo from another life, encapsulating a time of joy and fulfillment and completeness that would never come again.

Should never come again.

Vision misting, he tucked the photo back into its slot.

Vienna may have stirred up the embers of longing that were a by-product of his loneliness and grief, but he needed to extinguish them. He didn't deserve another chance at happiness.

Period.

So the sooner he left Hope Harbor and his lovely pro bono inn consultant behind, the better.

Trouble was, he had eight more days to go in a leave that had been earmarked for R&R but had instead dumped more stress in his lap. Eight days during which it would be impossible to avoid Vienna and the yearning she'd awakened in him.

As for any hopes Steve harbored that his partner would return refreshed and—

His phone began to vibrate, and he pulled it out. Skimmed the screen.

Why would Kay call him twice in one day? Had something come up in her conversation with Vienna that she wanted to discuss? Or was this about Cora?

He pressed the talk button and put the cell to his ear. "Hey, Sis. Everything okay?"

"Fine. Cora went to bed early and I was at loose ends. Are you busy?"

"Nope. Sitting on the beach."

A beat ticked by.

"It's almost nine thirty. Isn't it dark there?"

"The moon's out."

"Strange hour for a beach stroll. Everything okay on your end?"

"Fine." Hopefully she wouldn't see through that lie. "How did your chat with Vienna go?"

The slight delay in her response put a blip on his radar screen. "It was productive. We picked out bedding and a bunch of other items. Will there be room in the garage to store everything until we're ready to bring it into the inn?"

"I hope so. I started parking in the lot to accommodate all the deliveries."

"Sorry about that, but better a wet car than soggy furniture and soft goods. Vienna sounds nice."

He recalibrated at the non sequitur. "Uh-huh. You'll get to meet her in person after your Florence Nightingale gig is over."

"Yeah."

Her lack of enthusiasm about returning wasn't encouraging.

But if she wanted to sell the inn down the road, he wouldn't fight her on it. After the transformation Vienna was making, Kay should get top dollar for it.

"So how are you keeping yourself occupied when you're not helping Cora?" He rose and meandered back toward the inn. Tackling a discussion about the future of the inn would be too taxing tonight.

"There's more to do here than you might imagine. Cora tries to take on too much, so half my day is spent reining her in and keeping her entertained. But I've been getting away for a couple of hours most afternoons while she naps to visit Liz at the garden center. I've actually pitched in to help a few times. Working there has been therapeutic."

She proceeded to wax poetic about helping customers find the most suitable flowers for their gardens, caring for seedlings in the greenhouse, potting plants that were ready to be sold, and a myriad of other tasks. There was more animation and enthusiasm in her voice about her hours at the nursery than there'd ever been during their recent discussions about Sandcastle Inn.

As she wound down, he picked up his pace toward the welcoming lights of the inn in the distance. "I'm glad you're able to work in a break and get fresh air." Unless it was further undermining her resolve to be an innkeeper for the immediate future while she considered all her options.

"I've enjoyed the hours I've spent there, and Liz is shorthanded. Two people quit on her a day apart."

"It can be tough to find reliable workers these days. We lucked out with Andrew and Paige. Not to mention Vienna."

"I know. Listen . . . about Vienna."

His step slowed at her odd inflection. "What about Vienna?"

"While we were talking tonight, I mentioned . . . I mean, I assumed the two of you had shared a little background. I didn't realize she knew nothing about your past."

He stopped walking. "What did you tell her?"

"Just that Dana was a fabulous cook, and how you tried to pick up the slack after she died by making meals for . . . for Grace. I had no idea she was clueless about her."

Matt pinched the bridge of his nose. "How much did you say about Grace?"

"Nothing except her name. As soon as I realized Vienna didn't know anything, I backed off. Did you tell her what happened to Dana?"

"No. I haven't discussed my personal situation with her. Nor am I planning to."

"Why not? Locking everything up inside isn't healthy, and you won't talk to me."

"I'm doing fine, Kay."

"Then why did you take a whole month off?"

"Someone had to oversee the inn while you went to help Cora."

"Would Steve give me the same story if I talked to him?"

Matt called up his most daunting back-off tone. "Let it go, Kay."

His sister snorted. "Forget trying to intimidate me, little brother. I have a lot of years on you—and a ton of practice being both sister and mother-figure. But if you don't think Vienna would be an empathetic listener, forget I mentioned it."

"I didn't say that."

"So why not talk to her? It might be helpful to hear a third-party point of view on your issues, since you won't talk to me."

"I don't have issues."

"Says the man whose workaholic tendencies have multiplied as fast as tribbles over the past year and who hibernates in his condo when he isn't at his office."

He turned his back to the wind as a gust stirred up the sand at his feet. "How would you know any of that?"

"No matter how late I call you, you're either at the clinic checking on the four-footed patients you've kept overnight or holed up in your study at home with a medical journal."

Since that was true, denying it would be foolish.

"Fine. I work hard and I put in long hours. We all deal with grief in different ways." Despite his attempt to contain his irritation, it bubbled to the surface and spilled out. "But I didn't run out and sink my nest egg into a floundering B&B."

The instant the hurtful comment left his mouth, he cringed.

And the dead silence on the other end of the line spoke volumes about his sister's reaction.

He closed his eyes. Filled his lungs. Just because she'd hit too close to home in her assessment of him was no excuse to lash out at her.

"Kay, I'm sorry. I shouldn't have said that."

"Why not? It's true." Her voice was stiff. "At least I'm willing to admit I may have made a few mistakes while trying to deal with all of the upheaval in my life. I've also been spilling my guts to Cora. Liz too. And talking is helping me clarify my thinking about all kinds of stuff. You may want to give it a try. Now if I were you, I'd get off the beach before the tide washes you away. I'll talk to you tomorrow."

Without waiting for him to respond, she ended the call.

Stomach bottoming out, he slowly slid the cell back into his pocket.

Lambasting Kay had been a mistake. She was the only family he had, and after everything she'd sacrificed for him, he owed her compassion, not criticism.

So come tomorrow, he'd have to try to mend that fence.

As for the fence around his heart that was locking in all the emotions he didn't want to deal with—maybe Kay was right. Maybe the time had come to begin dismantling it.

Charley would no doubt offer him a sympathetic ear if he wanted a sounding board. The man radiated kindness and compassion.

Yet as Matt started forward again, toward the golden light shining from the windows of the inn, it wasn't Charley who was front and center in his mind.

It was a beautiful, caring hotel executive who'd trusted him enough to share her own darkest, deepest secrets.

Problem was, if he let his defenses down with her and opened the gate to his heart even an inch, there was a very real danger she'd slip inside and never leave.

Matt was back.

If she hadn't cracked the door to her room and been listening for his return, Vienna would have missed the faint snicker of the glass slider that led from the great room to the terrace.

She scanned her watch.

Ten o'clock.

He must have taken a long, late walk on the beach.

Prompted by the same excess energy pinging in her nerve endings, thanks to their almost-kiss? A need to clear his head? A sudden restlessness that had nothing to do with worry over his sister's purchase of an inn that was draining her financial reserves and everything to do with the hotel consultant who was a temporary occupant in said inn's premier room?

Hard to say. And further contact with him tonight hadn't been in her plans, despite the questions bouncing around in her mind after her conversation with Kay.

But she had news to share about the Thompsons, and it couldn't wait until morning.

Taking a steadying breath, she left her room behind and descended the stairs to the foyer.

A light was on in the kitchen, and she veered that direction.

Matt was rinsing out a mug at the sink, and she stopped on the threshold.

"May I interrupt for a minute?"

He swung toward her, surprise flickering in his eyes. "I didn't expect to see you again tonight."

Nor was he certain he wanted to, given the odd vibes wafting her direction.

"I won't keep you long." She passed on Andrew's message. "He said he'd be in touch tomorrow with an update."

"I'm sorry to hear about Paige's mother. I didn't realize either of them had family that close by."

"Me neither. I'm thinking they may be estranged, if her parents didn't help them out after all their troubles."

"That seems plausible." He wiped his hands on a dishcloth. "How was the livestream for your mom's award program?"

"Impressive. I'm glad she went. She was beaming, and her acceptance speech was vintage Mom. If the applause was any indication, the attendees loved it—and her."

"It's a shame you couldn't have gone."

"Someone had to keep the home fires burning. Or, in this case, man the desk at Bev's Book Nook." He didn't respond to that, so she took a step back. "Well, it's getting late. I'm going to call it a night." She began to turn away.

"I, uh, talked to Kay a few minutes ago."

She pivoted back.

Had his sister mentioned the breakfast issue, perhaps? Was that why he'd brought up their conversation?

It would be helpful if she had. The morning meal was a critical component in the inn's success, and Kay didn't seem up to the task in terms of either skills or interest. The issue had to be addressed, and it would be less awkward if her brother broached the subject.

"She and I had a productive discussion tonight. We hammered out a ton of details."

"That's what she told me." He leaned back against the counter and wrapped his fingers around the edge. "She also said she mentioned my wife and daughter."

Vienna blinked.

That had come out of left field.

And why had he shared that piece of information? Was it an invitation to ask questions? A signal he was willing to talk about private matters? A tentative reaching out to see if she was receptive to hearing his story? An indication he wanted to take their friendship to a deeper level?

"Um . . ."

As she grappled with those questions, he pushed off from the sink. "As you said, it's getting late. We should—"

"No. Wait." He must have interpreted her sudden speechlessness as a reluctance to dive into heavier subjects.

And maybe it would be wiser to back off if she didn't want to get involved with this principled man who'd come here to help his sister out of a jam while nursing his own hurts.

But it was impossible to turn away from the sorrow in the depths of his eyes.

"Yes, Kay did mention them. No details, though."

"She knows I don't talk about them much." He shoved his hands into the pockets of his jeans. "When you lose the two people who are the center of your world, it's easier to bury the pain than deal with it."

Her pulse stumbled.

Mystery of his daughter's whereabouts solved.

She wasn't with him because she had died too.

Sweet mercy.

How did a person cope with so much loss?

"I knew your wife had died. Kay told Mom. But I didn't know until tonight that you had a daughter. I can't begin to imagine how hard those losses must have been."

Bleak as his expression already was, the desolation on his face intensified. "It's even worse when the deaths are your fault."

As his confession hovered in the air between them, Vienna groped for the edge of the counter beside her.

Matt had caused the deaths of his wife and child?

No.

That wasn't computing.

Any guilt he carried had to be misplaced.

But whatever its source, it might need to be discussed and analyzed before it could be released.

"Sorry. I know that's a heavy subject to introduce." The corners of his stiff lips creaked up a hair, as if the tiny movement required supreme effort. "Kay read me the riot act tonight about keeping everything inside, and I guess her comments are still on my mind. She may be right, but it isn't fair to pull the first person to cross my path into the dark place I've been living for the past two years."

She scrutinized him.

Was that the truth? Would he have opened up to anyone who'd happened to walk into the room tonight? Or was it possible he felt the same connection between them that she did, and he was too scared to admit it?

Only one way to find out.

"Are you saying you'd have brought this up to Andrew or Paige if they'd come in instead of me?"

As he pondered her quiet question, his eyes reflected a serious internal debate.

She waited while he wrestled with her question.

At last, shoulders slumping, he slowly shook his head. "No. I haven't even talked about it in detail with my partner at our practice, and we've been friends since vet school. Kay only knows pieces of it. I brought it up to you because you shared your story with me, and . . . and I trust you."

Pressure built in her throat as the significance of his admission registered.

He trusted her not just with his story but with his heart.

Those may not have been the words he'd used, but that was what he'd meant.

She took a step toward him. "Thank you for that. And if you'd like to talk about your wife and daughter, I've been told I'm a decent listener. Sometimes having a third-party point of view can help bring clarity."

"That's what Kay said."

"Has she ever given you bad advice?"

"Not about personal matters. She's less savvy on the business side, as this indicates." He swept a hand over the inn. "But it's late, and the story isn't pretty."

Was he giving her an out, or getting cold feet?

If he wanted to bail, fine. But she wasn't going to be the one to back down.

"I stayed up far later than this working on projects for my previous job. Besides, I can take a nap tomorrow after services if I'm tired. And I'm not afraid of ugly."

After a moment, he slowly removed his hands from his pockets and motioned to the table. "Do you want to sit for a few minutes?"

In silence, she walked over and claimed the seat she'd occupied during their pizza dinner.

He joined her, stopping beside the chair he'd sat in earlier. "Would you like a cup of coffee?"

"No thanks. If I ingest any caffeine at this hour, I'll be wired all night." As if she wouldn't be anyway, after this late evening tête-à-tête.

He pulled out his chair. Sat. Knitted his fingers together on the table and stared at his knuckles. "I have no idea where to start."

Probably not, if he'd kept all of his guilt and pain and recriminations bottled inside for months—or years.

"Why don't you tell me why you decided to take a whole month off from your vet practice?" If he'd realized time away would be beneficial, talking about the reasons why should get him on track to discuss—

"I didn't. Steve, my partner, more or less twisted my arm. He suggested six weeks. We compromised on four."

So the break hadn't been initiated by Matt.

That put a whole different spin on his state of mind when he'd arrived in Hope Harbor.

She'd have to approach this from another direction.

"Why did your partner push you to take a leave?"

"I hadn't been sleeping, and it showed. Plus, I made a couple of minor treatment mistakes that fortunately didn't harm either patient. Steve thought some R&R would be helpful."

"Instead, you got This Old Inn on steroids."

"At least it's kept my mind occupied on things other than grief and guilt."

"Which may not be the most effective way to deal with either."

"So Kay and Steve have told me."

She studied him. "The grief I get. Not the guilt."

His Adam's apple bobbed. "This is where it gets uglier."

"Why don't you give me a bit of history? Tell me how you and your wife met?" Perhaps opening with backstory would ease him into the harder subject matter.

"Okay." He exhaled. "I was in vet school, and she was getting her master's degree in cybersecurity. We clicked right away, but we didn't get married until I was established in my practice. Dana landed a great job with an international firm, but after we had Grace, she became an independent contractor and worked out of the home. We had a perfect life." A muscle ticced in his jaw. "Then, in the blink of an eye, it was gone. All because of my mistakes."

Silence fell in the room, broken only by a jarring clatter as the icemaker in the fridge dumped a new batch of cubes into the bin.

Vienna waited, giving him space to collect his thoughts—and his courage.

Yet whatever mistakes he was about to claim he'd made, she

had a feeling he was being far harder on himself than anyone else would be.

When he at last picked up the story, a quiver ran through his voice. "Dana liked to run every morning. I'd watch Grace while she was gone. One Saturday two years ago, I wanted to sleep as late as I could. I had to be at the office by nine, but I'd been out the night before at a bachelor party for a vet school friend. To accommodate me, Dana started her run later than usual, and she cut it short by taking a different route home. According to the witness, a passing car swerved to avoid a squirrel that darted across the street, and the driver lost control. He hit Dana. She died two days later from her head injuries."

The pizza left in Vienna's stomach from their dinner began to churn. "I'm so sorry." Lame, but what could you say to a person who'd lost his spouse in such a senseless, heartbreaking tragedy—and who blamed his selfishness for the circumstances that led to her death?

"So am I." He loosened his fingers and flexed his white knuckles. "Grace is the only thing that kept me going, and she became the focus of my world. Until the nightmare repeated itself a year later." His voice rasped, and he swiped the back of his hand across his eyes. "I may have to stop here."

She reached out and covered the fist he'd clenched on the table with her fingers, gentling her tone. "If you want to pick this up another time, that's fine. I'm available. If you want to take a few minutes to regroup, I'll wait. You decide. But it may be easier to continue now than return to this later."

His gaze dipped to their joined hands.

For a moment, she thought he might pull away.

He didn't.

"I'll try to finish the story." He drew a ragged breath. "After a few months, Grace began to bounce back. She was excited about her fifth birthday, and I promised her we'd spend the whole day together. Morning at the zoo, afternoon at the beach, dinner at a kid-friendly place that sent every child home with a helium balloon. We had a fantastic day. The happiest since Dana died." His voice choked. "Sorry."

"Breaking down after trauma is allowed." The temptation to give him a hug was strong, but she settled for squeezing his hand.

Half a minute later, he continued. "After dinner, we went out to the car. I leaned in to put our leftovers on the backseat. Somehow, the balloon got away from Grace and she dashed after it. Right into the path of an oncoming car."

Shock reverberated through her.

Dear God.

Both his wife and daughter had perished in a tragic car accident.

"If I live to be a hundred, I'll never forget that terrible screech of brakes, or her little body lying s-so still on the pavement." He rubbed his forehead, as if he were trying to erase the memory. "I only let go of her hand for a few seconds, but that was all it took. I should have buckled her in first instead of dealing with the food. She didn't even make it t-to the hospital."

Vienna's vision began to swim.

Grace had died on her fifth birthday—and Matt blamed himself, just as he'd shouldered the culpability for his wife's death.

How did a man go on with that kind of grief and guilt lodged in his soul?

And what could she say in the face of such soul-deep sorrow and anguish?

But maybe words weren't what was needed here. Maybe it was time for the hug she'd been tempted to give minutes ago.

With a squeeze of his fingers, she slid out of her chair. "Let me give you a hug. Please."

He looked up, his eyes awash with such misery and self-recrimination her heart ached. As the silence lengthened, she thought he was going to refuse—but all at once, he pushed back his chair and stood.

When she extended her arms, he stepped in and pulled her close, tremors rippling through him, his respiration choppy, his pulse beneath her ear pounding as hard as if he'd run a race.

How many minutes passed, she had no idea. But she'd stay as long as he needed an anchor to cling to after the retelling of his harrowing tale.

At last he eased back. "Thanks for that. And for listening tonight."

"A sympathetic ear can make a huge difference. I don't know how I would have managed if I hadn't connected to that counselor in college."

His gaze locked onto hers. "Connections can be priceless." After a few charged seconds, he retreated a step. "Are you going to church tomorrow?"

She blinked.

That was an abrupt change of subject.

But it was understandable. Everyone had their emotional limits, and it was clear Matt had reached his.

"Yes. I am."

"Would you like to ride together and conserve gas rather than take two cars? I was planning to attend the early service and then dive into painting again."

His tone was measured, but could his suggestion be motivated by more than practical considerations? By stronger feelings?

No. Of course not. The man had spent the last few minutes telling her about his grief and loss over the woman and child he'd loved. His offer was pragmatic, perhaps prompted in part by gratitude for her willingness to listen as he unburdened his soul. There was nothing personal in the invitation.

Nor did she want there to be. Not here. Not now. The time and the place were all wrong for romance, for both of them.

So why not accept? The drive was short, and—

"Don't feel pressured. If you want to sleep in tomorrow and go to the later service, I understand. You've been working hard for days on end without a break."

She must have waited too long to respond if he felt compelled to give her an excuse to decline.

"I was just thinking over logistics and my plans for tomorrow. I'd appreciate a ride into town."

They agreed on a departure time, and after wishing him good-night, she left the kitchen and climbed the stairs to her room.

Yet late as it was, sleep was the furthest thing from her mind.

She could get a jump on gathering up all the personal items in the room, expend some energy until she got tired enough to climb into bed. Now that Andrew was finished with all the touch-ups in the other bedrooms and ready to start on the two that were occupied, she was scheduled to play musical rooms this weekend.

But with him and Paige in Portland, he likely wouldn't dive into her current space until Tuesday, at the earliest. There was no rush. What she didn't finish tonight, she could do tomorrow between church and opening the bookshop in the afternoon.

And while she was in the house of God, it couldn't hurt to ask for a bit of insight about how a handsome, hurting veterinarian was supposed to fit into her topsy-turvy world that had taken so many unexpected turns of late.

21

Dad looked so old.

As Paige paused in the doorway of the hospital waiting room, deserted except for the man pouring a cup of coffee from a carafe, her stomach knotted.

In the six years since she'd said goodbye to her parents and walked out the door of the home where she'd grown up, bag in hand, to marry Andrew, her father's hair had gone more gray than brown. Lines bracketed the corners of his mouth, and creases scored his forehead.

"Do you want me to wait in the hall while you talk to him?" Andrew spoke close to her ear, pitching his voice low.

"No." She tightened her grip on his hand. "We're a package deal. I made that clear when I left. If Dad didn't want you here, he wouldn't have let me know about Mom. He knew you'd come with me."

"I think it's your mom who wants you here."

"Tough. You go where I go. And if he—"

Her father turned toward them, his hand jerking as his gaze collided with hers.

She braced. "Hi, Dad."

For an infinitesimal second, his eyes softened. As if he was glad to see her. But then he dipped his head and peered at his watch in the subdued pre-dawn lighting. "You got here faster than I expected."

"There wasn't much traffic to slow us down. How's Mom?"

"Sleeping. Her doctor is going to stop by in the morning to discuss next steps. They've decided she had a TIA." He didn't acknowledge Andrew or make any attempt to close the distance between them.

That hurt.

But she could deal with his welcome—or lack of welcome—later. Right now she wanted information.

"What's a TIA?"

"Transient ischemic attack. Presents like a stroke but resolves fast with no lasting damage. Sometimes it's called a mini stroke."

"So she's going to be okay?" It was hard to think at three thirty in the morning after nothing but an hour or two of fitful sleep while wedged into the corner of the truck.

"TBD. The symptoms are clearing up, but her blood pressure spiked in the ER and they're waiting on test results."

"Can I see her?"

"Yes. But only two visitors are allowed at a time, and I'm already pushing it by being here after visiting hours." He flicked a glance at Andrew, finally acknowledging his presence.

Andrew angled toward her and motioned to a couch on the far side of the waiting room, weariness etching his features. "I'll grab a few z's here while you stay with your mom." He gave her a quick squeeze, then directed his next comment to her father, who remained several feet away. "If I can do anything to help, sir, let me know."

If he'd won an Olympic gold medal, Paige couldn't have been more proud of him. Instead of responding to her father's rudeness in kind, he'd chosen the higher road.

For a moment, her dad seemed taken aback. Whether by Andrew's offer to help or by his graciousness and civility despite the less-than-courteous reception he'd been given, it was hard to say.

Then he motioned toward the hall and addressed her. "I'll take you to her room. It's to the left."

He waited. As if he didn't want to pass by and get too close to Andrew.

Quashing a surge of anger, Paige rose on tiptoe and pressed a kiss to her husband's cheek. "I'll be back to check on you in a little while."

"Focus on your mom. I'll be fine. I'd like to clock some sleep before this place gets busier and noisier, anyway." After touching her face, he crossed to the couch.

Only then did her father take a step closer. "Let's go. I don't want to be gone too long."

Without responding, she exited the waiting room.

Dad fell in beside her as she walked down the hall, but she didn't look at him. Nor did she speak. If the doctor was coming in the morning for a conference, she could ask him or her all of her questions. She was here because Mom had asked for her. If Dad didn't want to communicate, so be it. She wasn't going to try to engage him in conversation.

They kept up a brisk pace down the hall, but as they approached the door to Mom's room, his step faltered.

She slowed her gait and peeked over.

"I hate hospitals." Rather than make eye contact, he directed his comment to the half-closed door ahead.

She didn't have to respond, but there was a plaintive quality in his inflection she'd never heard before. Induced, perhaps, by exhaustion and stress.

Or was there more to it?

He'd always been closemouthed about his past, making it clear his childhood was an off-limits topic. All he'd ever shared with her was that his parents had died within months of each other while he was in his late teens, leaving him to fend for himself with few assets to his name. If Mom was privy to any more than that, she'd been sworn to secrecy.

Could Dad's dislike of hospitals be sourced from that period in his past?

Why not dig a little, see what she could learn?

"Why do you hate hospitals?"

Slowly he transferred his gaze from Mom's room to her, an echo of sorrow filling his eyes. "I lived in a hospital for weeks when I was sixteen. Watching my mother die."

That was a piece of information he'd never shared.

"What happened to her?"

He wiped a hand down his haggard face. "She had strep throat as a child, which led to rheumatic fever. The fallout from that was heart valve disease, only discovered later in life. Too late to treat. And heart transplants weren't common yet. Watching someone you love slip away is . . ." His chest heaved, and he once again focused on her mother's door. "It's hell."

For a man who'd never expressed much emotion, that succinct admission spoke volumes about the depth of his feelings.

"I'm sorry you had to go through that, Dad. But Mom's prognosis doesn't sound as dire."

"I don't know. I've been googling the subject for hours, and one article said up to 20 percent of people who have a TIA have a full stroke within a week."

Paige's stomach began to churn. "That doesn't mean Mom will be one of the unlucky ones."

"I hope not." Dad straightened his shoulders and continued toward the door. "Let's go in."

She trailed along in his wake, trying to come to terms with the troubling statistic he'd rattled off—but talking with the doctor in a few hours might help reassure her on the TIA front.

The unexpected glimpse Dad had offered into his past, however, made all the questions she'd wondered about through the years bubble back to the surface. Like, what had happened to his father so soon after his mother died? Where had Dad lived after both parents were gone? How had he survived on his own at such a young age? What kind of sacrifices had been required to work a day job and go to night school to get the business degree he'd always prized? The one he claimed had opened doors and allowed him to rise on the corporate ladder despite the odds stacked against him after the early deaths of his parents.

But as she followed him into the quiet room, she put all that aside and directed her attention to the woman whose profile came into view.

Mom had aged too.

A lot.

Pressure built in her throat as she stopped beside the bed and scrutinized her mother.

As far as she could see, there was none of the sagging she'd expected in a stroke victim. But Dad had said TIA symptoms resolved fast. And Mom appeared to be sleeping peacefully. That had to be an encouraging sign.

"Go ahead and sit." Her father murmured the instruction and waved her toward a chair beside the bed.

"I don't want to take your seat." She lowered her volume to match his.

"I'll round up another one."

A nurse came through the door and crossed to the computer off to the side. "The room next door is empty. I'll get you a chair from there in just a minute."

"I'll take care of it. Thank you." Her dad disappeared into the hall.

"How is she doing?" Paige studied her mom's steady breathing, suppressing the urge to take her hand and risk waking her up.

"Improving by the hour. All her vitals are fine. Are you her daughter?"

"Yes."

The nurse smiled. "Thought so. I can see the resemblance."

Not surprising. Everyone had always told her she took after her mom. But she'd also inherited other, less visible traits from her dad. Like his fortitude and willingness to work hard to achieve a goal.

Dad returned and positioned his chair beside hers as the nurse disappeared again.

"How long has she been asleep?" Paige rested her hand on the bed beside her mom's fingers, close but not touching.

"Three or four hours. They may be giving her medication in the IV to relax her. The whole ordeal was stressful and exhausting for her."

"And for you."

He shrugged. "I'm not the one with a medical issue."

"Psychological stress can be just as draining. Why don't you go home and get a few hours' sleep? I'll stay with Mom."

He was shaking his head before she finished. "I'm not leaving. Besides, the doctor may come in at the crack of dawn. I don't want to miss him."

His definitive tone said he wasn't going to budge, so she didn't bother to argue.

They sat in silence, the even, reassuring cadence of her mother's breathing slowly untwisting the kinks in Paige's stomach. As the passing minutes became an hour and she began to relax, her eyelids grew heavier and heavier.

Since falling asleep in the chair and sliding onto the floor would be mortifying, she had to find a way to keep herself awake.

She peeked over at her dad.

His arms were folded, his eyes closed, but his taut posture indicated he was wide awake.

Was it possible that in the dark, early hours of this new day, he'd be willing to offer a few more glimpses into his past?

It was worth a try. If nothing else, a bit of conversation would help her stay alert.

"Dad." She waited until his eyelids flickered open to continue. "Why wouldn't you ever talk about your parents and what happened to them?"

His features contorted, as if he'd been dealt a physical blow. "I don't believe in dwelling on unhappy subjects or looking back."

"I get that, but why make all the details a state secret? It's not like there's anything shameful about your mom dying of heart disease."

"No, but my mother's heart issues and death set off a downward slide in our family that eventually spiraled out of control. It serves no purpose to revisit that terrible chapter in my life."

Paige zeroed in on the key phrase in his reply.

"What do you mean by out of control? I know your dad died soon after your mom, but illness isn't something most people can control. It's not like anyone would choose to be sick."

The steady, muted beep of the monitor beside Mom's bed was the only sound in the stillness.

He'd shut down again, as usual. Apparently, his parents would always remain a verboten topic, even decades after—

"Dad wasn't sick."

She frowned. "What do you mean?"

"He didn't have to die."

His answers weren't adding up.

"I don't understand."

He zipped up his yard-work jacket, the one he'd had for as long as she could remember. Pushed his fingers into the worn pockets. Hunkered deeper into the garment that had always been his refuge from the wind and rain and occasional sleet that could hammer Portland.

"This coat was my dad's."

That didn't clarify his comments, but it did explain why the jacket had always seemed outdated. It had to be decades old. It also explained why Dad had refused to get rid of the shabby, ill-fitting garment despite her prodding through the years.

"You never told me that, either."

"If I'd told you that, you would've asked questions about my father."

That was true.

"So why did you tell me now?"

"I don't know."

But she could guess.

When the foundations of your world were shaken, priorities shifted. In a mutating landscape, the need to strengthen connections took on new urgency—because love was what got you through.

As she well knew from the past few months.

Perhaps he hoped at a subliminal if not a conscious level that answering her questions and sharing some of the information he'd always guarded so fiercely would help them reestablish a connection.

Maybe that was a stretch born of hope, but whatever the reason, she ought to mine whatever he was willing to offer before the door swung shut again.

"Did your dad give it to you?"

"No. After he died, the house and contents were sold to pay debts. But I took a few of his things first."

"There was no money at all?"

"No. Dad's insurance didn't cover all of Mom's medical bills. He owed a chunk of money to the hospital and the doctors, and there was still a big mortgage on the tiny house they'd bought. The wages of a daycare aide and custodian combined didn't give them much to work with for a down payment."

She already knew that neither of her parents had come from families with money. Mom had shared that years ago. But she'd had no clue her dad had been burdened with such economic fallout after his father died.

Which brought her back to his earlier comment.

"What did you mean a minute ago, about your father not having to die?"

He removed one hand from his pocket, turned up the collar of the jacket, and sank deeper into the folds. When he spoke again, his voice was ragged. "Dad chose to die."

It took a few moments for his meaning to penetrate her fatigue, but once it did, her jaw dropped. "You mean he . . . did he commit suicide?"

"Yes."

Dear Lord.

Her father had said that period of his life was painful, but this crossed the line from pain to tragedy.

Losing his mother would have been bad enough. But after his father's death, he'd also been left to fend for himself as a teen barely on the cusp of adulthood.

What a terrible blow that must have been to a young man who could easily have interpreted his father's choice as rejection. As evidence that his love wasn't sufficient to motivate his dad to struggle through the dark valley and be the father he needed.

Instead, Dad had been left on his own to face the world.

And face it he had, growing up fast as he struggled to cope with the chaos that must have been his life.

Yet despite that rocky start, he'd gotten an education. Worked his way up the corporate ladder in the banking industry. Married a woman who loved him with utter devotion. Created a comfortable material existence for his family, keeping all the pain from his past in a locked corner of his heart where it could never hurt him again.

So many insights.

So much explained.

She leaned forward in her seat and reached over to rest her hand on his arm. "I'm sorry, Dad. I wish you'd told me all this years ago."

"It wouldn't have changed what happened. The past is the past."

"It could have changed the future, though. Knowing where people come from can create bridges to understanding."

"Are you saying if you'd been aware of all this, you wouldn't have defied our wishes and married that carpenter?"

She tried not to bristle. "No. I love Andrew. But maybe we could have talked about it more. Found a way to alleviate your concerns about my future with him."

"All of which came to fruition. You both ended up on the street. I've been there, and it's not a place I ever wanted anyone I love to be." Pain scored his words.

So her father knew about their circumstances. Not surprising, given his career and contacts in banking.

"We had a rough stretch, but we're on the upswing now."

"I thought you might ask for my help."

You could have offered.

But she left that unsaid.

Not that they would have accepted anyway. But knowing there was a safety net if the situation had gotten any more desperate would have relieved some of their stress.

"We managed. Andrew is a hard worker. Like you've always been."

"I applaud hard work when it leads to an education and a good job and financial stability. He'll never be anything but a laborer."

"He owned a company."

"Past tense. His judgment and common sense must be lacking if he hired a thief."

"Jack fooled everyone. He could even have fooled you."

"I doubt it. I'm a decent judge of character."

"Maybe not. You wrote off Andrew, and he's the finest man I've ever met."

He waved her comeback aside. "My concern with him wasn't about character. I hardly know the man."

"Your fault, not his."

"Be that as it may, my issue with him was related to career potential and the security he could provide. And I didn't take kindly to him derailing your college studies and depriving you of a degree. That piece of paper opens up doors and opportunities."

"I may go back to school someday. But I wanted to be part of the company Andrew started."

"Which is gone. A degree would have come in handy about now."

"We're doing okay."

He crossed his arms again. "Are you both working?"

"Yes. Andrew landed a major renovation job."

"What about you?"

"I'm helping him." No way was she mentioning the waitress gig at the Myrtle.

His mouth tightened. "You're doing manual labor?"

"Light labor. And exploring other options."

"There won't be many worth pursuing without a college degree."

She took a deep breath. Counted to five. "I know that was your road to success, Dad, and I'm glad it worked out for you. But not everyone needs a degree to create a secure life. Andrew has street smarts. Those count for a lot."

"I had street smarts too, but they weren't ever going to get me anything other than a blue-collar job."

"There's nothing wrong with a blue-collar job. Andrew loves what he does, and he's good at it. He's also experienced. That matters too."

"So does background. His wasn't the best."

So that was still a bone of contention too.

In hindsight, telling her parents about Andrew's abusive father and alcoholic mother had probably been a mistake. At the time, though, she'd thought his ability to succeed despite the odds stacked against him would impress them.

She tipped up her chin. "People can't help the circumstances they're born into or inherit, but strong people can overcome the challenges life hands them. Like you did. Andrew is a smart, caring, principled man, and I'm proud to be his wife. I would think someone with your background would appreciate and respect all he's accomplished and the amazing person he became despite formidable obstacles."

Her dad didn't respond to that, and she didn't attempt to continue the conversation.

Instead, she shifted away from him and settled back in her chair.

No worries anymore about dozing off after that intense exchange. She'd be wide awake for the duration. Thinking about all her father had shared.

And wondering if the crack in his armor that had let secrets about his unhappy past slip out might also allow receptiveness to a happier future with his daughter and son-in-law slowly seep in and soften his heart.

22

It was too early for a phone call.

As his cell rang on the nightstand, Matt forced his eyelids open and groped for it in the weak morning light. It couldn't be much past five thirty, meaning he'd only clocked three or four hours of restless sleep after his soul-baring session with Vienna last night.

He tried to focus on the screen, blinking to clear his vision.

When Kay's name popped up, he frowned. Pushed himself upright.

If she was calling at this hour, there was a problem.

He pressed talk and put the phone to his ear. "What's wrong?"

"I don't know." She sounded agitated. "I heard Cora moving around a little while ago and went to check on her. She said she wasn't feeling well. I took her temperature, and it's a hundred and one. I told her we should call the doctor, but she doesn't want to bother him at this hour."

He threw back the covers, stood, and began to pace. "How do her incisions look?"

"The one on her leg where they took the vein for the graft

seems fine. I don't know about the one on her chest. She's been taking care of it herself, and she won't let me see it. You know how independent and private she is. Will you talk to her? She may listen to someone with medical training."

"Yes. Put her on."

A shuffling sound came over the line, followed by an extended, muffled exchange. At last Cora took the phone.

"Matt, I'm sorry Kay bothered you at this ungodly hour. There's no cause for alarm."

Yes, there was, based on the threadiness in her usually strong voice.

He called up the calm but firm bedside manner he used with the owners of his patients. "Kay says you have a fever."

"I guess I do. She took my temperature a few minutes ago, and I assume the thermometer is accurate."

"Is there any redness around your primary incision?"

"Some. But what do you expect? They cut me from stem to stern."

"Is it warm to the touch?"

"A little."

"Does it hurt?"

"Of course it hurts! They pried open my chest, for pity's sake."

"Is there any pus or drainage?"

"In one small spot. It's not bad."

Given her symptoms, odds were she had a surgical wound infection. Hopefully one that was superficial rather than deep into muscle and tissue.

"Cora, you need to let Kay call the doctor. If the incision is infected—and all indications suggest it is—it should be treated ASAP. Otherwise, things can go downhill fast."

A beat ticked by.

"What do you mean by downhill?"

"Untreated infections can lead to sepsis."

"Is that blood poisoning?"

"That's a common name for it."

"I had a friend once who died of that." She sounded shakier.

Scaring her wasn't his first choice, but if it prodded her into action, he wasn't above using fear.

"That's why we have to catch this fast. How long have there been signs of infection?"

"A day or two."

That was a day or two too long.

"Let Kay call the doctor."

She sighed. "I suppose it couldn't hurt to have him weigh in."

"No, it couldn't." Since he was gaining ground, he pressed his advantage by adding on another tack. "Remember that the faster you recover, the faster you can come out here to visit Kay at the inn. The view is amazing, and you're going to love the fish tacos at the stand on the wharf."

"You're a smooth talker, Matt Quinn." A touch of humor softened her gravelly voice. "And speaking of smooth talking, are you applying those skills with that lady friend of yours out there?"

His lips quirked.

Even with a high fever, she'd managed to work in a reference to his love life.

"I'll discuss that with you after Kay calls the doctor and we get this issue taken care of."

"I'll hold you to that. I'm giving the phone back to Kay. Love you, Matt."

"Love you back." He pushed the response past the sudden constriction in his windpipe.

A moment later, Kay came back on the line. "I knew you'd convince her. I'll call the doctor as soon as we hang up."

"Keep me updated."

"I will. Sorry to wake you so early. Go back to sleep."

Not happening. Not with dawn minutes away and Vienna on his mind.

"I'll try. I wish I could be there to lend moral support."

"You're lending plenty of moral support by dealing with the inn. I can handle this situation with Cora. I'll get back to you as soon as I have anything to report."

She ended the call, and Matt set his cell back on the nightstand. There wasn't much point in staying in bed. Staring at the ceiling, rehashing the events of yesterday with Vienna, and wondering where he was supposed to go from here wasn't going to bring him any peace of mind.

A walk on the beach with God's inspiring creation all around him would be far more conducive to contemplation and discernment than a dark room and a blank ceiling.

If that didn't produce any results?

His visit to church in a handful of hours might help bring clarity to his muddled brain.

So as the barest hint of brightness began to lighten the dark sky outside his window, he pulled on his jeans, threw on a jacket, and tucked the slim volume by C. S. Lewis into an inside pocket to revisit a few of the passages that deserved a second read.

Because now that he was beginning to see a hint of illumination at the end of the dark tunnel of grief and guilt that had defined his journey for the past two years, he needed to use every tool at his disposal to reach that light.

Otherwise, there was no way his tomorrows could include the woman who'd given him a hug to remember last night.

Mom was awake.

As Paige returned to her mother's bedside after a quick trip to freshen up and a stop in the waiting room to peek at Andrew, who was out cold on the sofa, Mom greeted her with a smile.

"I'm sorry for all the drama and the long drive, but I'm so

happy to see you." She extended her arm. "Come closer. Let me look at you."

Paige crossed to the bed and took her hand, scrutinizing her face while her mother reciprocated. As far as she could tell, there was no evidence of a stroke in Mom's bright, alert eyes, clear speech, or symmetrical features.

Thank you, God.

Mom's irises began to glisten. "I didn't know if you'd come. Not after all these years and everything that happened."

"Of course I came. I never stopped loving you or Dad." She shot him a quick glance. He remained seated in the chair where he'd kept vigil all night. "I always hoped someday we'd find a way to get past the anger and hurt. That we could try to rebuild the relationship we once had."

"It was almost worth this TIA if it becomes the catalyst to make that happen." Mom squeezed her hand. "I've missed you so much. So has your dad."

"Ann." Dad scowled at her.

The mutinous gleam in Mom's eyes was new. "It's true. I've seen you paging through the family albums in the study when you think no one is watching."

Dad's cheeks grew ruddy. "There's no crime in looking at albums."

"I never said there was. The crime was letting Paige walk out the door six years ago."

Dad stood. "You're getting much too excited. I don't want your blood pressure to spike again, like it did last night in the ER. We can talk about all this later."

"I want to talk about it now. You ought to be glad this gave us an excuse to reach out to her. It's time to admit that this long estrangement was a mistake."

"This isn't the time or place for a discussion like this." Dad tugged his jacket closer around him. "We're in the midst of a medical crisis."

"We're also in the midst of a family crisis. We may as well address both at once." Mom kept a tight grip on her hand. "Your dad said you drove all night to get here."

"No. Andrew drove all night."

Her mom scanned the room. "Where is he?"

"Sleeping on a sofa in the waiting room."

"After he wakes up, bring him in here."

"Only two visitors are allowed at once." Her father folded his arms.

"Then you can wait outside. I want to talk to that young man."

Dad blinked. "I think the TIA muddled your brain."

"No. It cleared out the cobwebs, fortified my backbone, and gave me perspective. From now on, I'm—"

"Morning, folks." A fortysomething man in a white jacket swooped in, introduced himself, and got straight to business.

Paige tried to switch gears, but it was hard to take in all the information and medical lingo the doctor rattled off with machine-gun speed. Stenosis. Stenting. Atherosclerosis. Endarterectomy. She was still trying to assimilate all of it as he wound down and asked for questions.

Thankfully, Dad had absorbed more of the download than she had in light of the query he threw out.

"Isn't an endarterectomy more invasive than putting in a stent?"

"Yes, but it's the recommended procedure for patients with more than 70 percent stenosis. Your wife has 80 percent in both arteries. That, plus her high blood pressure last night, is one of the reasons we admitted her. In general, we send people home who've had TIAs and follow up with treatment, but 80 percent is dangerously high blockage. I'd like to get the first procedure done tomorrow morning."

"First procedure?" Paige's brain clicked into gear at that piece of information.

"Yes. We do one artery at a time. We'll repeat the procedure on the other artery in a few weeks."

"Is it dangerous?" Mom's forehead crimped.

"It's not considered high risk. It's done under local anesthesia and takes an hour or two. We'll keep you in the hospital twenty-four to forty-eight hours afterward."

"Does this help reduce the risk of a real stroke?" Dad moved closer to Mom and took her hand.

"Yes. We'll also be suggesting lifestyle changes and medicine to further decrease the risk. If you'd like to think about this, you can have the nurse contact me with your answer."

"Warren?" Mom looked at Dad.

"I think you should do it. A real stroke would have permanent consequences."

"I know. What do you think, Paige?"

"It's your decision, but in your place, I'd do it."

Mom nodded. "Okay. Let's proceed."

"Wise choice, in my opinion. I'll see you tomorrow morning at seven, and we'll get this taken care of. Try not to worry." The doctor's last comment encompassed all of them before he left as fast as he'd come.

"He's like a human tornado." Mom expelled a breath.

"Yes, he is. But I researched him last night. He's a top doc in his field, has a prestigious degree, and teaches at the medical school here."

Dad had been busy since Mom was admitted.

"If you're comfortable with his credentials, I am too." Her mom patted Dad's hand. "You've always been thorough about everything. I'm glad we were all here to hear what he had to . . . Andrew?"

Paige swiveled toward the door.

Andrew stood on the threshold, balancing a tray in one hand and three stacked Styrofoam containers in the other. "Sorry. I didn't mean to interrupt. I saw the doctor leave and thought I could stick my head in for a minute."

"You can do more than that. Come in." Mom motioned him into the room.

He complied but stopped two steps inside the door. "I went down to the cafeteria and got breakfast for the three of us. I'll just drop it off and eat mine in the waiting room."

"That was very thoughtful of you. Why don't you and Paige eat in the waiting room where there's more space? I'll keep Warren company here while he eats."

"I like that idea." Paige joined Andrew, took a cup and a Styrofoam container, and passed them to her father. Then she bent and kissed her mom's forehead. "I'll be back shortly."

"Don't hurry. Enjoy your food. I want to talk to your dad for a few minutes anyway. Andrew, it's nice to see you again. Thank you for delivering Paige here safe and sound last night."

Andrew seemed bewildered by the cordial reception from Mom, but he rallied and called up a smile. "I was happy to do it. And I'm glad your condition wasn't more serious."

"Let's go." Paige took his arm and tugged him toward the door.

He didn't protest. Nor did he speak until they were several yards down the hall.

"What did the doctor say about your mom?"

She gave him the condensed version.

"That all sounds encouraging."

"I think so too."

In the waiting room, they claimed one of the small round tables scattered throughout the space that was now occupied by a number of people.

Paige sat and flipped open the disposable container to find scrambled eggs, sausage, and a biscuit. "This is fantastic."

"I doubt that. It's hospital food." Andrew opened his own breakfast. "But you have to be as hungry as I am. Your dad too. So what gives with your mom? She seemed glad to see me."

"I think she's had a change of heart." She paused, her forkful of eggs suspended halfway to her mouth. “No. Correction. I think she’s finally acknowledged what’s been in her heart from the beginning. But Dad’s a strong personality, and she’s always let him take the lead. I think she regrets what happened between us six years ago, and the TIA is giving her an opportunity to fix the damage. I also learned a lot about Dad last night that I never knew.” She proceeded to fill him in as they ate. “I’d say there may be a change brewing.”

“I’m happy about that for your sake. I know how much it hurt you when they made you choose between me and them. I always felt guilty about that.”

“It wasn’t your fault. Dad owns the rift—and Mom, to some degree. But I know how hard it is to go up against my father.”

“Let’s hope the current trend continues.” He continued to shovel in food as if he hadn’t eaten in a week. “So what’s the plan? I can wait until after the surgery tomorrow to leave, but I should get back by end of day. I can pick you up later in the week if you want to stay longer.”

“No. I’ll go back with you tomorrow if the surgery goes smoothly. We have commitments in Hope Harbor.” She continued to chow down. Hospital food or not, it tasted wonderful.

“I’ll get us a room for tonight close by. I doubt we can check in this early or I’d take you there now. You’re exhausted.”

“You are too.”

“At least I slept for a few hours before it got busy in here. You didn’t.”

Truth be told, she was beginning to feel a bit shaky, and there was an odd vibration in her fingertips. Too much stress, too little sleep.

“I know, but I hate to spend the money on a motel.” They might both be working, but cash remained in short supply.

“Can’t be helped. We’ll need a decent sleep by tonight, if not sooner. But—” He glanced toward the door.

Paige twisted around.

Her father stood on the threshold. When he spotted them, he walked their direction.

Andrew wiped his mouth and stood as Dad approached, ever the gentleman.

"Don't get up." Her father waved him back into his seat. "Your mother asked me to give you this." He laid a key on the table. "Your bedroom is a guest room now, not that it's ever been used as such. You're welcome to go home after you finish your breakfast and get some sleep. Your mother thinks you both look tired after your long drive."

Paige stared at the key. "You're giving us a house key?"

"To use while you're here."

She raised her gaze. Searched his face, which was gray with fatigue. "You should sleep too."

"Your mother has the same opinion. I'll go home in an hour or two to shower and take a quick nap, and I'll sleep there tonight. The procedure is early tomorrow morning, and I want to be rested and back well in advance."

"So do we," Andrew said.

Her father cleared his throat and addressed him. "Thank you for driving Paige up last night. And thank you for breakfast. I'll see you both at the house."

He turned to go, and Paige called after him. "I'll be in to say goodbye to Mom before I leave."

Though he lifted a hand in acknowledgment, he kept walking.

Andrew picked up the key. "I never expected this."

"Me neither. The TIA appears to have been a blessing in disguise."

"You may be right." He reached over and folded her fingers gently in his calloused palm. "These last few months have been a roller coaster, but I'm beginning to feel like the track is finally leveling out."

"So am I."

"Let's finish up and go crash. We both need sleep." He went back to eating.

She did too.

But much as she appreciated the food that fed her body, she was even more grateful for the winds of change that seemed poised to refresh her soul and heal her heart.

23

Matt was waiting for her in the foyer on Sunday morning as Vienna started down the stairs from the second level of the inn, his sport jacket highlighting broad shoulders that jacked up her pulse and left her a tad breathless.

"Sorry." She picked up her pace and scanned her watch. "Did I have the departure time wrong? Have you been waiting long?"

"No to both. I was ready a few minutes early and decided to hang out here. The fog rolled in and cut my walk on the beach short."

She stopped at the bottom of the stairs. "You already took a walk on the beach? You must have gotten up at the crack of dawn."

"I did. Kay called very early. Cora appears to have an infection in her incision. We had to talk her into letting us contact the doctor."

"I'm sorry to hear that. Kay didn't mention anything about complications last night."

"She wasn't aware of the situation until a couple of hours ago. Cora's very independent and doesn't like anyone to fuss over her." His features softened. "But she sure fussed over us after she took us under her wing."

"Sounds like there's a story there."

"I'll tell it to you on the drive to town. Ready to go?"

"Yes."

He followed her out, settled her in his car, and circled around to take his place behind the wheel. "Are you certain you want to hear another tale from my past after everything I dumped on you last night?" He put the car in gear and drove down the gravel drive, his light tone at odds with his serious demeanor.

"I didn't feel dumped on." It was important to make that clear. "I was touched by your willingness to confide in me. And for the record, I think you're being harder on yourself about what happened than anyone else would be. The mistakes you made aren't the kind that usually lead to tragedy."

"But these did."

There was no disputing that.

Yet anyone looking at the situation objectively would realize his guilt was misplaced.

Hopefully he'd be able to accept that one day and put his gut-wrenching remorse to rest—but given the firm set of his jaw, this wasn't that day.

"I know." She took a deep breath and moved on. "To answer your question about Cora, yes, I'd like to hear about her. If two unrelated people are willing to disrupt their lives to the extent you and Kay have to help her out, she must be very special."

"She is. We think of her as our grandmother. I don't know what we'd have done without her after our parents died."

For the duration of the short drive through the fog, Matt filled her in on the woman he described as a bit rough-hewn in terms of manners and sophistication but endowed with world-class generosity and compassion.

"How old were you when she came into your life?"

"Nine. Kay was eighteen and at her wit's end trying to raise me and make ends meet. We were two lost souls in desperate need of nurturing. After we moved into the other side of Cora's duplex, she plied us with copious amounts of love and advice and chocolate chip cookies."

"She must be a wonderful woman."

"She is. I hate to think where we'd have ended up without her." As Matt concluded his tale, he swung into the lot at Grace Christian. "We weren't about to let her go through bypass surgery alone."

"After hearing your story, I can understand that. Do you think this infection is serious?" The caring, compassionate woman Matt had described didn't deserve a setback, and Matt didn't need any more loss in his life.

His forehead puckered as he pulled into a parking spot. "I hope not, but surgical site infections can be nasty. We won't know how serious hers is until she's evaluated. Sit tight and I'll get your door."

Before she could tell him not to bother, he slid out of the car.

Impressive.

Not many men practiced those kinds of basic courtesies anymore.

The display of excellent manners continued as he opened the church door for her, deferred to her on where to sit, and motioned her to precede him into the pew.

His wife had been a lucky woman.

Vienna sneaked a peek at him.

She was lucky too, for however long Matt was destined to be a part of her life.

But how long would that be?

A question that kept disrupting her concentration during the service despite her concerted effort to pay attention.

Hopefully God would understand and give her some guidance about where and how this man might fit into her world.

After the service ended, Matt again let her precede him down the aisle, but as they reached the vestibule, an older woman flagged him down and trekked over at a sprightly pace behind her walker.

She acknowledged both of them with a smile but spoke to Matt. "I'm so glad I caught you. I wanted to see if you'd be home this afternoon. I'd like to drop off a special delivery."

"Yes, I will. I'll be painting the rest of the day. Let me introduce you to Bev Price's daughter, Vienna."

As he did so, the woman took her hand. "Very nice to meet you, Vienna. Your mother's bookshop has been a godsend for me. Likewise for the conversation she provides. What a welcoming haven she's created in Hope Harbor. I expect she's delighted you came for a visit."

"Happy to meet you too, Ms. Cooper. And I agree about the bookshop."

"Make it Eleanor. We don't stand on formalities in Hope Harbor." She patted her hand.

"How's Methuselah doing?" Matt rejoined the conversation.

"Very well, thanks to you. Did you tell Vienna about him?"

"No."

Eleanor turned to her again. "Methuselah is my cat. He cut his paw on Friday, and Charley drove me out to the inn. Matt fixed him up in a jiffy. A house call in reverse, I suppose." Her mouth bowed, and a merry glint appeared in her eyes. "If you're in the neighborhood, he might share the treat I'll be delivering later. Small compensation for his expertise and kindness, but since he wouldn't let me pay him, it will have to suffice."

"I was happy to help," Matt said. "I don't want my skills to get rusty."

"You could keep them plenty sharp in Hope Harbor. I remember when our police chief's husband had to run his injured dog, Clyde, all the way up to Coos Bay. The poor pup could have died. Shep and Ziggy, the collies out at the cranberry farm, require regular looking after too. Then there's Toby, the cute beagle at the lavender farm. And Annabelle, Mrs. Schroeder's cat on Pelican Point Road, who's forever climbing trees and getting into fights. Not to mention Daisy, the border collie who belongs to our wonderful landscaper, Jon Gray, at Greenscape."

The corners of Matt's lips rose. "That's quite a menagerie."

"Indeed it is. If ever you want to relocate, you'll find a grateful market here. Now I must be going. Luis will be waiting out front. Happy to meet you, Vienna. I hope you enjoy your stay in our charming little town. Matt, expect me this afternoon at the inn."

As the woman trundled off, Vienna arched an eyebrow at her companion. "Not many vets do pro bono work."

"Nor do hotel consultants."

Checkmate.

"So what's the treat she's bringing?"

"A fudge cake that's apparently famous in these parts. Are you interested in sampling it later? I can't eat a whole cake."

"You could twist my arm. Chocolate is hard to resist. But I'm having dinner with Mom tonight, as usual, after she gets back. With all the stories she'll have to share, I'm not certain how late I'll—"

"Excuse me . . . may I interrupt for a moment?"

Vienna turned.

A slender, late thirtyish woman with long blond hair and accompanied by a tall man extended her hand to Matt. "I wanted to introduce myself. I spoke with your sister a few weeks ago about doing repairs at the B&B. I'm BJ Stevens Nash, and this is my husband, Eric."

"Kay mentioned you." Matt shook her hand and did likewise with her husband as he introduced Vienna. "She said you were booked for the foreseeable future."

"Yes, and I suspect I'll only get busier. Not that I'm complaining, but I wish I could have helped your sister out. I just wasn't able to meet her aggressive timetable with my present staff and workload. But I understand you found someone to do the job for you."

"I did. Andrew Thompson. He's phenomenal."

"Andrew Thompson." She shook her head. "I don't recognize the name."

"He's from Portland, but I think he's planning to relocate to this area."

"Uh-oh, BJ. Competition." Eric grinned and gave her a shoulder nudge.

She wrinkled her nose at him and nudged back. "There's ample work for everyone. I'd love to see how the B&B is shaping up, though. It has solid bones. Would you mind if I swing by sometime?"

"Not at all. In fact, if you're out and about today, I'll be there painting, and no one else will be on-site. You could wander around at your leisure."

"I may do that."

Eric took her arm. "We should go. Dad's expecting us for brunch."

"I know. A pleasure to meet you both."

As the couple disappeared into the crowd that had gathered in the vestibule, Vienna cocked her head at Matt. "You'll be having a fair amount of company at the inn this afternoon."

"Fine by me. I'm used to activity around the place." He pulled out his cell. Scrolled through his messages.

"Anything from Kay or Andrew?"

"No. Let's hope the old saying is true, and no news is good news. Ready to go back?"

"Yes."

They continued toward the door, pausing to say hello to Reverend Baker as they passed.

"Wonderful to see you both. You *are* together today, correct?"

"Yes." Vienna smiled at the cleric. "It was more environmentally responsible to take one car."

"Very civic minded of you." He gave a solemn nod, but his eyes were twinkling. "I'll have to let Father Murphy know I saw you today. I may have jumped the gun on your first visit, but it appears my instincts were sound."

His inference was obvious, and Vienna sent Matt a sidelong glance as her cheeks warmed. But her companion seemed to be taking the pastor's comment in stride.

When several congregants joined them, Matt took her arm, bid the man a pleasant day, and guided her toward the door.

As they returned to his car, and during the drive back, he kept the conversation focused on inn-related topics. Fine by her. They'd had enough heavy conversation in the past fifteen hours.

Unfortunately, he didn't mention the looming breakfast issue—and given Cora's new health problem, menus and recipe testing weren't going to be top of mind for Kay in the near term. A major concern with the soft opening less than two weeks away.

Vienna played with her seat belt.

She had to discuss the situation with Matt, develop a backup plan.

But adding another worry to his already overloaded plate felt almost cruel. Heck, as it was, the man was going to spend his whole Sunday painting to pick up some of the slack left by the Thompsons' crisis.

Painting.

Hmm.

An idea began to percolate in her mind that could give her the opportunity to broach the breakfast subject. And as she half listened while Matt talked about the new sign featuring the logo Marci had designed for the inn, which would be installed at the entrance as soon as the driveway was repaired, it solidified.

Maybe her approach wouldn't provide an immediate solution to the breakfast dilemma, but it might reassure him he wasn't alone and that she'd do whatever she could to help him see this mammoth project through to the end.

As Matt changed out of his church clothes and donned his spattered painting attire, his cell pinged.

Pulling his sweatshirt over his head, he strode across the room and picked it up from the dresser in the innkeeper's quarters.

The text was from Andrew.

Sorry we had to cut out last night. Hopefully Vienna passed on the news. Paige's mom is doing okay. TIA, not a stroke. We plan to come back tomorrow after she has a surgical procedure. Should be in Hope Harbor by six and back on the job Tuesday. Will still finish up on schedule.

Matt put his thumbs to work.

I'm glad it wasn't more serious. Continuing to paint, so we should be ahead of the curve on that. Thanks for the update.

At least he wouldn't have to worry about missing the completion deadline. With the tight timetable they were on, even a day or two lost would have caused a major glitch. Especially since the three rooms they were using for the soft opening were already booked.

He finished dressing, tied his sport shoes, and picked up the phone again.

As he began to slide it into his pocket, it rang.

Kay.

Pulse accelerating, he put it to his ear. "What's the news?"

"Not great. Her doctor wanted her to go to the ER. We're there now. Her temperature's up to 102. They're going to admit her and put her on IV antibiotics."

That wasn't what he wanted to hear.

He forked his fingers through his hair and began to pace. "Has her doctor seen her?"

"Are you kidding? It's Sunday." Kay made no attempt to hide her aggravation. "He said he'd come by early tomorrow."

"What have they told you so far?"

"Hang on a sec. Let me pull out my notes." A muffled noise sounded in the background, like paper being unfolded. "They're thinking it's superficial at this point. They also sent a sample from the infected area to the lab for testing. They seem concerned it may be something called MRSA. What's that?"

"A type of staph infection that's resistant to commonly used antibiotics."

"Then how do they get rid of it?"

"Certain drugs will work. That's why they took a sample. They want to identify the exact type of bacteria they have to tackle."

"So once they figure that out, she'll be okay?"

Not always. MRSA was tricky, especially in a patient already recovering from major surgery whose resistance was down.

But it would serve no purpose to further worry Kay.

"MRSA is treatable." Whether it would respond, or cause other problems before it did, was another concern.

"Do you think she'll be in the hospital long?"

"Depends on how fast they get the infection under control. If all goes well, maybe a day or two." But much longer if complications arose.

"I'm worried about leaving her alone. I'm supposed to come back to Oregon in less than a week."

And he was supposed to return to San Francisco.

Matt began to pace. "A brief stay at a rehab facility may be an option after you leave, if necessary."

"She'd hate that."

Yeah, she would—and truth be told, he'd hate it for her. Even the plushest places were institutional. There would be no family coming in and out to keep tabs on her and make certain everything was being done that was supposed to be done.

And to ensure a patient got optimal care in today's world, an advocate was essential while navigating the health care system.

"Matt . . ."

He knew what was coming, so he finished the sentence for her. "You want to stay longer."

"Yes. I could never repay her for everything she did for us. And leaving her alone feels all wrong. If you could extend your stay for one more week, it should get Cora over the hump. Could you ask Steve if he could spare you for five more days?"

"You won't be here for the inn opening."

"I know, but Vienna will. She told me she's staying for the bloggers' visit and until reservations begin coming in. She said she wants to be able to have a successful relaunch on her resume. To be honest, with her physical proximity to everything that's been happening out there, she's more in tune with the day-to-day details of all this than I am."

That was true.

And having an extra week in Vienna's company would be no hardship on his end.

"I can't make any promises, but I'll call Steve after we hang up and run this by Vienna. If she's not comfortable handling the opening without you present, we'll have to regroup."

"I understand. But if you can swing this, I think it would be in Cora's best interest."

"Did you tell her about the potential change in your schedule yet?"

"No. I want it to be set when I broach the topic. Otherwise, she'll tell me not to bother you with this and insist I go back to Oregon as planned. If it's a done deal, she can't refuse."

"Smart strategy. I'll touch base with Steve and Vienna today and give you an answer as soon as I have one. Until then, hang in and call with any news."

"Will do. I have to run. The ER doctor's coming out of Cora's room, and I want to flag him down. Talk to you later."

As the line went dead, Matt exhaled and checked his watch.

If Steve was following his usual pattern, he and his wife would be having a leisurely breakfast before leaving for the late service at their church.

It was either call him now and interrupt his meal or wait until this afternoon and intrude on another activity. Unfortunately, he couldn't defer this matter until their usual Tuesday check-in call. It required a faster resolution.

He dropped into a chair next to the window and tapped in Steve's number.

His partner didn't answer until the fourth ring, just as the call was poised to roll to voicemail. "Hey, Matt. Sorry for the delay. Vanessa's taking a bath, and my hands were immersed in bubbles."

Matt's lips quirked. "Did I want to hear that?"

A beat ticked by.

"I was washing the breakfast dishes. What did you think I was doing? Wait. Don't answer that. The more important question is, why would you think I was doing what you thought I was doing? Your mind hasn't tracked that direction for two years."

Steve had a point.

And the answer was simple.

He'd met Vienna.

But he wasn't introducing her into this conversation.

"Can't a guy make a joke?"

"Sure. But you haven't done that in two years, either. This trip has been good for you."

An ideal segue to the topic he wanted to discuss.

"Speaking of that . . . I may need an extension." He brought Steve up to speed on Cora's situation. "Kay and I are thinking another week should cover us. Can you manage that long without me if necessary?"

"No worries. Zoe's stepped up to the plate and picked up a huge amount of work. We should be fine."

It was reassuring to hear their part-time staffer was working out well, even if it made him feel a bit superfluous.

"Thanks. I'll let you know how this plays out. If all goes according to plan, I'll be back in the office August 1."

"No worries. We've got you covered. Just keep me in the loop. Now it's back to the bubbles for me."

Steve ended the call, and Matt slid the phone into the pocket of his jeans. The two of them were a great team, and he'd always expected their partnership to last until one or both of them decided to retire many years down the road.

But as Eleanor's comment from this morning about the large nonhuman population of Hope Harbor replayed in his mind, a different future than the one he'd envisioned suddenly tantalized.

From all indications, Steve and Zoe were doing fine without him. She was an excellent vet, despite her limited experience. If he ever decided to leave the practice, she could take his place.

Of course, a life-changing decision like that required serious deliberation. Look what had happened to Kay when she'd jumped too fast. Unless he was misreading her, she was having major second thoughts about being an innkeeper.

So he wouldn't make a mistake by moving in haste.

Besides, much as he liked Hope Harbor and felt at home here, the town itself wasn't the only draw. The people mattered too.

One in particular.

Problem was, once the inn was up and running, Vienna would be off to whatever glitzy job enticed her away.

Unless he could tempt her to stay by sharing another idea that was beginning to take shape in his mind.

24

Vienna stopped outside the bedroom Andrew had deemed ready for its finishing coat of paint, called up a smile, and stepped through the doorway. "Your painting partner, reporting for duty. Hand me a brush and point me to a wall."

As she spoke, Matt swung around, the paint in the can he'd been about to pour into a tray sloshing dangerously close to the lip.

He gave her faded T-shirt, worn jeans, and holey socks sans shoes a quick scan.

"I know, I know." She raised her hands, palms forward. "I won't win any fashion contests. But this is the only set of ratty clothes I threw into my suitcase for what was supposed to be a short stay. And I didn't bring any shoes I want to splatter with paint, hence the lack of footwear." She lifted her foot and wiggled her toes.

His gaze dropped to a polished nail peeking out a hole, then whipped back up as he cleared his throat. "I, uh, thought you were going to the shop."

"I don't have to open it until noon. I can put in an hour or two here. We need all hands on deck, with the Thompsons out."

"They'll be back tomorrow." He filled her in on the text he'd received. "You don't have to do this, Vienna. You've already invested too much time and effort into the rehab. Why don't you chill out, take a walk on the beach?"

"As someone once said to me, standing around watching other people work doesn't sit well." She grinned as she parroted back his comment from three weeks ago. "I'm glad for the good news about Paige's mother, but they'll still be a day behind. I'm happy to pitch in and help keep everything rolling—unless you'd rather work alone."

She hoped not. But if he balked at her offer of assistance, she'd have to bring up the breakfast issue faster than she'd intended this morning.

"No. The extra pair of hands is welcome. I had another inn-related issue to discuss with you anyway."

Could it be the breakfast problem?

That would be ideal. Coming from him rather than her would make the conversation less awkward. The last thing she wanted to do was sound critical of his sister.

"See? We can kill two birds with one stone. But put me to work first. That will let me be doubly productive."

"Would you like to edge or roll?"

"I've done both. While I was growing up, Mom repainted our apartment every other year. We went through the entire rainbow, though thankfully not all at once. Since I was a more precise edger than Mom, that job tended to fall to me—but I can do either."

"Edging it is. You can have your pick of brushes." He indicated several lying on the tarp beside the paint tray. "There are also damp rags down there. I have an extender for the roller, so the ladder is all yours."

She crossed to the tarp and selected a brush while he poured paint into the tray. After taking the can from him once he finished, she motioned to the other side of the room. "I'll start over there if you want to roll the opposite wall. That should keep us out of each other's way."

"Sounds like a plan."

She picked up a rag, positioned the ladder in front of a window, and set both the can and rag on the fold-down tray. "What's the issue you want to discuss?"

"I talked to Kay after we got back from church. Cora's been admitted to the hospital."

"Oh no. I'm sorry to hear that. How sick is she?"

"We don't have any details yet, but they've put her on IV antibiotics. We're hoping the infection is superficial and not antibiotic resistant. They'll know more after they get the lab results. Whatever the findings, though, this setback will extend her recovery." Matt dipped his roller in the tray, but instead of withdrawing it, he angled toward her. "Kay wants to stay in Boise another week to help her."

This must be what he wanted to talk about, not the breakfast issue.

She shifted mental gears, working through the ramifications of that change in plans. "She'd miss the soft opening and most, if not all, of the blogger weekend."

"I know. I told her I had to check with you before she commits to extending her stay. If you don't want to take on the opening without her, we'll regroup. But if it makes any difference to your decision, I can stay an extra week."

A bonus week with Matt?

Sold.

"That would be helpful." She stepped up on the ladder, trying to keep her tone businesslike despite the tingle of anticipation zipping through her. "Is your partner okay with that?"

"Yes. We have a very qualified part-time vet working with us who's been picking up the slack in my absence. I doubt they'll miss me."

"In that case, I'm fine with the arrangement. I imagine Cora will appreciate having Kay around a bit longer, given the complication that arose." She ran her fingers through the pristine bristles of the brush in her hand, which were about to get messy. Just like this conversation. "Did Kay happen to mention our discussion about the food at the inn?"

"No."

She dipped the brush in the paint. Took a deep breath. "We may have a problem. I'm not picking up a lot of excitement about or interest in creating the kind of gourmet breakfasts the inn clientele will expect. I know she bought in to the concept at the beginning, but I get the feeling she may have bitten off more than she can chew."

His resigned expression suggested he wasn't surprised. "I was afraid this would happen. She's a decent cook, but in my experience, she's rarely tackled anything I'd call gourmet. I assumed she'd up her game after she bought the B&B, but in the few brief discussions we had about food after she decided to go with the high-end concept, I didn't get a warm and fuzzy feeling."

"Me neither."

Grooves dented Matt's brow, and when he spoke again, he sounded annoyed. "Instead of spending a couple hours a day at the garden center her friend owns, she ought to be practicing in the kitchen."

The garden center interludes were news, but it was wiser to leave the criticism of Kay to her brother.

"Maybe she needs the break from caregiving duties. You said she loves flowers."

"She does, and I don't begrudge her an occasional change of scene. But now we're in a pickle."

Vienna sighed. "I feel like part of that is my fault. I assumed when she signed on for the upscale positioning that she was equipped for the job."

"Don't blame yourself. I think she had dollar signs in her eyes after she heard what kind of bucks that type of inn could bring in. If anyone's to blame, it's me. I know her—and I remember her skills in the kitchen during my growing-up years. I should have talked to her more about the food, made certain she was capable of rising to the occasion and wasn't overreaching."

Whoever was at fault, lamenting over the state of affairs wasn't going to fix their dilemma.

Vienna began stroking on paint. "I'd offer to pick up that chore if I could, but I'm no chef either. Plus, I'll be super busy with a million other details. In a pinch, I could probably pull off breakfasts and buy afternoon treats for the soft opening, but gourmet fare is essential for the bloggers."

The wrinkles on Matt's forehead deepened. "Any suggestions?"

"I'll ask Mom tonight if she has any chef connections in the area. The bookstore is a mecca for people from near and far, and it's possible she may be able to give me a lead."

"What if she can't?"

"We could hire a catering company in Coos Bay to provide the breakfasts and afternoon snack trays until we line up a cook. People at these kinds of places expect the food to be fresh and prepared on-site, but we have to get the inn open. The longer it stays shuttered, the longer it will be before your sister begins recouping her investment."

"Yeah. I know." He lifted the roller from the pan and began coating the dinged-up wall Andrew had patched with a masterful touch. "Let's hope your mom can offer a suggestion or two. If you'll follow up with her on that, I'll contact the landscaping company Eleanor mentioned at church this morning and see if they'll come by to spruce up the grounds. I'll also call the housekeeping service Kay was using and get us back on their daily schedule. This place will need a massive cleaning once Andrew wraps up too. There's drywall dust everywhere."

"Are you sure they'll have people available?"

"Kay said they promised her they would. It's a small, family-run company based in Bandon."

"Then aside from the breakfast issue, we should be set. I called the charity that's picking up all the furniture we're not repurposing. They'll be here later this week. Do you think Andrew will give us a hand putting all the new furniture in place once the bedroom carpets are laid?"

"I'll ask. I doubt he'll say no."

"What are his plans after this job is finished?" She worked her way around the corner of the window frame and started down the side.

"He hasn't mentioned anything specific. I know he's hoping it leads to more work in the area. I'm going to broach that with BJ this afternoon. If she's as busy as she claims, maybe she can divert a few jobs to him. I think she'll be impressed with his work."

"How could she not be? The inn looks great. All his repairs, inside and out, seem to be top notch."

"They are. And speaking of plans for the future . . . I've been mulling over Eleanor's comment at church this morning."

She leaned in toward the wall, working the brush as close to the edge of the wood frame as she could. "Which one?"

"About all the pets in Hope Harbor. It got me wondering if there's actually a market here for a vet."

Vienna stopped painting. Twisted toward him. "Are you suggesting that vet might be you?"

He shrugged, his nonchalant manner at odds with the sudden intensity vibrating in the air. "The idea has interesting potential."

"But you have an established practice in San Francisco." She was still trying to wrap her mind around his out-of-the-blue comment. "Wouldn't your partner be upset if you walked out?"

"Until Zoe came along, I'd have said yes. But she fits in at the practice. We all clicked from the get-go. It's possible we would have hired her permanently anyway."

Vienna swiped a wayward drop of paint off the back of her hand with the rag. "Have you ever considered a major career change like this before?"

"No." He dipped the roller in the tray again, taking care not to oversaturate and risk widespread splatter as he applied the paint.

"I think Steve and I expected to be partners until we retired. I realize a transition like this would shake up everyone's plans, but sometimes plans change—by choice or by chance. Choice is always preferable." He paused. Swallowed. Resumed painting.

He had to be thinking about all the plans he and his wife had made for their life together and the family they were creating.

"I hear what you're saying, but it can be hard to switch gears midcourse. There are so many unknowns."

"There are anyway. And the danger of being too locked into plans is that we can breeze right past forks in the road that could lead to an even better destination than the one we had in mind."

She scrubbed at the stubborn residue of paint clinging to her skin. "So are you seriously thinking about leaving San Francisco behind?"

"I wouldn't put it in the serious category yet. More like toying with an unexpected potential opportunity. I can see the appeal of living in Hope Harbor, can't you?" He locked onto her gaze as the intensity ratcheted up another notch.

"Um . . ." Was he asking her whether she found the attributes of the town enticing—or the idea that he might be thinking about calling it home?

"Sorry. I didn't mean to put you on the spot." He went back to rolling the walls.

"You didn't." Not exactly. "I guess I never thought about it. I mean, since there aren't any positions here that line up with my career goals, the possibility of staying hasn't been on my radar."

"I didn't think there were any opportunities in my line of work either, until Eleanor planted a seed. But nothing may come of it. A decision like that has a ton of moving parts, and if any of them are out of whack, it can deep-six the whole notion. If you need a paint refill, let me know."

He was done talking about a potential career relocation.

Vienna made a yeoman's effort to switch gears, but while the conversation shifted to other topics, one of his comments kept looping through her mind.

"The danger of being too locked into plans is that we can breeze right past forks in the road that could lead to an even better destination than the one we had in mind."

Mom would agree with that sentiment. Bev Price had never passed up a fork in the road without at least poking her nose down it.

But what happened if you followed one and it led to a roadblock or dead end?

Mom would dismiss that concern, of course. She'd say you just had to find your way back to the main road or forge a new path.

Vienna sighed.

For a woman who'd always planned her life out to the nth degree, courting such danger was a scary thought.

Yet sometimes, as Matt had said, you weren't given a choice about forks. Like with her previous job.

And that was turning out fine. The inn project had been fun, and it positioned her well for the sort of future she'd always envisioned.

Unless she altered that vision.

A headache began to throb in her temples, and she massaged her forehead.

Must be the paint fumes.

"Do you mind if I raise the window higher?" She tossed the question over her shoulder to Matt.

"No. Is the smell getting to you?"

"A little."

"You want to stop?"

"Not yet." She raised the sash and inhaled the fresh air.

Didn't help.

The smell must not be the culprit.

And in truth, she already knew that.

Her headache was the direct result of Matt's revelation about his potential career shift.

That was a curveball of the first order.

And she didn't like curveballs.

In baseball, they might add interest to the game and keep batters on their toes, but it was hard to get a home run out of them. A swing and a miss were more common.

Likewise in life.

Yet now that he'd thrown her one, she couldn't ignore it.

Because assuming Kay was in over her head here and having buyer's remorse, there might be a different career option worth contemplating for a certain out-of-work hotel professional—if she was willing to take a gigantic leap of faith.

And that was a huge if.

25

With a glance at his sleeping wife, Andrew quietly closed the door to Paige's childhood bedroom and padded down the hall in his stocking feet toward the kitchen, tongue sticking to the roof of his mouth. There must have been a ton of salt in the sausage they'd had for breakfast. He needed a tall, cold drink. ASAP.

He checked his watch and yawned. Four hours of sleep in a real bed had helped, but it wouldn't hurt to clock a couple more before he and Paige went in search of a very late lunch en route back to the hospital.

At the end of the hall, he hung a left into the kitchen. Halted.

Paige's father was sitting at the oak table, shoulders hunched, his hair in disarray as if he'd been running his fingers through it, a soda can sitting in front of him.

Before Andrew could beat a hasty retreat, Warren caught sight of him and straightened up.

"Sorry to interrupt." Andrew took a step back. "I was going to get a glass of water, but I can come back later."

"Help yourself now." Warren waved toward the refrigerator. "There's soda and iced tea too, if you prefer either of those."

"That's okay. I don't want to disturb you." He turned to go.

"Wait."

At Warren's weary directive, Andrew angled back.

The older man kneaded his forehead, pushed himself to his feet, and grasped the back of the chair next to him. "Ann told me I should bury the hatchet and make things right with you."

A few beats of silence ticked by, and Andrew shifted his weight from one foot to the other. What did Paige's father expect him to say?

Apparently nothing, because after a few more seconds he spoke again.

"I saw how hard it was on Ann in our early years, while I was going to night school to get my degree and holding down a day job that paid squat. We barely eked by, despite the long hours she worked as a waitress to supplement our income. We lived paycheck to paycheck, always worried whether we'd have the funds for the next rent payment. I never wanted that kind of life for Paige."

"I can understand that."

"Did she ever tell you I started a college fund for her the day Ann discovered she was pregnant?"

"No." But in light of Warren's history, an attempt to secure his child's future fit. Paige had probably kept it to herself rather than add to his guilt about taking her away from the cushy life her parents had provided.

"It grew to a tidy sum. Even during our toughest times, I managed to put a few dollars in it from every paycheck. I wanted her to have a first-class education that would position her for a good-paying job that offered financial security and a comfortable life. She was on track for that until she met you."

If Warren was trying to pile on guilt, he was doing an excellent job of it.

"I never wanted to come between her and an education, or cause a rift between all of you. But I love her, and I won't apologize for that."

"Love doesn't put food on the table."

"No, but it feeds the soul. And we've never gone hungry." Close, but not quite, over the past few weeks.

Warren's gaze didn't waver from his. "I'm going to be honest with you. When I heard what happened to your company, I was almost glad. I thought Paige might realize her mistake and come home."

"I thought she might too—and I wouldn't have stopped her if that had been her choice."

Warren's eyes narrowed. "Why not?"

"Because I've always wanted what was best for her."

"So have I." He exhaled. "I guess that's one thing we can agree on."

"I think we should also be able to agree that she's old enough to decide what's best for herself. Right or wrong, she chose me—but she never stopped missing you both. Even though she tried to hide it from me, I know she cried a lot the first six months we were married. That ate at my gut. Yet aside from that, we were happy and doing well."

"Until you weren't."

He squared his shoulders. "I take full blame for what happened. I trusted someone too much. It was a hard lesson, but it's one I'll never forget. And we're on the upswing now."

Warren picked up his soda. Wiped the condensation off the can with a napkin. "Ann and I talked about your situation. If you need a loan until you can get back on your feet, we can provide one."

Andrew blinked.

That was a huge concession.

"I appreciate that, sir, but I think we'll be fine."

"Make it Warren. And the offer will remain on the table if you change your mind. Ann also asked me to let you know you're both welcome to visit anytime, and that we hope you'll stay in touch while she recovers—and going forward."

Andrew's throat tightened. "I appreciate that too, and I know Paige will feel the same way. I'll tell her after she wakes up."

The older man drained his can of soda, crossed to the sink, and twisted on the faucet. "I plan to go back to the hospital about five. I'll order food for us at four. Is pasta satisfactory?"

"You don't have to buy us dinner."

"Yes, I do. Ann has never let any visitor to this house go hungry. I can't offer you homemade fare like she would, but there's an excellent restaurant nearby that delivers." He finished rinsing his can and set it in the sink. "I'm going to lie down for another hour. Help yourself to whatever you want to drink."

As Paige's father dried his hands and left the room, Andrew crossed to the fridge. A few moments later, a door clicked shut down the hall.

What an unexpected but welcome turn of events.

He selected a soda, pulled the tab to release the pressure, and took a long swallow, letting the cold liquid soothe his parched throat.

And as he walked back down the hall, his parched soul was also refreshed.

All these years, he'd lamented over the split between Paige and her parents. Now they seemed poised on the brink of a reconciliation.

Adding one more heartening development to the new chapter in their lives that had begun in the little town of Hope Harbor.

"Are you certain you want to go to Frank's? An award like this deserves a fancy celebration." Vienna lifted the handsome acrylic obelisk Mom had brought back from Seattle and examined the engraving again. "I could take you to an upscale place in Coos Bay."

Her mother waved that suggestion aside. "Frank's is fine. I already spent seven hours in the car today. A small price to pay for a fabulous evening last night, but I'd rather not drive back up to Coos Bay."

"Okay." Vienna handed the award back, and her mother carefully set it on the coffee table. "Where are you going to put that?"

"I thought I'd display it near the checkout counter at the shop for a while. Unless you think that would be too boastful?"

"Not at all. You should let your customers know they're patronizing an award-winning bookstore. By the way, I was able to download your acceptance speech." She pulled a flash drive from her purse and held it out. "It was worth preserving. Your comments were memorable."

"Thank you for saying that. It's hard to go wrong when you speak from the heart. I'll put this in my fireproof box in the closet. If I have a bad day at the shop, I'll pull it out to pep up my spirits."

"Have you ever had a bad day at the shop?"

"No, I can't say that I have. Every day has been a joy. But if I do have a clunker, this will come in handy." She wiggled the flash drive, then set it beside the award. "Now let's eat. I'm starving!"

During the ride to Frank's, Vienna peppered her with questions about the event, and Mom was more than happy to regale her with story after story. If she hadn't met every single person in attendance, she'd taken a Herculean stab at it.

Only after they were seated at the restaurant and had placed their order did Mom turn the tables and query her about the latest at the inn.

Vienna filled her in, ending with the food glitch she and Matt had discussed this morning.

"Matt and I both agree that Kay doesn't seem to have the culinary skill to create the sort of gourmet fare I had in mind, nor the interest in learning how to make it. Plus, she won't be here for the opening. So we have to come up with an alternate idea until we can find someone willing to cook on-site on a regular basis. Do you happen to know anyone who's talented in the kitchen and also has a bit of flair?"

"That's a tall order." Mom put her napkin on her lap as their pizza was delivered to their table. "I'm running names through my mental Rolodex, but the only cooks I can think of are at the Myrtle. Tasty as their food is, I wouldn't call it gourmet."

Vienna lifted a loaded slice of pizza, picking off an olive that had somehow strayed onto their toppings. "With all the people who come into your shop, I hoped you'd run into someone we could tap for temporary duty."

"I wish I had. I can put a few feelers out, though. I could also put a notice on my bulletin board. You never know who could come out of the woodwork. Matt connected with Andrew from an ad there."

"It can't hurt."

But the likelihood of finding a cook of the caliber they needed using that route was minuscule.

Mom studied her. "This is a major problem, isn't it?"

"Yes. Food matters, especially to the bloggers. What they write could make or break the inn."

"Do you want me to pinch hit? I can whip up a mean tofu frittata, and my soymilk waffles are very tasty. I'm not volunteering for regular duty, but I'll be happy to help if I can."

Kind as Mom's offer was, her cooking skills weren't at the level the inn needed, either. Nor would the menu items she'd proposed be to everyone's taste.

"I appreciate that, but you're already leading the bloggers on a tide pool excursion and you're busy at the shop. I'll work something out."

"Thank goodness Matt is staying through their visit. You won't have to man the ship—or the inn—alone."

"He may be staying longer than that."

"What do you mean?"

Whoops.

Maybe she shouldn't have let that slip.

On the other hand . . . Matt hadn't asked her to keep their conversation to herself, and it would be helpful to talk with someone about her reaction to his news as well as a potential fork in her own road.

Vienna scanned the restaurant from their secluded corner table. No one was paying any attention to them, and the noise level was in a decibel range to ensure privacy.

"This has to stay between us." She refocused on her mom.

"Goes without saying. I know I'm a talker, but I also know when to zip it."

Vienna uncurled a string of mozzarella and laid it across her slice of pizza. "I think he's considering staying here and making a new start. He's had more than his share of tragedy."

"I imagine the loss of his wife was devastating."

"It was—and there's more loss than that."

"Which he's shared with you?"

"Yes."

"You two must have become very friendly during the inn redo, despite the bad first impression he made."

"I've revised my opinion of him."

"I'm glad to hear that. He strikes me as a very nice man." She pursed her lips. "It's interesting that he'd give up his practice in San Francisco, though. Much as I love Hope Harbor and agree it's a wonderful place for a new beginning, I would think there'd be limited opportunities for a vet."

"Not according to Eleanor Cooper." She passed on the woman's comment from church this morning. "And I expect, once word spreads, he'd draw from the surrounding area too."

"That's true. And now that I think about it, I suppose if one is interested in settling in a place like this, there could be more opportunities than you'd expect. There are plenty of examples of that in town."

"Such as?"

"Well . . . you know about Zach at The Perfect Blend. And his wife gave up her Hollywood career to become a chocolatier, with some acting on the side. But not everyone who's come opted for a new profession. Eric Nash, BJ's husband, continued his law career here by opening his own practice. I expect it's very different than his days in Portland at a high-end firm litigating on behalf of corporate clients from all over the world, but he's still in the same business."

Pizza poised halfway to her mouth, Vienna stared at her. "How do you know so much about everyone?"

Mom shrugged. "Lots of the residents come into the bookshop. They talk, and I ask questions and listen. It's amazing how much people will share once they realize you have a sincere interest in them." Mom took a slice of pizza.

Sincere interest described Mom to a T. Like Will Rogers, she'd never met a person she didn't like.

"I didn't realize how many of the residents had made a new start here."

"And that's just the tip of the iceberg. Of course, not all of them intended to stay when they came. Take Ben Garrison, Marci's husband. He's an orthopedic surgeon. He came to town to settle his grandfather's estate and had a plum job waiting for him in Ohio. Then he met Marci and ended up joining a practice in Coos Bay. From what I can tell, he doesn't have a single regret."

So Matt was only one of many who'd succumbed to the town's charms and thought about relocating here.

Perhaps because all of them had also been charmed by someone *in* the town.

Could she be one of the moving parts Matt was factoring into his decision? Had he been subtly trying to let her know that with his question about whether she could see the appeal of living in Hope Harbor?

"You have an intriguing look on your face." Mom stopped eating to inspect her. "What are you thinking? Or is this one of the times I should zip it and concentrate on my pizza?"

"No. I was just mulling over everything you said. I have to admit I was taken aback when Matt brought this up. Giving up an established practice would be a huge leap of faith."

"I imagine he'd do a great deal of investigation before he

jumped—unlike his sister, from what I've been picking up. Poor Kay. It sounds like she leaped before she looked."

"I get the same impression. Matt says she seems happier working in her friend's garden center in Boise than she does about the prospect of coming back to the inn. I can tell from my own conversations with her that she's not excited about tackling the breakfast challenge."

Mom shook her head. "That's a tough spot to be in. Based on her comments during our few meetups in town, she sank most of her nest egg into the inn."

"I think she did. From what I gather, her reserves are also running low. That's one of the incentives to get the inn up and running and generating income ASAP."

Expression speculative, Mom took another slice of pizza, picked off a pepperoni, and popped it in her mouth. "I wonder if she'd be open to an offer? Now that you've fixed it up and rebranded it, Sandcastle Inn could be a plum opportunity for someone with know-how in the business. Imagine running a world-class inn." Mom's eyebrows peaked as she bit into her pizza.

"Are you suggesting that someone might be me?"

"The inn has your touches all over it. Don't you already feel a sense of ownership?"

They were tracking the same direction.

"Yes. But that was never the intent. This was supposed to be a pro bono job to help Kay salvage a floundering B&B. A temporary gig, nothing more."

"But wouldn't it be amazing to own a fabulous inn? You'd also be your own boss."

There was that. Not only could she write the rules, but no one could ever fire her again.

"I do like the sound of that."

"And the icing on the cake would be Matt, if he ends up staying."

"We're not involved."

"You could be."

"He's never indicated he has that kind of interest in me." Not counting the electricity that sizzled in the air whenever they were together.

Mom gave her a get-real look. "The man told you the secrets of his heart. What do you need, writing in the sky?"

Vienna forced up the corners of her mouth and lightened her tone. "Are you trying to marry me off? The woman who dismissed the idea of tying the knot years ago?"

"You're cut from different cloth than I am. Marriage would suit you—to the right man, naturally. Matt could be him."

"He hasn't said he's staying for sure."

"It may be contingent on other factors."

Yeah. He'd implied that.

Like her staying too.

"Could be." That was the most she was willing to offer at this stage.

"You may want to discuss it with him. Or at least let him know you're receptive and give him an opening to bring it up if you're reluctant to broach the subject."

Vienna took a deep breath.

This day was ending on an unexpected and somewhat unnerving note.

"I don't know, Mom. My previous salary was excellent, and I socked away a hefty amount, but buying the inn would probably eat up all my savings and then some. Aside from whatever Kay paid for it, she's sunk a chunk of change into repairs and updating. The dollar amount could be a roadblock. I don't want to go into debt."

"Think of it as an investment. As for roadblocks, you'd have those with any venture. I suppose it comes down to how much you trust your instincts and experience and knowledge, and whether you think you can make a success of the inn. But if I can offer one piece of advice, don't base your decision on Matt's plans.

Buy the inn because you want it and you'll be happy here even if a romance fizzles."

That was sound counsel. There were no guarantees of a happily-ever-after at this early stage of their relationship.

"Advice appreciated."

"I'll tell you one other thing, sweet child." Her mom wiped her fingers on a napkin and reached across the table to touch her hand. "Your mama would be in seventh heaven if her little girl lived close enough to go with her on walks to the tide pools every week or two. And that relationship will never fizzle."

Vienna's vision misted. "I'd like living closer too." She filled her lungs. Exhaled. "I have a lot to ponder."

"The answers will come in time."

"Time is in short supply. The clock is ticking. Besides, you know how I've always agonized over every decision."

"Let the idea percolate for a few days. Do some of that due diligence you always talk about. Explore the possibilities with Kay and Matt. In the end, the answer may be easier than you think."

Vienna wasn't as confident of that as Mom.

But as her mother had said, she didn't have to decide anything tonight. The whole concept was new as of this afternoon.

So she'd sleep on it. Think. Pray.

And hope that whatever path she decided to take would lead to an exciting new journey and not a dead end.

26

"You'll come again soon, won't you?"

At her mom's anxious question, Paige exchanged a glance with Andrew.

"Yes, we will." He joined her beside the hospital bed. "If our work schedules allow, we'll stay for a long weekend."

"I'd like that. Wouldn't you, Warren?"

Paige looked across the white sheet that covered her mother to where her dad stood on the other side of the bed.

"Yes." He took Mom's hand. "The room will be theirs whenever they want it."

Grateful as she was that Dad had begun to mend his fences with Andrew and for his attempt to converse at dinner last night, he hadn't said a word to her directly about all the heartache between the two of them. Nor offered an apology.

But perhaps that would come eventually. Her father had held his emotions close to his vest in the best of times, and the two of them were only just beginning to emerge from a very rocky stretch.

In the meantime, his actions spoke volumes about his change of heart.

"You'll be careful going back?" Mom reached for her hand. Gave it a squeeze.

"Yes. Andrew's an excellent driver. I'll text Dad after we arrive." She bent down and kissed her mom's forehead. "I'll call you later tonight too."

"Hearing your voice will help my recovery more than any medicine the doctors prescribe."

Paige straightened up. "Goodbye, Dad."

"Safe travels."

Andrew said his goodbyes too, and as they skirted the bed and walked toward the exit, the murmur of conversation followed them, too soft to decipher.

As they were about to step into the hall, her father spoke.

"I'll walk with you to the elevator."

Paige swiveled toward him as he exchanged a look with Mom and joined them at the door.

What was that all about?

He followed them down the hall, pausing at the door to the waiting room. "You may each want to take a coffee to go. It will keep you alert on the drive. We were all up at the crack of dawn."

That was true, but until she had something more substantial in her stomach than the piece of toast she'd wolfed down at the house this morning, any more coffee would play havoc with her stomach. And Andrew had already downed a gallon of the stuff.

She opened her mouth to dismiss the suggestion, but Andrew took her hand and spoke first. "That's not a bad idea." His next comment was directed to her. "I'll get the truck while you fix our coffee. You can meet me outside the main entrance after your dad sees you off at the elevator."

The message in his eyes was clear.

He was giving her and Dad a few minutes alone, in case her father wanted to say anything to her in private before she left.

"Okay." She nodded. "I'll be down fast."

After telling her father goodbye again, Andrew veered left in the hall toward the elevators while she and Dad entered the empty waiting room.

Her father didn't speak as she prepared an unwanted cup of coffee for herself and one for Andrew.

Apparently he wasn't going to take the opening Andrew had provided.

But maybe the conversation between the two men yesterday in the kitchen was a sufficient start. From what Andrew had told her about it, the exchange had been difficult for Dad.

Stifling her disappointment, she snapped on plastic lids. She ought to be satisfied with the progress that had been made. There would be other opportunities down the road for her and Dad to mend their fences.

She turned toward her father. "This should set us up for the trip. Thank you again for dinner last night and for making us feel welcome. Especially Andrew."

Dad fiddled with the zipper on his father's jacket. "I'd like to get to know him better."

"I'd like that too. I think you'll be impressed." When her father didn't respond, she reached for the cups. "I should go. We have a full week ahead of us and—"

"What your mom said yesterday about me missing you . . . that was true."

She stopped. Looked over at him.

"I never really thought you'd walk out that day six years ago." He zipped the jacket up to his neck, his tone subdued. "But you called my bluff. Then I thought you'd realize you'd made a mistake and come home. But you didn't. And as time passed, it was harder and harder to figure out how to reconnect. I've never been good at admitting mistakes."

Yet he was admitting one now, at what had to be a high cost. The only thing Warren Reynolds had had left after his father died was the pride he'd always guarded and the iron will that had seen him through more adversity than most people ever faced. They'd been his defenses against the world. Allowing either to crack would have left him vulnerable to hurt and rejection.

Which put a whole different spin on his reaction the day she'd walked out, given the story he'd told her yesterday. Her departure must have felt like a replay of the nightmare with his father. Yes, she was still alive, but he could easily have interpreted her choice to marry Andrew against his wishes, to leave the safe and secure world he'd worked hard to create for her, as rejection and abandonment.

Vision misting, she touched the sleeve of his worn, tattered jacket. "I just want us to get back together, Dad. I love you and Mom. I appreciate all you both have done for me, and I know you always wanted what was best for me. I'm sorry we didn't agree in the end about what that was, but maybe we can start fresh."

"That would make your mother happy. Me too." He straightened up. "I should get back to her."

"And Andrew will be waiting." She hesitated. Dad had never been much into physical affection. That had always been Mom's purview. Her father had demonstrated his love in more practical ways—working hard to provide a comfortable life for them, planning family vacations each summer and driving her and Mom all over the country, helping her with gnarly math homework. The hugs he'd dispensed had been few and far between, and always stiff. Usually they'd been initiated by her.

But he'd loved her the best way he knew how.

And thanks to Mom's influence, she was a hugger.

Throwing caution to the wind, she stepped closer and slid her arms around him.

For a moment he froze. And then he wrapped her in the awkward embrace she'd missed for six long years and gave her a squeeze.

"I love you, Dad. Take care of Mom." She spoke the words against his chest.

"I will." His voice hoarsened.

After a couple more seconds, he disengaged and turned aside to pick up her coffee. "I'll carry these to the elevator for you. It will be hard to press the button with both hands occupied."

She gave him the space he needed to get his emotions under control.

Truth be told, she could use a few moments too.

He followed her into the hall and to the elevators, waiting until she was inside and had pressed the button for the lobby before handing her the two cups.

As the doors began to slide shut, he tucked his hands into the pockets of his jacket and met her gaze. "I love you, Paige. Always have. Always will."

Throat clogging, she sniffed as the doors closed and the elevator began its descent.

But another door had opened.

And God willing, it would never shut again.

The taco stand was open for business.

C. S. Lewis book in hand, Matt left his car behind and strode toward the food trailer beside the pocket park on the wharf.

Charley raised a hand in greeting as he approached. "You must have been reading my mind. I was going to swing by the inn today and ask if I'd left a book there when I drove Eleanor and Methuselah over on Friday."

"Yes, you did." Matt lifted the bag. "I've been stopping by the stand every day since, but the window was shuttered. Sorry you had to do without your book for four days."

"No worries. It wasn't for me. I bought it for a friend. It's hard to go wrong with C. S. Lewis if a person is in need of deep insights on any number of subjects."

"This is chock-full of them." Matt handed over the bag. "I hope you don't mind, but I read through it. More than once. I was careful not to bend the spine or leave fingerprints, though." He called up a smile.

"I'm delighted you found it worthwhile. I've always considered that particular volume to be especially perceptive. Probably because Lewis was writing from raw personal experience."

"It does have some excellent insights." Only someone who'd been there would know that grief was a long, winding valley, where any bend could reveal a new landscape. Or that sorrow was a process, not a state of mind.

"Yes. Lots of food for thought, no question about it." Charley tucked the bag under the serving counter. "Speaking of food, can I interest you in an order of tacos before the lunch rush hits?"

"I'd like to say yes, but I have to confess that I ate a huge chunk of Eleanor's fudge cake for breakfast. That will hold me to dinner or beyond."

"I've been known to overindulge on her cake too, though rarely for breakfast." Flashing him a smile, Charley picked up a rag and wiped the pristine counter. "How's Vienna these days? I haven't seen much of her."

"She's meeting herself coming and going trying to get the inn ready for the opening."

"I can imagine. When will Kay be back?"

"Not soon enough." He gave Charley a quick recap of the change in plans. "We're lucky Vienna was willing to take the lead on the opening."

"She strikes me as a very competent and dedicated woman."

"I'd say that's a spot-on description."

"Will she be on her own for the opening? Aren't you leaving soon?"

"I've extended my stay so she won't have to go it alone."

"That was kind of you." Two seagulls fluttered down near the food trailer, and Charley leaned out the serving window to take a gander at them. "I see my feathered friends have decided to drop in."

"Are they after a handout?"

"No. Floyd and Gladys aren't moochers. They're romantics. Did you know seagulls mate for life?"

"No. I'm not an avian specialist."

"They're fascinating creatures. Floyd lost his first partner and mourned her for a long time. He was a pathetic figure. A shadow of his former self. Then he met Gladys and got a new lease on life."

Matt eyed the two seagulls snuggled up together on the pavement a few yards away, their attention fixed on him. "I'm glad his story had a happy ending. Not everyone's does. And not everyone deserves one, if they've made mistakes." Frowning, he turned his back on the lovey-dovey twosome. Why had he made such a revealing comment? Charley didn't know his history. Only Vienna was privy to his darkest secrets.

"I don't know." Charley rested his forearms on the counter and leaned down, bringing him closer to eye level. "To err is human, as they say. God doesn't hold our mistakes against us. He knows humans are an imperfect species. And mistakes aren't an intentional infliction of injury, which is a different matter altogether. So why should we hold them against ourselves? In truth, expecting perfection may be a bit arrogant. Only God is perfect." He straightened up and motioned in the direction of Dockside Drive. "Maybe our Hope Harbor clerics can weigh in on this theological discussion."

Matt angled toward the street.

Father Murphy and Reverend Baker, dressed in golf shirts and slacks, were approaching from a few feet away.

"I'm at your service for help with any theological questions." Father Murphy gave a mock bow as he stopped beside the food trailer.

Reverend Baker's lips twitched. "Based on all the time he spent on the course today battling through the rough, digging himself out of sand traps, slicing the ball, and missing putts, he may be your man if the question is about accepting our imperfections."

"Ha. This from the man who hooked his first tee shot so badly it wound up on the adjacent fairway." The padre rolled his eyes.

"I was just getting warmed up."

"Then how do you explain your encore on the ninth hole?"

"That was a fluke." Reverend Baker gave a dismissive wave and shifted his attention to Charley. "I only caught the end of your comment, but from a theological perspective, I concur with what you said. Mistakes by definition are innocent, made without malice. God doesn't expect us to be perfect. All he expects is that we do our best."

"For once I agree with my clerical counterpart," Father Murphy chimed in. "Too many people carry heavy burdens of guilt over mistakes, and that can snuff the joy from the glorious gift of life God has blessed us with. A life he wants us to live fully and without regret."

"Well said." The minister gave an approving nod.

"I knew you men of the cloth would shed light on this topic." Charley adjusted his Ducks cap. "I'm glad you played golf today and wandered by, but what happened to your standing Thursday date? Tuesday is out of pattern for you."

Father Murphy grimaced and hooked a thumb toward his companion. "Blame it on my friend here. He volunteered us as drivers for a youth group outing on Thursday that our churches are jointly sponsoring."

"Where are you going?" Charley tossed a scrap of fish to Floyd and Gladys.

As the banter continued around him, Matt sneaked a peek at his watch. He had more walls to paint, and with the finish line for the project looming, it was wise to stick close in case Andrew needed a hand with anything.

At the first opportunity, he jumped back into the conversation. "It was nice to see all of you, but I have to get back to the inn. The grand reopening is approaching at warp speed."

"By all means. Don't let us hold you up. If you have any other theological questions, give me a ring." Father Murphy winked at him.

"I'll do that."

The three continued to chat as he dug out his keys and hustled back toward his car.

While there was plenty to keep him busy at the inn, if Vienna had a few spare minutes this afternoon, maybe he'd try to coax her into a quick coffee break by bribing her with another piece of Eleanor's fudge cake. That would be a pleasant interlude to—

"Matt!"

At the summons, he stopped beside his car and glanced across Dockside Drive.

Paige waved at him and hurried over.

At this rate he was never going to get back to the inn.

"I'm glad I ran into you." She stopped in front of him, a tad out of breath. "I just got off my shift at the Myrtle, and I have a few errands to run in town for Andrew's birthday. It's tomorrow."

That was news.

"I'm glad you told me." He'd have to detour and pick up a card at Bev's Book Nook before he headed back.

But the timing on the birthday couldn't have been more ideal. While Andrew would likely have refused a bonus at the end of the job, it would be harder to say no to a birthday gift. So he'd tuck a check inside the card, along with a slip of paper that would be an even better present.

"I wouldn't have under normal circumstances, but with all of us living under the same roof, it would be hard to keep it a secret. Especially since I'd like to surprise him with a special breakfast. I wanted to ask if it would be okay for me to use the kitchen early in the morning for longer than usual."

"Have at it. I'm not doing any cooking, and Vienna never has more than a bagel and coffee."

"I was hoping the two of you might join us. It would be more festive and party-like."

"Are you certain you wouldn't rather have a private meal? Vienna and I wouldn't mind making ourselves scarce."

"No. I'd like you both to be there."

"In that case, count me in. I'm sure Vienna will accept too. But don't you have to be at the Myrtle?"

"I switched with someone on the afternoon shift tomorrow. Is seven too early for breakfast? I know Andrew wants to keep pushing through on the inn."

"That's fine."

"If you could let Vienna know, I'd appreciate it. I'm afraid Andrew might walk in on me talking to her about it at the inn."

"I'd be happy to."

"Thanks. Now I have groceries to buy." With a wave and a sunny smile, she hurried toward the truck, parked farther down Dockside Drive.

Interesting that she'd arrived back from Portland last night upbeat and glowing despite her mother's health issues. Perhaps, if there had been an estrangement with her family, they'd repaired the rift.

Too bad he couldn't tap into a little of her good cheer.

He turned back to his car and slid behind the wheel for the short trip to Bev's Book Nook, mulling over his funk.

The source wasn't hard to identify.

Vienna.

She hadn't exactly seemed overjoyed Sunday when he'd told her he was considering relocating to Hope Harbor. Nor had she answered his question about whether she found the town appealing.

And she hadn't brought up the topic yesterday either.

It was possible, of course, that she'd been discombobulated by his bombshell.

Truth be told, it was still kind of shocking to him too. But perhaps it was time to make peace with his guilt and to accept that while his grief would be always with him, it was okay to start looking to the future instead of dwelling in the shadows of the past. To embrace the glorious gift of life Father Murphy had referenced. To welcome joy back into his world. To open his heart to love again.

And perhaps it was time to tell Vienna all of that too.

27

Wow.

As Paige set a plate in front of her early Wednesday morning in the inn's kitchen, Vienna's jaw dropped at the artfully presented food with an edible nasturtium floral garnish.

"I hope everything's okay." Paige continued around the table to Matt and placed a plate in front of him too. "I'm a little out of practice."

Vienna looked over at him. He was staring at his plate, apparently as stunned as she was.

"You haven't lost your touch, honey." Andrew rubbed his hands together. "This is what I call a birthday breakfast."

Paige deposited a basket of blueberry muffins with streusel topping in the center of the table. "In case you're wondering what all the food is, it's eggs Benedict, roasted garlic rosemary potatoes, a raspberry compote over yogurt, and roasted asparagus sprinkled with parmesan cheese."

Double wow.

After she got her eyeballs back in their sockets, Vienna sent another glance toward Matt.

He was still fixated on his plate, but as if sensing her perusal, he lifted his chin—and hopefully read her mind.

Could this be the answer to our food dilemma?

It could if everything tasted as delicious as it looked. And if Paige was able to figure out how to reconfigure her schedule at the Myrtle. And if they could convince her to help them out.

Lots of ifs there.

"This is amazing." Vienna directed her comment to Paige as the other woman took her seat. "Where did you learn to cook like this?"

She gave a self-deprecating shrug. "No special training. I'm self-taught. I've always loved cooking and would have been interested in going to culinary school, but my parents wanted me to get a business degree. They thought that would lead to a more practical and higher-paying job. In the end, I didn't do either."

"That was my fault." Andrew speared a piece of potato. "She married me instead, much to her parents' regret."

"But we're mending our fences now." Paige reached over and squeezed his hand. "And it wasn't your fault. I chose you over school. I can always go back someday if I want to."

"Or pursue a career in food." He took a bite of the eggs Benedict. Closed his eyes. "This is great."

"I may see if I can pick up a few catering jobs once we're settled in, like I did in Portland until the company got busy and required all of my time."

Catering jobs?

Yes!

The solution to their food problem at the inn could very well be sitting at this table.

Vienna worked her way around her plate as they all conversed. Every item had an intriguing blend of flavors, including the yogurt topped with compote.

"What's in this, Paige?" Vienna lifted her yogurt-filled spoon. "It seems simple, but there's a unique combination of flavors that gives it a zing."

"My secret ingredients—a hint of lemon zest, a sprinkle of cinnamon, and a touch of ginger."

"It's a winner."

"I second that." Matt was already halfway through his meal. "Vienna, this is restaurant worthy, don't you think?"

They were on the same page.

"Or high-end inn worthy."

"Agreed."

They both looked at Paige.

She stopped eating. "Is something wrong?"

"On the contrary." Vienna cut another bite of her eggs Benedict. "It may be very right, if you're willing and able to help us out." She proceeded to explain their breakfast and afternoon snack challenge. "Based on this meal, you have the skill and the flair to give the inn exactly what it needs until we can find someone to take on the job permanently. Unless that would interest you too."

"You mean, like . . . be the chef at the inn?"

"More or less. It wouldn't be a full-time job. Just breakfast and the afternoon snack. Would the snack part be an issue? It should be fancier fare than chocolate chip cookies, though it would be nice to have those on hand too."

"I used to do hors d'oeuvres for some of my catering customers. Like baked brie with a maple syrup and brown sugar topping, and avocado bruschetta, and crab salad tapas, and three-cheese crostini. Is that the sort of thing you're thinking about?"

This was a miracle.

"Yes. Any and all of the above."

As Paige's eyes began to sparkle, Andrew took her hand. "Why don't you do it? This would be right up your alley."

"I'd love to—but what about the Myrtle? I made a commitment there to fill in until the regular waitress gets back from maternity leave."

"Would someone be willing to switch shifts with you, like they did today?"

"I could ask."

"It would be a lifesaver for us. Or rather, for Kay and the inn."

Vienna took a muffin and broke it apart. Nibbled a tender bite. Bliss. "These would have to be on the menu on a regular basis."

"The thing is, we need an answer as soon as possible." Matt took a muffin too. "With the opening breathing down our neck, we have to make arrangements fast. Vienna was thinking of having a caterer in Coos Bay provide the food on a temporary basis, but that's not ideal."

"I could ask the server who switched with me today if she'd keep doing that until the other woman comes back. If she says no, I could call the Myrtle and see if they think anyone else might be willing to exchange shifts."

"That would be fantastic." Vienna continued to eat her muffin. Maybe the tastiest one she'd ever had. Every bit as good if not better than the breakfast sweets at the inns in her former company's collection.

The talk shifted to other topics during the remainder of the meal, and at the end Matt handed Andrew an envelope. "What's a birthday without a present?"

Andrew wiped his mouth on his napkin and took it. "Thank you."

"Or at the very least a card." Vienna withdrew an envelope from the purse she'd hung over the back of her chair and handed it over too.

She and Matt must also have been on the same wavelength about recognizing Andrew's special day.

The birthday boy opened hers first, read the sentiment she'd penned, and smiled. "Thank you, but I think I was the lucky one the day I got this job." He set her card aside and picked up Matt's.

From her seat, Vienna could see two folded pieces of paper inside as Andrew flipped it open.

One of them was a check. No doubt from Matt's coffers, not Kay's.

What a thoughtful and generous gesture.

Andrew opened the check. Blinked. Angled it for Paige to see as he shook his head. "I can't take this."

"Yes, you can." Matt sipped his coffee. "It's not polite to refuse a birthday gift. It's also a token of my appreciation for all your hard work here. You were a lifesaver. Besides, the other enclosure is the real gift."

Andrew set the card on the table and opened the other piece of paper. Raised his eyebrows at Matt after he skimmed it.

"That's the contact information for BJ Stevens Nash, who owns the local construction firm." Matt set his mug back on the table. "She came by Sunday and poked around. To say she was impressed with your work would be an understatement. She's staffing up for a big project, and she asked me to let you know she'd like to talk to you about possibly coming on board."

"Oh, Andrew!" Joy suffused Paige's face. "What a wonderful birthday present! I knew Hope Harbor would give us a second chance. There are opportunities here for both of us."

"I don't have this job yet." Andrew waved the piece of paper with BJ's name on it. "And you may not be able to change your shift at the Myrtle." Despite his caveats, excitement and enthusiasm and hope filled his eyes.

"I'm not worried. I have good feelings about this. After what happened in Portland over the weekend, anything is possible."

"True." He gave her a quick kiss and pushed back his chair. "That was a fantastic start to my birthday, but now it's back to work for me—after I call BJ."

"Can I help you with the cleanup, Paige?" Vienna stood too.

"No, thank you. I have it covered. I've been cleaning as I cooked, so there isn't much to deal with."

"In that case . . ." She turned toward Matt. "Before you dive into whatever is on your to-do list today, could you spare a few minutes? I have something I want to discuss with you."

"Sure." He rose. "It's a beautiful morning. You want to sit on the terrace?"

"Or walk down the beach. After that huge breakfast, I wouldn't mind burning off a few calories."

"I hear you."

After they both thanked Paige again for the meal and wished Andrew another happy birthday, he followed her out.

Since her dinner with Mom on Sunday, her mind had been in a whirl over the idea of a change in ownership for Sandcastle Inn and a permanent move to Hope Harbor.

And the more she'd played with the idea, the sweeter it had sounded.

The possibility that Matt might make a similar move was icing on the cake, but even if he didn't . . . even if nothing ever came of the voltage between them . . . Hope Harbor wouldn't lose its appeal. The town was idyllic, her mom lived here, and she'd be her own boss at a world-class inn.

That was a win all around.

The time had come to explore the possibilities with both Kay and Matt.

"Can you believe a cook of Paige's caliber was right under our noses all these weeks?" Matt fell in beside her as she struck off up the long stretch of sand. "It's almost like a miracle."

"I know. And lots of other mind-blowing stuff has been happening lately too. Like a well-established vet thinking about leaving his big-city practice behind to open an office in Hope Harbor. And a very ambitious hotel professional getting involved pro bono with a floundering inn and falling in love with it—and the idea of being her own boss."

Matt stopped walking.

She did too.

"What are you saying?" His expression was difficult to read as he turned toward her.

Her pulse picked up, and she drew a steadying breath. "You asked me the other day if I could see the appeal of living in Hope Harbor. I didn't answer you then, because I'd never given it any serious thought. But I have in the days since, and the answer is yes. I love the town, and I love the inn. If Kay would be willing to let it go, I'd like to consider buying it." Here came the put-yourself-on-the-line part. "My decision isn't contingent on anything else, but it would sweeten the deal if that vet I mentioned also followed through and relocated here."

He stared at her, and as the seconds ticked by, heat crept across her cheeks.

Mom must have been wrong.

Matt's decision to share the secrets of his heart didn't appear to be writing on the sky about his feelings for her after all. He must have simply reached a stage in his grieving where he needed someone to—

"Are you saying what I think you're saying?" His inflection was tinged with caution . . . and hope.

Might as well go for broke.

"That depends on what you think I'm saying. If you think I'm saying I like you and am open to exploring a relationship that goes beyond inn business, your instincts are correct."

A slow smile curved his lips. "One of the moving parts in my decision just clicked into place."

Joy bubbled up inside her.

"I don't know that I've ever been called a moving part before, but I'll take it. However, that comes with a certain amount of pressure. As my mother advised me, a life-changing decision shouldn't be based on a new relationship that could peter out. You should do this because you want to live here. What if nothing ever happens between us? I wouldn't want to have to deal with a boatload of guilt if you upend your life for me."

"Trust me, I know all about guilt—and I wouldn't wish that burden on anyone. I like Hope Harbor. From my very preliminary investigation, it appears a vet clinic would fill a gap here. But there's one piece of research I haven't tackled yet."

"What's that?"

He slowly lifted his hand. Ran a gentle, tentative finger along the line of her jaw.

Her lungs locked.

"It has to do with electricity." He fingered her hair. Tucked it behind her ear. Let his hand slide around behind her neck to cup her head.

Then he bent and guided her lips to his in a kiss that set off sparklers and fireworks and thunderous, ground-shaking reverberations. And did she somewhere hear the booming strains of Tchaikovsky's *1812 Overture*?

When he at last eased back, she clung to him. Otherwise, her shaky legs would have collapsed, and she'd have ended up face down in the sand.

"That was . . . incredible." Her breath came in shallow gasps.

His respiration didn't seem any steadier than hers. "Yeah." He inhaled. "I don't think there are any worries on the electricity front."

"No." She made a mighty effort to engage the left side of her brain. "But there's more to a successful long-term relationship than that."

"Agreed. For the record, I'm attracted to you for many reasons beyond the obvious physical ones. You're an amazing woman, Vienna Price, and I can't wait to get to know you better."

"I feel the same about you. But what if Kay doesn't want to sell? Or you discover the market here for a vet isn't as promising as you thought?"

"I'll call Kay this afternoon. To tell you the truth, I think she'll jump at the chance to unload the inn. And if I find out Hope Harbor isn't an optimal place for a vet clinic, a town like Coos Bay ought to be able to support another vet. That would be a very manageable commute."

"So are we really going to do this?" Excitement and anticipation thrummed in her nerve endings at all the delicious possibilities ahead.

"I'd say we're both leaning that direction—but we have an inn to open first. I don't want to lose sight of that. If the blogger weekend doesn't bring in the kind of bookings you're hoping for, you may change your mind about buying it."

"I don't think so. The inn is a treasure waiting to be discovered, and I'm confident I can make that happen even if the initial promotion doesn't do the trick. But I think it will. Besides, I have a huge incentive now to make sure Sandcastle Inn lives up to its promise."

"It seems the two of us will be very busy for the next ten days."

"I don't mind busy if it leads to good results."

"Neither do I." He took her hand. "You want to head back?" He nodded toward the inn, only fifty yards away. "We both have work to do."

"We didn't get very far on our walk."

"No, but we made huge strides elsewhere."

At the warmth in his eyes, her heart melted.

That was true.

And as they started back toward the inn, she gave a contented sigh.

For who could have known that while she'd been refashioning the inn to represent fantasies and dreams and fairy tales and happily-ever-afters, she'd find herself poised to discover those very things herself in this tiny town on the Oregon coast?

Assuming all went well over the next ten days.

28

As Matt began to paint the final wall in the last bedroom of the inn, his phone vibrated in his pocket.

Finally.

He set the roller down and pulled out the cell. Checked the screen.

Yep. It was Kay.

He put the phone to his ear and watched through the window as two seagulls soared overhead. "Hey, Sis. You're a hard person to reach. How's Cora now that she's been home for twenty-four hours?"

"She's doing wonderful. The antibiotics knocked out the infection, and she's back to her feisty self."

"I heard that." Cora's gravelly voice was muffled in the background.

Matt grinned. "I can tell. I want to talk to her before I hang up."

"She wouldn't have it any other way. So what's up? I talked to you last night. You don't usually call in the middle of the day. I ran over to the garden center this morning to help with a special order for a couple of hours, and I had my phone on mute."

"I have some news."

"Good or bad?"

"Not bad. Could be good. Depends on your perspective."

"What is this, a riddle?"

"No. It's a possible offer on the inn."

Several silent seconds ticked by.

"Okay, you're going to have to back up. What are you talking about?"

"I'm talking about a potential sale. Vienna may be interested in buying it if you'd like to get out of the innkeeping business. Assuming you two can come to terms."

More silence.

He waited her out while she digested that shocker.

"Is this for real?"

"Yes. After all the work she's put into the place, she's fallen in love with it." And was maybe on the verge of falling in love with him too—but he left that unsaid. He'd delivered enough startling news for one day.

"Wow." Kay blew out a breath. "I never expected anything like this."

"I don't think Vienna did either. She had her sights set on a high-level job somewhere with a glitzy hotel chain. But Hope Harbor is special, Sandcastle Inn has tremendous potential, and her mom lives here."

"Yeah. I can understand her motivation. I mean, I think she's done wonders with the inn and I like the town too, but it was kind of lonely for me. I really missed Cora."

"You could stay in Boise if you sold out. Spend more time with Cora and your friend at the garden center."

"Funny you should mention that."

"How so?"

"Liz was talking this morning about how she'd like to expand, but she said it was too much for one person to take on. I think she'd be thrilled to find a partner. Matt . . . it would be a fun business. She and I click, and you know how much I love flowers and gardening."

A caution flag began waving in his mind.

"Puttering around in a home garden is different than working with plants and flowers all day, every day."

"I know, but I've been at the garden center on a regular basis over the past few weeks, and I've enjoyed every minute I've spent there. Much more than I'd enjoy making gourmet breakfasts at an inn."

That, he could believe. Her interest in fancy culinary chores had been underwhelming.

"You could always hire someone to do that."

"I guess."

Zero enthusiasm, suggesting she was also fast losing interest in running an inn.

That didn't mean she should jump headfirst into another venture, however.

"Kay, you've been down this road once, with the inn. You're incredibly fortunate that someone came along who may be willing to take it off your hands. That won't happen a second time."

"I know. But the garden center opportunity seems like a gift from God. Think about it. What were the odds someone like Vienna would appear out of nowhere and not only tackle the redo but be interested in buying the place so I would be free to pursue a different future? That alignment is too perfect to be coincidence."

She had a point.

"I'll concede it seems providential, but I wouldn't recommend jumping into anything without a great deal of thought and research up front, plus due diligence that includes a thorough examination of the property and the books."

"Trust me, I'm done leaping before I look."

Good to know.

"If Vienna does end up buying the inn, I'd also suggest you work at the garden center for six months before you put a dime into it. That would give you a chance to see if you like dealing with plants and flowers as well as the business side of the operation day in and day out."

"That sounds reasonable to me. Should I call Vienna today to discuss this?"

"Why don't you let me tell her you're receptive and have her call you when she has a spare minute? She's got a full plate until the opening's behind us."

"Okay." Kay exhaled. "Listen, if this all comes to pass, I should apologize for asking you to leave your practice behind to babysit a property I probably never should have bought in the first place."

"No apology necessary. I've enjoyed my weeks here."

"Right." She snorted. "Being a construction foreman and painter is exactly how you'd have chosen to spend your precious vacation days."

"There have been other compensations."

"Like what?"

"The town is charming, and I've met a lot of nice people." One in particular.

In fact . . . should he begin laying the groundwork with Kay for his possible relocation to the town?

Maybe.

Putting it off would serve no purpose.

He propped a shoulder against the window frame as the gulls wheeled overhead. "To tell you the truth, I wouldn't mind living in Hope Harbor."

"I thought the same thing. But now that I'm back in Boise, I realize how homesick I was. And you have a life and a career in San Francisco."

"My skills could find a market anywhere."

"I doubt a place the size of Hope Harbor would support a vet practice."

"You might be surprised."

A few beats ticked by.

When she spoke again, there was a note of caution in her inflection. "We *are* talking hypotheticals, right?"

"Not necessarily."

"Matt." Caution had been replaced by alarm. "Aren't you the one who just told me not to make any big changes without a great deal of thought and research?"

At least she'd been listening to him.

"I didn't say I was going to be rash. I said I'm considering it." Even if he was already past the considering stage. But unlike Kay, he had another incentive for a major move.

Namely, Vienna.

"You're full of surprises today."

"All happy ones." He turned away from the window. "I should get back to work. The carpet layers are waiting in the wings, and I want all the painting finished before they show up. Let me talk to Cora for a minute first, though."

"You got it. Promise you'll have Vienna call me ASAP?"

"Yes."

"Here's Cora."

As the woman greeted him, Matt smiled. Kay hadn't been exaggerating. The spunk was back in her voice.

"How's my favorite chocolate-chip-cookie baker?" He wandered back to the paint tray.

"Improving by the day and on the mend. But I don't want to talk about me. Tell me how you are."

"Busy. No complaints, though. The inn's shaping up. Vienna's done a terrific job redoing the place. Kay wouldn't recognize it. It's an innkeeper's dream."

"From what I picked up of your conversation with Kay, I got the impression she may not be an innkeeper much longer. Which I believe would suit her fine. She's in the kitchen, by the way. We can talk freely."

"I'd say her innkeeping days could be numbered. Vienna may be interested in buying the place."

"Ah. That would explain why you're thinking of opening a practice in Hope Harbor. I did pick that up correctly, didn't I? Not that I was eavesdropping or anything."

His lips flexed. "Perish the thought. And yes, I am. But Vienna isn't the only reason for that."

Whoops.

Slip of the tongue.

And of course Cora homed in on it, astute woman that she was. "*Only* suggests she's one of the reasons, though—and I'll wager a big one."

"Cora, before you get carried away, I—"

"Matt."

He shut up. When she used that tone, it was better to let her speak her piece.

"I don't think I'm the one who's getting carried away. Which isn't a criticism, mind you. If I had all my energy back, I'd stand up and cheer."

"Just don't get too carried away *yet*."

"Duly noted. But at least you're moving forward. That's what counts. I want to meet this young woman."

"That can be arranged as soon as you've recuperated and are able to travel. Assuming she and Kay come to terms on the inn."

"They will. Kay is probably doing a happy dance as we speak. I think if she can get most of her investment back, she'll be ecstatic. So what's your plan? You can't walk out on your partner with no notice."

The very subject he'd been thinking about as he rolled paint onto the walls today.

"No. I expect it may be a four to six month transition. But we do have a competent vet on staff who can take my place. In the meantime, I have to research the area here and find the optimal location for an office."

"I want regular progress reports."

"Will weekly updates suffice?"

"I'll let you know if they don't. Love you, Matt."

"Love you back, Cora."

Smiling, he ended the call and stowed his phone.

If everything worked out as he hoped, it appeared Sandcastle Inn was going to be launched with several of the happy endings it was designed to promote already under its belt—even if all of them weren't romance-related.

As Vienna waved off the final blogger she'd entertained for two and a half nonstop days, she exhaled.

The last two weeks had been a whirlwind, but everything had come together flawlessly and with dizzying speed. There'd been only a few minor glitches during the soft opening earlier in the week with paying customers, and the blogger weekend had been phenomenal. If the inn didn't get superlative coverage from all three of them, she'd be dumbfounded.

Once the dust from the departing car settled on the newly smoothed-out driveway, she turned back toward the front door.

Matt was watching her from the threshold, a suitcase behind him in the foyer.

Her stomach dropped.

This was the moment she'd been dreading.

Yes, she understood why he had to go back to San Francisco. He had loose ends to tie up there, as she did in Denver—and his would take longer. You didn't walk out of a long-term practice with two weeks' notice.

She, on the other hand, was set to become an innkeeper as soon as all the paperwork was ready to sign. Back in Denver, there was only an apartment to pack and moving arrangements to be made. A short shutdown of the inn to give the bloggers a chance to post about it and to let reservations begin to roll in would give her ample opportunity to take care of all her business.

The corners of Matt's lips rose. "You did it."

"No. *We* did it—and I'm including Andrew and Paige in that."

"Rightly so. We couldn't have managed this without them."

She walked over to him. "I guess you have to leave."

"Soon. Unless I want to be driving late into the night."

"I wish we'd had more time together these past two weeks."

"We snuck in stolen moments here and there—and we'll make up for it going forward. I do have a few minutes to spare if you want to sit with me on the terrace before I take off. I'd open a bottle of champagne to celebrate a successful launch, but you told me the bubbles tickle your nose."

"Having a few minutes alone with you will be intoxicating enough."

His smile broadened, and he waggled his eyebrows. "I'm flattered. Unless you say that to all the guys?"

"Nope." She stopped in front of him and rested her hands on his shoulders. "Only you."

His eyes darkened, and he leaned down. She rose on tiptoe to meet him, letting her eyelids drift closed and—

"I'm getting ready to—oh."

Vienna pulled back and peeked past Matt as he twisted around.

Paige stood in the doorway that led from the foyer to the back of the house.

"I was, uh, getting ready to go and wanted to give this to Matt." She lifted a white box like the ones she'd prepared for each blogger as a parting gift, filled with goodies to nibble on during their trip home. "I can, uh, leave it in the kitchen."

She started to retreat, but Vienna stepped out from behind Matt, willing the heat in her cheeks to subside. It wasn't as if she and Matt were going to be able to keep their relationship a secret for long in a place the size of Hope Harbor, anyway. Especially since the building he was eyeing for a vet office was at the edge of town on 101, and everyone would soon be seeing them together on his weekend visits.

"Matt was saying goodbye."

"Yes. I saw that." Paige seemed to be having difficulty keeping a straight face. "I should be going too. Andrew promised to hang curtains in our new apartment, and I don't want to keep him waiting." She crossed to Matt and held the box out to him. "In case you get hungry during your trip."

"Thank you."

"That was an inspired idea, Paige." Vienna motioned to the box. "One final positive impression to leave with the bloggers. All the food you made was also fantastic. Thank you again for working everything out at the Myrtle so you could handle that for us."

"It was my pleasure, believe me. And don't worry about the inn while you're back in Denver. Andrew or I will swing by every day to do a walk-through. Now that he's working for BJ, his hours are more regular."

"I appreciate that."

"Safe travels, Matt." Paige wiggled her fingers, pulled her keys from her purse, and sidled past them to exit through the front door.

When it clicked shut, Matt held out his hand.

Vienna took it and let him lead her toward the back of the inn, through the spacious great room that looked even more airy and large without all the excess furniture she'd ditched. Past the beautiful flower arrangement Kay had sent after they'd agreed on a price for the inn that included her original modest investment plus a significant share of the cost of improvements.

The deal had been a win-win for both of them.

Out on the terrace, Matt tugged her to the far side, where the sea stretched to the horizon unobstructed by the boughs of the evergreen trees that sheltered the inn. "Alone at last."

"Not quite." She motioned to two seagulls, sitting side by side on the flagstones a few yards away.

"Those kinds of witnesses I don't mind. They won't tell tales. Except maybe to Charley."

"What?" She arched her eyebrows.

"He seems to have a special connection to birds."

She gave the two gulls a skeptical survey. "I'm not too worried. Besides, I don't care who knows about us." She angled toward him. "Now where were we?"

"I think we were at the part where I sweep you off your feet and the soundtrack is supposed to soar."

"Swept off my feet—check. As for the soundtrack, I'll settle for the waves and the wind."

"I'm with you." He touched her cheek. Sighed. "It's going to be tough not being in the same place for a while."

"You'll be here on quite a few weekends, though."

"But the weeks in between will be long and empty."

"So let's use the time we have together to make memories that will carry us through until we're together again."

"I like that plan. What do you say we start with a kiss to remember?" He held out his arms.

She moved into them. "Ready whenever you are."

He didn't need a second invitation to dip his head and capture her lips in a kiss that was filled with dreams and magic and stardust.

And as the avian duo serenaded them in the background with a sweet coo that was most unusual for gulls . . . as the distant boom of waves against the craggy offshore sea stacks pounded in tempo with her pulse . . . as the tangy salt air swirled around them and the warm breeze caressed her skin . . . joy bubbled up inside her.

For even though they were still in the early stages of a romance neither of them had expected, and it was a bit difficult to clearly see the road ahead, she knew with absolute certainty that wherever it led, she'd be traveling it with this special man beside her.

Now and forever.

Epilogue

"Mmm. Can we stay here forever?" Vienna shaded her eyes and looked up from the double chaise lounge.

Matt handed his bride one of the glasses of lemonade he'd retrieved from the kitchen of the private little casita he'd reserved for their Sedona honeymoon. "Sadly, no. You have an inn to run, and I have pets to take care of."

She sighed. "I know. And I do love my job." She shifted onto her side, tenderness suffusing her features. "But I love you more."

"The feeling is mutual." As he'd tried to prove not only over the past eight months but every day of the blissful honeymoon that had been distraction free.

Except for the very major distraction his wife represented.

He stretched out beside her, soaking up the warmth of the March sun on their secluded balcony.

"I'm definitely not ready to go back in two days." She stroked a finger over his lips.

He captured her hand and pressed a kiss to her palm. "Me neither."

"At least I didn't have to worry about the inn while we were gone. Paige has the routine down after her stint as substitute host last fall while Mom and I were gone. I'm grateful she was able to work inn duties around her blossoming catering business. She told me she has two new bookings lined up at Edgecliff. Apparently the historic estate is on a roll since it opened to the public for private events. But she assured me that preparing food at the inn will always be her priority."

"That's good to know. I'm happy for her—and for Andrew. I saw BJ at The Perfect Blend the day before our wedding, and she was singing his praises. I got the feeling he was in line for a foreman slot as soon as one opens up."

"They deserve all the success that comes their way."

"Amen to that." He took a sip of his lemonade and swept a hand over the casita. "I know we both agreed to go low-key on this trip, but are you certain this was nice enough? I would have taken you anywhere in the world, to the fanciest spot on earth, if that's what you'd wanted."

She smiled and traced the line of his jaw with her index finger, leaving a trail of warmth on his skin. "I live in a luxury inn. Soon we'll both be living there. The only luxury I wanted on this honeymoon was uninterrupted quiet time alone with my groom. This place fit the bill, and it's met every expectation I had. As has the groom." Her eyes softened in invitation.

Pulse picking up, he motioned to her lemonade. "Are you going to drink that?"

"I suppose I should. I don't want to get dehydrated after our hike through the glorious red rocks this morning. And all this sugar may bolster my energy for any other glorious activity we might want to engage in this afternoon." She arched her eyebrows, then tipped her head back and sipped the frosty drink, giving him a close-up view of her elegant profile.

He lifted his own glass and took several large gulps. The sooner they finished their lemonade, the sooner they could move on to the other activity she'd mentioned.

"Isn't this weather wonderful?" She leaned back again, raising her face to the rays of the sun. "Mom and I would have loved these cloudless blue skies and balmy temperatures while we were in London last fall on her other bucket list trip."

"I don't think the weather dampened your enjoyment."

"It didn't—and London was a much better location for me than Vienna would have been. I know Mom was thrilled when I suggested we go together. I think she was afraid that once you and I got involved, she'd be a third wheel."

"No more so than Cora or Kay are. Family is important."

"Yes, it is. And I think it's great that Kay decided to accept Cora's invitation to move in with her. That beats living alone for both of them. I'm just glad she could break away for the wedding, with the ink hardly dry on her buy-in to the garden center."

"She wouldn't have missed our big day for the world."

"I talked to her at the reception, and she seemed thrilled about her new venture. You really think she'll be okay this go-round?"

"Yes. She worked there for six months to make sure it was a fit, and the accountant who audited the books gave the operation high marks. She should be fine." He finished off his lemonade and set the empty tumbler on the table beside him. Enough chitchat. The clock was ticking down on their honeymoon, and he didn't want to waste one more minute focused on anything but the woman he loved. "Are you going to nurse that all afternoon?" He tapped the glass in her hand.

She peeked over at him with an impish glance that supercharged his libido. "Do we have somewhere to go?"

"Mm-hmm." He leaned over and nibbled her ear. "It's not far in terms of distance, but a whole different realm awaits through that portal." He motioned toward the door in the adobe wall of the casita. "Want to step through with me?"

In response, she drained her glass and stood. "I could be persuaded." She held out her hand and smiled.

A millisecond later he was on his feet. He twined his fingers with hers, pressure building in his throat as he gazed at her beautiful face. "Have I told you lately that I love you?"

She edged closer, until nothing but a whisper separated them. "I believe I've only heard that four or five times today. You're slipping." An enchanting dimple dented her cheek.

"Maybe I should let actions speak louder than words."

"Maybe you should."

When he tugged her toward the door, she followed without protest.

And as he led her inside, his heart overflowed.

For with her sweetness and generous spirit, this special woman had refreshed his soul and illuminated his world—as she would continue to do for all their tomorrows in a tiny seaside town with the appropriate name of Hope Harbor.

A magical place where his heart had healed . . . and love had bloomed.

Author's Note

This is a milestone book—number ten in the Hope Harbor series.

Amazing.

When I began this series in 2015, I hoped readers would come to love my small town on the Oregon coast as much as I did. But the reception was beyond my wildest dreams. Readers around the world have embraced this charming seaside community that *Publishers Weekly* calls "a place of emotional restoration that readers will yearn to visit." I am grateful beyond words to everyone who has read these books and asked for more.

There are always certain people I thank at the end of a book, and top on the list is my husband, Tom, whose steadfast support for my writing career is a treasure beyond price. He is always there for me, on good days and bad, and his faithful, sustaining love feeds my soul and adds joy to my days.

My deepest thanks also to my parents, James and Dorothy Hannon. They're both gone now, but the memory of their love, encouragement, and unwavering belief in me are tucked in my heart forever.

As always, my gratitude to the amazing team at Revell, especially Jennifer Leep, Brianne Dekker, Laura Klynstra, Kristin Kornoelje, and Karen Steele. I've been with this wonderful publisher for more than fifteen years, and I count our partnership among my cherished blessings.

Peeking ahead in my publishing schedule, the Hope Harbor series will continue with book 11 in April 2025. And in October 2024, watch for book 2 in my Undaunted Courage series, in which a police detective must determine whether a traumatized murder witness's claim that she's being targeted is true—and if it is, figure out who is behind the relentless campaign that seems designed to destroy her credibility . . . and perhaps her life. I hope you'll add both of these books to your TBR list!

Thanks for reading *Sandcastle Inn*!

Love Irene Hannon's writing? Turn the page for a sneak peek at the next book in the

UNDAUNTED COURAGE SERIES

OVER THE EDGE

That was odd.

Lindsey Barnes eased back on the gas pedal and surveyed the empty bay in the three-car garage at her client's upscale house. The one used by the female half of the power couple.

If Heidi Robertson had gone out, why hadn't she closed the door to her spot?

Whatever the reason, her absence was welcome news. It should be simple to dash in and grab the knife roll she'd left yesterday, with no one the wiser.

Unless the other half of the couple was home.

But according to Heidi, James lived at the office. From what Lindsey had gleaned during her interview for the personal chef position four months ago, running a commercial real estate development firm was a 24/7 occupation.

So odds were this would be a quick in-and-out.

Nevertheless, she continued toward the concrete pad out of sight behind the garage, where the help parked. If her client happened to return during this brief visit, she wouldn't be happy to discover an out-of-place car. The lady of the house liked her instructions followed to a T—a lesson learned via a taut email after the new personal chef forgot to use the woman's preferred font on the heating instructions for each dish.

Rolling her eyes, Lindsey rounded the garage.

At least she didn't have to deal with Heidi beyond their menu planning emails. All she had to do was slip into the kitchen once a week, do her thing, and leave. Plus, the Robertsons paid their bill promptly—an important consideration if you were still establishing your business and cash flow was sometimes an issue.

Lindsey tucked her older-model Focus next to a pickup truck bearing the name Allen Construction.

Chad must be on the premises.

Good for him.

He deserved every plum job he could get after all the hardships he'd endured.

Lindsey set the brake, pulled out her phone, and dialed Heidi's number again on the off chance the woman would pick up. But as it had half an hour ago, the call rolled to voicemail.

So much for the courtesy of informing her she was on the premises. But Heidi had told her to let herself in whenever she came—and she needed those knives. Besides, the woman had assured her that neither of the Robertsons hung around in the kitchen.

After stowing her phone, she opened her car door and slid from behind the wheel. The faint sound of contemporary music came from the vicinity of the pool house, the driving beat pulsing through the unseasonably cold early November air.

That must be Chad's work site for the day.

Shoving her hands into the pockets of the puffy, quilted coat that hit her mid-thigh, Lindsey lengthened her stride. The bright noontime sun hadn't put much of a dent in the St. Louis pre-winter chill, and after years in more temperate South Carolina, it was going to take longer than eighteen months to adjust to the harsher fall and winter temperatures here.

At the back door, she dug out her key, inserted it in the lock, and prepared to tap in the security code.

But the high-pitched *beep, beep, beep* that always sounded was absent as she twisted the knob and stepped inside.

Huh.

Was someone home after all?

She paused on the threshold. Listened.

All was quiet.

Maybe Heidi had forgotten to activate the security system. Or she could have left it off, if Chad was scheduled to do a job in the house too.

No matter. All she had to do was grab her knife roll and make a fast exit.

Mentally running through the recipes she'd be preparing this afternoon for today's client, she hurried through the large mudroom, past the half bath, and into the spacious kitchen replete with granite countertops and high-end appliances. All for show rather than utility, though. From what she'd gathered, the only real cooking that happened here occurred on the days she came.

Except . . .

She sniffed.

The distinctive smell of charred bread—along with another faint scent, indistinct as it mingled with the stronger odor—suggested someone had used a toaster very recently.

She glanced across the center island, toward the sink.

Yep. A crumb filled plate stood on the counter beside it.

But cleanup in the Robertsons' kitchen wasn't on her agenda today.

Lindsey continued to the island, where she always did her mise en place. And there'd been a ton of it yesterday, thanks to the complicated menu Heidi had selected. But chopping, cutting, peeling, slicing, and grating all the ingredients upfront was superefficient.

One of the many valuable lessons she'd learned in culinary school.

She scanned the island that ran parallel to the sink.

No knife roll.

Propping her hands on her hips, Lindsey gave the large room a once-over.

Ah. There it was. Over on the coffee bar in the far corner, past the second island with stools that faced into the kitchen and doubled as an eat-in counter. She must have put it there while she was cleaning up.

Sport shoes noiseless on the tile floor, she hurried across the room. If a chef without her knife roll wasn't akin to a surgeon without a scalpel, she could have skipped this unplanned detour. Wedging it in after shopping for today's ingredients had cut into her afternoon cooking schedule.

She rounded the corner of the island, strode toward the coffee bar—and jerked to a stop as a scream bubbled up in her throat.

Between the other island and the sink, a man lay sprawled on the floor, his vacant pupils aimed her direction. Beneath his center mass, a crimson pool stained the white tile. A half-eaten bagel lay beside him.

It was James Robertson, based on the photos she'd found of him on the internet while researching the couple after securing this chef gig.

And he was dead.

Even worse?

The location of the blood suggested he hadn't died of natural causes.

Lindsey grabbed the edge of the island to steady herself. Tried to suck in air.

She had to call 911.

And she would. As soon as the room stopped spinning and she could—

The toilet in the guest bathroom flushed.

As her brain did the math, another shockwave rolled through her.

The person responsible for James's demise was still here.

And the murderer was between her and the back door.

Heart stuttering, she clutched the countertop and gave the room a frantic sweep.

Could she make a run toward the front of the house? Try to—

The knob on the bathroom door rattled, and panic squeezed the oxygen from her lungs.

Too late.

She was trapped.

Letting her instincts take over, she dropped to her knees, edged the last two stools closer together, and tucked herself under the island.

Please, God, don't let whoever is in here find me!

As that plea for deliverance looped through her mind, she crouched lower and peeked through the shelving between the end of the cabinetry and the decorative column that held up the granite slab on top of the island.

A figure entered the kitchen, but a long coat, ski mask, latex gloves, and boots hid every identifying feature.

When the person walked her direction, Lindsey stopped breathing.

The murderer rounded the granite at the end of the other island. Paused when something clunked to the floor and skidded her direction.

It stopped sliding less than three feet from her, on the other side of the island where she'd taken refuge.

She froze as the killer walked toward her, bent down to grasp the sparkly item that lay almost within touching distance, then continued toward the dead man.

From her vantage point, only the person's jeans-clad lower legs were visible as one of them nudged the body with the toe of a boot.

No reaction as James's lifeless eyes stared at her.

Every nerve in her body vibrating, Lindsey snaked a hand toward the shelves at the end of the island and curled her shaky fingers around the rim of the Daum crystal vase Heidi had pointed out during their tour of the kitchen. The one she'd said had cost more than $4,000.

But with her knives out of reach on the coffee bar, the pricey decorative piece was the sole weapon at hand. Better to risk her client's wrath if she broke it than certain death if the killer spotted her and she had no way to defend herself.

Best case, the murderer had finished what they'd come to do and would leave through the back door.

If they had more business to attend to in the house, however . . . if they walked past the island that was her refuge . . . they could spot her no matter how small she tried to make herself.

And if that happened, her career as a personal chef would likely come to a very sudden end.

Along with her life.

Irene Hannon is the bestselling, award-winning author of more than sixty-five contemporary romance and romantic suspense novels. She is also a three-time winner of the RITA award—the "Oscar" of romance fiction—from Romance Writers of America and is a member of that organization's elite Hall of Fame.

Her many other awards include National Readers' Choice, Daphne du Maurier, Retailers' Choice, Booksellers' Best, Carol, and Reviewers' Choice from *RT Book Reviews* magazine, which also honored her with a Career Achievement award for her entire body of work. In addition, she is a HOLT Medallion winner and a two-time Christy award finalist.

Millions of her books have been sold worldwide, and her novels have been translated into multiple languages.

Irene, who holds a BA in psychology and an MA in journalism, juggled two careers for many years until she gave up her executive corporate communications position with a Fortune 500 company to write full-time. She is happy to say she has no regrets.

A trained vocalist, Irene has sung the leading role in numerous community musical theater productions and is also a soloist at her church. She and her husband enjoy traveling, long hikes, gardening, impromptu dates, and spending time with family. They make their home in Missouri.

To learn more about Irene and her books, visit IreneHannon.com. She occasionally posts on Instagram, but is most active on Facebook, where she loves to chat with readers.

"*Hope Harbor* . . .
a place of emotional
restoration that readers
will yearn to visit."

—*Publishers Weekly*

THREE-TIME RITA AWARD WINNER
IRENE HANNON
Blackberry Beach
A Hope Harbor Novel

THREE-TIME RITA AWARD WINNER
IRENE HANNON
Sea Glass Cottage
A Hope Harbor Novel

THREE-TIME RITA AWARD WINNER
IRENE HANNON
Windswept Way
A Hope Harbor Novel

Revell
a division of Baker Publishing Group
RevellBooks.com

Available wherever books and ebooks are sold.

Meet

IRENE HANNON

at www.IreneHannon.com

Learn news, sign up for her mailing list,

and more!

Find her on